Dear Reader,

Welcome to the w̶o̶n̶d̶e̶r̶f̶u̶l̶ world of *Scarlet*!

This month sees the launch of our exciting new romance series, offering you books I'm sure you'll enjoy reading as much as I've enjoyed selecting them for you. From June 1996 onwards, become a *Scarlet* woman and look out for four brand-new titles every month, written exclusively for you by specially selected authors we know you'll love.

At the back of this book you'll find a questionnaire and we'd be really happy if you'd complete and return it to us as soon as possible. Returning your questionnaire will earn you a surprise gift.

*Scarlet* is *your* list and we want *your* views on whether or not you like our selection of titles. So . . . feel free to drop me a line at any time, as I'd be delighted to hear from you.

Till next month,
Best wishes,

*Sally Cooper*

SALLY COOPER,
Editor-in-Chief – *Scarlet*

## About the Author

**Angela Drake** is a Chartered Psychologist currently practising as a freelance consultant. She is the published author of several romance and mainstream novels and has also written for the young adult market.

In her spare time, Angela enjoys reading, going to the cinema and listening to music.

Angela is married with one grown-up daughter and lives in Harrogate with her husband and other assorted pets!

*Other **Scarlet** titles available this month:*

DANGEROUS LADIES by Natalie Fox
FIRE AND ICE by Maxine Barry
PARTNERS IN PASSION by Ann Kelly

# The Mistress

# ANGELA DRAKE

# *THE MISTRESS*

SCARLET

*Enquiries to:*
Robinson Publishing Ltd
7 Kensington Church Court
London W8 4SP

First published in the UK by Scarlet, 1996

A copy of the British Library Cataloguing in
Publication data is available from the British Library

ISBN 1-85487-476-4

Printed and bound in the EC

10 9 8 7 6 5 4 3 2 1

*Part One*

# CHAPTER 1

Saul Xavier had not conducted in London for three years. The mere rumour of his coming to the city's premier concert hall to do an all Brahms concert set the box office into a flurry of activity. Advertised prices went to an all time high and ticket touts patrolling the street outside the hall on the night were asking five times the advertised price and getting it.

Xavier lost no time in making his presence felt. Within minutes of arriving for the afternoon rehearsal the worst fears of the apprehensive manager of the hall and his staff were realized when Xavier abruptly stopped the orchestra almost as soon as they had started playing. Spinning round on his stool he peered frowningly into the gloom of the almost empty hall. The manager ran quickly towards the elevated stage. Two of his staff hurried after him. Xavier stared down at them from his eagle's perch.

'There is a noise,' he said softly, sending prickles of anxiety down the manager's neck.

Everyone fell silent, listening intently.

Xavier held up his hand. 'There! Do you hear it?'

3

They all nodded. Yes, there was something in the background. It was very faint, but it was there. The manager groaned internally. What could it be? What could be *done*?

'We'll look into it, Maestro,' he said reassuringly.

Xavier smiled, his aristocratic, remote features registering only a shadow of movement. 'I would not complain if it were in pitch with the music,' he commented politely. 'But it isn't!'

The hall staff laughed nervously.

Xavier spun back to the orchestra, dispatching the hall staff with a swift gesture of one hand.

'So!' he told them, raising his baton. 'We have a problem of extraneous noise, ladies and gentlemen. But the show will go on!'

A low collective chuckle reverberated across the rows of players. A sensation of anticipation and elation was already building in each member of the orchestra. Even those who had not worked with Xavier previously recognized instantly that they were in the hands of a master of his craft. No matter that he was a stern disciplinarian, that he would not hesitate to be brutal if he thought it necessary; they sensed that he was about to put an emotional depth charge beneath them. When they played for him tonight it would be the music of angels.

Xavier looked along the rows of instrumentalists, making eye contact with each individual as he conducted, giving the slightest of nods in recognition of players he had worked with before. He gave the impression of being able to see, and more importantly hear, each player personally, of being *inside* each player's mind. In front

4

of an orchestra Xavier was the living embodiment of law, the ruler of the world.

In front of an orchestra Xavier was also at his happiest. His life had been moulded around music since early childhood. At the age of six he had played a Mozart rondo in concert.

Today, on the eve of his fortieth birthday, he exuded physical fitness and well being. He was a handsome man, perhaps at the very height of his sexual potency and attractiveness. Whilst his upbringing and native language were English, an international pedigree gave him a mingling of Greek, Austrian and Spanish blood. It was perhaps the Grecian influence that could most easily be traced in his carved, classical features and his smooth olive skin. His hair was a thick sable mane, greying pleasingly at the temples and mid-forehead in a manner that nature does better than art. His eyes were clear grey, an innocent enough colour, belying his ability to hypnotize or terrify with one glance from beneath his deeply hooded eyelids.

Standing erect he was just over six foot, with a body tightly muscled and compact from a lifetime of skiing and swimming. His iron will with regard to the intake of food and alcohol was legendary, having been respectfully described in a variety of fawning magazine articles through the years. In fact Xavier appreciated fine food and wines just like any other human being. But he was never greedy. And he never drank on the days before he planned to be at the controls of his TBM 700 turboprop aircraft. Which meant that in the past few years he had drunk comparatively little.

At the break in the rehearsal the hall manager gave

Xavier a report on the noise. It came from the pump powering the massive boiler in the basement of the hall. 'I have to confess that I've never noticed it before,' the manager said ruefully.

'It will have to be turned off during the concert,' Xavier decreed without expression. There were never any tantrums with Xavier, never any rages or storming. He kept himself in tight control. Just occasionally he would strike – with all the stealth and venom of a poisonous snake.

The manager knew better than to protest. He expressed a mild hope that the operation of the hall's bars and cloakrooms would not be totally disrupted.

Later that evening, as the audience assembled, the air in the hall was on the chilly side but the psychological atmosphere was quietly smouldering. International celebrities were turning out in force, the men in black ties, the women in a shimmering array of peacock-bright silks and taffetas.

Half-way down the auditorium a young woman clad in black lacy tights and huge scarlet sweater curled her legs up onto her seat, hoping to make herself taller so that she could see the stage. The gaze from her big green eyes was intense as she watched the orchestra assembling.

Her ears thrilled to the insistent throb of the instruments tuning up, the rich steely sound of the strings, the clarity of the notes bursting from the brass section so sparkling and bright that she could imagine the great horns had been washed to gleaming brilliance in a torrent of thunderous rain.

She closed her eyes in anticipation. Soon the orchestra

would sing, the music would wind itself into every crevice of the auditorium like the mist of an autumn morning.

A minute before the concert was due to start a small party processed down the auditorium causing a flurry of interested speculation amongst the already seated audience. The woman leading the group was tall and exaggeratedly slim, her long blonde hair worn dead straight in a manner which only the very beautiful can get away with. She was dressed in a classically cut white crêpe gown and matchingly simple diamonds. Before taking her seat she looked around her, bestowing a faintly mocking and capricious smile on the watchful audience. By the time her party was seated and settled the starting time of the concert had been exceeded by three minutes.

There was an agitated rustling in the auditorium. A woman sitting behind the latecomers whispered to her husband that the woman in white was Saul Xavier's wife. 'I suppose that gives her the God-given right to make all the rest of us wait!' he whispered back with a wry smile.

Then suddenly all agitation was stilled and an electrifying hush fell on the auditorium as the tall figure of Saul Xavier appeared on the stage, threading through the orchestra and moving to the podium. A deafening storm of applause broke out.

Ignoring the acclaim from the audience Xavier mounted the podium, planted his gleaming black shoes in line with his shoulders, raised his baton and started straight away. His gestures were those of a man of great restraint, a man who knows how to extract the maximum from his followers without any indulgence in hysterical gymnastics.

7

Exhibiting scarcely any movement at all he set the orchestra off on a journey of pure musical delight.

He guessed that he must have played the work around fifty times in his extensive career. And yet there were still new things to discover about it. A great piece of music was always receptive to further interpretation. It was like a great ocean: one could dive down and down and never reach the gravel bed.

In his early days as a struggling young conductor, trying to coax performances of Mozart's *Don Giovanni*, or Puccini's *La Bohème* from ragged local orchestras and singers in the north of England, Xavier would fantasize when conducting that he was actually composing the piece himself. A heady experience!

But in recent years he had finally recognized that the gift of composing had not been granted to him by whatever divine force shaped the world. Acknowledging and accepting this, he had driven all his energies into perfecting the art of conducting. And he had not failed. Indeed one of the most influential music critics in New York had once remarked that on the podium Xavier was a true artist, one of the great baton virtuosos who could, with a flick of the wrist, do what others could not have achieved with the aid of a bulldozer.

Acclaim had been showered on him all over the world as he progressed from continent to continent, enticing penetrating performances from a host of great orchestras. In Germany the Chancellor summoned him to dinner. In Japan electronics magnates became his disciples. One of Britain's top defence manufacturers was regularly flown by company jet to wherever he was conducting and the

United Nations Secretary-General had gone so far as to create him an Ambassador of Good Will.

Conducting fees, television appearances and royalties from over a hundred recordings in current circulation provided an annual remuneration comfortably into seven figures. Careful selection of financial advisers to help him play the world markets and navigate his way through the complexity of international tax laws meant that his overall net remuneration was vast. He was a man of immense wealth.

There were many who envied him: who would have given anything to match his musical ability, his lifestyle, his money, his seductive and absolute power over the world's finest orchestras.

Yes – much had been achieved he thought as he stood before this magnificent London orchestra, noting the velvet timbre of the string section, sensing the slight tightness of feeling it brought to his throat.

And yet, and yet . . .

There was this fear growing inside him; this embryo flexing its limb buds, nodding its bulbous head, demanding to have life. At the approach of this fortieth milestone Xavier was menaced by a sensation of emptiness, a terror of the future where the days collided together in frightening sameness, where there was nothing to look forward to beyond a replication of the glories of the past. He recognized that it was unrealistic to hope for anything more than the continuation of his work as a brilliant interpreter. He had brought countless great works of music to life, but he had never created anything of his own. He had never painted or sculpted or written. He had created nothing lasting.

He had no child. And now it was too late.

Xavier had a sudden sharp image of himself as an eagle caged at the height of its strength. Panic thrust within him. The silent, unseen face of time mocked him. What should he do? Should he go back to the beginning? Look again at the great classical repertoire through the fresh eyes of a new ensemble? Maybe he could find some rag, tag and bobtail group somewhere. Bradford? Hull? He would take them over and shape them into a great orchestra. It would be his creation.

The thought kindled a frail flame of inspiration which flickered uncertainly but failed to ignite.

A chill shot down his spine.

His hands moved with automatic precision but his spirit fluttered away from the music. He felt his eyes close. For a moment there was a faltering in the strings section. Infinitesimal, no more than a split second. Only the most sensitive of trained musicians would have noticed.

Xavier's eyes snapped open with a jerk. He turned the whiplash of his iron will upon himself. Self pity played no part in his personal repertoire. And losing concentration was an unforgivable sin. That must not happen to him again. He might never be a composer, but he was never going to be anything less than a supreme virtuoso conductor.

Next week there were to be two further concerts; an evening of Sibelius and Britten and after that a dip into Edwardian nostalgia with David Bronfenbrenner playing the Elgar Violin Concerto. He made himself a grim promise that those performances would be nothing short of superb, they would be faultless. The mealy-mouthed British critics would eat their tight-lipped words.

The applause at the end of the evening was persistent and tumultuous, electric with acclaim. The audience had loved every minute. And they had loved Xavier.

Four times they brought him back to the podium. Staring out over the feverishly applauding audience he inclined his head gravely. His austere features registered only the faintest of smiles. Whatever Xavier's feelings were about the performance he was keeping them to himself.

Then suddenly he had had enough. Having savoured the applause, now he was sated. With an abrupt flick of his hand he dismissed the orchestra and strode off the stage, seeking the temporary solitude of his dressing room.

The audience began to sweep out, carried on a wave of dizzy excitement.

The green-eyed girl made no move. She sat motionless, curled in her seat, staring up at the empty stage.

# CHAPTER 2

Georgiana Xavier watched her husband leave the platform and smiled with satisfaction. With the hurdle of the concert over she could now devote her mental energies fully to the celebrations she had planned to mark his birthday the following evening.

She had listened only half-heartedly to the music. After reviewing the menu for the party supper her mind had wandered away into the past, reflecting on the twenty years of her marriage to Xavier. She was pleased with her marriage. In the world of the performing arts there were many couples who failed to stay the course; separations and divorce were commonplace. But she and Xavier were still together, a glittering couple on a rock solid foundation.

There had been only one frightening moment, a split second of horrified panic when she had feared that foundation might crumble and split.

She recalled the fateful occasion with perfect clarity, every detail intact: the sultry sky of a summer afternoon in New York, the luxurious beige and gold hotel suite filled with the scent of fresh flowers.

She had spent the afternoon shopping whilst Xavier rehearsed at the Carnegie Hall. Clothes, jewellery and other assorted trinkets littered their bedroom, spilling out of bags stamped boldly with the names of fashionable stores.

Georgiana had sunk into a chair feeling utterly exhausted, not so much with the journeying through the shops, as the long years of travelling with Xavier on his endless conducting tours of Europe and America. In the beginning she had been happy enough to trail after him like an eager young groupie on his yearly tours, but after his showdown with the English Symphonia with whom he had been chief conductor and music director for over a decade, he had become almost demonically restless, tearing round the globe, shaking the dust of one great city after another from his feet before it had even had time to gather. It was becoming impossible to keep up.

Xavier, lying prone on the bed relaxing between rehearsals and a big performance that evening, heard her weary sigh. He had looked up at her, surveyed the spoils and smiled indulgently. 'You haven't been enjoying yourself, darling?' he enquired with indulgently mocking incredulity.

'Yes, of course.'

'But?'

'I was alone. I'm always alone,' she said bitterly. 'You have your work, your orchestras, music . . .'

'So?'

'I need my home, my friends, my own life.' She sighed with mingled wistfulness and impatience, knowing that her words sounded trite and unoriginal, knowing that

Xavier would never understand the depth of her need for her social circle, her group of women friends, the crackle and thrust of female gossip. Shopping – like many other luxurious pastimes – had a limited attraction when you were doing it solo. What was the fun of shopping for wonderful, outrageously expensive things if there was no one with you in whom you could kindle a spark of pure envy?

Xavier raised himself slowly into a sitting position and held his arms out to her. 'Darling! You have me. We have each other.' His eyes beckoned her to approach him. When Xavier beckoned, it was hard – no, impossible – to refuse him.

Georgiana moved slowly towards the bed and allowed him to curl his long, strong arms around her slender hips.

His hand moved and strayed over one slim buttock and toned thigh. His fingers pressed into her flesh. She stiffened – she couldn't help herself. She prayed he had not noticed.

He reached up and stroked her face, tracing the lines of her high cheekbones. He drew his fingers around her lips and stroked her hair, parting the long blonde strands gently. As always his iron control went some way to reassuring her. Xavier was astonishingly controlled. He could maintain a quiet, courteous demeanour throughout what seemed to Georgiana the eternity it took to prepare for sex, and then when he eventually penetrated her he could keep going seemingly forever before eventually exploding deep inside her.

He was an exquisitely sensitive, careful and courteous lover. He had never once alarmed her with violent passion,

14

even though she sensed an undercurrent of longing within him for just that.

His hands reached inside her silk shirt. Mentally she shuddered. Her hands dutifully stroked his neck and chest. She hooked her fingers hesitantly in the band of his trousers. Her mind slurred away from what lay beneath them, that terrifying pole of masculinity: swollen, throbbing, dangerous.

In her head her thoughts tumbled wildly. It was no good. Some time, some time *soon* he would have to accept it. She was just dead as far as sex was concerned.

Georgiana groaned. She had noted the way women groaned with pleasure in the recent spate of 'sexually frank' films. She had trained herself to make all the appropriate noises but in truth her groans merely expressed her horror at the inevitability of yet another coupling, yet a further invasion of her identity and her most deep and private self.

She wished she could switch off. Just allow the husband she loved to pierce her flesh with his and gain the satifaction he was entitled to. But increasingly the act seemed an invasion, not just of the body, but of the soul.

Sex! All that writhing and groping and stickiness. All that gasping and screaming and clutching. And then the endless obligatory mutual congratulations afterwards.

The words *ultimate invasion* screamed silently through her mind as he plunged into her. The ultimate invasion of the self. That was it! That was sex in a nutshell.

Personal identity was hard to cling on to with a husband as successful and revered as Xavier. Trotting around in his shadow was one of the problems, although she judged she

15

could deal with that. But to be expected also to yield up the freedom to cling to the privacy of her own body and spirit was simply asking too much.

And yet he was so gentle, so restrained, just for her sake. She wanted to do better. A wife had a duty to do better. He was a wonderful husband she told herself, stroking the long carved bones of his face. But even as she registered the thought a spark of hate flashed through her head. She was locked to him, her body shackled to his flesh. He was her friend, her husband, her lover – but he bound her in chains and tortured her. Regularly.

He expected far too much. And deserved so much more. How she loathed the guilt and inadequacy he made her suffer.

Her teeth clamped together like a vice.

And then – oh mercy, oh joy – he gave one final thrust and suddenly it was over.

She cradled his head to her girlish half-apple breasts, blissful with the sense of renewed freedom. It might be another whole week before she need perform the task again.

She felt his hand stroking her softly. She breathed in deeply. The release she felt, the incredible relief became more intense each time he performed sex on her. Sometimes she thought she would have to run away and leave him rather than go through the awful charade yet again.

There was a moment of silence.

'Do you hate it *that* much?' he asked carefully sending her into a flurry of confusion. She had never dreamed that he would guess. No, not that. She had never dreamed that he would *confront* her. She had believed things were

16

skilfully balanced. She stared at him, uncharacteristic anxiety in her wide blue eyes.

Might everything suddenly fall apart?

'Do you want to go back to London?' he enquired.

'Yes.'

He nodded. 'Yes, I see that now.'

She held her breath. Her heart ticked loudly in her chest like an antique clock. She had a swift unnerving image of herself banished from his court: a queen dethroned. The thought of losing him was like a sword in the side. She reminded herself that trotting in his shadow was only one side of the coin. The flip side was basking in his glory.

She couldn't bear to be cast off, couldn't survive outside the role of being his wife. And she loved him. She did. Yes she did!

'Will you see a therapist?' he asked, his grey eyes frighteningly steady. He'd suggested this before, making delicate allusions to her need to 'find herself', have the opportunity to explore the deeper aspects of her personality. She had suspected that finding herself had meant getting herself into gear sexually. But he had never gone so far as to say this, nor had he pressed the point about therapy, merely repeated the suggestion once or twice in a casually solicitous manner.

'Yes. Yes, I'll book an appointment straight away.' She tried not to sound too eager.

He nodded. 'Good. Good.' His tone held the measured and courteous tenderness which characterized their relationship.

'Alfreda will know someone,' Georgiana volunteered, desperately seeking to retrieve her cool composure as

17

though wrenching a silk wrap around her shoulders having been caught naked – which she still was.

He smiled. 'Alfreda knows *everyone*.' His mockery of her rich, idle friend was open but not malicious.

'It was the miscarriages,' Georgiana told him, apologetic but on the defensive. 'Things have never been the same since the miscarriages, have they?'

Xavier smiled, his eyes distant and cool. 'No. So – that will be your starting point to begin your work with a good therapist. The miscarriages? Mmm?'

She nodded, half believing her own desperate excuses, almost certain that her husband did not.

Xavier stood up, lifting the naked Georgiana off his knee and placing her gently on her feet. She expected him to reach down and pat her firm smooth bottom but he turned away and crossed to the window, staring out. She knew that some kind of milestone had been reached.

She gathered up her satin négligé and slipped her arms through the sleeves, covering her nakedness before moving to stand beside him. 'I do love you,' she said quietly.

'Yes,' he agreed after a long moment of silence.

A sudden tenderness for him swept over her and she touched his arm with light fingers.

'What are you thinking?' she wondered.

'The Brahms Fourth,' he said. 'I've suddenly realized for the first time how I must conduct the last part.'

'You've done that piece time and time again,' she replied, exasperated and wounded. Bloody Brahms, barging in and busting up what she had believed was the beginning of a discussion of her marriage.

18

'I've always taken it too slowly,' he mused. 'Now I know!'

Bloody Brahms, bloody Mahler, bloody Stravinsky, Schubert, Beethoven, the whole lot of them. Georgiana rang down to the desk and instructed them to book her on a flight to London.

Xavier helped her pack, his face calm and abstracted. He handed her into the cab and leaned down to kiss her.

When she got back to London she telephoned Alfreda and asked her to recommend a good therapist. Then she arranged to meet Alfreda for lunch, planning to ask for her advice on a rather more intimate kind of service.

That had been four years ago. And Alfreda had not let her down thought Georgiana as she went back-stage to join Xavier in his dressing room. In fact her recommendations had led to one of the most fascinating projects of Georgiana's life.

# CHAPTER 3

Leaving the city centre after the concert, Tara felt in no hurry to get home – whichever place she decided would be home that night. Her head still reverberated with the magical last movement of Brahms's Fourth Symphony. She wanted to hold onto the marvellous sensation it had stirred in her, cling to the feeling until it evaporated like a precious dream in the harsh white morning. She made her leisurely way to the embankment and stared into the broad glinting girdle of the Thames. Under the autumn evening sky the shifting water was inky black. The moonlight reflected on the choppy ripples looked like broken fragments of silver which had fallen from somewhere high above.

Tara stood and watched the glittering, empty motorway of water. In her head she saw it reaching away to Tilbury, then the sea, the oceans and the rest of the globe. Its relentless timelessness mesmerized her. The stirring closing chords of the symphony tumbled over and over again through her mind.

Various passers-by, all males, eyed her with speculation – a tiny, decidedly tasty looking young woman on her own in the heart of London at gone eleven at night.

A variety of possibilities passed through an assortment of minds.

Tara was well aware of the dangers of the big city, having been sternly lectured on them by a number of people who had her best interests at heart. She was utterly indifferent. She could take care of herself. Just let anyone try anything! During her year in London she had already seen off two flashers and psychologically crushed a slavering drunk in the tube who had told her that she had kind eyes.

She stared into the swollen flow of water, then upwards to the glitter of the lights strung out along the embankment. Suddenly she wanted Bruno, wanted his big comforting body, his kind treacle-brown eyes, his unquestioning devotion.

An hour later found her tiptoeing down the hallway of one of University College's residential blocks, a pair of clumping studenty shoes clutched in her hand, an expression of wicked stealth in her eyes. Arriving at his room she scratched on the door with small, short-nailed fingers.

A rangy and rumpled young man eventually opened up, blinking in the light as he fixed thick-lensed, wire-framed spectacles around his ears. He peered down at Tara and then broke into a smile of delight.

'Hello there!'

'It's only me,' she said. 'No need to look as though you'd just discovered buried treasure.'

Beaming with happiness he bent down and kissed her tenderly on the mouth.

'Well – can I come in?' she asked impatiently.

'Yes. Yes.'

He cleared a space for her on the chair beside his small desk, both of which were littered with books and papers.

Tara sat on the bed.

Bruno sat next to her. His face was filled with concern as he examined the expression on her face, trying to read her feelings. He would hate to say anything that would upset her. 'Did you see him?' he asked eventually.

'Yes.'

'How did he look?'

'Weary. Resigned.' Tara screwed her face up, concentrating on the image in her head. 'He looked – *old*.'

'Well, he is in his fifties,' Bruno pointed out, wanting to reassure her. At twenty Bruno held the reasonable view that after a person hits forty life is basically downhill all the way.

'How long is it since you saw him?'

'Ages. Last Christmas.' Guilt squirmed inside Tara like a wriggling snake. 'He looked fine then. Great.'

Bruno reached out and squeezed her shoulder sympathetically. He understood what it felt like to have been the cause – however reluctantly – of a rift with parents.

'I thought about going back-stage, giving him a surprise,' Tara said regretfully. 'I almost did. But I felt . . . well, I felt shy!'

'You! Shy?'

'Incredible, isn't it? He seemed so stern and remote up on that platform. Untouchable. I couldn't believe he was my lovely daddy who used to swing me round by my arms until I was all dizzy and laughing.'

'Sweet memories of childhood,' Bruno smiled.

'Oh – there were some pretty good bits here and there.'

22

Tara agreed, her face screwed up with a number of conflicting feelings. 'It was just so awful that last row. I said some terrible things. I must have hurt him so badly.'

Bruno's face glowed with total loving compassion as he gazed at her.

'I'll go and see him soon,' she burst out. 'I will, I really will! Before the next Xavier concert at the very latest!'

'Aha – Xavier!' Bruno exclaimed, his eyes lighting up. 'The great man himself! He really did turn up then?'

'Oh yes. In the actual live flesh no less!'

'What did you make of him?' Bruno asked curiously.

'A master of audience manipulation. The people in the seats next to me were gawping at him with that slushy sort of reverence people usually save for the Royal Family.'

Bruno laughed. 'But the music was good?'

'The music was *heartbreakingly* wonderful. I wish you could have been there,' she said, turning to smile at Bruno, her green eyes slanting up at him from long black lashes, making his heart contract with desire.

'So do I.'

'How was your evening? Did you get to meet anyone influential?' she asked teasingly.

Bruno had had to forgo the concert in order to attend a social gathering in the Law Department, which offered students the opportunity to meet practising solicitors and barristers who could well be helpful to them in their future careers. It was a function students were advised not to miss, which was the only reason Bruno had gone along. He would have much preferred to go to the concert, or indeed almost any other function he could think of.

Bruno Cornwell hated being a law student. He hated the

23

great fat grindingly boring tomes to which he was tethered day and night. He hated the whole idea of a career in law.

Bruno wanted to be a musician. His parents, always keen to further any youthful interest they considered worthy and cultured, had been happy to pay for individual piano tutoring at school and had religiously attended school concerts and recitals in which Bruno took part.

But when it came to a career, they had put their dual parental foot down. Music was not a serious occupation; there was no security for an aspiring young man in the artistic world. Bruno must study for one of the professions. It might be hard grind and a bit boring for a few years, but it would all be worth it in the end. And once he became established in a respected profession – well, then he could think about music. There were plenty of amateur groups putting on quite decent concerts like *The Merry Widow* or Gilbert and Sullivan, sometimes even a little piano concerto or something of that kind.

Bruno's parents knew little about music. And virtually nothing about the world of classical music which Bruno ached to become part of.

Bruno's parents knew a great deal about the back-aching grind of running two local confectionery shops and the constant anxiety attached to being in trade. For their son they wanted the security and prestige afforded by one of the great professions – which in their eyes meant medicine or the law.

The final decision had been outwardly polite but inwardly bitter as Bruno came to terms with the fact that his parents would not be prepared to finance him through any form of higher education in the field of music.

24

He had no way of financing it himself and in any case he felt a strong duty to fulfil his parents' wishes. They had been decent, kindly parents. They had made 'sacrifices', sending him to an expensive private school.

They had ensured that Bruno never felt inferior to the other, richer boys. When they visited on sports days Bruno's father would not dream of embarrassing him by turning up in the rusting works van with Cornwell's Bakery written on it in flowing blue letters. He had always hired a shiny new Rover.

Watching his father drive up to the school, his mother sitting beside him dressed up in a new two-piece suit and matching accessories, Bruno would sense something faintly pathetic and ridiculous in the way they tried so hard to be something other than they were. It was that blend of parental pathos, imagined inadequacy and grim determination that made it almost unthinkable for a sensitive child like Bruno to take issue with them.

'Influential?' Bruno mused, giving his darling Tara a wry grin as he considered a suitable response to her question. 'Oh, I doubt if there was anyone in the Law Department tonight who will throw a shadow over my future life.'

Tara shook her head at him in exasperation. 'How long are you going to go on with this farce of studying law? Cut loose, Bruno. Dare to be a rebel. Fly a little!'

'Like you, my dearest, gorgeous, scrumptious darling?' he grinned, reaching out and pinching her smooth round cheek.

'Oh sure, like me. Part time waitress extraordinaire at the local wine bar! That really is cutting loose!'

'No, no,' he chided. 'You're a student of philosophy – that's your true identity. Waitressing's just a little hobby. An endearing foible.'

'It's a way of earning some spare cash,' Tara declared with some ferocity. From the start of her university career a year ago she had refused to eke out an existence on her student grant cheque. She needed money for her razor cut at Vidal Sassoon and her fat bottles of Miss Dior eau de parfum. And even with the wine bar remuneration she was struggling to stay solvent, which was why she was currently working on getting hired to serve in the dining room of one of the big hotels: the Ritz or Claridges. You could get simply fantastic tips in those places.

'And I doubt if studying philosophy has anything to do with my "true identity", whatever that is!' she exclaimed mockingly, entertained by Bruno's delightfully innocent earnestness. 'I haven't been to more than a couple of lectures this term. I haven't written an essay. And I haven't opened a single book apart from the odd trashy novel.'

'Well, you are a very bad girl then.'

Tara narrowed her eyes. 'So what are you going to do about it?' she whispered provocatively.

Bruno got to his feet and scooped her up into his arms, threw her over his shoulder and tapped her jutting round bottom with light fingers.

Tara squealed and bit his ear.

'Shut up!' he hissed lovingly. 'The whole corridor will be outside the door listening!'

'So what!' She planted a ferocious kiss on his mouth and slotted a wriggling tongue between his neat white teeth.

26

Chortling with mirth and lust they fell together onto Bruno's bed, their limbs entwined in some kind of furious wrestling match.

'Quick! Quick! I can't wait!' Tara breathed.

Their sex was spontaneous, warm, guilt-free and candid – a glorious celebration of high-spirited youth and genuine affection.

It was over in six and a half minutes flat.

'Mmm!' said Bruno, tucking Tara into the curve of his arm amidst the tangle of half-shed clothes and crumpled sheets.

'Mmm back!' Tara murmured, already nearly asleep.

In the porter's lodge at her hall of residence the telephone pealed out urgently at regular intervals through the night.

# CHAPTER 4

At seven o'clock the following evening, Georgiana stood in the doorway of her elegant drawing room with her friend Alfreda and surveyed the preparations for Xavier's fortieth birthday celebrations. Silently she congratulated herself on the clever and subtle way she had side-stepped the threat to her marriage and transformed her relationship with Xavier into something precious, lasting and unique.

Alfreda had been a constant source of help of course. As one therapist after another failed to unlock the mystery of Georgiana's soul, yet another was suggested. Alfreda was never at a loss, had always heard of a 'simply miraculous new man'. Georgiana had found the whole business utterly intriguing.

She stepped forward to patrol the majestic displays of food – pyramids of glazed ducks, bread braided like the coiffure of a Regency beau, pink prosciutto curled around open amber figs, an entire marzipan orchestra complete with 'Maestro' sculpted in sugar candy and a great cake in the shape of a treble clef decorated in white and gold icing. She smiled in satisfaction.

'Too gorgeous to eat,' Alfreda murmured, sipping her

champagne cocktail – 1973 Bollinger poured over sugar crystals saturated in vintage Armagnac.

'Tonight is going to be really special,' Georgiana purred. 'He will be over the moon. Ecstatic. Brahms and Mahler can eat their hearts out.'

'So what have you got for him on this special birthday?' Alfreda enquired in her lazy drawl, sipping her drink and smoothing the skirt of her crimson silk gown with elegant white fingers.

Georgiana, ethereally beautiful in cream crêpe, draped in the Grecian manner – a favourite style of Xavier's – gave a husky laugh. '*Who* have I got, you mean?'

Alfreda stared down into her drink. So Georgiana was still playing her little games. Her lips twitched. 'Naturally. I should have remembered that you have superbly original taste when selecting gifts for your husband.'

'This one is exquisite, the best one yet. And there have been some gorgeous ones,' Georgiana commented, her voice vibrating with satisfaction. 'But nothing to touch this one.'

'Good God!' exclaimed Alfreda, uncharacteristically rather shocked.

'Mid twenties,' Georgiana mused, 'tall, elegant, stunningly beautiful.'

Alfreda raised her eyebrows.

'In fact, darling, it was the best turn you ever did me recommending that agency,' Georgiana remarked lightly to her friend.

'Good,' Alfreda said slowly. The name and address she had discreetly supplied to Georgiana, following their momentous lunch meeting all that time ago she had in

29

turn acquired from a friend of her husband's; a cabinet minister who was familiar with the supply markets for just about everything you could think of.

Even the worldly Alfreda had been rather surprised at the ready supply of quality young women available to act as escorts and sexual partners for men rich enough to hire them.

Georgiana had been astonished. Her first contact with the agency had been hesitant and nervewracking. But she had soon been soothed into a state of relaxed confidence by the voice on the other end of the telephone. A female voice; cultured, sympathetic and, most importantly, apparently completely unshockable and stripped of any hint of moral censure.

After a tentative start Georgiana had warmed to her theme. She required a sympathetic, cultured, beautiful young woman to care for the needs of her husband whilst she herself recuperated from a debilitating illness. Georgiana had managed to feel suitably sorry for herself as she spoke these words. Well, after all she *had* suffered a miscarriage three years previously and had never been really well since and she was booked in to consult a psychotherapist in Harley Street the very next day.

The voice on the agency phone had been instantly understanding and sympathetic. There had been a lengthy series of relevant – but extremely discreet – questions to be answered before further action could be taken, and this had reassured Georgiana immensely. A registration fee was required of an amount which suggested exclusivity and a luxury product, and this served to increase Georgiana's confidence further.

The voice on the phone judged that the agency had a young woman on their list who would meet Georgiana's requirements. Once her cheque had been cleared arrangements could be made immediately.

Georgiana wondered at this point if the whole thing was a big confidence trick for extracting money. But she was a rich woman in her own right, quite apart from Xavier's wealth, and was not especially concerned about losing the amount quoted – indeed, she was more than willing to take the risk for what seemed a miraculous gift from heaven.

On the first occasion, which took place just after Xavier returned from the USA tour which Georgiana had so suddenly quitted, it was agreed that the young woman hired would be included on the guest list for one of Georgiana's famous dinner parties for twelve. She would be invited to attend the pre-dinner cocktail party and if Georgiana had any reservations about her suitability would leave discreetly on the nod from the hostess before the company progressed to the dining room. Her fee was to be paid in full whether or not she stayed on for the dinner and subsequent duties with Xavier, an arrangement Georgiana found both clever and sensitive, enabling her to feel quite at ease about the project; freed from any anxiety or embarrassing guilt should the hired girl prove ill matched to the occasion.

In the event things had gone better than Georgiana could ever have imagined. The young woman was smooth, poised and charming, clearly at ease with the fashionable company Georgiana had assembled in her fine drawing room.

She was coolly beautiful in a understated English Rose

style, wore classic clothes, a minimum of jewellery and very little make up. She also had the long straight blonde hair that Xavier so admired.

Georgiana watched her from across the room and saw some reflections of herself twenty years back. But although there were many similarities she was pleased to conclude that she still had the edge over the younger woman for sheer perfection of bone structure. Georgiana had the high cheek bones that made it impossible for her ever to appear anything but beautiful. She had always regarded them as her greatest natural gift, something God-given and precious. Not even the most skilful cosmetic surgeon could construct bones like hers. And women with good facial bones went on looking good right into old age she reflected, noting that the younger woman's looks were mainly based on a swell of cheek flesh and full lips which would most likely collapse when she was in her forties.

Georgiana had arranged the seating so that the young woman was on Xavier's left at the head of the table, whilst she presided regally at the opposite end, flanked by the Secretary General of the Arts Council on one side and a devoted royal admirer of Xavier's conducting on the other.

Standing now with Alfreda, sipping champagne before the first guests arrived, Georgiana recalled her mingled feelings of nervousness and tense anticipation as she watched the young woman gently seduce her husband over a simple English dinner of saddle of lamb and Bramley apple tart.

She recalled the letter she had written to him, placing it unobtrusively into his hand as the ladies retired to the drawing room and left the men to their port.

32

It was a loving letter, telling him how much she adored him, how she longed to make him happy, how it would please her to feel that he could gain the satisfaction she had denied him with the lovely young guest she had included at her dinner. She had let him know that she would be staying with friends that night, that he should use the privacy of the house to do whatever pleased him. She entreated him not to be angry with her. She was his true and loving wife. She had acted out of the purest motives. But if her actions had made him angry she knew that he would forgive her. Etcetera, etcetera.

It was really rather a good letter Georgiana thought, hitting just the right note for a man like Xavier – a true romantic who would warm to the lush sentiments in her tender message. He would know, of course, that her tongue had been partially in her cheek as she wrote, and he might not be inclined to go along with her generous offer. But she felt reasonably confident that he would not be disapproving or insulted.

But until the men rejoined them she had felt her nerves to be jagged with tension and anticipation.

One glance at Xavier's face, a swift connection with his glittering grey eyes, told her instantly that all was well.

He was not angry in the least. He was amused, entertained, intrigued. He was going to play the game.

The image of Xavier and the beautiful, fresh young woman naked in each other's arms stirred Georgiana more than actual sex had ever done.

She hardly slept that night, envisaging the two of them making love, conjuring up scenes of combined violence and tenderness which made her heart beat thick and fast.

33

When she returned home the next day she found Xavier relaxed and amiable, making plans to take her on a short holiday to St Tropez, her favourite resort.

The young woman had disappeared. He made no mention of her. The incident might never have occurred. But Georgiana sensed that she herself had risen in his affection and his estimation. He admired her consideration, her imagination and her tact. From feeling faintly inadequate as a wife, suddenly she saw herself as some kind of heroine: a woman not afraid to take risks, cross boundaries, break new ground in the cause of her man.

She judged that he would like her to repeat the exercise, although perhaps only on rare occasions. She would have to be very sensitive about her timing. It seemed to Georgiana that she had hatched a golden scheme and now she was living her life in a luminous glow.

That feeling had persisted and each encounter that she arranged had brought Georgiana ever increasing excitement and fulfilment.

Tonight was going to be special, not only because it was Xavier's birthday, but also because the young woman Georgiana had recruited was more beautiful than any she had recruited before.

Georgiana had requested the opportunity to meet and talk to several possible escorts and had enjoyed some entertaining lunches where she had vetted the young women individually whilst feeding them exquisite food and inviting them to share a bottle of fine white burgundy, her own favourite wine.

They were all wonderfully desirable but the woman

34

Georgiana chose stood out from the others, being a match for herself in slenderness, elegance, bone structure and feminine grace. Her eyes were deep violet blue and her voice soft and rich. But more than that, there was an aura around her, a sense of presence. It was hard to believe that she was not a member of an old aristocratic family.

Georgiana had asked about her work. The woman had answered with calm directness, explaining that her clients were gentlemen in every sense of the word, that she felt no sense of shame about her work, that she performed a useful function in the tradition of any artist or entertainer and that she was earning annually five times as much as she would have been had she entered the profession of teaching for which she was fully qualified.

Georgiana was very impressed. 'It's you I want for the job,' she told the woman with cool decisiveness at the end of the lunch. She gave her a vellum envelope filled with high value notes. 'This is a token from me personally. A thank you in advance. You will get your fee from the agency in the usual way.'

The woman smiled graciously and inclined her head in thanks.

Georgiana's heart had registered a faint flutter as the taxi bore the woman away into the jumble of London's traffic. She recognized that in this young female she had met her match in physical perfection. And she was going to hand her over to Xavier on a platter.

It was dangerous. Foolhardy, some would say. It was breathtakingly, heart-stoppingly, dizzily exciting.

It was proof that their marriage was impregnable and eternal.

35

'She will be wearing hyacinth blue,' Georgiana told Alfreda. 'Xavier loves that colour – after cream and white of course,' she added, fingering her own divine gown with a calculating smile.

'I hope Xavier's up to it,' Alfreda commented drily. 'After all he's hardly a young man any more. And he's had a punishing few years on the work front.'

'He's the definitive workaholic,' Georgiana commented dismissively. 'The only ways he knows how to relax are by being active – flying his plane, skiing and sailing. I would guess that sex is fairly low key in effort and stress compared to all of those.'

Alfreda winced invisibly. This casual mention of sex in relation to one's husband and other women disturbed her. She privately considered that the whole idea of finding high-class call girls to satisfy your husband's sexual hunger was a decidedly dangerous business. And if you were hoping to stay married it was definitely asking for trouble.

'Where *is* Xavier by the way?' she asked, looking around the room, which had now filled with an assortment of glossy metropolitan celebrities drawn mainly from the worlds of art and politics.

'Hospital visiting. One of the Tudor Philharmonic players he used to work with years ago had a heart attack just after the concert last night. It's touch and go.'

'God! How tragic.'

'Yes, I believe he's only in his early fifties. Still, to go out on a burst of Brahms . . . Xavier will probably be madly envious.'

Alfreda glanced at Georgiana and reflected that she really was rather an unusual woman.

The party was in full swing when Xavier eventually arrived. He stood in the doorway surveying the scene; a tall, remote figure, austere and chillingly inscrutable until he allowed his features to register a gentle smile in acknowledgement of the respectful attention he was commanding from every person present. All heads had turned, all eyes watched.

Xavier had long ago taken for granted his ability to walk into a room and command instant attention. He was also perfectly capable of creating a complete silence if he chose, but tonight was a celebration, a special birthday. This was a time to dig into his reserves of charming affability. That was what Georgiana would want and this party was much more hers than his. He moved forward into the throng.

Georgiana surveyed him with pride, as though he were a priceless work of art in the same league as the set of Picasso sketches he had recently given her. How *noble* he looked, she mused, how well the years sat on him. He was the sort of man who would simply get better and better as he grew older.

Forty was a marvellous age for a man of quality she decided. Forty had a roundness and weight to it not present at thirty. At forty a man was at the peak of his powers and could look ahead to a burnished decade of further glories.

She watched Xavier progress smoothly through the ranks of guests until eventually he came to stand beside the exquisite blonde woman in her tasteful yet seductively cut blue gown. She saw his dark head incline towards the gleaming fair one, could sense the spark of delighted anticipation that had sprung up within him. When he turned to make a brief connection with Georgiana's gaze she smiled in delicious conspiracy.

Oh, she understood him so well! And she was grateful to him for appreciating her requirements in return: the need to remain untouched. Which was why he deserved the splendid gift she was presenting him with tonight.

Walking into the dining room to make a last survey of the supper arrangements Georgiana found it difficult to focus her attention on the laden table. She was awash with sensation: electric currents of excitement rippled through her flanks. She threw her head back and breathed in deeply. A dark throbbing had started up between her legs and the reverberating thrills of ecstasy which shot through her hips and thighs made her gasp aloud in sudden desperate pleasure.

Alone in the gracious airy room Georgiana allowed her hands to travel over her slender colt-like body whilst her mind exulted in its fragile perfection.

In the most chaste of caresses her slim fingers moved across the fabric of her gown, lightly moulding the shallow domes of her breasts, the narrow pedestal of her waist, the gentle swell of her hips.

A small sigh leaked from her lips.

She knew herself to be perfect. Exquisite. And utterly pure.

When the last guests had left and Georgiana too had been borne away in Alfreda's chauffeur-driven Mercedes, Xavier poured himself a double measure of Laphroaig and paced softly in front of the long windows which spanned the south-facing drawing room.

The young woman in the blue dress waited quietly, standing at a respectful distance, one golden-tanned arm resting against the marble fireplace.

'Would you like to hear some music?' Xavier asked softly.

Her body straightened slightly. 'That would be lovely.' She waited. She looked around for the inevitable music-producing technology which all her clients owned. There was nothing immediately apparent. Maybe the necessary equipment was discreetly hidden in one of the splendid lacquered cabinets. 'Shall I put on a compact disc? Where do you keep them?'

He gave a dismissive wave of his hand. 'No, no. I meant live music.' He sat at down at the nine-foot concert grand which stood in the corner of the room.

Of course! She should have guessed.

His eyes flickered over her. 'What do you like? Mmm?'

She licked around her lips, feeling strangely apprehensive.

'Ask for what you *want*,' he said. 'Not what you think would please me.'

'West Side Story,' she responded after a brief pause. She had a vague idea that the music from the show had been composed by some famous conductor or other. She couldn't remember his name, but Xavier probably knew him. '"Tonight" – that's one of my favourites. Do you know that?'

Xavier gave a low grunt. His strong fingers picked out the tune and then began to improvise an accompaniment. The harmonies were subtle and complex.

His listener was a little baffled, but very impressed.

39

'Quite a nice little melody,' Xavier commented, pausing. 'Do you sing?'

The woman shook her head. 'I'm sorry. Making music isn't one of my talents.'

Xavier turned back to the piano, polished off 'Tonight' and then embarked on a spot of breathtaking Liszt. It entertained him to show off a little. Especially to a beautiful young woman who was clearly a blank sheet as far as music was concerned.

On completing his short recital, he got up and crossed the room to stand beside her. 'So what *are* your talents?' he asked pleasantly.

The woman smiled. She raised her arm and laid a gentle and undemanding hand on the lapel of Xavier's dinner jacket.

Xavier stared down at her for a long moment, then reached for the switch behind him and flicked off all the lights. The curtains were not drawn and a broad sword of moonlight lit the room with a bluish silver gleam.

'So – you have no talent with music,' he said softly. 'That is of no importance my dear. You are extremely beautiful.'

She basked in the silky caress of his praise. What a marvellously magnetic man he was. And he was going to be hers for the whole night. Her heart quickened. And this was work!

'One of *my* talents is undressing beautiful women very slowly and skilfully,' he informed her in a lazy husky whisper.

She tilted her head back with a little sigh, giving him an unrestricted view of her smooth throat.

Xavier bent his head towards her and touched her cheek fleetingly with his. As she breathed in deeply and leaned slightly towards him he placed his hands on her satin-skinned shoulders and turned her around very gently. He stroked her half-naked back lingeringly and cupped his hands around the base of her neck, cradling it softly and moving his thumbs tantalizingly beneath the fall of blonde hair.

Another soft sigh.

Now Xavier permitted his hands to travel down over her hips and thighs bending his long frame so as to enable him to trace the curve of her calves and touch the chiselled bones of her ankles.

'These are instruments of torture,' he commented, his hands grasping the narrow shoes with their punishing four-inch stiletto heels. 'I shall set you free without delay.' With firm fingers he eased the soft cream suede from her pretty slim feet. The shoes were tossed away to lie on the carpet.

'Mmm!' she sighed, wriggling her toes. 'Bliss!'

'So – from what can I free you next?' he enquired.

She stood perfectly still; a passive vessel to be used in whatever way he wished. Xavier was both touched and outraged.

He reached for the discreetly inserted central zip of her gown, grasped it in steady fingers and pulled the zip head down the row of tiny teeth with exquisite delicacy. A frail, tantalizing sound like the ripping of silk pierced the silence.

The woman gave a small moan.

Xavier lifted her bodily so that her feet cleared the ring

41

of fabric lying around her legs. Very carefully he picked the gown up, folded it neatly and laid it on the sofa next to the fireplace.

She started to turn to face him. His hands gently re-directed her to the position he had placed her in.

He surveyed her lovely back and her beautiful rump. She was wearing some kind of corset; boned, lacy, frilled and snowy white. It accentuated her figure, exaggerating the waist, pushing up the breasts which he could see to advantage from his superior height as he glanced over her shoulders.

He was heavily aroused now. But not so carried away that his hawk-like eye for detail was failing to register the fact that her stockings were hooked onto long suspenders attached to her corset and would require releasing before things could proceed further.

'You're terribly good with suspenders,' she murmured with a charming chuckle. 'It's easy to get in a dreadful muddle.'

'Is that so?' he commented drily, thinking that she was both skilled and tactful not to have referred to the many men of her acquaintance who *had* got into that kind of difficulty. He rolled the stockings down her lovely long legs and placed them with the gown.

'Well now, and how does this wonderful garment yield up its treasures?' he enquired, fingering the top of the corset, lightly touching the line of vertebrae running from her neck into the white lace.

'Press studs,' she whispered. 'Dozens of them.' She wondered what his reaction would be when he saw her naked breasts. She judged she could give his skinny

42

wife at least four inches in bust measurement.

Patiently Xavier undid the unending row of press studs. He was beginning to feel weary. It had been a trying day and the visit to the hospital had laid some sort of cloud over him.

Dutifully, politely he removed the lace garment, tossing it to lie with the rest of her things.

There was a long pause. She wore only the tiniest of white lace panties now.

He surveyed her dispassionately. She was a perfect specimen of western womanhood. The body could not be faulted. It was the embodiment of an image; an ideal which countless women strove to emulate.

Long legs, a soft mound of hips and buttocks, a curved waist, breasts as firm as oranges, bones as delicate as the wood carvings in an altar screen.

And clearly she was eager. He could hear her breathing, a little jerky, a little increased in tempo.

He brushed his hands over her nipples and let them trace a line over her skin from there to her manicured toes.

Lifting her into his arms he laid her tenderly on the sofa, over whose fatly upholstered arms her clothes already lay.

She looked up at him, her face silvered in the moonlight.

Her arms reached out. 'Come to me!' she urged.

Somehow her insolence in presuming to command him made things easier.

Xavier ran a skilled finger down the centre line of her chest, over her navel and down into her panties which he now removed in a single graceful movement.

Parting her legs with ceremonial courtesy he allowed his

43

finger to skim inside the pink fleshy lips beneath the soaking hairs.

She cried out, slippery with desire.

He thought of Georgiana's dry crotch and that last occasion when he had forced his way into her. And now this beautiful young woman was dripping with lust for him.

Xavier stared down at her for a long moment. 'Thank you for a perfect finale to a splendid evening,' he told her, his voice cool and even. 'Please feel free to have another drink and use the telephone when you require a taxi to take you home. There is no rush, of course. But perhaps you would excuse me now. I have two concerts in the next week. There is work to be done.'

Turning his back on her he closed the door quietly behind him and went upstairs to his room, took a brisk shower and fell into bed, his skin still damp. Within seconds he was deeply asleep.

# CHAPTER 5

The day marking Xavier's fortieth birthday was significant for Tara also.

It started in carefree happiness with her and Bruno whiling away the morning in bed. When they eventually rolled out the sheets had the appearance of a rugby scrum having taken place in them.

'Let's take a day off!' Tara suggested impulsively.

Bruno attempted a protest. 'I've lectures this afternoon.'

'Oh, come on! Live dangerously. Cut them!'

They spent the day like tourists, taking a leisurely walk along the embankment, impulsively jumping on a train bound for the Surrey countryside and discovering a little inn that served beer well into the afternoon after licensing hours.

Afterwards they made love beneath a fiery autumn sun in the corner of a golden stubble field before returning to the inn for a supper of sausages and chips.

It was approaching eleven when Tara arrived back at her hall of residence. The night porter let her in. She was rather a favourite of his and never got any stick about being late and not having a special pass key.

'The phone's been hot for you, lovey,' he told her.

Tara glanced up at him, her heart quickening. Something was wrong.

'Since last night,' he went on, his face kindly but faintly chiding.

'Oh God!' She stared up at him, her face white now with anxiety.

'Your mother needs to talk to you,' he said softly. 'You'd better ring right away sweetheart. Use the phone in my little cubby hole behind the desk. You'll have a bit of privacy there.'

Her hands shuddering Tara dialled the number of her home in Kent.

Her mother's voice answered. 'Tara! Where the hell have you been?' She sounded beside herself with anger.

Tara felt suddenly disoriented and bewildered as though she had suffered a swift blow to her head. 'Out. On the river. I was out.'

'You've been uncontactable for twenty-four hours. Did you realize that?'

'I didn't think . . .'

'No. That's your problem. You never *think*. Not of the important things.'

'Mummy, tell me! What is it? What's the matter.'

'Daddy. He had a heart attack.'

Tara gripped the receiver. 'When?'

'Last night. Just after I picked him up from the concert. In the car.'

'Oh no!'

'I took him straight to the hospital. He was asking for

you. All the time, he was asking for you,' her mother said bitterly.

Already Tara knew the worst. Her heart was even now trying to absorb the blow.

She heard her mother's voice again, flat with resignation and despair. 'He had a second massive coronary at four this afternoon. Dead. That was it!'

Tara screwed up her face, trying to fight off the shock and pain. 'Look, I'm coming home. Rightaway. I'll get a taxi.'

'No point. I've taken two sleeping pills. I'll be flat out in a few minutes. Come tomorrow. Or better still, go to your lectures for a change and come home at the weekend.'

'Mummy!'

The line clicked off. The dialling tone purred in Tara's ear. She started to re-dial and then thought better of it.

'Bad news?' the porter asked sympathetically as she walked, zombie-like, back to the desk in the lobby.

'Yes. My father. A heart attack.' She stared unseeingly ahead of her, appalled at the tragic waste of it. Fifty-two and such a wonderful person. Such a brilliant instrumentalist, far too good to have been buried in the second row of the violins all those years. And now there would be nothing else for him, his future cruelly snuffed out.

The porter shook his head. 'Oh dear, oh dear.'

'Have you got any daughters?' she asked him.

'Just the three lads. Your father was a lucky man having one like you,' he told her with a fond smile.

If only you knew, Tara thought with bitter self-reproach.

'Are you going home then?'

'Tomorrow.'

'That's right. No good dashing off now. Go and get some sleep – best healer in this world.'

Tara forced a smile, waved good-night to him as she walked to the stairs with leaden legs. It seemed difficult to imagine ever sleeping again.

She lay in the narrow bed, her arms by her side, cold – like a corpse.

Her father had gone. She kept hearing her mother's voice: 'Dead. That was it.'

Dead. His body would be wrapped up in a plastic bag and slotted into a chilled steel drawer like an anonymous cardboard file in a cabinet. His body would be there in the mortuary – or maybe already at some undertaker's – unmutilated with no abrasions or external abnormalities. His body was there just a few miles away from her. She could go there and seek it out and embrace it as she used to when she was a little girl. She could embrace it through eternity, but he would not be there. Where was he? The essence of him: where had that gone? How could all that spirit and talent and skill suddenly be nothing? How could a life be rubbed out so swiftly?

There were no answers to the torturing questions. And there was no sleep either. She sat up and wrapped her arms around her knees and rocked herself to and fro, softly moaning his name. 'Daddy, Daddy, Daddy.'

Bruno travelled home with her. She told him she could not face her mother on her own.

My mother's a widow, she thought in horror, fearful of

the change she might see in the parent she had always considered the most psychologically tough.

But her mother was reassuringly the same; not openly ravaged by grief nor pink-eyed and tearful. She welcomed Bruno in a pleasantly neutral manner, told him to call her Rachel and fed him hot buttered muffins and slabs of chocolate cake. She said she had been keeping herself occupied cooking and shopping. It numbed her brain. And in any case there would probably be a stream of callers needing to be offered snacks.

Bruno and she got on famously. She insisted that he stayed on over the weekend and got up at six to drive him to the station to take the early train to London on the Monday morning.

'I've invited him to come to the funeral,' she told Tara over breakfast.

'Thanks.'

'Is it serious? You and Bruno?'

Tara paused, considering.

'He seems to think so,' her mother observed.

'Yes. I know.' That was the problem really.

'I just hope you don't hurt him.' Her mother stared hard at her daughter before rising to clear the table.

'Like I hurt Daddy. Is that what you're trying to say?' Tara demanded, stung and resentful.

'You're very powerful Tara. You grab at life and squeeze it as if it were a great big juicy orange.'

'What the hell does that mean?'

'It means you're capable of being very selfish and very ruthless.'

Tara gasped. 'Thanks for the character assassination.

49

You were always rather good at that, Mummy.'

'You needed squashing by someone. From around the age of eighteen months.'

'God! Now I know why I left home and didn't come back.'

'You left home because your father finally confronted you with some harsh realities about yourself.'

Tara breathed deeply as anger burned inside her. She knew she had been wayward and self-centred. She knew she had been bolshie and difficult. They had expected so much. *He* had expected so much. She had felt stifled, harnessed and handcuffed. She didn't think they could ever have had any idea how she felt.

It was all Freddie's fault. If Freddie hadn't gone and died when he was only ten, they wouldn't have been so fragile and bitter. They wouldn't have needed to make her so precious and special, to mould her into the genius who would tread in her father's musical footsteps and far beyond.

Tara's large green eyes swam with tears as she confronted her mother's dignified, weary face. 'Don't let's fight Mummy. Please.'

Her mother smiled. 'Well, it's too late now.'

'If I'd any idea he was going to be ill, I'd never have stayed away. I just didn't know how to build a bridge back.'

'I know,' her mother agreed absently. 'I just wish he could have seen you before he died.'

Tara thumped the table with her fist. 'Oh God! Don't! DON'T!'

'No. I'm sorry.'

Tara wanted to jump up and wrap her arms around her mother and for them to weep together. But her mother was being very brave and sensible and it seemed important not to disturb the outer shell of calm self-possession. A fragile truce held until the day of the funeral later in the week.

Tara put on a navy dress which had been a favourite of her father's. It flared softly from a deep neckline yoke and had a big white puritan-style collar. With it she wore her new red skyscraper heels, bought from the proceeds of her wine bar earnings. An incongruous and startling mixture.

Her mother was in dark burgundy, a neat suit with a cream silk blouse beneath. Tara thought she looked both lovely and brave.

'I hope I'll be able to sing,' Tara said, feeling a thick choking sensation in her throat as she sat beside her mother in the vast black saloon car and watched the hearse, with the flower-decked coffin, move sedately in front of them on its journey to the church.

Bruno was there with them, a solid and comforting presence, already bolted on to the nucleus of the family.

'I should hope you will,' her mother responded drily. 'It was you who made such a fuss about doing it. The organist will be pretty fed up if he's been practising day and night and doesn't get to play his party piece after all.'

'Daddy would have been pleased,' Tara said, suddenly feeling like a small girl desperate to please a beloved parent. 'Wouldn't he?'

Her mother smiled. 'Yes. He would.' She sighed, a long quivering expulsion of air.

'Oh God! This is so awful!' Tara wailed, fearful of exploding in a storm of unstoppable weeping.

'Yes. It's called mortality,' her mother said in a matter-of-fact voice. 'It shouldn't happen to one's own darlings. They should live for ever. But in time I suppose we'll adapt to the idea.'

Tara looked at her mother's composed and dignified face and wondered if losing a child made you almost immune to every other thing that life threw you afterwards.

The church was crammed with people. Tara had been to one or two funerals recently and had been distressed to see how few mourners had been present. She felt her heart curiously soothed and uplifted to see this outward sign of the way her father's life had been valued.

She found herself able to sing the hymns sturdily and when it came to the time for her solo, following the vicar's address, she mounted the altar steps with a feeling of resolute calm.

It was the *Pie Jesu* from Fauré's *Requiem* that she had chosen, a piece her father had always expressed a great fondness for. She remembered him playing his 1950s recording of it to her when she was a small child. The themes lingered in her mind, triggering off those fragile forgotten childhood feelings that were perhaps more commonly aroused by *Away in a Manger*.

Her clear, pure voice leapt out into the still cool air of the church, creating a ripple of feeling and bringing a thickness of regretful sensation to a great many throats.

'*Pie Jesu, Domine, dona eis requiem; dona eis requiem sempiternam.*'

Blessed Jesus, O Lord, grant them rest; grant them eternal rest. She recalled the English translation as she sang. Oh yes, let him rest, she thought. He'd had a pretty hard time of it all in all. 'Don't I ever get a moment's peace?' he used to joke.

Rest now Daddy. There'll be peace stretching on for ever and ever.

Her voice swelled with feeling as she faced the congregation, free now of all apprehension or restraint. As her glance swept along the rows a figure seated alone in a side pew beneath the stained glass windows seemed to spring out at her, demanding attention. A coil of shock spun inside her as she recognized the great conductor Xavier; austere, remote, chillingly inscrutable.

Her composure faltered for a second and there was a small break in her voice as she lingered on the closing note.

Returning to her pew, her task completed, the tears began to roll unrestricted down her cheeks. Her mother pressed her hand and smiled, her own eyes still dry. Bruno gazed at her with unequivocal adoration.

Tara threw her head back, not ashamed to be seen weeping openly. From the edge of her vision she was painfully aware of the dark rigid form of Xavier. A satanic figure at my father's wake, she thought with quite unfounded aggression.

Back at the house the rooms seemed to be thronging with people: family, neighbours, players with the Tudor Philharmonic.

Her mother decided to serve sherry and whisky. 'Make them doubles,' she instructed Bruno who was proving indispensably helpful in the kitchen. 'I can't bear all that hushed whispering.'

Tara circulated, dutifully greeting relatives, gritting her teeth as she attempted to absorb their sympathy, deftly fielding the inevitable questions on the progress of her career.

Yes, she was studying philosophy. Yes, it was fascinating. No, she didn't quite know yet what one *did* with philosophy. She was sure something would turn up.

As she conversed her attention was caught by the high-pitched whine of a car's engine passing the house. Glancing through the window she registered a sleek grey Porsche, glimpsed a flash of wraparound red and blue stripes.

Moments later the doorbell rang. Throwing open the door Tara stared up at the tall grim-faced man, taking in the familiar saturnine features which adorned the sleeves of millions of discs. It seemed curious to see them here in close up, in the flesh.

'Saul Xavier,' he said, extending his hand courteously. 'And you're Richard's daughter.'

It was a statement not a question.

'Yes.' She was discomfited by the effect of his proximity.

When his strong fingers unclenched from hers she felt dampness in her palms and her heart was bounding. It was ridiculous. She'd met plenty of famous people before, had never been the slightest overawed.

She ushered him in and went to find her mother. 'The King of the Maestros is here,' she announced. 'Correction – Emperor.'

'Xavier?' Her mother appeared unsurprised. 'He phoned earlier to say he might come.' She smiled. 'Well, well!'

Tara watched her mother walk up to the great man, allow her hand to be sympathetically retained in his as he inclined his dark head to her blonde one.

'Rachel – my dear,' Tara heard him say. 'Georgiana sends her very deepest condolences. We both remember Richard's playing from way back.'

'God, he's smooth,' Tara hissed to Bruno who was eyeing the conductor with undisguised wonder. 'Positively glistening.'

Bruno patted her affectionately in a there, there kind of way. He loved her when she was indignant. 'It's good of him to come. Your mother will be really pleased.'

Tara grabbed a nearby glass of sherry and drained it in one gulp. She felt exhausted and dangerously on edge after these few days at home trying to be the kind of daughter she felt her parents had always wanted. She watched her mother talking with Xavier as though they were guests at some elegant cocktail party and felt a growing dislike for him. Her father used to tell stories of his occasional brutality at rehearsals: singling out individual players and humiliating them, creating an atmosphere of fear rather than comradeship. Although she recalled that her father had always considered that the ends justified Xavier's means.

She doubted that her father had ever had anything to fear from the likes of Xavier. He had been a superbly technically skilled player, although sadly never one of the lucky few who had that extra spark of talent that brought them out of the grinding ranks of the orchestra into the sphere of individual stardom.

'Bruno!' her mother called, beckoning him towards her.

'Come and meet one of Richard's old sparring partners.'

Bruno hurried forward, a flush springing to his smooth youthful cheeks. Tara heard the word 'Sir' as he shook Xavier's hand.

Turning away she went into the kitchen and started on the task of washing up. She felt dizzy and disoriented. The sherry was already working in her brain and there was an insistent humming in her ears. She reached across to the table and picked up another full glass.

The party began to disperse. Tara skated in and out of the kitchen, smiling gamely whilst an assortment of now jolly people kissed her cheek.

'Are you all right darling?' Bruno murmured, sliding out of the departing crowd and winding an arm around her.

'Fantastic,' she snapped. 'Never better.'

Following her into the kitchen he picked up a cloth and started on the task of drying the chaotic pile of crockery and cutlery stacked on the draining board.

This helpfulness had the effect of exasperating Tara beyond endurance.

'Oh for God's sake! Leave me to do it. Go and comfort my mother. You do it much better than I seem to manage.'

Bruno ignored her. He understood her only too well.

'Xavier was asking about my musical exploits,' he told her. 'He thought there might be an opportunity to do some playing with the Tudor Philharmonic. They sometimes need stand-ins in the percussion section.'

Tara glared at him. 'Grow up Bruno. There'll be a waiting list a mile long to stand in at the Tudor Phil. You've only been playing the kettle drums for a year. He's just being polite. Or most likely showing off how powerful he is to impress my mother.'

'No,' Bruno countered mildly. 'The timpanist is here and Xavier got him over to talk to me. A really nice old chap. He's invited me to go and have a session with him in the next week or so.'

Tara looked up at Bruno's boyish eager face and melted. 'Oh, that's marvellous. I'm sorry I'm being such a rat.'

Bruno smiled. 'Xavier's a splendid chap. Really he is!'

'OK. But for goodness sake stop calling him "sir!"'

'Sorry! It just came slipping out.'

'I don't like him being here. It's all a sham.'

'No. He really admired your father. And he *is* pretty splendid.'

'Stop being so impressed!'

'Sorry!'

'And stop saying sorry!' they chorused in unison, breaking into laughter.

Her mother came in. 'Xavier's staying for supper. Bruno – be a darling and fish out a couple of bottles of claret from the crate in the cellar. You'll have to search among the dust!'

'That's Daddy's claret!' Tara blazed.

Her mother gave her a curiously arch look. Calmly she turned to open the fridge and inspect the contents.

Tara was on fire with feeling. She drained yet another sherry. Alcohol never made her incompetent or slurry, in fact Bruno frequently marvelled at her capacity to put away the drink and stay perfectly lucid.

What it did to Tara was connected more to feelings than

reasoning, which was why she now felt about to explode with churning emotions.

Her mother laid four thick slices of steak on the table and prepared a vinaigrette to dribble over them. Then she took a knife and began to slice an onion with great precision and skill.

Tara looked into her mother's face. Even poised over an onion her eyes were still entirely moisture-free.

'Why does he have to stay?' Tara hissed, rounding on her mother like an angry, snarling terrier. 'What has he to do with us? This should be a night when you and I can be together and grieve.'

Her mother looked up. Her face was still and strangely serene.

'Why can't you weep?' Tara demanded furiously. 'Why are you so blasted cool and collected?'

Her mother turned back to the onion.

'You bitch!' Tara yelled. 'You bloody cold-hearted bitch with your neat highlighted blonde hair and your neat receptionist's job with that greasy doctor. No wonder Daddy felt he had to make the final exit!'

Her mother straightened up, her face a wasteland of emotional wounds.

Saul Xavier, standing silently in the doorway, stepped forward and took Tara by the arm. 'Stop it,' he told her softly.

He guided her through into the sitting room where Tara shook him off and swore under her breath. She flung herself into a chair. 'I want to howl,' she said. 'I want to roar and sob and moan. Right from *here*.' She thumped the base of her stomach.

He looked down at her, his eyes stripped of any readable feeling. 'Go on then. Initiate a flood. It will prevent years of painful and futile leaking in the future.'

Even in her rage Tara saw the sense in his words. But she had no intention of weeping at his command. 'Not here. Not now,' she said, coldly.

'Whilst *I'm* here?'

'Yes.' Tara glared fiercely up at him.

Xavier, who was unerringly attracted to cool slender blondes, felt a primitive blast of sexual heat radiating from this minute, volatile elf who had eyes like peridots and breasts as round and firm as small melons.

He stared down at her, commanding his face to be blank. She would think that he scorned her, that he held only contempt for a young woman who was indulging in a small temper tantrum at her father's funeral. Turning away from her he walked over to the fine Bechstein upright piano that had originally belonged to Tara's great-grandfather. Its inlaid walnut top was submerged under a mass of flowers – gifts of condolence, still in their cellophane wrapping. Beside them was the battered case in which lay her father's latest, most precious, violin. Idly Xavier tapped his fingers on the battered leather. Slowly he opened the case, took out the instrument and stroked its gleaming belly thoughtfully.

'He never made it to a Stradivarius or a Guarneri,' Tara remarked bitterly.

Xavier plucked the strings. 'This is a very close relation. A most beautiful instrument. Your father was an excellent player, a true and loyal servant of music.'

59

'He played his guts out in that orchestra!' Tara said angrily.

Xavier raised his eyebrows. 'Many players do. That is what they choose.'

'They get paid peanuts, slaving away day after day in rehearsals, night after night at concerts. And what do you do? Stand in front of them waving a stick, then pick up your great fat fee and fly off to some far-flung corner of the world to bully the next lot of poor suckers.'

Tara felt enormously pleased to have got that off her chest. She resented Xavier's continued presence bitterly. He should have pushed off with the rest of the guests – or whatever you called people at a funeral bash. Did he truly believe that he was above ordinary human conventions, that he had no need to observe the usual social niceties? Scrutinizing his carved aristocratic features she was certain that he imagined himself to exist in some atmosphere far above ordinary mortals, breathing rarefied air.

'The cost of your car would probably represent double his annual salary,' Tara continued unstoppable, vaguely recollecting fragments from a debate in the students' union concerning the uneven distribution of wealth. 'Whilst my mother will probably have to sell his violin to cover the costs of this funeral and make ends meet.'

'Not at all,' her mother said, coming into the room and regarding her angry daughter with long-suffering resignation. 'Your father left that to you. I shall never sell it, and neither will you.'

'If it's mine then I can do what I like with it,' Tara fumed. 'I'll sell it and give you the money. And then I'll be free.'

'From what?'

'Trying to be something I'll never be. Never being *good enough.*'

'Tara, what is all this about?' Rachel said in genuine bewilderment.

'I don't know.' Tara went quiet. Her throat filled with remorse and grief.

'So – Richard's daughter is not only a singer,' Xavier commented, looking interested. 'I meant to compliment you on your singing in church by the way,' he told Tara. 'I always prefer the boy treble sound in the *Pie Jesu* rather than the full blown soprano.'

'You think I sounded like a boy treble?' Tara demanded.

'Very much so. Charming.' His smile was laced with mockery. No aspiring female singer over twenty should sound like a boy treble.

'You're absolutely right. Tara is no singer,' her mother stated flatly. 'She's a violinist.'

Xavier glanced sharply at Tara from beneath his cowled eyelids. 'Ah!'

'No!' Tara bit fiercely into her lip.

Bruno came in bearing bottles of claret and cut-glass goblets on a silver tray. 'She's terribly good,' he agreed fondly.

'Yes. She just won't practise, that's the problem,' her mother said evenly.

'Mummy! For goodness' sake.'

'Goodness has got nothing to do with it. You could have been a brilliant player. As good as your father. Better. Instead you decided to let your stubborn,

61

mulish, wilful behaviour stifle all your potential.'

Tara gasped. 'Why are you attacking me like this?'

'As a last ditch attempt to stop you throwing yourself into life's dustbin.' She turned to Bruno and Xavier. 'Shall we eat?' she suggested pleasantly, leading the way to the dining room.

The unease caused by Tara's outburst was rapidly dispelled during the meal by Xavier's smooth flow of anecdotes about the famous and quirky in the world of music.

Bruno was agog, his face shining with enthusiastic interest. Xavier's charisma, together with the consumption of generous quantities of sherry and claret, made him wonder how he would ever bear to go back to his law books.

Tara's mother listened with quiet appreciation, smiling abstractedly from time to time.

Tara, her eyes seemingly fastened to Xavier's carved face by invisible wires, found herself smouldering with inner turbulence.

She was furious to have to admit to herself that Xavier was compellingly magnetic, that an almost tangible psychological power emanated from him. There was something softly menacing about him also, something stealthy and cat-like that both alarmed and stimulated her.

Damn him to hell! she thought, liking to have the measure of people and situations.

Over coffee the conversation turned to the art of conducting.

'Isn't that whole thing about Maestro power just a myth?' Tara declared. 'I mean look at poor old Otto

Klemperer. He used to sit in front of the orchestra like a man under anaesthetic whilst the players all followed the first violinist and asked each other now and again if the conductor was dead yet.'

Rachel sighed and raised her eyes heavenwards.

'Daddy used to tell that story.' Tara told Xavier sweetly. 'It's absolutely true.'

'I do apologize for my daughter,' Rachel interposed. 'I'd like to say she is not herself tonight – but unfortunately she is just that. I'm afraid she needs taking firmly in hand.'

'I'm working on it,' Bruno said gamely.

But Tara's mother was looking at Xavier, something Tara did not fail to notice.

Xavier leaned back in his chair and narrowed his eyes reflectively. 'You know when I was a young music student I once had the good fortune to attend a lecture in Milan given by Arturo Toscanini.'

'Before he went gaga I hope,' Tara muttered under her breath.

'Just before his final illness in fact. When he was a very old, very experienced and very wise man,' Xavier countered, throwing Tara a mildly admonishing glance.

'Sorry. Go on,' she said grudgingly.

'He still had the energy to curse and rage about German and Austrian conductors who ruined Mozart's two/four time works by beating four beats in a bar instead of two. Toscanini himself always beat two you see.'

Xavier hummed a Mozart tune from one of the composer's later symphonies. 'You know it?' he asked his interested audience. 'Of course you do. Now – Tara,

Bruno you sing it for me and follow my beat.'

Fixing them with his penetrating grey eyes and using just one long curved finger, he conducted their singing, first beating with the accent coming on each fourth note, then more slowly with the accent coming on the second note.

As she sang Tara understood in a moment why Xavier had this power over orchestras. Watching his moving, mesmerizing finger she had the growing sensation that a steel belt had been placed around her waist, a slightly flexible steel belt which allowed her to be held on the point of that finger, making it impossible for her singing to deviate more than the tiniest fraction under the sparse amount of liberty that he was permitting.

The sensation of intense control brought an equally intense excitement. She found herself wanting to be free and at the same time longing to be held even more firmly.

She wondered if Bruno felt the same, but they were not able to compare notes as Bruno gratefully accepted Xavier's offer of a lift back to London, anxious not to be late for his nine o'clock tutorial the next morning.

Tara accompanied the two men out into the road, where she embraced Bruno lovingly. As she listened to the high whine of the Porsche's engine accelerating into the distance she let her fingers move over the stiff white card which Xavier had unobtrusively placed in her hand as he stepped outside the door. She considered tearing it up without even looking to see what it said.

Having dropped the younger man off at his college, Xavier turned his car towards home and Georgiana.

He felt deeply satisfied. He had done the young man a good turn: he had set up a meeting for him with the timpanist at the Tudor which he was sure would bear fruit. And anyway the young fellow had a career in law all mapped out. Xavier had no need to concern himself with him further.

It was that small fireball of green-eyed rebelliousness that interested him.

Ah, yes. There was much to be considered in respect of that fleshly nymph, delightful manoeuvres to contemplate. And he judged he had already set the ball rolling very nicely.

As he navigated the night-time streets of London he felt himself energized and revitalized, his spirits surging with a sense of anticipatory exhilaration which he had begun to despair of ever recapturing.

# CHAPTER 6

Georgiana lay on the chaise longue, her body and limbs tension-free and peaceful as she looked out of the windows of her therapist's consulting room to the line of cherry trees beyond. Their few remaining leaves had turned to vivid lime-gold.

'I had such a beautiful sleep last night,' she told him. 'Ten whole hours. There were no dreams, no sounds, no movements. Nothing. It was the sort of sleep I used to have when I was a child.'

Dr Daneman, sitting at an angle a few yards away from her, made no immediate response, giving Georgiana time to reflect on her statement, the opportunity to make some analysis of her own – even though he seriously doubted her capacity to do so. His eyes rested on her long stockinged feet and her gazelle-slim ankles before moving slowly over her body, alluringly draped in a cunningly fitting dress of some soft jersey fabric which clung to every contour.

After a short interval of silence he asked, 'You have not slept like that since you were a child?'

Her eyes stared unseeingly ahead of her. Ignoring his question she continued with her own thoughts. 'After I lost the babies I had these terrible nightmares. They were full of blood and pain – ghastly, horrible. I used to force myself to lie awake so they wouldn't come again.'

Yes, she had told him that before. She had been coming to him for some weeks now, at first once each week and now twice. She raked constantly over the ashes of her miscarriages. In fact she was reluctant to talk of much else. He had to admit that he was not making very much progress with her. But it was early days yet. There was time – weeks and months of it stretching ahead. And the prospect of sitting quietly just out of her view, with all the freedom in the world to let his eyes linger over her delicious person was distinctly pleasing.

'You did not dream then when you were a child?' he asked, wondering if she might at long last be persuaded to speak of her childhood. Usually his patients were only too eager to delve into their past. After all, in this modern, fast-moving, money accumulating society it was a luxury to be granted the licence to talk at length about oneself. Especially to someone who not only listened without interrupting, but seemed to care.

In the four years of his practice as a psychotherapist (the 'Doctor' tag came, not from medical qualifications, but from a complex thesis on the merits of contrasting methods of mind therapy for which he had gained a Doctorate in Philosophy) Dr Daneman had heard countless stories of childhood – most of them unhappy and brutal. This was hardly surprising as his patients came to him because they had problems, the underlying causes of which were inevitably rooted in their childish past. The problems that rose to the surface – alcoholism, drug abuse, anorexia, depression, poor sexual performance – were merely symptoms of something far deeper. It was his job to discover the demons in the hidden caverns and gently reveal them to the patient in an attempt to purge their power. He judged that his degree of success was satisfactory and steadily improving.

'Just sometimes I would dream,' she said suddenly. 'I used to see my parents' faces. They would be smiling at me just as they did when I was awake. They were the gentlest parents, the most loving. We were all so happy.'

Dr Daneman looked across at the winking red light on his tape recorder on his desk. He would be interested to listen to those words played back when she had gone. Statements of that kind were simply too good to be true. What was she concealing from him? From herself?

'My mother was very beautiful. Golden-skinned, lovely ash blonde hair. Not as tall as me, but everyone said we were unmistakably mother and child.' She smiled, taking obvious pleasure in the memory, closing her eyes like a cat responding to a soft caress.

Dr Daneman directed his attention to her face. She was indeed beautiful with her firm jawline, her high cheekbones and her fashion model's straight nose. Beneath her bronze-shadowed lids were eyes as blue as a summer sky and her straight baby-soft hair was not the strawy white blonde produced in a hairdressing salon, but a thick buttery shade which he assumed must be entirely natural.

'She's still alive,' Georgiana continued. 'Seventy now and still very lovely.' Another smile.

So the daughter need have no undue fears about the ravages of the ageing process, Dr Daneman thought.

'You seem to feel great affection for your mother,' he suggested.

Georgiana gave a low loving murmur of assent. 'Yes. Oh yes. And my father, of course. He was a wonderful man.'

'He's dead now?'

'Two years ago. Poor Daddy. He used to call me his own lovely darling.'

'And what did he call your mother?'

'His own precious darling. They were terribly loving to each other. And to both of us.'

'Both of you?' Dr Daneman enquired.

'Me and my brother Raymond.'

Dr Daneman leaned forward slightly, clasping his manicured hands loosely together, considering how to frame the next question which he hoped would stimulate Georgiana to make a start on the intimate biography of her past.

He was an excellent listener: concerned, calm, sincere, unshockable. He liked his patients to feel that he took them seriously, that he truly cared about them as people, not just as one more item in a conveyor belt of human misery and anxiety.

'So that was your family? Your mother, your father and your brother Raymond. Anyone else?'

'Just the four of us. The perfect family.' Georgiana allowed her mind to drift away into the idyllic lost world of her childhood. As she began to translate her thoughts and images into words for the handsome, personable Dr Daneman she felt a warm glow of well-being suffuse her body. Suddenly there was licence to be a cherished little girl all over again.

69

Dr Daneman listened to the faintly metallic, flat voice with growing pleasure. Georgiana Xavier was beginning to have an appeal for him that none of his other women clients had evoked.

And now at last she was opening up. Another few sessions like this and he would have enough information to begin to frame a hypothesis as to the true nature of her troubles.

Dr Daneman saw Georgiana as an innocent, partially blind creature confronting a sheet of darkened glass, seeing only her own reflection, her own feelings. In time he would clear that glass for her, wipe away the darkness and enable her to see clearly into the outer world beyond the inner turmoil.

The prospect of exercising such tender and healing power was utterly seductive.

# CHAPTER 7

**X**avier waited a week and then he telephoned Tara's home number. Taking into account the tantalizing message he had scribbled for her on his personal calling card he was intrigued and rather impressed that she had not been on the line to him before.

He recognized her voice immediately, was struck afresh by its curious blend of grating assertiveness and husky seduction.

She, in turn, knew immediately that it was him. 'Oh!' she exclaimed.

'You did not go back to college?' he enquired pleasantly.

'No. Packed it in.'

'It was not for you?'

'No.'

'That is because you are a musician.'

Her answering silence was bold and deliberate.

'I've been making some enquiries,' he continued. 'Your former teacher for a start.'

'What!'

He took pleasure in imagining her shocked and indignant expression. 'I have something important to tell you Tara. My old friend Monica Heilfrich is here in London giving some master classes and I want you to take part.'

'Me? Play for the great Heilfrich. Is that a joke?'

'I'll take you along myself.'

'Is that supposed to make things better? Do you think you're any less terrifying than her?'

Xavier was delighted at all this unashamed frankness. For years he had been surrounded with fawning sycophants and had become heartily sick of their evasive style of speech. He could almost hear their minds squirming and wriggling as they painstakingly weighed every word for fear of offending him.

'So how often have you been playing your father's instrument since last week – mm?' he asked Tara, conjuring a detailed visual image of her in his head, the shaggy elfin haircut, the wayward fringe flopping over those wonderful glinting green eyes. And her figure – so tiny, yet so rounded, so firmly fleshed.

'Around three to four hours a day.' This was a lie; she had been playing for seven at least.

A smile of triumph tilted the corners of Xavier's long stern lips. 'I'm very glad to hear it. Now! Listen to me! This is no joke. I've been talking to Monica and she is most interested to hear you play. She's invited you to join her little group next week. Tuesday I think. She starts at two in the afternoon. So I'll pick you up at eleven, we'll have a little light lunch together and then I'll drop you off at her place.'

Tara breathed in deeply. 'No.'

'Tara! This is an opportunity not to be missed.' He

wondered whether to exert a little extra pressure in the form of dropping in a reference to her father, but decided against it.

'Oh, I'll come to the master class. But I'll get there under my own steam, thanks all the same,' she added.

'I see. Very well.' His voice was chilling.

'Will you be there?' she asked.

'Yes.'

'I'll be scared out of my wits. I'll probably play like a donkey.'

The line clicked abruptly off, leaving Xavier high and dry.

Dropping the phone deftly back on the cradle, he smiled with devilish speculation. Of course the spiky young sprite might be absolutely useless and he would have a little egg on his face, for which Monica would tease him without mercy.

He doubted however that Tara Silk's lack of musical skill would be a problem. Her teacher had spoken of Tara's interesting potential in her childhood and early teens and, even if the wayward nymph had not been motivated and practising for a while, that was unlikely to have vanished. True talent was never lost – ruling out brain damage or psychological breakdown.

No doubt Tara would present plenty of problems outside the musical sphere, but he rather looked forward to dealing with those.

And what could be more tantalizingly exciting than playing god in the conception, gestation and eventual birth of a coruscating new talent?

\* \* \*

'Saul Xavier seems to have taken it into his head to be my Svengali,' Tara told her mother drily when she returned home from work that evening.

As Rachel listened to the full story a spark of hope leapt inside her at the prospect of the re-awakening of Tara's buried musical aspirations. Concern about Tara had temporarily almost stifled the grief of Richard's death. Rachel saw that her daughter was desperately adrift, stumbling around in some private wilderness, searching wildly for the odd signpost to re-direct her on a path of purpose.

Rachel wondered where she and Richard had gone wrong with this bright, iron-willed offspring who had been so full of shining hope and promise as a child. She supposed they had been preoccupied with the intensity of their sorrow for a time after Freddie's death and maybe that had had some harmful effect. But they had tried so hard not to let their private torment affect their relationship with their remaining child. Indeed when Tara had become their *only* child she had been even more precious than before.

And Richard had always been so encouraging about her musical potential; her singing and her violin playing. He had spent hours tutoring her himself in addition to the expert teaching she received at one of the country's leading music schools for which she had gained a scholarship at the age of eight. He had even composed short pieces for her practice sessions so as to provide extra interest.

And after all that, at seventeen, when her talent seemed on the point of breaking from the bud into full blossom, she had suddenly turned her back on it. She had gone wild, sampling all the temptations of the stereotypical teenage culture: booze, boys, all-night parties. And raucous, full-blast pop music that throbbed through the house and made Richard wince with horror.

Her violin lay untouched in its case and her voice was directed into yelling at her parents rather than developing musically.

Scraping into London University to do philosophy had been a last resort rather than a choice, affording no more than temporary parental relief. Clearly that had never been right for her. And now she had thrown that in as well, with no apparent plans to do anything else. Even her waitressing job had gone – her boss did not take kindly to employees taking time off, even for family bereavement.

Rachel supposed Tara would be reduced to signing on for unemployment benefit. Her heart wept.

There seemed only Bruno at present who represented some stability.

'Aren't you pleased Mummy?' Tara demanded. 'For me to be playing again?'

'Of course I'm pleased.'

'Daddy would have been, wouldn't he?'

Rachel sighed. 'You must do this for yourself, not for Daddy.' She looked at Tara and saw the confusion and conflict in her face. Anger too. There was this constant undercurrent of anger. Rachel couldn't understand it. Why?

Later in the evening as they watched the late night news programme, Tara said suddenly, 'I think I was crazy to agree to go to this master class. Do you really think I should?'

Her mother frowned. 'Yes. Yes, I think you should go. What's to be lost?'

'My self-respect?'

'Xavier's faith in you?'

'Yes.'

'I'm surprised you're admitting to caring about that!'

'So am I,' Tara agreed with feeling.

Monica Heilfrich held her master classes in the pink and gold drawing room of her Belgravia flat. She maintained that the intimate, home-like atmosphere helped her students to relax.

Tara was the last to arrive, her bus having been delayed in the snarl of city traffic. She found two other nervous and hopeful violinists present, a boy who looked about fourteen and a young woman her own age – but no sign of Saul Xavier.

Monica welcomed her as though she were a long-lost relative, overwhelming Tara with a huge hug which made her instantly uneasy. In fact the moment she walked into the womb-like room with its plumply upholstered sofas and extravagantly swagged curtains Tara wanted to escape.

Monica, sixtyish, Junoesque and flamboyantly arrayed in a flowing pink caftan, served coffee and fragile continental biscuits whilst in the background her stereo system played a 1959 recording of the Brahms violin concerto.

'Is that you playing?' Tara asked, listening intently.

'Naturally. Can you guess the orchestra, the conductor?' Monica enquired teasingly.

Tara frowned. 'A mid-European orchestra. Not the Vienna Phil, you can't mistake their elegant mellow sound. This is a real deep throat sound, a bit on the stern side. So maybe a German orchestra?'

Monica's eyes sharpened. 'Go on,' she encouraged.

'The Berlin Philharmonic,' Tara decided. 'My father used to say that if angels had sterling silver harps the skies would be filled with the sound of the Berlin Phil's string section.'

'What a marvellous thought! Now, what about the conductor?'

Tara considered. There was not enough to go on from what she had heard. It was, of course, perfectly possible to detect certain conductors' styles from an orchestra's playing. Her father had demonstrated that to her years ago, both from his unending fund of stories about conductors and their idiosyncratic styles and also his vast collection of recordings which he used to invite the young Tara to enjoy with him. But from this snatch of the music, which was mainly designed as a show case for Monica's brilliant violin playing, it was not possible to do more than guess.

'Herbert von Karajan was the boss then at the Berlin Phil,' Tara observed. 'I'll go for him as the most likely.'

Monica handed her the record sleeve to check for herself. Her hypothesizing had been entirely correct. 'I'm rather impressed,' Monica said, raising her eyebrows.

The other assembled instrumentalists glanced at Tara with respect. But there was a tinge of envious rivalry in their eyes which made her wish she'd kept her mouth shut.

Monica gave them an A on the piano and invited them to

tune their instruments. Tara took her father's precious instrument from its case and settled it under her jawbone. Suddenly the essence of its previous owner overwhelmed her. For a few seconds she felt her father as a living presence in the room and then just as suddenly the image died and she found her eyes brimming with tears.

'A little ice breaker!' Monica decreed, taking up her own instrument and plucking the strings provocatively before launching into the opening theme of the Mendelssohn concerto. 'Every aspiring violinist has a go with this one,' she told her admiring audience. 'It is simply too tempting not to have a little try. Such a sinuous, tantalizing melody.' She wriggled her ample shoulders like an elderly overfed kitten. 'Let's see if I'm right.' She beckoned to the boy, inviting him to continue where she had left off.

He stood up, a pale oriental beanpole with a curtain of silky black hair.

As he started to play the door opened softly and Xavier walked in. Settling himself silently in a far corner of the room he gave a floppy wave of his hand indicating that the proceedings should continue without interruption.

Tara listened in fascination to the boy's playing. His talent was huge, his technical skill awesome, and his ability to wring emotion from the music equally stunning. She was consumed with admiration. But despite the intensity of her concentration on this young boy's phenomenal ability she found herself unable to ignore the still, silent presence of Saul Xavier. Her eyes flickered constantly across to his, desperate not to miss any clue as to the nature of the Maestro's response to what he was hearing.

But Xavier gave nothing away. His face was perfectly

still and blank and remained so throughout the next thirty minutes, during which Monica tutored, tortured and teased the gauche intense boy, drawing from him ever more evidence of a massive musical potential.

Tara found herself growing increasingly apprehensive at the prospect of being placed under the merciless spotlight of Monica's tuition. It was not so much her sure knowledge that her own skill in no way measured up to what she had heard so far, but more an intense reluctance to be shown up as mediocre in Saul Xavier's eyes.

Her nerves began to sing with tension. Stage fright churned in her stomach.

When Monica eventually called on her to take up her violin her hands were trembling so much she feared she would not be able to pull the bow over the strings.

Monica listened to her playing solo for a few seconds before stopping her abruptly. 'That's good. Quite nice. But there's too much tension. Relax my dear. Watch me – deep breaths. Come along now, deep breaths.'

Tara felt there was no alternative but to do as she was told. She felt humiliated and stupid stood there in the middle of room huffing and puffing.

She started again. Some Bach this time, one of the partitas.

Again Monica stopped her. 'Still too much tightness, too many nerves. Listen, it happens to all of us, these wretched nerves. *I'm* nervous!'

'No you're not!' Tara shot back at her firmly.

Monica laughed. 'OK. It's different for me. Of course it is. Why don't you go and sit down for a few minutes, get your breath back and then we'll try again?'

Her face hot and crimson, Tara did as she was directed whilst the other young woman was put through her paces. Tara wondered whether to leave now. Very quietly, no fuss, no drama. She knew she had no chance of showing whatever talent she possessed in these surroundings. And certainly not under the hawk-like gaze of Saul Xavier whose silent presence seemed to permeate the room.

In fact Monica did not demand a second performance from her but invited her to join in a final group session where the three instrumentalists played together whilst Monica accompanied them on the piano.

At the close of the session Monica spoke to her three pupils, making a brief appraisal of what she had heard, making it clear that she was interested in tutoring the young man further. She told the young woman that she should persist with her present engagement with a London orchestra and that she was going to recommend her to her own agent as a prospective client.

She turned last to Tara. 'Quite nice decisive playing once you got rid of those nerves. Very *physical* playing in fact,' she observed carefully. 'A nice tone as well.'

Tara felt herself stiffen. This was definitely a case of damning with faint praise.

'You must go away, get some good tutoring and practise for around a year,' Monica smiled. 'Then you could well try for a place in one of the provincial orchestras. They need young players of spirit like you. All in all, I think you will do very well my dear!'

Tara packed away her instrument. Her stomach still churned. Her brain felt numb. She cursed herself for having laid her head on this particular chopping block.

She hoped desperately that Saul Xavier would continue to show little interest in her presence. With relief she saw that he was fully engaged talking with Monica, frowning and nodding his head gravely.

Unobtrusively nodding her goodbyes Tara moved towards the door and slipped through, gaining an immediate sense of release. Out in the street she breathed deeply, savouring the fresh, sharp air. She debated going on to see Bruno, but hesitated, thinking it would be unfair to disturb him if he was studying hard.

A strong purposeful hand grasped her elbow. 'I'll take you home Tara.'

Her heart jumped. Looking up she connected with Saul Xavier's impassive gaze. In the still-bright afternoon light she noticed that his eyes were flecked with streaks of deep sapphire. They glinted in the depth of his cool grey eyes, suggesting some underlying wildness of personality which contrasted strongly with his remote and rigidly contained exterior.

Still touchy and on the defensive after the session with Monica Heilfrich, Tara's initial instinct was to refuse his offer. But as he steered her firmly towards his car parked just a few yards away, she found herself curiously unresisting. She felt drained and weary, in no mood to fight him for her right to grapple with London's public transport.

He started the engine, a throbbing beast with a roar in its belly and the distinctive whine of precision engineering in its throat. Tara felt her back pressed against the seat as Xavier accelerated. She had never realized before that it was perfectly possible to drive fast in London's jumble of traffic – as long as one was prepared to ignore the rights and demands of all the other drivers.

'You are sorry you went along to that little event?' he enquired conversationally.

'It was a farce. A disaster,' she responded with feeling.

'To be told you could make it into a civic orchestra. That is a disaster?'

Tara jerked her head round so as to examine his expression.

As she might have foreseen it gave nothing away. 'As a matter of fact, yes.'

He nodded. Said nothing.

'Would *you* have been pleased at twenty to have been told you might make it to the rear section of the violins in a second-rate orchestra – *if* you practised?' she demanded.

'I was never a violinist.'

'Hah! Sliding out of the question.' She turned to stare out of the window. She felt wretchedly bleak. The master class session had not only unnerved her but had dug deep into the rawness of her grief. It was as though her father had been there with her during those fateful minutes and she had been powerless to prevent herself letting him down.

'What were you hoping for? To be told you had a future as a soloist?' Xavier asked.

'Probably.' She felt a fresh stab of pain as the flame of ambitious optimism that had glowed throughout the years of her childhood was finally snuffed out. 'Yes. I used to hope for that. That is what *he* wanted for me.'

'And were his hopes realistic?'

'You've just heard me play. You should know,' she responded aggressively.

'I did not hear you as a child. A great deal could have happened since then.'

Tara did not reply. She did not want to talk about it; her childish potential, the anxiety to match up to her father's hopes. She wanted to cry again because she had lost him forever. She wondered how long it would be before she stopped feeling like that.

They were out of the city now, on the dual carriageway leading to the west-bound motorway. She glanced at Xavier. 'Why aren't we going straight home?'

'I enjoy driving. And you're not busy are you?'

She shrugged. She glanced at the rev counter. The rpms were up at 4000. The car was doing ninety and still accelerating.

Her eyes moved to Xavier's profile, travelled over the lithe supple body and the slender powerful hands placed at ten past ten on the small steering wheel. She found that she could not keep her eyes off him. Against her will she was fascinated. There was something unfathomable in those steely cold eyes with their deeply cowled lids. And his face was disturbingly arresting, troubling even. The long carved bones were those of a medieval knight, the deep forehead reminiscent of the stone heroes who lay on marble-topped coffins in great cathedrals.

Something stirred and uncoiled in her body, something dark and primitive, giving her an uneasy premonition of some basic and fateful change about to overtake her.

Briefly he turned to her, his long lips curved into a smile as though he were relishing a private joke. She did not smile back.

They were on the motorway, in the outside lane. Behind

them the snaking trail of cars was rapidly swallowed up in the disappearing distance.

'It's illegal!' Tara breathed, exhilarated and a little fearful.

'I know all the radar traps. And no police car could catch us if we really started moving.'

Tara moulded herself back in her seat and watched the countryside spin past.

'I love speed,' he told her. 'In the summertime I judge the quality of my driving by the number of flies I kill with the side windows!'

Tara felt a lurch of nausea. The speedometer now registered one hundred and thirty.

'Are you afraid?' he enquired softly.

She moistened her lips. She looked again at his face. 'No. Was that what you wanted?'

He laughed. 'I'm glad that you trust me.'

Tara's fingers were curled against the raised leather seams of the seat, her knuckles white. She said steadily, 'I trust you because you're the sort of man who values himself very highly. You believe your life is important. You would never put yourself at real risk.'

His lips curled into a slow smile. 'What a curious little speech.'

Tara judged she had hit the nail on the head and felt herself relax.

Xavier turned off the motorway at the next exit, easing the car to a sedate seventy miles an hour. He reached out and pressed a small black button on the dashboard.

Music surged from an array of speakers: Bach, the Brandenburg Concerto Number 2. Tara's uncertainties and unease began to fall away from her with the smooth swiftness of rain coursing down sheet glass. A spring of sheer joy bubbled up inside as the clear notes of a flute, oboe and violin intertwined their voices in a musical conversation of radiant beauty. Her lips curled into a smile of pure pleasure.

'I used to play bits of the Brandenburgs with my father,' she told Xavier.

He nodded.

'Years ago, when I was just a kid.'

'Before you shot yourself in the foot,' he observed drily.

'What?'

'Rejected your musical talent and also *him* for some incomprehensible reason, murdered your future prospects as a player.'

Tara was utterly dismayed.

'You've been a stupid fool, haven't you?' he said softly.

She flinched, angry and wounded. 'Oh God, you don't begin to understand!'

'I most certainly do not. Do you?'

She stared at him, her eyes wide with pain. 'No,' she said slowly.

He drew up beside her house and switched off the whining engine.

Tara turned to him. 'Thank you,' she said solemnly.

'Today was helpful?' he wondered.

'Yes. Playing for Monica, being scared out of my wits, realizing how much damage I've done . . . all of it.'

'So – what will you do with your life?'

Her eyes swam with tears. She shook her head.

'I'll see you into the house,' he said.

He stood in the hallway, a tall impassive figure looking down at her, his face blank and clinical. 'Will you be all right?'

'Yes. Would you like some tea before you go?'

He inclined his head graciously.

Tara went into the kitchen. The telephone on the wall rang.

'Tara, it's Mummy. I've had to stay late at the surgery.' A pause. 'Donald has suggested we go and get something to eat together.'

Tara heard the hesitation in her mother's voice. It had the effect of irritating her intensely, just as Bruno did when he skirted around her, anxious not to offend. 'Donald's invited you out to dinner! Well that's great. Have a lovely time,' she said cheerily.

'Yes, well look . . .'

'Mummy! You're perfectly entitled to go out for a meal without getting my approval. I'll expect you when I see you. Right?' Tara put the phone down and looked at it thoughtfully.

She found Xavier sitting motionless on the sofa, his hands folded on his lap.

Tara handed him a steaming mug, then sat down opposite him staring into her own drink. 'My mother's got a date with her boss. He's a smooth-talking doctor who just happens to be a lonely and available widower. Isn't that nice for both of them?' she said sarcastically.

'It probably is,' Xavier agreed evenly.

The bitch! Tara thought, her eyes narrowing with resentment at the thought of her mother swanning off to some restaurant with another man when her father was

86

hardly off the scene. She glanced up at Xavier. She sensed that he was acutely aware of the hostility and bitterness that churned inside her, but that he would probably choose to ignore it.

She had never come across anyone like him. His detachment was such she could imagine herself feeling free to reveal anything to him, however vile or shocking.

Moving her gaze from his icy grey eyes to his long slender hands the question of his sexuality suddenly crossed her mind, making her wonder how he ever managed to let go enough to perform the undignified contortions involved in the sexual act.

The telephone rang again. This time it was Bruno, anxious to know how she had gone on.

As she began to respond in guarded tones, Xavier got up quietly and, raising his hand in a small gesture of farewell, slipped out of the room. She heard the front door click shut behind him and then the high whine of the car's engine.

'Darling are you all right?' Bruno enquired kindly after she had completed her story and they had progressed to more general subjects.

'Perfectly,' she snapped.

'When can I see you?'

'Oh, soon. I don't think I should go out too much. It's not good for Mummy to be on her own just at present.' She was not sure of her motivation in telling this lie.

'Yes, of course. What about the weekend?'

'Fine. We'll fix something definite next time we talk.'

'Are you sure there isn't anything wrong? It isn't me, is it? Have I made you cross?'

Tara grimaced in exasperation. 'No. No – it isn't you.'

When Bruno put the phone down he found that he was taking deep heavy breaths. He sensed that something had happened, that some fundamental change had taken place which might alter his life.

The terrifying possibility of losing Tara spun in his head, and his steps were dizzy and uncoordinated as he walked down the corridor back to his little room and the book-laden desk.

# CHAPTER 8

Georgiana was agitated. The air around her seemed to crackle with feeling as she approached the chaise longue.

Dr Daneman watched her closely as she slipped off her shoes and swung her long thin legs onto the velvet plateau of the therapy couch.

'Can you cure me?' she asked him abruptly, her blue eyes wide open, glittering with a mingle of emotions.

He attempted to identify them. Anxiety? Indignation? Or perhaps something stronger. Terror? Outrage?

'You are not ill,' he told her mildly.

'Then why do I come to you?'

'To learn more about yourself.'

'I come because I am frigid,' she told him, spitting the last word out with contemptuous emphasis.

This was interesting. Georgiana had never used that word before. She had told Dr Daneman with wistful regret that she and her husband had not slept together for a time, that he was a very busy man and did not find it easy to relax, that his tension in turn strung her up so she found it hard to respond as a loving wife should. She had been tenderly regretful as she told him this, emphasizing to Dr

Daneman how much she loved her husband, how she longed to make him happy, to be the perfect wife.

'You feel guilty about that?' he asked her.

Her breasts rose and fell rhythmically as she struggled with some intense feeling, which looked to Dr Daneman like red-hot rage.

'I have *nothing* to feel guilty about. I have done my very best to make my marriage perfect. My parents always used to tell me that it was the trying that counted, not the outcome. *They* understood me,' she finished bitterly.

Georgiana felt as though the inside of her head was on fire. Xavier had never understood her. He had been a considerate, admiring and generous husband, but he had never idolized her, fêted her, placed her on a golden pedestal. And now he had rejected her very best efforts on his behalf.

She heard again his calm, cool words; so polite, so totally controlled and reasonable. Those words rang on in her head, punishing and humiliating her.

Xavier's gentle directive had come out of the blue, just a few days after that last wonderful gift she had offered him, just as she was congratulating herself on her continuing ingenuity in breathing life into her marriage.

'No more charming "gifts", darling – mm?' he had told her lightly. 'Little games are entertaining for a while, but I think it's time to stop now.' He had taken her very gently in his arms, terrifying her with the prospect of a fresh assault on her virginity – for it was as a virgin that she saw herself after the years of chastity.

Dr Daneman watched her contorted face. He waited.

She wrapped her arms lovingly around herself. Her

facial muscles relaxed as she took herself back to the old, lovely world that was now lost. She said, 'When I was small my daddy used to sing me to sleep.' In a husky, not very tuneful voice she began to sing:

> 'Hush little baby don't say a word,
> Daddy's gonna buy you a mocking bird.
> If that mocking bird don't sing,
> Daddy's gonna buy you a diamond ring . . .'

She went on humming, the words becoming less clear. 'Do you know,' she said suddenly, 'my mummy and daddy used to say that nothing would ever harm their little baby; if the cold east wind so much as tried to touch a hair of her little blonde head then they would trap it in a bottle and put the cork on so tightly it would fizzle away to nothing.'

Dr Daneman believed her. Over the weeks Georgiana had painted him a vivid verbal portrait of her childhood. Gradually, he had come to the conclusion that Georgina's problems lay, not in dealing with the loss of her babies, but in finally accepting the loss of her childhood.

A seemingly idyllic childhood, a time when she appeared to have been sublimely happy. At first he hadn't believed a word of her eulogizing. But then the picture began to fit together and make perfect sense.

There had been no cruelty, no traumas, no poverty, no illness or untimely deaths.

Home had been a warm pool of love peopled by parents who made a goddess of her, who unquestioningly adored and protected their beautiful little trophy-daughter. There had been no competition from the elder brother who was painted as an equally adoring acolyte – not threateningly clever and obligingly moderate in terms of looks.

Clearly Georgiana had had a wonderful time controlling them all. Whatever she wanted they had given her: love, approval, praise, attention. And material goods – oh, lots of material goods.

The adult Georgiana went about the world in disguise, presenting herself as a passive object of idle leisure and exquisite beauty. Trophy-offspring transformed into trophy-wife. There was no career, no children to care for.

But Dr Daneman judged that the outward picture of passivity cunningly concealed a ferocious inner drive. Georgiana was still the narcissistic baby who had sought the control of her world and gained it. Why should she give it up?

A job would have been out of the question. A job would have made demands on her. Georgiana would only be happy as the boss. *She* must control. But she had not learned the necessary skills in order to be in that position.

The act of sex would be even more damaging than a job, far too passive an activity for her mammoth child's ego to withstand. To be penetrated by a powerful man would be deeply painful psychologically. Perhaps physically also.

And ironically she had chosen to marry the dynamic, dominating Saul Xavier, who would have no intention of being anything but in full control himself.

Georgiana would have had no way of understanding that. She would, of course, have regarded the snaring of him as a great achievement.

A beautiful girl child gets presents. She gets dolls and

clothes and puppies and diamonds. And when she is old enough she must get a man worthy of her feminine perfection. She must prove to other women how superior she is.

Xavier must have been a real catch: brilliant, talented, famous and wildly attractive. A modern day hero.

Entirely worthy.

But now Georgiana's marriage was faltering as she and Xavier struggled for power and refused to bow any longer to the demands of a wife who was a sexual failure and had a pathologically undeveloped appreciation of the way her fellow human beings ticked.

Dr Daneman found himself fascinated. He longed for Georgiana to give him details of her sexual encounters with Xavier but she remained stubbornly silent on that subject.

'Do you want to change?' he asked her. 'As a person?'

Her eyelids flickered. A slow smile crept over her face. 'No – no, no, no.'

Dr Daneman smiled.

He doubted that she would ever change. What motivation was there? She truly believed herself perfect. It was simply that on occasions the world annoyingly refused to accommodate itself to her view.

He looked at her hands, delicate with tapering fingers and coral-lacquered nails, resting on the flat of her stomach just above the navel. He imagined her naked; smooth-skinned and clean-boned. There would be a gentle haze of blonde hair at her crotch, a childlike rosy tip to each dainty breast. Her buttocks would be soft ellipses; if she turned her back to him and bent over with her long legs together those globes would form the perfect heart.

His pulse quickened.

As the light on his tape recorder winked and Georgiana's flat voice chimed in the background he allowed his mind to play out a fantasy where he delicately peeled off her clothes and, using the most gentle, most leisurely touches of his lips and fingers brought her to a shuddering orgasm that made her his slave.

# CHAPTER 9

Bruno walked with Tara along the embankment. Looking down at the top of her head, at the adorable sheen of spikily cropped chestnut hair, he felt a painful lurch of tenderness.

He had known as soon as she arrived at his room earlier on that his terrifying premonition of losing her was about to become reality. The sadness welling up within him – to be concealed at all costs from Tara – formed a liquidy swelling at the back of his throat.

She had spoken hardly a word in the past hour. Her face was still and solemn.

'You can tell me, darling,' he said gently. 'Anything – whatever it is, I'll understand.'

She shook her head, squeezed her eyelids together tightly. 'I don't know. I honestly don't know.' She stared up at him, her eyes glistening with tears.

'It's hardly any time at all since your father died, it's only to be expected . . .'

'No,' she interrupted quietly, sending a chill to his heart. 'No, not that. I just feel . . . well, I just think we should stop seeing each other for a while.'

It was incomprehensible to him. They got on so well. He loved her so much. There would never be anyone else. Never. Unthinkable.

He took her hand. She held on to him tightly, trying to make things easier for him.

Bruno sensed her pity for him. He did not want her pity. That only made the hurt worse. He simply wanted to have her with him for ever – body and soul. *For richer, for poorer. Till death us do part.*

'There's no one else,' she said truthfully.

He winced silently. It was three weeks now since they had made love and his body ached for her. The mere thought of another man possessing his treasure engulfed him in a fresh wave of bleak misery.

He smiled down at her. 'Good! Because I'd have killed him. Grievous bodily harm at the very least!' He forced the words to emerge with delicate irony. On no account was she to guess the extent of his grief.

'I'm being such a bitch!' she wailed. 'I just don't seem to be able to get anything right at the moment.'

'You got *everything* right,' he told her tenderly. 'For me – being with you was . . . perfect. This last year has been the best of my life. I'll be eternally grateful.'

Getting it right, he thought. What an odd, indefinable concept that was. He recalled asking her on the telephone if he had done anything wrong. He had pondered it endlessly and eventually come up with the answer. He knew that if it were possible to start right back at the beginning the one thing he should never do was let her guess at the extent of his adoration. It had smothered her, given her no space to breathe. Even

96

that last little speech had been just the kind of thing to chase her away. He had, in fact, done everything completely wrong. He saw it all with perfect clarity. And at the same time he knew that even with the miracle of a second chance with Tara he would make exactly the same mistakes.

If you really loved someone, there was simply no way of concealing it. And, on the whole, that meant you were doomed to suffer.

He took her to the train. He kissed her gently and told her she was terribly brave to have been so frank with him.

As the train lurched into movement he saw the tears rolling freely down her beloved face.

'Cheer up,' he mouthed to her, waving, smiling, keeping his own emotions locked tightly behind the required façade of manliness as he made his way out of the station. Squaring his shoulders he plunged bravely into the road beyond.

For a year now Tara had been his friend, his lover, critic, judge and ally. He had allowed her to mould his identity. Without her he would not be the same person.

Tara spent a miserable day or two trudging round the local restaurants and eventually got herself an evening job waitressing in a small Italian trattoria ten minutes' walk from her home. It was hard work, but better than being unemployed and queuing up with the sad procession of life's losers every Wednesday morning to argue the toss about state benefits.

With her earnings and tips she was able to give her mother a small amount to contribute to the housekeeping bills and was now saving in order to book a number of sessions with a reputable violin tutor.

Having broken her father's heart by rebelling against his lifetime ambition for her in the world of music, now all she wanted to do was play.

During the day, whilst her mother was at work, she practised non-stop. Holding and playing her father's precious instrument fulfilled some deep need. There was no clear aim behind her punishing regime, no identifiable goal to work towards. She was simply driven, compelled. It was as though in a few weeks she had to make up for all the lost time of the past two years.

She would start with some basic exercises, working on the technical bits and pieces of playing that her father had always claimed should be in impeccable working order so that one did not have to think about them once there was the interpretation of a complex piece to concentrate on. After that she would move on to some short pieces of Bach, and then something from one of the great violin and piano sonatas. Occasionally she would permit herself the luxury of a grand, full-scale concerto – played against the orchestral background of one of the old vinyl records from her father's vast collection.

It was whilst she was engaged on one such an undertaking – the work being Elgar's mighty concerto which was making her sweat with effort – that she was astonished to see the tall figure of Saul Xavier standing outside the window staring in at her.

A coil of shock spun inside her as his eyes made contact with hers. She stared at him blankly for a few moments.

He gestured towards the door, requesting that she should open it.

He walked straight in and stood in the hallway looking down at her. A faint, ironic smile flickered over his features.

She flung out her arms in a gesture of mock despair. 'I'm not dressed for entertaining,' she protested, her mind racing with conjecture as to why the hell he had turned up like this.

She was struck afresh by the psychological power of the man, the magnetic, subtly menacing charisma that clung to him like a soft halo of light so that his presence illuminated everything around him. As he watched her in calm silence she had the sensation of standing under a spotlight, with all the little human flaws and faults mercilessly revealed.

'Elgar,' he said, tilting his head in the direction of the stereo speakers from which the music surged.

She nodded. 'I was playing along to the recording. I know it's not the approved method, but it seems to help.'

He raised his eyebrows slightly. Offered no opinion.

'I've come to put a proposition to you,' he said, ushering her in front of him to the sitting room and settling himself on the sofa.

Tara turned the music off. It unnerved her to have been discovered practising in this way. And the recording was not even one of Xavier's!

She looked at him. 'Oh?'

'You have no job at the moment I take it?'

She told him about the restaurant and he waved a dismissive hand. Clearly that did not count.

'I've been approached to take on the job of music director and chief conductor with the Tudor,' he told her. 'I'm considering it very carefully.'

'You haven't been with one particular orchestra recently, have you?' She stood before him, her face intent with speculation; a small barefoot figure clad in faded old jeans and a well worn arran sweater.

'There have been links with one or two, but I've been mainly guest conducting as I'm sure you know.'

'Jet-setting round the world picking up the loot!' Tara suggested mischievously, not being able to stop herself.

His features registered no response, but his grey eyes pierced her relentlessly, never leaving her face for a second. 'It will mean settling down here in London, having a base again, taking up the cause of a great orchestra. There are a lot of advantages to consider.'

'Yes. I can see that. And orchestras like it on the whole having one guy at the helm. As long as the bloke in question isn't a malevolent despot.' Her eyes held his boldly. Verbal fencing with Xavier took a lot of nerve, but she judged she was up to it.

'Is that your own opinion, or your father's?' Xavier enquired.

'His, of course. How else would I know?'

He paused. 'For the record Tara, I am indeed a despot. But not, I think, malevolent.'

She nodded, holding his gaze firmly, refusing to be the first to drop her eyes.

'I think my decision is made,' he stated evenly. 'I shall take on the Tudor Philharmonic and shape it into one of the finest orchestras in the world. It will have a repertoire second to none. And the players will be rewarded not only artistically but also financially. We shall gain recording contracts that will make them all rich enough to drive to rehearsals in Mercedes and when we go on tour they will stay in the best hotels. Because that is what they will have earned, that will be what they are worthy of.'

'And what will you do on the second day?' Tara interjected wickedly.

He paused. The hint of a smile hovered around his stern medieval features. 'I'm sure I shall think of something.'

'I'm sure you will. So what is your proposition?' she demanded.

'I came to say that I'd like you to take over the future publicity and promotion of the orchestra.'

Tara was astonished. She forced herself to say nothing. The automatic responses – protests of lack of experience, unworthiness and so on were to be avoided at all costs.

Xavier was no fool. If he was asking her to do this – and he was serious, which she judged he was – then he must believe her capable of it. And if he believed it, then she could believe it too.

But did she *want* to? It was playing that she wanted, not an administrative post – however exciting and prestigious.

'There is no need to give an answer now,' Xavier said softly. 'I merely wanted to introduce the idea to you. You can have time to think it over and I'll set up a meeting with the orchestra's management board sometime next week so that you can meet them and find out more.'

'Is it in your power to hire and fire me?' Tara asked.

A muscle flickered at Xavier's temple. 'You know about the management and politics of orchestras. Of course I don't have that power. But with your father's reputation as a backing and with my recommendation, there will be no difficulty about securing the post for you if you decide you would like it.'

Tara frowned. She was hugely flattered, and immensely suspicious. 'Are you trying to do me some sort of good turn?'

His eyes sharpened. 'I don't do "good turns". I'm surprised you asked that.'

'Sorry.' She stared ahead of her. He was right. She needed time to think. But the idea was by no means unattractive; she was not going to reject it out of hand.

Xavier stood up, unfolding his long frame with athletic grace.

Tara experienced an unexpected desire to hang on to him. She did not want him to go. She was hungry for companionship. The full extent of her present loneliness hit her with painful force.

When she split from Bruno she had imagined she was making a fresh start, cutting herself adrift from all the ties of the past two rebel years. In some curious way she had thought that by doing so she would get in touch with the old Tara, the child who had shown such musical promise, who had delighted her father with her youthful talent.

She had wanted to create a space in which to fulfil that wish. And in some ways she had achieved that. But what she had thought of as a clean slate was beginning to look like a simple void.

A few moments of the company of even the arrogant, nerve-jangling Xavier seemed preferable to solitude.

He made no move towards the door however, but

walked across to the piano and fingered the keys. 'How is your mother?' he asked.

'Surprisingly well.' There was an edge to Tara's voice.

'And the widower doctor?'

'The same.'

'Ah. And how is your young friend Bruno?'

Tara held back for a second, then changed her mind. What was to be gained by concealing what had happened? 'I don't know. We're not seeing each other at the moment.'

Xavier turned to glance at her and Tara stared resolutely back.

He drew in a long breath. 'Ah.' He turned back.

On the stand in front of him was the score for César Franck's violin sonata in A major, the paper well thumbed and pencilled all over with handwritten comments and directions. Xavier flicked over the sheets. 'This piece can be played in so many different ways,' he mused. 'A truly amazing work.'

'I used to play it with my father,' Tara said. 'He took the piano part and I wrestled with the rest!'

'You know this first movement takes a gigantic hand,' Xavier commented. 'Look at this!' He played a chord, his long fingers only just spanning the notes.

'Yes, Franck must have been a huge chap,' she chuckled. Xavier seated himself at the piano and played the soft opening piano introduction.

Tara felt a shiver of pure ecstasy creep over the bones of her shoulders and raise the hairs at the back of her neck. Without conscious thought or intent she took up her violin. Over Xavier's shoulder her eyes followed the score, watching for the entry of the violin.

'Now!' he commanded softly, giving a brief nod to bring her in with the violin's first wistful pensive melody.

Tara drew her bow across the strings. Now the theme passed from his hands to hers, the melody gaining in pace and assertiveness. Soon the piano took over again, Xavier making the music ride boldly along on light chords. Tara hummed when she wasn't playing, keeping the rhythm flowing through her mind, whilst at the same time her eyes glanced down at Xavier's flying fingers, fascinated, awed and admiring.

'Do you want me to go on with this?' Xavier enquired, pausing.

'Yes. But don't listen to my pathetic attempts!'

After they had negotiated the climax of the first movement Xavier said evenly, 'I liked the way you played that. Moving things along a bit. Not too reverential. That's good. Shall we go on?'

Without waiting for a reply he was plunging into the next section. 'This should be played very fast,' he said, 'a terrible task for the pianist. I don't know how I'll manage without a page turner. You'll have to be patient.'

Tara came in once more, the violin beginning on the G-string. 'Lots of agitation and passion,' Xavier decreed, making the piano thunder.

'I don't know if I'm gutsy enough for this bit,' Tara gasped.

'YES!'

She lost him a few bars later. He stopped. 'Should I have slackened pace there? Did I gallop off?' He flicked the pages back.

'No, I got lost,' Tara confessed smiling, her confidence flowering by the second.

They tried again. Stayed together. Pure happiness began to steal over her as she concentrated on the wonderful task of playing great music with a like-minded and great musician.

Playing together like this, the gap in age and experience between them was stripped away. They were on the same musical wavelength. There was some exciting collective energy being generated between them – a golden thread binding them together in the music.

The last movement had always struck Tara as intensely touching and as she played she felt her heart merge into the music. All sensation of apprehension, of being put to the test, had left her now. Playing with Saul Xavier she felt no anxiety, no competitiveness, she was able to play without restraint from the very depths of her being. And that must be about the most seductive thing on earth she thought, as the last piano trill rang out and the piece finally came to end with one long note from her violin.

She gave a long sigh. Sweat oozed out of her from the sheer physical effort she had expended. 'Not only a maestro, but a virtuoso,' she told him. 'You were fantastic!'

'And you were extremely "gutsy",' he commented, spinning round on the stool and shooting her a glinting glance which sent a bolt of electric feeling through her body.

'Playing music,' she said, closing her eyes. 'That's all I want to do now. That's all there is really.'

'Really?' He watched her very carefully.

'And I've blown it,' she mourned.

'Maybe not,' he told her softly.

'Oh yes. Monica was right. She was horribly brutal – but quite justified.'

Xavier smiled. 'Monica was entirely infatuated with that young Japanese boy, who may or may not stand the test of time. I've seen plenty of young prodigies all burned out by the time they're twenty-five.'

'I don't think I shall even have ignited by then!'

She longed for him to sprinkle a few more little crumbs of praise on her, but predictably he kept quiet. He seemed to be pondering some problem, his head angled slightly away from her as though he had forgotten her presence.

Tara allowed her eyes to move slowly over his profile. She felt she would like to gaze at him forever, he was as exquisitely carved as a Michelangelo statue, as finely drawn as a portrait by Holbein. 'You have beautiful hair,' she said softly, her eyes lingering over the thick dark strands.

He stared gravely at her, the streaks of sapphire glimmering in the depths of his cool grey eyes.

'These silver linings here and here,' she murmured, her eyes moving over his temples, 'nature couldn't have arranged them better!'

He stared at her. A long deep intimate stare. Her blood felt suddenly hot; singing and pulsing in her veins.

'Tara,' he said, his voice low and even, 'there are other things to make besides music.'

Tara froze into stillness, digesting the full significance of his words. She ran her tongue over her lips, momenta-

106

rily stunned and bewildered, for instead of feeling outraged she had the sense that a great burden had been lifted from her, a wide pathway shown, a licence given to snatch at all manner of previously unconsidered joys.

The complexities and confusions of the past years, months and weeks suddenly slipped away from her. There was no sensation of astonishment, no shiver of apprehension. This moment seemed to have arrived in the same inexorable way that the seasons follow one another; serene and inevitable with all the naturalness in the world.

He gazed at her steadily, making no move to reach for her, to stroke or probe. His still anticipation was more arousing than a whole battalion of breathless grasping embraces.

Tara placed her hands around his face, tracing the line and angle of every bone. Her heart beat with primitive desire for this austere, ferociously talented man whose hooded eyes burned into hers.

He pulled her down onto his knee. Everything went into slow motion as Tara's fingers travelled lingeringly over his face, exploring each minute detail. The sensitive pads of her fingers touched him with the softness of a breath of air, lingering across his deeply cowled eyelids, then moving languorously over the length of his forehead and down into the silver tendrils of hair she had just admired.

His face twitched with spasms of pleasure.

Now she parted her lips softly and took them on the same tender journey that her fingers had just completed. She breathed softly on his skin and allowed her tongue to slither tantalizingly over the tips of his ears, touching and withdrawing with mischievous teasing.

He linked his hands behind her head and pulled her towards him.

A violent tremor shook her as their lips joined. She felt herself floating in a warm pool of darkness as her tongue linked itself with his.

Long moments slid by.

She pulled back a little and looked deep into his eyes. It was as though she were gazing into the very heart of him. It seemed to her that this linking of eyes was as deep and intimate as any physical caress.

She felt herself opening up inside, as though some sensitive wound deep in her hips was throbbing with anticipation.

She drew back and smiled at him. 'Saul,' she breathed softly. 'Saul.'

He sighed. 'Ah, Tara. My bright, lovely elf.' His hands passed tenderly over the wisps of hair framing her face.

Tara took his hand and placed it on her throat.

'Are you sure?' he whispered huskily, making her heart contract. Always before she had seen in his face an awesome and uncompromising iron strength mingled with ruthless determination. She had recognized that a man of his calibre, a great musical interpreter, might need to be a cruel taskmaster in his search for excellence. But looking down at him now she saw much more – his great sensitivity, his compassion, his vulnerabilities.

They stared at each other. There was a shimmer of ultimate fusion and blending between them.

'Where?' he demanded, masterfulness regained.

She took him by the hand and led him upstairs into her bedroom.

They threw off their clothes — arran sweater, jeans, black silk shirt, brief panties, expensive Italian shoes. Then they threw themselves into each other's arms.

He's not hungry, Tara thought with astonishment as he began to burrow into her flesh, teasing with his tongue, massaging with his fingers — he's starving! He's like a wild creature who hasn't eaten for days.

She stared up at him. Stripped of his clothes, desperate with desire, he had lost not one shred of his authority. His body was like a gun; at the same time iron hard and velvety smooth.

His hands were all over her. Fingers squeezing her nipples, kneading her inner thighs and then his tongue teasing her, drawing pleasure from every warm crevice.

But Tara was not willing to be passive, that was not in her nature. She twisted in his arms, making loving assaults back; she wriggled, as slippery as a fish. As he touched her her breathing accelerated wildly. Sparks of burning, stinging sensation cannoned through her consciousness. She felt herself rolling and tossing in a sea of ecstasy, almost fainting in the troughs, then riding high on the crests: great curling waves of unimaginable sensation. His dark male presence seemed to engulf her. His hands and lips were everywhere on her skin, the essence of him burrowing deep inside her with punishing insistence.

He was an expert, a craftsman. He delved and carved and sculpted. He used her mercilessly. He roamed over her flesh as though he would leave none of it intact, hewing ecstasy out of every hollow and curve.

And for all that he was on fire with desire, his control

was such that he was able to hold himself back from his own climax for what seemed to be an eternity.

At last he gave a low groan and shuddered inside her. She let herself relax, sore and aching with pleasure.

'Well?' he said softly. 'Well?'

'Oh, very well,' she replied.

When at last she slid out from under him and swung her legs over the side of the bed her body was so stiff and bruised it was painful to walk. 'God!' she exclaimed.

He moved across to her, supporting her with a strong arm around her shoulders. 'My sweet little sprite, what have I done to you?' he asked.

She twisted herself to and fro in front of the mirror, looking at the livid marks of passion. Inside, her flesh seethed with heat.

She laughed, turned and punched his chest lightly. 'Don't worry, I'm tough. A survivor.'

He took her in his arms, rubbed gentle soothing hands all over her. 'What time does your mother come back?'

'Not for ages. It's her late night working. And then Donald usually wines and dines her. In ever more lavish style from what I can gather.'

His grip tightened on her. She gave a sharp yelp of pain as his fingers brushed tender flesh.

He released her instantly. 'My little love!' he exclaimed.

'You are a malevolent bastard after all,' she laughed. 'Oh come on Saul. It's OK. I'm not an innocent virgin.'

'Don't talk about other men,' he growled softly.

'Just *one* other. I'm not a tart!' she flashed back. 'Don't you dare start on any of that hypocritical male bullshit!'

He recoiled, momentarily stunned that she should turn

110

on him so aggressively. 'Explain what you mean!' he demanded, his eyes blazing down at her.

'You know the sort of thing. Accusing the woman you've just shagged very thoroughly of being the kind who sleeps around. Making a woman feel like a slag if she's eager and willing. Branding her as frigid if she's virtuous.' Tara had read the challenging and questioning feminist literature that every female student was morally obliged to assimilate. Its message had made her burn with rage at the 'no-win situation' most women found themselves in in the sexual arena, even now in the latter half of the so-called enlightened twentieth century.

She was also alarmed to find herself still a victim of exactly those old prejudices she so despised; terrified that Saul Xavier would brand her a trollop because she had fallen so easily into bed with him and enjoyed herself with such transparent abandon.

Even now she could not believe it had happened, could not understand *how* it could have happened. And at the same time, deep within her there were no regrets. She would like to make love with him for an eternity.

Oh HELL.

'Tara!' He grasped her tightly. 'I don't want to make war. Just love. And we have all evening . . .'

'No,' Tara said. 'No. I've my job to go to.'

'You've no need to do that any more. That's over.'

'It is my job, Saul. It's my only source of income at the moment. I need it.'

'You are a fool to do it. Wasting your talent. Demeaning yourself.'

Still naked, they confronted each other fiercely. She

snorted like a cross pony and turned her back on him. He came to stand close to her and wrapped his arms around her firm fleshy body. Tara felt the hardness of his stomach and thighs against her back and buttocks. Her innards turned liquid with fresh desire.

With a superhuman effort of will she wrenched herself free.

'It's honest work. It gives me a tiny shred of independence.'

He made a contemptuously dismissive gesture.

'At least I don't have to be anybody's kept woman,' she continued angrily. 'No man's pampered performing monkey – or mistress or wife for that matter.'

A terrible silence filled the room.

Wife. Saul's wife. Tara felt a physical breathcrushing shock. Her brain began to race like a fleeing panic stricken animal who senses danger on all sides.

She stared up at Saul. 'You've just committed adultery. And so have I!'

Her body became chilled and icy. She began feverishly burrowing amongst the heap of clothes beside the bed, wrenching out what was hers and pulling them on with trembling fingers.

Making love with another woman's husband. How tawdry. How cheap. How *despicable*. Oh God! Oh God! Oh God!

Unable to bear being in the same room with him for another instant, she flew across the hall and into the bathroom, trying to blot out the horrible reality of what had happened. The room dipped and swam before her eyes and her stomach lurched. She ran to the sink and vomited violently into the basin, her whole body shaking.

As she hung over the edge of the bowl, she heard Saul come up behind her, saw his hand reaching in front of her to turn on the tap and swirl the nastiness away. His firm strong arm brushed hers and against the depths of her will Tara felt a fresh shaft of desire darting through her with white heat.

She heard his voice. 'Tara . . .'

'Don't!' she moaned. 'Don't say anything. Don't do anything.' She wanted him to cease to be a presence in this room, in her house, in her thoughts. She wanted him to cease existing as an image in her brain, for the memory of him to be erased and expunged forever.

He grasped her, his fingers digging deep into the soft flesh of her upper arms. 'Listen to me – I am no womanizer. No adulterer either. If only you knew the truth of it Tara,' he said bitterly.

She stayed silent, her whole body stiff and unyielding.

'My marriage is dead,' Saul told her. 'I shall deal with whatever needs to be done and then we can be together.'

His cold and ruthless decisiveness appalled her. 'Get rid of your wife you mean?' she said with icy derision. 'You must have a heart of granite and an ego the size of the Albert Hall. What makes you think that I would even give a second's thought to being a party to all that?'

'Because now that I've tasted the first delights of making love to you I shall make sure that you do,' he said. 'I've no intention of letting you slip through my fingers.' And those fingers tightened on her, the pressure remorseless. 'And you won't be able to help yourself.'

She looked up and saw his face reflected in the mirror

above the basin. She shivered, seeing the hard relentless purpose in his eyes. She knew that he meant what he said. And that he was used to getting his own way in all things.

She would need the strength of Hercules to resist, on that score alone.

His eyes held hers in the glass and she winced as the pressure of his hard fingers slowly increased, digging in deep.

She bit her lip and tasted blood. 'Get out!' She said slowly and deliberately. 'Get out now!'

He released her.

She tensed, wondering if he would sweep aside her resistance and take her by force.

A part of her urgently wanted that and she felt a wave of sickening self disgust.

There was a breathless moment of stillness and then he stepped back away from her. She heard his footsteps on the stairs, heard the front door open and then close firmly.

Flying back into the bedroom she watched the tall figure walk down the road to the low sleek car.

He did not turn to look back.

# CHAPTER 10

Georgiana paced up and down the length of her bedroom. On the floor were half a dozen suitcases, partly packed with clothes.

Alfreda, armed with a large gin and tonic and a long slender cigar, rifled through the clothes in Georgiana's vast wardrobe, eyeing them speculatively whilst at the same time keeping a close watch on her friend about whom she was more than a little concerned.

Georgiana kept insisting that nothing was wrong, that she was merely restless and excited at the prospect of flying off for a marvellous holiday in the Canary Isles. Lithe and elegant in trouser suit of turquoise crêpe she paused by her dressing table and fingered a long rope of milky pearls whilst exclaiming that it would be so gorgeously hot and sunny out there at this time of year. She would get a fabulous golden tan. Xavier always said she was at her most beautiful with just a touch of extra gold about her.

The more she protested the more certain Alfreda was that something extremely serious was wrong.

'What about your therapy sessions?' she asked Georgiana. 'Won't you miss them? And that gorgeous doctor?' Alfreda sometimes called for Georgiana at the end of her sessions with Dr Daneman. She had spotted the doctor briefly on one or two occasions and wondered how long a female patient would be able to resist him. Although thinking it over she had then wondered about her friend's capacity for falling in love.

'Yes I shall miss the sessions,' Georgiana admitted. 'I've got used to them.'

'Well, a break might be no bad thing,' Alfreda remarked. 'In fact I'm surprised you've stuck at it so long.'

'Xavier wanted me to,' Georgiana said simply.

Alfreda laughed. 'Since when did you do things because Xavier decreed it?'

'I take notice of what he says. I've always valued his advice. You know that.'

'Has it *really* made things any better? All that talk and stream of consciousness stuff?' Alfreda screwed her eyes up against the smoke from her cigar as she watched Georgiana's reaction carefully.

She shrugged. 'On balance – I think so.'

Alfreda was pretty sure that whatever else the therapy had done it hadn't got Georgiana back in the sack with Xavier. She was frequently dying to ask directly but something in Georgiana's manner when the subject was touched on always restrained her.

'So you'll go back when you're in London again?'

'Oh yes.'

'Shall I keep an eye on Xavier while you're away?'

Alfreda enquired. 'I've got one or two little dinners coming up.'

'You can invite him by all means. But he's frightfully busy. Since he took over at the Tudor Phil, he's had hardly a spare minute.' Georgiana's lovely features were temporarily distorted with a touch of peevishness.

The phone pealed out. Georgiana gave a little start. It rang twice and then stopped.

A few moments later it rang again. Georgiana stared at the instrument, making no move to pick it up.

Alfreda watched her curiously. She looked at the phone. She looked back at Georgiana. She was intrigued.

'You answer it,' Georgiana said. 'I'm in no mood for chatting.'

Alfreda picked up the phone. 'Hello,' she said in her lazy ripe voice.

'Could I have Mr Saul Xavier please?' It was a woman's voice. A young woman. Assertive but unmistakably anxious. Alfreda glanced up at Georgiana who had turned away and was now fiddling around with the bottles on her dressing table.

'Could you *have* Mr Xavier? I shall have to ask his wife. I rather think he belongs to her,' Alfreda drawled tantalizingly, enjoying herself. 'Shall I ask her – she's right here?'

'No! Could you tell me where I can reach him please? Give me a number to contact him?'

Alfreda was impressed. She appealed with her eyes to Georgiana to take the call. Georgiana turned, shaking her head vigorously.

'Is it a business matter?' Alfreda asked the caller. 'You could contact his agent.'

A pause. 'Yes. Yes, I'll do that.'

'I presume you have the number?'

'No. I haven't.'

Of course not, Alfreda thought. Business matter, my foot! 'Mr Xavier's agent is Roland Grant,' she said sweetly. 'You'll find the number in the book.'

'Thank you.'

'You're welcome!' Alfreda replaced the receiver and drew deeply on her cigar.

'Well?' Georgiana asked.

'I suspect that was one of the delightful escorts you hired for Xavier. Obviously wanting some more of the same. Of whatever it was that he did to her,' she added wickedly.

Georgiana sank down onto the bed, her face chalk white.

'Darling, I warned you it was dangerous,' Alfreda said gently. 'It's got to stop. You could lose him.'

'No. NO! That will never happen.' The agitation in Georgiana's face was in direct opposition to the confidence suggested in her words.

'She's phoned before, hasn't she, that young woman? You were expecting her?'

Georgiana flinched. 'No!'

'Come on sweetheart. Confide in me. Use me. I'm your friend.'

'No one has phoned. I just have this feeling. This awful feeling.'

'About Xavier?' Alfreda demanded.

'He's never at home, always working.'

'So? He's behaving normally.'

Georgiana's wary blue eyes sharpened with a curious mixture of bewilderment and calculation. 'He's abstracted. He forgets things when you talk to him.'

Alfreda took a sip of her drink. That was definitely *not* like Xavier. He was always in total command. 'You think he's fallen for one of these women? It's hardly surprising. But don't worry, he'll soon come through it. After all they're no more than high-class call girls. Hardly Xavier's style.'

Georgiana couldn't help but agree. But then Alfreda did not know about Xavier's cool cancelling of Georgiana's 'gifts'. Alfreda did not know that Xavier wanted nothing more to do with those delightful girls she had hired for him. Only Dr Daneman knew about that.

But not even Dr Daneman knew that Xavier had suggested to Georgiana that they had a trial separation, that maybe in the circumstances it would be better to review their marriage from a position of distance. *In the circumstances*, he had said. She knew exactly what he meant. His voice had been laced with deeply sexual meaning when he said it. But he had made no move to take her in his arms this time.

A sudden terrible panic seized her. Could he really just toss her aside? Surely not. No, she would never let it happen. Never. Never. She was only thirty-six and more beautiful than she had ever been. He would never be able to let her go. It simply would not happen.

'Have you any evidence that he's got another woman?' Alfreda enquired.

'No,' Georgiana replied truthfully. But he must have, mustn't he? There would be no other possible reason for his wanting to change things between them. One of those girls must have got her hooks into him. That must be why he wanted no further new gifts.

'Look darling. It's more than likely that he hasn't,' Alfreda reassured her. 'He's a workaholic and he's choosy, which narrows down both the opportunities and the field. Neither is he a fool. This girl on the phone is almost certainly a one-night stand from the agency, and she simply won't be an issue as long as you play your cards right.'

Georgiana pressed her lips together.

'Things have to change,' Alfreda told her. 'Before it's too late. And you can *make* them change sweetheart, you *can*!'

Georgiana stopped pacing. She looked steadily at her friend, her eyes wide with a sense of foreboding.

'You've got to start sleeping with him again,' Alfreda said bluntly. 'And if the idea still makes you wince, knock back a few stiff vodkas before he comes home.'

'He doesn't look at me any more,' Georgiana complained. 'Not . . . properly.'

'He will, darling, if you're on that bed with your knickers off and your legs spread,' Alfreda said brutally. 'There are very few men who wouldn't.'

Alfreda's comment on male desire was generalized to include all available females, but Georgiana interpreted it very personally, knowing that no man would be able to resist her.

Revulsion passed over her perfect features as she

thought through the possible scenario with Xavier. She would need more than a few vodkas. She would need to be anaesthetized.

She could not bear to lose him. But could she bear to do *that* again, even to keep him?

# CHAPTER 11

Tara felt like a new woman: scarred, tainted and shabby.

Also bereft. The image of Saul Xavier's face was still lodged in her head for almost every waking minute. Constantly she heard his voice and relived the sensation of his touch.

Listening to and playing music – always a refuge before – now seemed like torture. She was always wondering how *he* would have reacted to a certain piece, how they might have shared it together.

Her appetite deserted her and her firm ample flesh began to melt away. Bones appeared which she had never seen before, little spikes at her hips and ribs like plate racks. But her breasts, which she had always considered rather absurd and clearly designed for a much bigger girl altogether, stubbornly refused to change. If anything Tara thought they were even fuller than before, tender and slightly swollen, the nipples enlarged and deep rose coloured.

She was astonished at the way emotional stress could translate itself into such obvious physical changes.

She raged at herself for being such a fool as to have fallen into Xavier's arms so easily. It was not as if she had even been hankering after him in that way. Well, not consciously at least.

And now all she could do was moon around longing for him like some dreadful lovesick bovine, whose brains were lodged somewhere between her knees and her navel.

She hated herself. She hated him. She took his letters to the bottom of the garden beside the compost heap and set fire to them. The daily barrage of flowers he sent she took to adorn deserted graves in the churchyard nearby.

She stopped answering the phone. She made an arrangement to use the practice rooms of her former school when she wanted to play so that she was never in the house alone.

She carried on with her job. She was always cheery and hard-working. Customers took to her. She made more tips than the rest of the staff put together.

And she never let her mother suspect for a minute what had happened.

This went on for some weeks after which she felt completely exhausted.

'Tara, isn't it time you stopped dieting?' her mother asked, as they ate supper together on one of the rare evenings they were both at home.

'I'm not. I just don't feel very hungry. It's working at the restaurant that does it. Seeing all that food – and the smell! Ugh! It churns me up.'

'Is it Bruno?'

'What?'

'Are you pining?'

Tara looked genuinely amazed. Bruno had not figured much in her thoughts at all recently. 'No.'

Rachel looked at her anxiously. 'I think you should have a word with the doctor.'

'Donald Giovanni?'

'Tara!'

'Are you two sleeping together yet?'

'Yes,' Rachel said evenly. 'Is that all right?'

'Not really.' Tara felt a nauseous lump in her stomach. She looked at her mother's concerned, lovely face. 'But then why shouldn't you? Yes, it is all right.'

'I'm sorry.'

'Don't be. Will you get married?'

'Probably.'

'Let Daddy get cold first?'

Rachel flinched. 'My God, you can be so cruel.'

Tara sighed. 'I don't want to be. Really.'

'You're not well. Will you go and see the doctor? Please?'

'All right. But not Donald. Too embarrassing.'

'There's Dr Critchley on Mondays and Tuesdays. She's lovely. Grey hair. A bun.'

'Sounds just the job. OK. Book me in.'

After supper Tara went to the bathroom and flushed the toilet to conceal the noise of her vomiting.

Dr Critchley was sympathetic. Also immediately perceptive.

'You say you've lost nearly a stone,' she commented. 'That's rather significant for a tiny person like you.'

'Yes.' Tara lay like a rock under the doctor's kind yet impersonal hands. It was five weeks and one day since any other human being had touched her in an intimate way.

Five weeks since *he* had touched her. Her body felt shrivelled and rejected.

'Are your periods regular?' Dr Critchley asked, pressing cool gently probing hands on Tara's stomach.

Tara tried to think. 'A bit mixed up. I came off the pill a couple of months ago after I broke up with my boyfriend.'

'So what's happened since then?'

'A few dribbles here and there.'

'And in the last four weeks?'

'Nothing.'

Dr Critchley slipped on some transparent gloves. 'I'm going to make an internal examination. Just relax.'

Tara felt fingers slide inside her. And suddenly an amazing, utterly terrifying idea hit her.

'Relax!' the doctor said. 'Have you had the opportunity to become pregnant?' she asked as she straightened up.

Tara recalled the dark animal pain and pleasure of her love-making with Saul, the way he had driven deep inside her and pounded without mercy. 'Yes. So that's what's wrong with me!'

'I suspect so. And there's nothing wrong with you. Pregnancy is entirely healthy and normal.'

'But losing all this weight?'

'That's quite usual in the early stages. And don't forget you've had a big emotional shock to contend with recently. Grieving is often associated with weight changes.'

Tara's mouth went dry. 'How soon can you be sure?'

'Leave a urine sample and come back before evening surgery.'

\* \* \*

125

Dr Critchley was able to confirm the pregnancy. 'What do you feel about it?' she said, looking at Tara over her half-moon glasses and lacing her fingers together to form a neat steeple.

Tara felt temporarily numb. 'Scared witless. A stupid fool.' She paused. Now that it was a certainty her thoughts and feelings were different to those which had raced around her head all afternoon.

Conjectures about abortion, ways to tell her mother, fantastic schemes to go ahead and have the baby. Cope somehow.

Tara looked at Dr Critchley. This calm mature woman must have had hundreds of this kind of interview. She was so wise, so serene.

Whereas she, Tara, was nothing more than a randy little fool who'd got herself in the club, up the spout.

I'm having Saul Xavier's baby, Tara thought suddenly, and a strange thrill of excitement pierced her self-disgust and terror.

'It's a miracle isn't it?' she said to Dr Critchley. 'I've "got caught" or whatever they call it. It's an utter mess. But it's magic! Fantastic!'

Dr Critchley smiled. 'Indeed it is.'

'Do you want to consider a termination?' she asked Tara after a long silence.

'I don't know. I suppose so. No, I don't think so.'

'There's no rush. You can take a few days to think it over. It's early stages as yet.'

Tara placed her hands on her stomach. 'How old is it?'

'About five weeks.'

'It's a real life. A little person. I couldn't kill it.'

'You could consider adoption, of course. There are lots of couples longing to have a baby and so few babies to go round since the Abortion Act.'

'I need to talk it over.'

'Of course. I'm sure your mother will be very helpful.'

'With the baby's father,' Tara said.

'Yes. Naturally.'

Tara looked at Rachel's worried face and said, 'It's OK Mummy. I'm perfectly A1 fit. I just need to try to eat plenty of good food and start thinking positively.'

She waited until the next day, until Rachel was safely at the surgery.

She prowled round the telephone, Saul's professional card in her hand. The one he had handed her after the funeral. The one that had his private phone number hand-written on it in black ink and underneath the message: 'Don't waste your potential. Accept a helping hand. S.X.'

She re-read the message with a grim smile of irony.

Several times she dialled the number and then slammed the receiver down before the connection was even made.

Then she let the number ring out. On hearing the rhythmic purring she felt she would be sick. Her fingers pressed on the connectors, annihilated the purrs.

'God! DO IT!' she raged at herself, placing her finger on the dial once more.

A woman's voice answered. His wife. Oh sweet heaven.

She willed her voice to be steady, to follow the clear, unadorned little script she had written out. One which would cope with all eventualities, whoever answered her call.

The person on the other end did not conform to any of the possibilities she had foreseen.

Nor was she Saul's wife apparently.

At the close of their brief and amazing conversation Tara found herself desperately unnerved, her heart drumming hotly against her ribs.

She got the agent's telephone number from Directory Enquiries. The secretary who answered sounded terribly amused to be asked the whereabouts of Mr Xavier. 'Oh, we don't keep a tail on his movements I'm afraid! And in any case, I don't think he would be pleased for us to give out that kind of information.'

Tara's heart sank. 'Right,' she said wearily. Desperately she made her mind sharpen and focus. 'I'm a relative,' she said.

A disbelieving pause. 'Look, hang on!' The voice relented. There was a shuffling of paper. 'The Tudor Philharmonic are giving a concert tonight. He'll be in rehearsal now most likely.'

'At the Festival Hall?'

'No. The Royal Albert. Hope you find him. Good luck!'

Tara made no preparations. She simply set off.

An hour and a half later, her heart having failed her at the main doors to the great hall, she made her way around the side of the building and eventually found herself in its backstage depths. She remembered the place well from the countless times she had visited to hear her father rehearse. Even now, despite her sick apprehension, she still felt a spark of excitement as she made her way up the the long narrow corridor wryly nicknamed 'the bullrun' by keyed-up players – which led to the back of the main auditorium.

Music poured from the stage: Beethoven's Seventh Symphony, the last movement, throbbing with zest for life and sheer unadulterated joy.

Tara felt a smile creep over her face. The positive thrust of the music gave her the courage to step out of the gloom of the corridor onto the partially lit stage.

Her eyes leapt over the ranks of the orchestra and made an instant connection with Xavier. Dressed entirely in black, shirt sleeves rolled up his muscled forearms, he was utterly absorbed in his task. Completely composed. Calm and cool. Living the music.

Even when he halted proceedings, and entered into a dry dialogue with the string section he was fully in control.

She heard his low velvet voice teasing and cajoling.

'So, we have a twenty-bar crescendo, ladies and gentlemen. In five bars you're already there. Fortissimo! What have I done to encourage you into this indecent haste? Mmm?'

A murmur of laughter.

They set off again.

Tara was intensely aware of the personal force of strength flowing from Saul Xavier into each player. Under those compelling eyes, no player would stand a chance of straying from the magnetism of his will. Whatever it was that Xavier wanted musically, the players would have no option but to give him.

She recalled the sensation of being held in a steel band when he had directed her and Bruno's singing on the day of her father's funeral. As she watched him a dark ripple of thrills shot through her muscles and nerve endings.

At the close of the rehearsal he was heavily in demand

129

from all sides. Tara sat quietly, waiting, watching. She was not even sure that he had seen her.

In fact after half an hour she was seriously concerned that he had no idea at all of her presence and that he might simply walk away, leaving her to seek him out all over again.

Or maybe he had seen her but wanted nothing to do with her. She had, after all, rebuffed him very soundly. And the letters and flowers hadn't been coming for a week or so now.

A sickening anxiety droned inside. It occurred to her that she had hardly stopped feeling sick ever since she met him. Eventually the stage emptied.

She began to breathe more deeply.

Xavier was talking with a tubby silver-haired man. They turned their backs to her and began to walk away into the huge auditorium.

Tara slumped on her seat with despair.

Minutes passed. She felt rooted, unable to move.

And then she saw him returning, making his way to the platform. He vaulted up onto the stage and moved across to her.

He stood very close, almost touching. Looking down. Silent. Immobile.

'This has taken a hell of a lot of courage,' she said.

He sat beside her. He took her hands in his. 'And the waiting has taken a hell of a lot of restraint.'

She looked at him. Drank him in. She felt that she was jealous of the air he breathed. That if he asked her to lie down and die for him she would.

These were not the thoughts of a liberated woman, she told herself.

'So?' he said.

'So.' She gazed deep into his eyes, holding nothing of herself back. 'I'm having your baby.'

Utterly incredible words.

Xavier's eyes sharpened. Tara experienced a moment of piercing terror. And then his lips curved into a smile of pure delight. All the dialogue she had prepared became null and void. The ins and outs of terminations and adoptions. All unthinkable.

But she supposed those issues would have to be discussed anyway.

'What do you want me to do?' she asked him. Humble now. Placing herself entirely in his hands.

'Come to me. Be with me. I need to look after you. Both of you. What else?'

'Just like that?' She was astounded. Unable to think clearly. Of the many responses she had imagined from him, this was the simple and obvious one that had eluded her.

'Of course. Why not?'

'Your wife might not be too keen.' Dear God, Saul, she thought. This is dangerous. You're talking about revolutionizing lives. Yours, mine. Your wife's.

Not a muscle of his face flickered. 'This is nothing to do with her.'

'The house you share must be something to do with her.'

'I have more than one house.'

As if that were the issue. She stared at him, astounded by this brutal, single-minded clarity of purpose. Afraid too.

'Tara!' He rattled her arm. 'What are you thinking? You haven't thought of killing it?'

'Of course I have.'

'Tara!' His eyes were like guns.

'I could just have done it,' she said, facing his relentless gaze. 'You would never have known.'

'So why didn't you?

'It's yours as well as mine. Equal rights for parents.'

He was incensed. 'Is that a real feeling, or something you read in a philosophy book?'

'What do you think?'

He looked at her, assessing and then understanding. His smile came from deep inside. 'We're going to make a wonderful pair you and I.'

'I hope I'm up to it,' she said drily.

And then, with a force entirely out of her control, the belief that they could do this thing came suddenly flooding in. For days she had felt herself motionless and still. She had been the deep inanimate pool that collects at the head of a death-fall cliff. And now she was the roaring cascade of water, all sparkle, movement and shimmer.

She and Saul. They *were* truly a pair. They matched each other, understood all that was unspoken. For all that he was so ferociously talented, for all that the chasm between their life experiences was formidable, they would be soul mates.

She reached out and touched his face. 'I want it too. More than anything. Your baby growing inside me.'

He looked as though he would like to devour her with adoration. 'I'm forty years old Tara,' he said in a low voice. 'I am past my youth.'

'And I am eighteen,' she replied. 'There's a generation between us, Saul. And that situation is unlikely to change. So?'

She telephoned her mother. There was no reply. One of Donald's nights obviously.

Saul was heavily engaged with a multitude of musical personnel.

Tara wandered through the auditorium, renewing acquaintance with its broad expanses and its hidden nooks and crannies, sniffing it out in the manner of a dog long banished from its home.

A number of players recognized her, recalling the little girl who used to trot along beside her father, Richard Silk, holding tightly to his hand and looking around her wide-eyed at the huge stage and the vast amphitheatre of the auditorium with its gilded balconies banked one on top of the other.

In this curious lonely hour, suspended between her old and new life she felt no connection with the previous Tara: the innocent little girl, the rebellious young adult. In this hour she felt like a latter day child bride, a Dauphine or an Infanta, sent to attend on her husband-to-be in the country of which he was ruler.

What had just happened between her and Saul was still in the realm of fantasy. She had not yet fully adjusted to the incredible idea that a new life was growing inside her. To be now faced with the unfolding of a whole new life for herself was almost too awesome to comprehend.

Saul secured her a prime seat for the performance. The view was magnificent.

The orchestra came trickling in, laying itself out before her to form a vast black and white chequered board. Tuning up commenced, that familiar confused din that had thrilled her with anticipation from being a tiny child. Short brays from the clarinets, tiny shrieks from the piccolos, the boom of drums and double basses underneath.

And then, as though an unseen hand had moved over them, the noise faded and subsided. The audience stiffened, sat upright.

Saul cut a swift path through the players. Tall, upright and unsmiling, a hunter on the attack. As was his custom, the applause from the audience was neither registered nor acknowledged. It was yet to be earned.

His two taps on the rostrum rail caused the hum of the auditorium to sink to a sigh. And from a sigh to total silence.

The overture to Mozart's *Abduction from the Seraglio*. It started innocently enough. And then exploded into the auditorium, all flash and dazzle, grabbing the audience by the throat, sending electric impulses down the spine. Another sudden change and the audience were lapped in sweet melody. Love music from the yearning sigh of strings, the water-clear purity of woodwind.

The house lights went right down, leaving only the low-intensity lights on the music stands to bathe the orchestra in a soft glow. The neon bulb in Xavier's podium light illuminated the Maestro from below. Tara stared in fascination at the chilling image created: a harsh, macabre mask darkly shadowed and menacing, its frowning eyes glinting in the cold light like steel balls. Xavier's mouth was drawn in a tight, thin line as he conducted and his jaw worked furiously with concentration.

Tara felt her breath coming in thick gasps.

Then something began to happen in her belly, some horrible crawling turbulence; a rhythmic droning that rapidly progressed from sensation to pain.

She felt snakes of wet stickiness come slithering from the roots of the grinding torment, dark oily trickles sliding between her thighs.

She sat transfixed, trying to control reality, to push away the evidence of sensation. Stop! she shrieked silently to her disobedient body. Stop this!

Wildly she sprang from her seat, stumbling mindlessly up the sloping aisle and out into the broad stairway, desperate for cool air. Somehow she got herself to the foyer.

Her head was filled with terror. She lurched into the street, instantly attracting the attention of a taxi. 'A hospital,' she moaned urgently. 'Any hospital. Quickly. Please, please!'

# CHAPTER 12

Rachel tried not to look at the phone.

It was past midnight. Tara was not at home and this was not one of her working nights.

She's an adult, Rachel kept telling herself, her mind filled with visions of rape and blood and death. She's probably out with friends.

But what friends? Tara had been distressingly alone, almost hermit-like since Richard's death.

Should she try to contact Bruno? She paused, her fingers stroking the smooth plastic of the phone. Something told her there would be nothing to be gained from that.

She tried to forget about the phone and poured herself yet another large whisky. The liquid slid like fire down her throat. Still her imagination continued to torture her with the maimed and mangled body of her only child.

When the outer bell rang and she saw Xavier standing there in the doorway, the only thing she felt was tremendous relief. It was the arrival of a member of the police force she had been dreading. *I'm very sorry madam. I have some rather bad news. Perhaps you'd like to sit down . . .*

'Is she here?' Xavier said. He looked wild. Desperate.

'No.' She frowned, her brain clearing itself of the previous fears and suspicions and starting to frame fresh ones.

'Come and join me in a drink,' she commanded him.

She watched him rotate the glass in slow agitation. 'Has she told you?' he asked.

'She tells me very little,' Rachel commented. 'Is she safe?'

'I hope to God she is.'

Someone stop this agony, prayed Rachel. She had dared to hope Xavier would be able to reassure her on that one thing – even if some other disaster were about to spring itself on her.

'She was fine a couple of hours ago at the concert,' he said, his voice thick with apprehension.

'When you have a girl you worry about murder and attack and rape and unwanted pregnancy,' Rachel said. 'Is that what I should know about? Is she pregnant? I've had my suspicions.'

'Yes.'

'It's yours!'

'Yes.'

'You unspeakable bastard,' she said flatly.

He made no reply. 'Where would she have gone? To that young man?'

'No. That's all over. He's not old enough yet to deal with someone like Tara.'

'Quite.'

Rachel felt hollow and sick. When the telephone rang she grasped at it as though it were a raft in a rough sea.

'Yes!' She listened for no more than a few seconds. 'Yes. I'll come. Right away.'

She turned to Xavier. 'She's in St Stephen's Hospital. Bleeding. Suspected miscarriage.'

'I'll drive you,' he said.

'I think I'd rather accept that favour from anyone in the world but you,' she said bitterly, 'But I'm well over the limit now. And there's no one else is there?'

They were there in fifteen minutes.

Xavier drove like a madman. Sitting in the car with him Rachel began to realize that his feelings were violently aroused. A sense of impotent desperation seemed to fill the car.

This was not the picture of a mature man who has been fooling around with a sexy young girl and now regrets his actions and his wife's anger.

This was the picture of a man in real pain.

She supposed she should be grateful that at least her daughter had not been used as a casual plaything by a man who had no real appreciation of her.

Or was there some other, more devious reason?

Rachel did not know. She could not be bothered to think. All that mattered was Tara coming through this. Regaining her strength. Rediscovering her zest for living. Coming home.

'Who takes preference here?' Rachel asked Xavier as they progressed down the corridor towards the room the night sister had indicated. 'The father of the unborn child or the mother of the suffering daughter?'

His grey eyes were utterly bleak and Rachel saw that it would be unthinkable to play the possessive parent, even if that had been in her nature.

Tara was lying stretched out under the sheets. The bed was tilted, so that her feet were higher than her head.

Her eyes, watery dark with the aftermath of panic and pain, leapt between mother and lover, anxiety and defiance jostling one another for position.

She nodded towards her raised feet. 'They're trying to stop it leaking out,' she said shakily.

Rachel was almost weeping with the blessed relief of seeing Tara alive.

Saul was holding back, his massive self control stretched to the limit as he looked at this miracle of femininity on the bed: death white, gaunt, grey crescents of puffy skin under her eyes. Hair sticky with sweat. Entirely without artifice.

Utterly, heart-stoppingly desirable.

'It's still there,' Tara told them with a tight little smile. 'Fighting like hell to hang on.'

'Oh God!' said Rachel.

'I'm sorry Mummy.' Tara looked at Rachel appealingly. 'I should have told you.' Her gaze rested only briefly on her mother and then switched longingly to Saul.

Rachel felt her heart crushed. 'I'll leave you two alone for a few moments,' she said quietly, moving out into the corridor where she walked up and down without purpose.

Tara took Saul's hand and drew it to her face, kissing it

139

tenderly, inhaling the smell of his skin with a look of drugged bliss.

'I'm not going to lose it,' she told him. 'I won't let it go. I promise you. The doctor said my cervix hasn't dilated, so there's every chance.'

He stroked her head. Never in his life had he experienced anything approaching the depth of emotion that was aroused in him now. Even his greatest moments of musical elation and triumph were eclipsed. He would move the earth for this small, astonishing creature who was battling so determinedly for the life of his child. *Their* child.

'How long will they keep you here?' he asked. 'If I didn't think it would be dangerous I'd steal you from them right now.'

'I don't know. A few days. The doctor said they had to be sure the bleeding had stopped. Not long.'

'Far too long,' he smiled. 'And then I shall take you to my house in Oxford. You'll like it there.'

She smiled. She was too weak to put up any opposition to this breathtaking masterfulness. And even if she were stronger she doubted if she would make a stand. The temptation to be with Saul, to exist in the glow of his presence, to rest in his arms and his bed was simply too powerful to resist.

In the depths of her conciousness some little spark of premonition suggested to her that some older Tara, in some future moment, might look back on all this with tolerant amazement.

But just now all she wanted was *him*.

And, like Saul, Tara had a strength of belief in herself

140

that allowed her to pursue her own ends long after other people would have bowed to the demands of compromise.

Rachel came to see her on her own the next day.

She brought some early daffodils and sprays of mauve chrysanthemums. Beside the six dozen red roses and the huge wicker basketful of freesias which Saul had sent earlier they looked mundane and insignificant.

Breathing in the heavy scent of Saul's flowers Rachel felt queasy.

'Well?' She looked down at Tara with a gentle smile.

'Still there,' said Tara cheerily. Her colour had all come back, her hair was washed and shiny and her eyes sparkled with the renewed joy of living. 'I think it's a survivor.'

Rachel tried to think of ways to say what she knew she had to say. Seconds passed.

'Are you sorry I didn't lose it?' Tara asked. 'Well, at least this way you're spared the embarrassment of wondering whether to say something about it "being for the best".'

'When did I ever make that kind of comment?' Rachel asked, deeply hurt.

'You'd have thought it though, wouldn't you?' Tara challenged.

'Yes. I'm afraid I would.' Rachel hesitated. 'I'm on your side you see.'

'Which means?'

'Which means I think it's crazy for you to be having a baby when you're no more than a child yourself, when you're not married to the father and he happens to be a man twenty years your senior about whom you know scarcely a thing.'

'Well! That certainly puts it in a nut-shell, Mummy. Thanks a lot!'

'Was it just a mistake darling?' Rachel enquired, already miserably aware that whatever battle it was they were embarking on, she was going to lose it.

Tara stared at the riot of roses. 'That question is so inappropriate to what happened and how it felt that I can't even begin to answer it.'

Rachel winced, hearing an echo of the teenage scorn that Tara used to heap on her and Richard three, four, five, six years ago.

'Oh Mummy, that was cruel. I didn't mean it to sound like that. But it was just such a stupid thing to ask!'

'You're really in love with Saul Xavier?'

'Yes. I know it sounds ridiculous. But yes. And I know I shouldn't have made love with him. It was wrong and stupid – irresponsible too. But I just feel . . . like a changed person.'

A black cloak of helpless gloom settled around Rachel at the prospect of her sparky Tara's spirit being tamed by pregnancy, childcare and dependence on a rich man's protection.

If only Richard were here, she thought automatically. But she knew that it probably would not have made the slightest difference.

'He has a wife Tara. Have you thought about that?' Rachel demanded. 'Thought about her?'

'Of course I have. What do you think I am? Some sort of monster?'

142

Rachel felt physically assailed by Tara's anger. 'What is he offering?' she enquired calmly. 'Marriage? Or setting you up as an expensive mistress in a luxury Knightsbridge flat with a charge account at Harrods?'

'Now who's turning the knife?' Tara flashed at her. Her face became wistful. 'I don't know the ins and outs yet. He may not be able to get a divorce. Not straight away.'

Rachel sighed. Refrained from comment. If only the young didn't always have to learn all the most commonplace and obvious pitfalls through experience.

'Look darling. I admit I'm shocked. A bit dismayed as well. You're letting yourself in for a lifetime of responsibility. Children are chains and fetters even if totally wonderful. I should know. And you could have had years of freedom to achieve something for yourself before all that.'

'Oh please!' Tara threw her eyes to the ceiling.

'But I'm glad as well, because there's a new life coming along. A life that belongs to you and me and Daddy as well as Saul. This baby is good for me too in a curious kind of way.'

A pause. 'Yes.' Tara sounded less than enthusiastic. 'I suppose it's a bit like a re-birth, a resurrection for Daddy.'

Rachel smiled, warmed by a new feeling of closeness.

'When you're home we'll be able to make all kinds of plans,' Rachel said, suddenly enlivened by the prospect of visits to baby stores and the chance to nurture Tara through this problematic but tremendously exciting period.

'Mummy, I'm not coming home,' Tara stated brutally. 'I'm going to live with Saul.'

Rachel stared at her.

'From now!' Tara said, making things crystal clear, digging the knife in deep.

Rachel felt anger surge inside her in a beating red wave. Oh the brazen effrontery of youth, she thought looking at her daughter, buoyant and irrepressible, completely restored to the delightful task of planning her life when less than twenty-four hours before she had been at the gates of hell. A daughter who was about to go home with a man whose wife – cast off and probably perfectly innocent – had shared with him sufficient years to represent a lifetime. Tara's lifetime certainly.

'Don't look at me like that!' Tara warned.

There was worse to come. As they blazed at each other with eyes and wills, Saul Xavier appeared in the doorway.

'Rachel!' he said in deep soft tones, just as he had done at the funeral. He placed his hand lightly on her shoulder. 'Rachel!' His voice was deep with sympathetic understanding.

'Don't make things more difficult,' Rachel told him caustically. 'I want to hate you.'

Saul smiled. He moved to the bed, stood looking down for a while, then bent and took Tara in his arms.

Tara felt his tongue invade her mouth like a weapon. Piercing trills of longing shot through the nerves of her hips and thighs.

She looked at him with deep admiration. Any other man in this situation, confronted with the bitter and angry mother of the girl he had knocked up – and her mother was quite capable of coming out with that kind of phrase – would have been diminished and shamefully exposed, stripped psychologically naked and humiliated. But Saul Xavier's dignity shone through the cringing embarrassment of the scenario, his self esteem and integrity were entirely undented.

'I was just saying to Tara that if I were your wife I should feel like committing murder,' Rachel observed.

Saul nodded thoughtfully. There had been a particularly distasteful scene with Georgiana in the early hours of the morning. Rachel probably had a point about her feeling murderous. 'I think she will find that she prefers living her own life once she gets used to the idea of my being with Tara,' he said calmly, refuelling Tara's admiration and sending chills of horror down Rachel's spine.

'So when did this amazing love affair spring into life?' Rachel enquired.

'When I heard Tara in the church singing the *Pie Jesu* for her father,' Saul responded without hesitation. 'If I thought a child of mine would sing like that at my funeral I would die a happy man!'

'I hope your child brings you happiness whilst you're alive,' Rachel said drily. 'I wouldn't wish it even on you Saul for your child to grow up and throw her or his youth away!'

There was a brittle silence.

'It's time I went,' Rachel said, 'before I say things I really mean.'

'Oh Mummy!' Tara's eyes filled suddenly with tears. 'You'll come and visit us lots won't you?'

'Oh yes. I'll soon get used to the idea of all of this – just like Saul's wife. And of course I can always find consolation in Don Giovanni's arms.' She smiled archly at Tara.

She bent down and Tara hugged her fiercely.

'Good-bye Saul,' Rachel said, straightening up. 'I can see that you're already infatuated with the idea of your child. Please don't forget to cherish mine.'

# CHAPTER 13

Georgiana awarded herself an especially self-indulgent day.

At the hairdresser's she was trimmed and highlighted, blow-waved and manicured. After that she moved through to the Body Beautiful salon where she had her bikini-line waxed, creating a satin smooth finish on her inner thighs. And for a final luxurious treat she placed herself under the soothing fingers of the chief masseuse, enjoying a long, sensuous massage designed to soothe away all tension from her muscles. Georgiana knew that she had tension in her muscles for the masseuse always told her so.

Bodily refreshed she then went for her weekly session with Dr Daneman, the last she would have before setting off to the Canaries. Although, of course, when she got things worked out with Xavier he would probably want her to stay at home with him.

Georgiana was not sure what her feelings were about that.

She lay on Dr Daneman's couch, her dove-grey suede boots neatly parked beneath her. Just out of her vision he waited for her opening words.

He thought she was looking particularly delicious today, swathed in soft charcoal grey wool, her baby blonde hair gleaming, her white hands clasped together just above her slender waist, like a dove of peace.

As was often the case with Georgiana he felt no agitation or anticipation for her to speak. He was perfectly content just to sit close by her and gaze.

'It's a time of change,' she said at last.

He waited.

'A new year. A new start.'

'Those are the kinds of things we are trained to think as one year merges into the next,' he agreed softly.

'We have to *make* things change. We have to do it ourselves,' Georgiana said, surprising Dr Daneman a little. She was normally so passive; expecting things (good things naturally) to happen to her in the manner that the sun comes up each morning.

'Whose voice says that to you?' Dr Daneman enquired.

'My own,' Georgiana countered, believing that to be the case, forgetting the words of Xavier and Alfreda and the countless other strong-willed, successful people who filled her social life. It was a popular modern doctrine, wasn't it? You were responsible for your own good fortune. It was a doctrine never shared by her parents, of course. They had always held the view that certain chosen people are simply destined for good fortune, come what may.

Dr Daneman waited, hopeful of some interesting development on this theme. But as usual Georgiana denied him gratification. She often teetered on the brink, but rarely put so much as a foot in the water.

She steered the talking and the thinking back to her

early days. On she went, over the old idyllic ground. It seemed to Dr Daneman that with every week Georgiana's childhood became suffused in ever more golden light.

But his attempts to hold up the mirror of life to her eyes and persuade her to confront the changing reflections were always charmingly and stubbornly resisted.

'How do you think I've done?' she asked unexpectedly at the end of the session?

'Since when?'

'Since the beginning?'

'You've made good progress,' he said carefully.

She smiled. 'Yes, I have, haven't I?'

He could not tell if she really believed that, or if she was desperately persuading herself that it was true.

'When I come to see you next, I will have something very special to tell you,' Georgiana confided with a light in her eye. Her smile now had a new quality. Something he had not seen before.

As she prepared to leave he felt concern for her. He reminded himself that her actions were not his responsibility. Neither had he had any reason – logical, theoretical or intuitive – to believe that she might be about to do herself harm.

But would she have the potential to do someone else harm? That was a question which had occasionally crossed his mind.

But never before, in anything but theory.

Georgiana had a light supper with Alfreda; there was a mousse of poached salmon, some slivers of lightly toasted brown bread, a fresh fruit salad.

149

She hinted to Alfreda that tonight was the night when she planned to make changes, but would say no more than that. Alfreda had arched her eyebrows, speculative and approving.

When Alfreda left her to go on to the theatre, Georgiana made her way to the Albert Hall to watch Xavier conduct the New Year concert: a heady programme of Mozart, Sibelius, Ravel and Beethoven. All very accessible, although the whole thing promised to be tediously long.

However Georgiana found herself entertained by the innovative and dramatic lighting effects; the dimly lit orchestra, and most especially the dramatically highlighted Maestro.

Seeing Xavier like this at a distance, theatrically presented and magical, she could almost imagine that she lusted after him. It was the reality of closeness that alarmed her and switched off desire. Xavier was so powerful, his tongue like a steel rod, his long fingers cruel batons, his thighs hard millstones to crush delicate flesh.

Revulsion quivered in her veins, coursing from head to toe.

And yet when she looked at him, a towering figure of authority, so dark, so compelling, so aristocratic, she felt a contrasting shiver of anticipation. Maybe it was the knowledge that so many other women wanted him that thrilled her. He was known the world over; a sex object for discerning and cultured women, a latter day god of Greek mythology.

Of course she wanted him, she told herself. What had she been thinking of these past few years? She had suffered

150

some hormonal imbalance probably. Those sort of things could play havoc with a woman's sexuality.

Even as she reasoned with herself she knew that her feeble arguments were self-deluding lies and deceptions.

But she would not be deflected from her purpose. There was more at stake here than the simple issue of sex. Which after all had never been a real issue for Georgiana, simply a distasteful inconvenience.

The Mozart tinkled and thundered capriciously. A young girl nearby got up and staggered out, obviously ill. Georgiana almost envied her her early escape. She felt sorry for the girl as well, just as she felt sorry for the majority of women who were physically unremarkable. And how awful it must be to be small and dark and so top heavy.

At the end of the concert she took a taxi home and opened a bottle of Bollinger. Xavier was particularly fond of Bollinger, relishing its yeasty fragrance and doughy aftertaste. Georgiana would have preferred something a little lighter but tonight was to be one hundred per cent geared to *his* preferences.

She drank two glasses and felt suitably unwound.

It never occurred to Georgiana that her chosen methods of seduction were clumsily crude, cringingly commonplace. Ultra stylish – and much admired – for her taste in clothes and her amusingly original dinner parties, Georgiana was little more than a child when it came to sexual sophistication. She was sure she was doing everything that was expected, that it could not fail to please.

Arrayed in a peach satin nightdress, and a cloud of *Jolie*

*Madame* eau de toilette, she waited for Xavier to return, mercifully oblivious of the disastrous mismatch between the scene she had set and the emotional upheavals of Xavier's day.

He did not return until four in the morning, looking uncharacteristically haggard and exhausted.

Georgiana, stretching out languorously on the sofa, saw him stare at her blankly. It was as though she were someone he had seen once or twice before but could not quite place.

Having waited tensely for him since midnight, she was inwardly incensed.

He had been with one of those girls. One of his own choosing, at his own instigation. An assignation that had nothing to do with her, Georgiana, his *wife*.

She fumed. She willed herself to be calm.

'You're still up,' he said.

'I wanted to see you,' she told him. 'I never see you these days.' She smiled. She tried to recapture the feelings and demeanour of the young bride Georgiana who had been so in love with her famous, stern bridegroom.

'No. I'm sorry about that.' He sat down, his upper body slumped forward, his long arms hanging between his legs.

'You've been working so hard,' she chided him. 'You're getting to be a workaholic!'

Xavier looked at her, noted the brittle, girlish coquetry glittering in her eyes. His mind was full of Tara and their child, he did not want to think about Georgiana. He had lost all motivation to expend mental energy on her problems. He suspected she had not been very happy recently. Maybe not very well. He wished she would simply dissolve. Get a lover, a potential new husband. Go away somewhere and be happy.

'Have some champagne,' she said, coming across and sitting beside him.

He took the glass.

She raised her glass and chinked it delicately on his. 'Happy New Year, darling.'

'Happy New Year.' The response was automatic.

'A new year, a new start,' she went on.

He paused. 'Yes.' If only she knew. He considered the kindest way to tell her.

'I do love you very much Xavier,' she said, sounding a little pathetic.

He said nothing.

She put her glass down and placed her hand on his crotch.

Xavier could not have been more surprised and dismayed if she had pulled a knife on him. Slowly she began to rotate her hand, her blue eyes staring into his.

Xavier felt revolted. He wanted to swat her off like a troublesome insect.

Still smiling she slipped her arms out of the straps of her nightgown and allowed it to slither down to her waist. Her small, girlish breasts gleamed like creamy pearls in the soft light from the lamps.

Xavier thought of Tara's gorgeous, succulent, Rubenswoman globes. Heavy and voluptuous like ripe fruits trapped in an invisible net.

Vaguely he registered Georgiana getting to her feet, wriggling out of her gown and presenting to him her perfect, blemish-free body.

She stood for a moment, triumphant and yet uncertain. And then, incredibly, she was taking the initiative, reaching for his hand and guiding it between her thighs.

Xavier felt the texture of her, greasy and perfumed, anointed with some expensive lubricant. His hand rested in hers and then as she withdrew it so his own dropped away from her, dead as a stone.

Georgiana looked down at him in bewilderment. Her face showed the pain and confusion of a child whose much considered gift has been roughly rejected.

Reluctantly, and with a huge effort of will, Xavier forced his mind to focus on the woman before him with whom he was sharing this awful moment.

Holding back the impulse to fell her with a single violent blow, he schooled himself to be gentle, for it was not her fault he no longer felt any emotion for her, and instead pulled her to sit beside him on the sofa. He let his arm rest around her shoulders.

And then he told her.

She sat very still, unflinching, wordless. Her face became closed and unreachable.

He fancied she had simply shut him off. His wife had an awesome capacity to ignore that which did not please, which did not fit with her view of the world. 'Georgiana,' he insisted, shaking her shoulder. 'You must listen.' There was no kind way to do this. He must be honest. Honesty was often brutal and cruel, but he had never shirked from it.

'This isn't some sudden whim of mine. I have been thinking about it for weeks. I have hardly slept. Georgiana!'

154

Her face was white as death, the china blue eyes blank and glassy.

He lifted her in his arms and shook her as though attempting to wake someone from drug-induced sleep. She was limp and yet in some curious way ferociously resisting him.

'Our marriage has been sick and ailing for some time now,' he informed the beautiful, marble-like features. 'We are not doing ourselves any good to carry on in this way.'

It was like trying to communicate with a corpse. He groaned with weariness and mounting frustration. 'For God's sake, Georgiana. Our marriage is dead!'

He fancied he saw a flicker in the blue stare.

'We shall still see each other, still be friends,' he coaxed, cringing at the notion. 'And you'll have nothing to worry about on the money side. You can have anything you want my dear.'

Still nothing.

His patience was at an end. 'Tara is having my child,' he said, the cruellest cut of all.

There was a long silence.

Suddenly she let out a chilling and primitive scream. A howl of animal rage. Just one. After that there was silence.

He could do nothing with her. She was encapsulated in some impregnable world of her own.

He gave up. He picked up the crumpled nightdress and manoeuvred it onto his wife's body, moving her limbs as though she were a doll.

He carried her to her room and laid her in bed.

She turned on her side and closed her eyes, shutting him out.

He had wondered for some time now if Georgiana were ill. He had no idea how serious it might be. He would make contact with her therapist, ask his advice.

He sat beside the bed, keeping watch over her. In his mind he was several miles away in a clinical hospital room where a small marvel of female humanity was suffering in the struggle to save the life of his child.

# CHAPTER 14

Saul's house on the outskirts of Oxford was a mock Tudor pile set in four acres of ornamental garden.

Tara chuckled with mockery as he drove the Porsche through the splendid wrought iron gates which opened automatically and then closed with a ringing clang behind them.

'Shut up,' he growled, loving her refusal to be impressed with the trappings of success, 'I don't take it seriously either.'

'But you bought it!'

'I have to have a place somewhere outside London.'

The drive was a smooth grey road, bordered on each side with tall bushes whose glossy leaves gave every appearance of having been polished by hand. The road swooped and curved, revealing glimpses of spreading lawns beyond the thick foliage of the bushes. Tara registered the trailing branches of weeping willows, the stiff fingers of a huge monkey puzzle tree.

There was a distant glint of turquoise water promising the opportunity of some relaxing swims.

The grey road ended in a circular gravel sweep. The

house presiding over it was huge with a high front door of heavy oak, arched and studded like the entry to a castle.

Tara stared at it and then burst into laughter. 'Will the staff be lined up waiting? Is there an evil, jealous housekeeper who will strike terror into my bones?'

Saul smiled. 'There is Mrs Lockton. She comes in every day from the village where she lives with her husband and children. I very much doubt her capacity for serious wickedness.'

Inside the house smelled of beeswax polish and freshly cut flowers. The huge hallway was panelled in dark oak. There was a honey marble floor, on which one solitary silken rug from the former Persia lay in softly glistening ripples.

Tara looked around her. For a moment it was hard to think of anything suitable to say.

Saul took her in his arms and kissed her face. He then took her on a tour of the eleven-roomed house.

'Who dusts the skirting boards?' Tara enquired, having regained her usual spiky assurance.

'Not you.' He spoke in a manner which prohibited all challenge. 'Mrs Lockton organizes people to come in and do all that, also the cooking. I'd advise you simply to steer clear.'

'So what do I do all day? Apart from being a brood mare?'

'Oh – I have a few plans,' he said softly.

'What about the promotion job with the orchestra?' she asked tentatively.

He looked down at her. 'No.' His eyes were hard.

'No longer on offer? Don't get the idea my brain's about

to turn to porridge just because I'm pregnant.' She stared up at him with warm challenge.

His face was stripped and austere. 'You almost lost this baby, Tara. There is no question of taking any risks. You need peace. You need calm and rest. Then after the baby – well . . .' His hand curved in an upwardly spiralling gesture suggesting the possibility of all manner of un-limited heights to be scaled.

She realized there was little point in protesting. And secretly she was relieved. Just for the moment she wanted to concentrate on very little besides loving Saul.

In the huge main bedroom Tara rushed at him like a playful calf, surprising him with a sharp lunge, catching him off balance so that he fell onto the king-sized bed. Kneeling over his hips she declared love on him with a vengeance.

Their lips and tongues entwined. He gazed at her with his mysteriously remote yet deeply sensual eyes. She could feel their hearts beating in rhythmn, their breathing perfectly synchronized as they lay together like one body.

'How did you get so bony?' he murmured, his fingers tracing over the spikes of her rib cage.

'How do you think?'

'Pining? Mmm?'

'Shame on me,' she grimaced. 'When were you going to come for me?'

'When you'd had long enough time to sweat.' He smiled at her. He loved all the verbal fencing. She was so sure, so resilient. But then suddenly her breath-catching young vulnerability would show through the self-assurance like a flash of naked flesh beneath torn fabric.

She narrowed her eyes dangerously. 'I'm going to make *you* sweat.' She reached down.

He grasped her hand, stilling it. Holding it prisoner.

'Saul!'

'I'm sure I don't have to remind you what the doctor said,' he told her, his eyes suddenly icy.

Tara recalled the interview with the gynaecologist before they left the hospital.

He'd been a smooth, patronizing jerk. On one occasion he had even referred to her as 'the little lady.' And he'd made coy remarks about play pens when he meant vaginas.

'Wise to leave the play pen empty for the next month or so if you want to make sure it's going to be full later,' he had jested.

Tara had interpreted this as a warning to refrain from strenuous sex. At least for a while. If possible.

With Saul lying next to her now she didn't believe it was.

She looked into Saul's eyes and saw the resolution of purpose there.

'You're not suggesting we don't make love for weeks and weeks,' she gasped in horror. 'My God, Saul, I'd go mad. I couldn't bear it!'

His eyes held hers, compelling, magnetizing. In total, awe-inspiring control. 'You are having a child, my darling. That means that you yourself are no longer a child. You have to learn patience. Restraint. I'm quite used to it,' he informed her drily. 'A little more privation will make very little difference. Besides which, anticipation always sharpens up the appetite.'

This last statement he believed to be true. The one

before was an outright lie. He did not know how he was going to keep himself from penetrating her wonderful firm body and losing himself in the ecstasy of making love to her. But Xavier knew that he would just have to exercise the greatest self control of his life if he was to ensure the safe delivery of his baby and the continued adoration of his new lover. He would also have to find other ways to entertain her.

He smiled down at her, his outward mask of control now firmly back in place after his anxiety during those first few terrible hours when he did not know if she and his baby would live or die.

'Oh my God!' said Tara, looking up at him in awe and despair. 'Oh Saul,' she wailed, enough to break a heart of iron.

He bent to kiss the pulse beating in her neck. 'Turn over,' he whispered. With languid reverence he released her from her white cotton tee shirt and her bright turquoise jeans. He unhooked her bra and watched her squirm with pleasure as he brushed the darkening nipples with dry fingers.

Pulling away the ridiculous tiny panties he placed an arm beneath the swell of her belly and raised her hips. Then he kissed her firm smooth buttocks. All over. Lingering, tantalizing until she was gasping like someone drowning.

His fingers found every throbbing crevice, every welcoming eager fold of flesh. His lips traced the paths his fingers had drawn. His tongue flicked and darted.

Tara was heated and feverish. Such power he had.

Almost, almost, almost, she chanted silently. Then

finally, 'Oh my God!' as the ecstasy pulsed and swirled in the secret dark centre of her femininity.

Rachel arrived with a carload of Tara's belongings.

'Is he here?' she asked.

'No, he's at the Paris Conservatory, talent spotting. He's flying back later this evening.'

'And you're waiting here for him like some good little wife?' Rachel arched her eyebrows.

'Don't be a cow Mummy.'

'I'm jealous,' Rachel said, squinting up at the magnificent house. She knew also that she was just a tiny bit triumphant to see Tara a little tamed.

'It's a bit of dog,' Tara grimaced, eyeing the mock Tudor beams and the lattice paned windows, sprinkled with burglar alarms.

'Perhaps a little opulent for your taste,' Rachel agreed drily, recalling Tara's previous scorn for anything that smacked of ostentation and conspicuous consumption. 'Did he choose it?'

Tara shrugged. 'I haven't asked. I can't imagine so.'

Inside the house Rachel followed her daughter around, observing thoughtfully, declining to comment if there was nothing good she could find to say. She stared up at the extravagantly swagged and tasselled curtains in the bedrooms, at the draped silk canopies adorning the beds. 'Very Homes and Gardens!' she ventured at last.

'Oh, come on! Be honest. It's unbelievably frightful,' said Tara.

'Taste is a matter for each individual.' Rachel commented evenly. She was thinking of the woman who had chosen all this pampered luxury. Was such a woman to be despised as merely spoiled and underemployed? Or was her need for self indugence a reflection of some deeper longing? What was she truly like, this woman? The one who had been cast off. Saul's wife.

Rachel looked at the top of Tara's gleaming chestnut head as she followed her down the stairs and knew that she could not bring herself to voice these questions, nor be confronted with her daughter's opinions.

Tara took her into the drawing room, a vast salon of thirty feet long, perfectly proportioned as a double cube. Rachel stared at the stark white walls and the gleaming, unadorned oak block floor. There was no clutter here, no ornaments, no dainty little antique pieces, just one arresting, fabulous painting from Picasso's blue period which drew the eye and held it like a magnet. Other adornments were of a directly practical nature: a stereo system with controls like the cockpit of a small aircraft. And on a slightly raised platform beneath the windows a nine-foot Steinway grand piano.

'Now *this* is definitely his choice,' Rachel said. 'You can see his hand all over this room. Spare, aesthetic.'

'Yes, it's perfect,' Tara murmured. 'I spend nearly all my time here.'

'So what about your friends? Do they come here to see you?' Rachel enquired.

'No. Well, they seem a bit young and crass . . .'

'Are you worried he would object?'

'Oh for heaven's sake say his name Mummy. Even if he is the low bastard who impregnated your daughter.'

Rachel sighed.

'Sorry, sorry,' Tara said impatiently. 'No, truly – my not inviting any of the old gang here is nothing to do with Saul. He makes me feel free to do whatever I like here. As long as I don't seduce the milkman.'

She had to make a joke about sex. The reality of the situation was driving her a little mad.

Saul indulged her shamelessly in games of gratification. She never knew when he was going to reach for her. Any room in the house could be a chosen scene for a swift divesting of her clothes, some sensual stroking, massaging, kissing, rubbing. Sometimes these encounters were titillatingly risky with the staff present in the house, quite likely to disturb them at any moment.

Saul undressed her with his eyes across the tables of elegant restaurants. He slithered his hands over her erotically during other conductors' concerts. And then he would reach for her in the car whilst driving at crazy speeds.

She felt she must be experiencing more heady orgasms than the rest of the world's women put together.

But he refused to play mutually masturbatory games.

One morning, waking early she had looked longingly at his beautiful stern face and then burrowed down the bed and wrapped her lips around him, rousing him into rapid, gratifyingly throbbing life.

He had pulled her head away. 'No!'

'Why? Saul, let me pleasure you. Like you do me. So very beautifully.'

'No.' He had slid from the sheets, his taut body a rod of determination. She had heard the rush of the shower.

He must be in control. He must have the power. Thinking of it had made her ache for him.

Then he had come back to bed and brought her to a thundering climax in one minute flat. She had wanted to throw herself at his feet and kiss them.

His self control was truly awesome. He could go without food for days if he decided he needed to fast. Cut out the drink completely if he chose.

But it was his sexual control, given his capacity for passion, that was truly mind chilling. This ability to hold himself back drove her to the brink of desperation and also excited her deepest admiration.

The ache was constant.

'Come and see the kitchen,' she said to Rachel, taking her through and filling the kettle.

'We're quite safe,' Tara chuckled. 'The army of staff are all on temporary leave.'

Rachel sat down at the oak refectory table. A spear of late winter sunshine picked up some new auburn lights in her hair.

'You've had a tint,' Tara said noticing.

'Mmm. I thought it was time to get rid of those blonde highlights you so despised.'

Tara grimaced, recalling her sudden verbal attack on her mother at the funeral. All that seemed like another life. She used to be such a rotten little bitch sometimes. Poor Mummy.

'Does Donald like it?'

'I think so.'

'He wouldn't mind even if you dyed it green?'

'Something like that.'

165

'Has he moved in yet?'

'Yes.'

Tara smiled. 'Me knocked up by Saul and you shacked up with Donald Giovanni. Randiness must be in the blood!'

Rachel looked down at her hands. Her resolute light-heartedness suddenly evaporated. She didn't know quite how to interpret Tara's constant jokiness, feared it was a ploy to hold her at a distance.

It simply didn't feel right; Tara being here in this huge and serious middle-aged house. A solitary little figure, cut off from her own generation. Obviously pregnant now. And not married.

It was no joke.

There were other, more public worries. Rachel was well aware of the talk going around amongst Richard's former colleagues in the Tudor Philharmonic. Especially amongst the men. And face it, orchestras were still male-dominated tribes. *The Maestro's done all right for himself there, got himself as juicy a bit of tender young meat as he'll have tasted in a long time. Nice work if you can get it eh?* Rachel heard the jests in her head, could visualize the sly winks and pulled lips. She winced internally.

Most certainly not a joke.

'Do you like him?' Rachel asked. 'Do you like Saul?'

There was a fractional pause. 'Yes. I do.'

'But not in the way you liked Bruno?'

'Bruno was so *nice*. He used to drive me potty he was so kind and patient.'

Rachel felt like weeping. For Bruno, for Tara. For all lost young love.

Tara stared at her mother suspiciously. 'I'm perfectly aware that you don't like Saul. It's always cringingly obvious.'

'I don't know him well enough to offer an opinion,' Rachel said carefully.

'Balls! And it was you that started all this.'

'Balls ditto!'

'Inviting him back after the funeral. He left me his card, offering to help me with my playing. That's what kicked everything off.'

'Dropping his calling card?' Rachel commented with a smile of irony. 'I thought that was something tom cats did.'

Tara breathed heavily. 'And then you were all for encouraging me to go with him to that ghastly geriatric violinist's place.'

'Are you playing much now?' Rachel asked, willing herself to call a truce and keep calm.

'I get in four hours practice most days. And then I sit in on most of Saul's rehearsals and there's a lot to learn there.'

Rachel tried not to allow her smile to register too much motherly pleasure. Tara was so ambivalent about her playing that if she suspected she was pleasing her mother by picking up the threads of her musical endeavours she might decide to pack it in again.

'Saul's always inviting musicians round,' Tara went on. 'We play chamber music. I've been playing quartets and quintets with some of the most famous names you can think of!'

'Really!'

167

'Yes. It's fantastic!' She looked at Rachel. 'You'll be pleased about that.'

Rachel saw the flash of childish anxiety in Tara's big green eyes. *You're pleased with me aren't you Mummy?*

What a mixture Tara was. Touchy and brittle one minute, soft and pleading the next. Rachel wondered how Saul managed with her. But of course it would all be so different for him. For one thing he was not her parent.

'I know it's not the same as playing in my own right,' Tara said, voicing Rachel's own thoughts exactly. 'But after the baby I'm really going to think seriously about developing a career for myself. Saul has already introduced me to his agent.'

Rachel reflected on the benefits to be gained when one shared a bed with the famous and influential. She felt pain to realize that Tara had long ago left her and Richard behind. Now she belonged to Saul. Body, soul, ambition – everything.

Tara walked with Rachel to her car. Before stepping in Rachel reached out for her daughter and pulled her against her. She longed to cradle her in the easy yet fierce embrace with which she used to comfort the infant Tara when she had had a fall, or yelled herself exhausted after an explosion of toddler rage.

She felt the slight stiffening in Tara's body as she hugged her. Tara offered her cheek for a kiss and then drew away.

Rachel arranged her face into a cheery smile. She started the engine.

The gates at the end of the drive swung open. Rachel tooted. Tara waved.

On the opposite side of the road a woman with long blonde hair sat motionless in a parked blue Mercedes and gazed steadily at the house.

## CHAPTER 15

Looking back on the night of the all Brahms concert, the night of Richard Silk's sudden death from which everything else seemed to have sprung, Saul realized that his sensation of emptiness as he had stood on the podium had been nothing more than a simple longing for the love of a true mate and the gift of a child.

It had taken long enough to find that out he thought, grimacing at his own obtuseness. For years he had deluded himself with a number of other ideas – a wish to promote a shining new talent, a need to dominate and control a magnificent orchestra. And to provide himself with an heir, someone to carry his torch. Those things had been real, been true. But not until he knew Tara, not until she told him that she was carrying his child had everything fallen into place.

And now he was almost obsessed with the notion of his lover and his child. He loved his Tara. He adored her. He wanted to make her vitally and endlessly happy – and he knew that he had the vision and the means. The idea of the child held him in a grip of fevered anticipation that governed his thoughts and feelings in a way he had not experienced before. He longed for the day when he would see the child in reality, hold it supported in his hands and arms and feel the breath of its life against his skin.

In the meantime he was indulging his darling Tara in a barrage of adoration – and music.

It had delighted him to discover that Tara was a true lover of music. She was not just a sensitive and competent player who used music as a vehicle for her talent. She penetrated to the warm beating heart of a piece. She untangled the skeins of feeling, sensed and expressed every flickering change of mood that had passed across the composer's mind as he wrote. Her emotions were fully engaged.

Saul had spent a good deal of time and thought in the planning and engineering of regular gatherings of musical artists who would stimulate Tara's interest and augment her confidence. These were lively occasions, filled with laughter and musical gossip, accompanied by a variety of delicious cold suppers prepared by Mrs Lockton. The champagne would be plentiful.

And then the music would start. Violins, oboes, clarinets would be taken from their cases. Fragments of themes would ring out. There would be noisy discussions on the pieces these gifted musicians might favour with their skills. It was all tremendous fun. And yet fiercely serious.

Saul would sometimes participate, playing supporting piano parts, offering dry observations, pinpricks of jesting criticism. But usually he chose to remain in the background, a silent assessing figure, revelling in the pleasure he was offering his young lover through the chance to play the violin which had once been her father's in the company of some of the greatest instrumentalists in the world.

And after the parties came to an end, and the house was still and silent, he would request her to take up her violin once more, just for him.

'So – are you good enough yet?' Saul asked her as they stood together at the front door in the early hours of a dewy morning, supervising the departure of their guests. A procession of cars weaved down the driveway, their red tail lights gleaming against a sky already tinged with dawn apricot.

'Good enough?' she looked up at him.

'Don't you remember?' he asked evenly. 'At your father's funeral how you got in a terrible rage with Rachel, shouting about not being "good enough". I've often wondered what you meant. Because, you know, you really are becoming rather a good player.'

'Am I? Truly?'

'I always suspected that dear Monica would have to eat her words.'

Not being good enough, Tara thought. That old recurring theme which had pulled her down, killed motivation. What had it meant? She frowned, her thoughts active. A spark of insight flashed across the surface of her mind. She grasped at it, but it was instantly gone.

'I was always ranting and raving about something or other when I was at home,' she explained to Saul. 'I was still a kid. Poor Mummy and Daddy.'

'Yes, your poor mother!'

'Saul!'

'You were an *enfant* truly *terrible*,' he informed her, nipping her ear.

'Yes. And now I've grown up. OK?'

'Very well. Would you like to play for me then? A little nightcap?'

'I think I feel too nervous.'

'How so?'

'Because you said I was good. I might not live up to it. Did you really mean it?'

'Yes.'

'Better than the second chair in the back row of the violin section?'

'Yes.'

'Soloist quality?'

'Possibly.'

'Ugh. Down to earth with a bump.'

'Wait until this bump is out in the open,' he said, glancing at the growing swell of her body. 'And then we'll see what the possibilities are.'

She turned to him and stretched up to kiss him hard on the mouth. 'Thank you for being honest with me Saul. Thank you for not flattering me into thinking I'm something I'm not.'

He was immensely touched. 'There will be a great future for you in music, I'm sure of it. Just be patient.' But maybe not as a solo violinist, he thought privately. Maybe musical journalism, criticism. She had a good ear and a sharp witty tongue.

She poured him a whisky. They sat together on the sofa. She placed her hand over his, squeezing it with tender affection. 'What would you say if you thought we were

173

going to have two babies?' she said in matter of fact tones. Inside she was tensing. There was always that tingle of apprehension about Saul's reactions to significant news. A glitter of sparkling anxiety.

He turned his head slowly.

She nodded, confirming her statement, parting her lips. His hand lay beneath hers still and firm. A smile stole onto his face.

The thought of pleasing him like this made her insides warm and liquid with desire.

'Say something,' she demanded.

'Are there increased risks?' he asked.

'Yes.'

'For you? For the babies?'

'A little. For me. For all of us. It's nothing to worry about.'

'I shall worry,' he said quietly. 'Until the three of you are safe.'

She heard the rasp of his breathing. She took his hand and placed it on her belly, right over the two small beating hearts. She shared none of his fears. She had not yet thought of herself, or any part of her biology, as mortal.

In bed later she lay in his arms. At peace. Entirely contented.

'Saul,' she said, suddenly remembering. 'Is your wife an elegant gazelle with long blonde hair?'

Saul's body froze. 'That's a fair description. Why?'

'I think I saw her the other day when I was driving out through the gates.'

In fact Tara had seen the Mercedes most days in recent weeks. Always in the late afternoon when Saul was never at home. Always parked just out of sight of the house. But Tara could see it very clearly from the tiny window in the roof space.

'What was she doing?' Saul enquired tersely.

'Just driving past slowly, looking in. I'm sure I'd have done the same in her shoes.'

'Is it a problem?'

'Not at all. You could invite her here you know. I wouldn't mind.'

'Unthinkable. And she would mind very much.'

Tara had the impression there was nothing more to be said on the matter. And in any case she had been separated from sleep for much too long. She sighed, turned over, burrowed into her pillow.

Looking back later she supposed she had been very naïve.


The next day Saul telephoned Dr Daneman and expressed insistent concern about Georgiana's condition. Dr Daneman was courteous and sympathetic. He was not, however, prepared to be bullied by a man clearly used to having all his own way. He answered every question posed but in such a way as to maintain a very proper professional reticence. He made it plain to the icily furious husband that there was to be no discussion on the contents of the revelations offered by his wife in the therapy sessions. Such information was entirely private between a patient and her therapist, as Mr Xavier would, of course, appreciate.

Dr Daneman declared himself generally pleased with Mrs Xavier's progress. He saw no cause for anxiety about her actions. It was quite natural that a woman should want to take a drive past one of her former homes, from which she had been virtually barred.

Saul felt nothing but contempt for the man's bland reasonableness. He listened for a while and then softly replaced the receiver, cutting the doctor off in mid sentence.

Soon afterwards Saul telephoned Georgiana herself, intending to speak very kindly, very gently, whilst spelling things out to leave her in no doubt. But there was no reply from her number. Neither was she with Alfreda, who reassured him that Georgiana was fine and coping surprisingly well with the separation.

In the afternoon Tara saw the blue Mercedes draw up opposite the gates just after four-thirty. She watched it for ten minutes or so. Her natural warmth and sympathy were strongly aroused. She struggled to put her own feelngs on one side and to step into the mind of a rejected wife.

Suddenly she had had enough of passive reflections. She must act, do something positive. Aware that Saul would have restrained her by force, had he been on hand to guess at her intentions, she slipped out of the front door and started on the long walk down the drive.

She was nervous. Her heart drummed in a jagged rhythm. It was the courage of youth that spurred her on, a belief in her capacity to heal rifts and make the world a better place.

She walked out through the gates, then crossed the road and bent down to the driver's window.

The woman turned her face up. Her eyes were brilliant and startling. Sky-blue irises and whites as smooth and unblemished as the flesh beneath the shell of a freshly boiled egg.

She is simply beautiful thought Tara, experiencing a bolt of shock. Such wonderful bones. And those thick dark lashes, an arrestingly dramatic contrast against the magnolia petal skin and the swing of pale hair.

'I am Georgiana,' the woman announced.

'Yes, I guessed. I'm Tara.'

There was a long silence.

Tara licked around her lips. Her mind darted and bucked like an alarmed animal. *I'm sorry I've taken your husband Georgiana. I'm so sorry. But I'd do it all over again if the choice were there. Oh God!*

'Would you like to come in?' she said to Georgiana. 'Mrs Lockton is just making some tea.'

Georgiana gripped the steering wheel, staring straight ahead through the windscreen.

Tara fancied it would be no more than a moment before Georgiana would simply activate the engine and drive away. She fancied that was what she would have done, given the same set of choices.

It was with some astonishment that she watched Georgiana Xavier open the door of the car, and swing two breathtakingly slender legs over the sill.


Saul had told Tara that the term of a pregnancy was a small time to contemplate celibacy. In the event the waiting time was less than he had thought.

In the August of that year, only days after Rachel and Donald were married, Tara gave birth to twins four weeks prematurely. Both babies, a male and a female, were tiny and frail. The little boy, Saul Richard Aristotle, died at the age of thirty-six hours.

*Part Two*

# CHAPTER 16

The Violin Concerto of Edward Elgar is one of the greatest and best-loved works in the virtuoso repertoire; a mighty piece lasting almost an hour, full of technical subtleties and complex emotions.

Tara had been practising it relentlessly in the last few weeks, fitting in her playing schedule around the demands of one-year-old baby Alessandra, and the rediscovering of the delights of lovemaking with Saul. Following the birth of the twins she had been advised to wait for some weeks before resuming what the doctor termed marital relations. Advice she instantly discarded. She could not wait. She hungered for him. And he had devoured her.

Her twentieth birthday was rapidly approaching and Saul had masterminded a spectacularly imaginative and wholly wonderful gift to mark the occasion. On that day the Tudor Philharmonic was to give a huge charity concert. The proceeds were to be given to the Great Ormond Street hospital where Saul's and Tara's baby son had been given exceptional care throughout the hours of his short life.

Saul had put the suggestion to the orchestra's managing

board that they might consider inviting the mother of the child whose memory had sparked off the project to be their soloist. There had been whole-hearted approval.

Tara had been amazed when Saul told her, had stared at him with incredulous delight and pure terror.

'You can do it,' he told her softly, pulling her to him and breathing kisses into the skin of her neck.

'You'll be there on the podium, Saul?' she asked, part mocking, part wracked with genine anxiety. 'You won't leave me to the mercy of some rogue guest conductor?'

He chuckled. 'I shall be there. So you'd better deliver the performance of a lifetime my sweet angel, otherwise you'll be dead meat.' She tingled. God, how his menaces turned her on.

Tara watched him later on playing with their baby daughter; teasing, cajoling, directing, teaching. Alessandra adored him. Her huge shining eyes followed him around, tracking his every move, transparent worship on her features.

Tara tuned in exactly to that feeling. She herself was still hopelessly in love with him, totally in thrall, utterly bound. He was always near to her, in her blood and in her eyes, waking, sleeping and dreaming. The rest of the world seemed to have fallen back into the distance, the people in it existing in a shadow out of the circle of his light.

Occasionally she sensed that she was in the grip of some kind of disease, laid low in its attack, helpless to do anything to counteract it and ignorant of the appropriate antidote.

She loved his masterfulness, the cutting edge of his

opinions, his utter belief in himself. And yet she was not blind to his faults: stern intransigence and ruthless dominance. She waged a constant teasing battle with him in order not to be utterly subjugated to his will. It was hard work, but wildly exciting and all in all she judged that she was managing to keep her head above water.

Over time she had learned never to take anything he did or said at face value. Saul was a strategist, a shaper and planner. Although a passionate man he was rarely impulsive. Behind all his deeds and words was a purpose.

She could not help musing on Saul's motivation in setting up this marvellous opportunity for her to play in public with the great Tudor Philharmonic. Maybe it was a simple desire to give her the most wonderful gift he could think of, but as things were rarely simple with Saul she suspected there was something more subtle behind it.

She was also well aware that in accepting his gift she took the risk of making a fool of herself, making a total mess of things through her lack of experience or hopelessly jangled nerves. Although, of course, as the event was for charity, it would not be a disaster if her performance went no further than basic competence.

And maybe that was what he was giving her the opportunity to find out. For once and all. Whether or not she was any good as a solo player.

One never knew with Saul. Which was why living with him was so endlessly thrilling, like an eternal ride on a dizzy roller coaster.

He had been deeply moved by the birth of the babies. The death of the tiny boy child had temporarily stunned him, but Alessandra's sturdy growth and development had in time become a compensation.

Tara saw the three of them now as a tight, entwined unit.

Tara, Saul and Alessandra – all interdependent, all needing each other fiercely.

Alessandra was developing into a beautiful young child. She had the long face and straight nose of her father and the huge green eyes of her mother. However, whereas Tara's irises were green lit with gold, Alessandra's were heavily flecked with tawny brown, deepening the overall tone of her eyes and forming a startling contrast with her pale blonde hair – a feature that neither Tara nor Saul could trace in their ancestry.

Tara felt that it was curiously ironic that her baby should have this beautiful blonde hair – a childish replica of the mane of Saul's wife.

Georgiana had been deeply puzzled by Saul's mistress's directness, right from those first moments in the spring of the previous year when she had leaned into the car and invited Georgiana to join her for a chat and cup of tea!

It was quite simply not the sort of thing that should happen. But it had happened. And she had not been able to see any way of refusing the invitation without seeming graceless. She had found the younger woman curiously compelling.

Georgiana had never spent much time at the Oxfordshire house, preferring her house in London or the apartments in Florence and the south of France. She did not like the country house. Its situation was isolated and its decor and furnishings too sparse and simple for her taste.

Saul had given her a little licence in furnishing the bedrooms, but he had been adamant in having his own way in the main rooms on the ground floor. It had always been Georgiana's view that the Oxfordshire house was a man's place. Saul's place.

The mistress had invited her to bring her car up to the house. She had encouraged her through the front door, smiling and friendly. She had ushered her in to the monk's cell of a drawing room, given her tea and afterwards mixed her a very good gin and tonic.

Whilst Georgiana sipped, desperate for the solace the alcohol would bring, the mistress had apologized to her for stealing her husband and becoming pregnant with his child.

As Georgiana winced to hear such words spoken out so plainly, so nakedly, the mistress had said softly, 'I didn't plan it to be like this for you.' She had said it in a way that was almost believable. And then she had said, 'I wouldn't blame you for hating my guts.'

Georgiana had looked hard at her. At the girl's ripening bulge: the sickening badge of her triumph. At her full, heavy breasts. At her candid face. She had a vague recollection of having seen her before somewhere. She could not place it. The mistress was like so many girls of her generation – no dress sense, no feeling for jewellery or make-up. No style.

That was something to be grateful for at least. But as Georgiana listened to the girl talking and saw the life and spirit in her mobile face, she had begun to see why a man might be attracted to her. It was probably nothing more than raw animal sexuality. But then, you could snare a man with that. Keep him maybe, at least for a while.

And, of course, the girl was *young*. There was no competing with that. The years were simply too cruel.

The girl talked about her background; her parents and her efforts on the violin.

'Do you play?' she had asked Georgiana suddenly. She was so open. So quick.

'No. Not at all. I used to be a model.'

'Yes. I should have guessed. You're incredibly beautiful.'

Georgiana had been caught off balance. Disarmed.

The mistress had seemed to be genuinely interested in her. She had asked Georgiana to tell her about her family, her interests. The ups and downs of a modelling career. She had virtually invited Georgiana to recount her life story.

Relaxed and encouraged by the gin, Georgiana had found herself not only complying with the request, but beginning to enjoy herself.

The mistress had listened with such attentiveness. She had broken in with questions from time to time, clearly fascinated by what she heard.

And then, to crown all, as Georgiana eventually got up to leave, she had asked if she would like to visit again sometime. Not when Saul was there if she would rather not.

'You could meet me in town,' Georgiana had said after consideration. 'We could have lunch.' She had looked at Tara, her fastidious eye seeing in that small figure a desperate need for sartorial guidance. 'Afterwards we could have a browse round the shops.'

And so a tentative and unorthodox relationship had begun.

Saul had taken the news impassively. 'You're free to plan your own social life,' he had told Tara, his grey eyes cool. 'Be careful!'

'Fraternizing with the competition,' Alfreda had exclaimed at the end of Georgiana's story of this first encounter. 'You must be out of your mind!'

# CHAPTER 17

The rehearsal was about to begin.

Tara was already on stage, chatting and joking with the violin section, making a valiant job of concealing her nerves which seemed to have gathered in her stomach in a hard curdled lump.

Saul had been delayed for a few moments, talking with the orchestra's manager. Now suddenly he was there on the podium, standing erect, motionless and yet charged with energy. A hush fell over the orchestra and all eyes were trained on the remote, tall figure before them.

His eyes took their customary assessing journey across each section of the orchestra, then briefly rested on Tara, giving a special acknowledgement of her presence.

'Ladies and gentlemen!' he smiled. 'May I ask you to welcome Tara.'

A huge cheer went up. A round of applause. A roll from the kettle drums. Everyone was loving the occasion: welcoming a soloist who was not only the daughter of an old colleague but now romantically and scandalously shacked up with their charismatic music director.

There was something in all of that to appeal to everyone.

Saul waited for silence. And then, just as he was about to say something about Elgar's concerto and the way it was going to be played, there was a mischievous interruption from the leader of the orchestra, a mild-mannered man affectionately known as the Chief Toreador.

'Maestro. Aren't you going to give Tara the newcomer's cautionary story? It's something she shouldn't miss.'

Saul narrowed his eyes and then smiled. 'Ah yes.' He looked down at Tara and she looked up. 'The initiation story. It's about a bassoon player I knew once in an orchestra in Munich,' he explained. 'A wily old devil. He knew all there was to know about the playing of great music. He used to sit in darkened beer cellars telling stories about conductors.'

He paused. Tara looked up at him. 'Go on!'

'He claimed that when a new man faced the orchestra they knew straight away whether *he* was the master or *they*. Before the poor man even picked up his baton they knew whether he or they would call the tune.'

'I think I know who calls the tune with this orchestra,' Tara interposed sweetly, her eyes sparkling with the thrill of combat. 'Is this a story with a happy ending?' she wondered.

'Oh indeed. As long as all the players are competent and obedient. Including the soloists.' He arched his brows.

'So anyone with a faint heart, a rebellious spirit or inadequate technique may leave now? Is that the moral of the tale? Well, I'm staying!' Tara responded smartly, eliciting a roar of delighted approval from the players.

'Good. Now, shall we get down to business?' Xavier was suddenly the indomitable conductor again, his face steely with purpose. 'The Elgar Concerto, ladies and gentlemen. A great work of art. A silk purse. Let us not make a sow's ear of it.'

He rested his hands on the curved brass rails of the podium. His face had become distant, absorbed and intent. 'Edward Elgar was a composer of immense charm,' he told his audience softly. 'His music has a taste and breeding that belong to a bygone age. It has great dignity, great beauty, genuine nobility. It is filled with a nostalgic longing for the past.'

His words created a picture in Tara's head: a dreamy June afternoon in an old English garden. She saw elegant slender women in white muslin – an older Alessandra, a younger Georgiana maybe – drifting over silky lawns murmuring companionably to each other.

Saul was still speaking. 'This great concerto we are going to bring to life is loved and renowned for its poetry and romanticism.' He paused and gazed intently at Tara for a moment. 'I want our audience to feel the spirit of a bygone England as they listen. I want them to experience the same regrets that the composer felt when he wrote this music, contemplating the closing years of his life and the glories of the Edwardian age, an epoch already closed.'

My God, he's inspirational, Tara thought, a lump rising in her throat.

'And remember,' Saul continued, his voice calm and hypnotic, 'that Edward Elgar was himself an accomplished violinist and would know all too well the pitfalls of this piece.' Again he looked at Tara.

Saul! Are you trying to scare me out of my wits, she thought. But she knew that he was not playing games now.

This was Saul at his most serious, his most intense and genuine. His soul was bared and he would expect everyone else's to be in the same state in the pursuit of musical excellence, not only technical but spiritual.

'Elgar was well into his fifties when he wrote this piece,' Saul continued. 'Tara is still very young. She will need all her skill and sensitivity to capture the emotions of an ageing man.' He stopped and stared at her with his penetrating, remorseless eyes, making her heart sway.

'I'm sure she will do it beautifully,' he concluded, his voice almost a whisper. His eyes held Tara's for a few moments and she felt herself spellbound, utterly magnetized. Even after living with him for all these months he could still work this powerful magic on her.

She knew that all his wealth of experience and musical perception, all his strength of purpose would be generously put at her disposal in order to draw out the performance of a lifetime.

Whenever she played for Saul she was always at her peak, going far beyond the abilities she believed herself to have when she was without him – in the cold light away from the orbit of his sun.

Play your heart out for him Tara, she murmured to herself, knowing that she had the power under his direction to give the quality of performance that would satisfy even his exacting requirements. And she was sure that the orchestra felt similarly energized and empowered.

Emotions stirred within her. Warm, prickling sensations swelled through the veins of her fingers as she placed her violin against the skin of her jaw . . .

* * *

The following minutes and hours swam unrealistically by, an unbroken dream of playing and listening and preparing to play yet again.

And then it was time to play for real. The audience had assembled, the overture had reached a climax and swirled to a close. Applause resounded through the auditorium.

Tara waited behind the stage, her nerves singing with tension and anticipation. She tried to fix her mind on nothing but the piece she was about to play.

Her head swam with mingled images of the music and of Saul's beloved aesthetic features.

Beyond fear now, her mind drained and almost numb, she waited for him to leave the orchestra and escort her onto the stage.

Then suddenly he was coming towards her, his face intense with concentration as though he had not yet quite returned to earth after the surging crescendo of the orchestra.

In his long tailored jacket and classically plain white shirt he looked every inch the aristocrat: remote, passive, inscrutable.

How little she really knew about him.

And how fascinating that made him seem.

He extended his hand towards her, taking in the low-cut tight-waisted scarlet gown from which her full breasts swelled temptingly.

'The audience will love you,' he said enigmatically, taking her hand in his.

And now they were walking onto the platform together, Saul shepherding her with pride through the ranks of the orchestra.

A roar of approval went up. Tara's heart bucked with mingled exhilaration and terror. She forced herself to smile, giving a brief inclination of her head in acknowledgement of the warm reception.

Planting her feet firmly on the platform, she straightened her back and breathed deeply. Now, at last, the moment had come. A moment dreamed of for years. By her, yes – but most especially by her father. His face swam briefly before her inner eye, that beloved face of the past.

She took up her bow and looked towards Saul, the living man who now filled her present. His eyes held hers in a long naked stare, making her recall some of their most intimate moments together, the marvellous unfettered love-making hovering on the exquisite borders of pleasure and pain. A glow of heat suffused her body.

'Tara!' Saul whispered harshly, pulling her away from her inner thoughts, 'are you ready?'

His face was urgent and intense. He was thinking only of the performance ahead, of his responsibility to ensure that it went perfectly. Nothing but the music mattered now.

She drew her bow across the strings. Energy flew into her fingers.

In front of her the tall figure of Saul bent the orchestra to his will, binding them together in a silken net, drawing Tara into the golden circle.

Now they were all breathing a purer air, soaring up into the heights and carrying the audience along with them on a carpet of magical sound.

Sweat began to stream off her. At the end of the first movement Saul paused to look at her enquiringly. Gravely he reached into his pocket and took out a white cotton handkerchief. 'I think you need this,' he said, leaning down to hand it to her. 'And you're playing wonderfully.'

Tara mopped her face and ran the stiff firm cloth around her neck and breast bone.

She looked up at Saul, seeing that he was still again, his face a stern mask in preparation for the next movement.

This was the most emotionally touching part of the concerto in Tara's opinion and as she played she felt her heart merge into the music.

All the fear of anticipation had left her now. With this orchestra – her *father's* orchestra – and under the iron guidance of her lover, Saul Xavier, she felt utterly safe. Able to play without restraint from the very depths of her heart and soul.

An orchestra, a soloist, a great and sensitive conductor all sharing in the re-creation of wonderful music. That must be one of the most seductive things on earth Tara thought, as she strove to dig out every ounce of energy and emotion to give to this great piece.

When at last the final notes of the concerto rang out she felt her mind and body swell with joy.

The audience reaction was ecstatic. The applause roared and thundered, washing over Tara like warm waves on a tropical beach.

She smiled and bowed until her jaws ached and her back felt like that of a puppet jerked on a clockwork string.

Saul stepped down from the podium and took her hand. As their eyes connected a great bolt of feeling shot through her body like a huge electric current.

'You're not going to get away without an encore,' Saul murmured into her ear. 'How about a Beethoven Romance – the one in G?'

She turned back to the audience. Energy surged through every vein and nerve of her body. She could go on playing for ever if they asked her.

At the end of the encore the applause still went on and on. Saul led her off the stage. They had to come back. Twice, three times. To and fro they went.

'That's it!' he decided suddenly, dismissing the orchestra with the single sharp flick of the hand she had seen him use on the night before her father's death. 'Enough.'

He propelled her down the bull run and out into the dressing room area.

'We're going home,' he said abruptly, his hand tightening around her shoulders.

Tara glanced up at him, bewildered and disconcerted. Behind her players were streaming past into the bar. As a matter of course she had expected to join them. They would be waiting for her. For Saul also.

His fingers dug into her flesh. 'To bed!' he commanded softly.

She considered putting up a fight. And then she sensed the urgency of raw sexual desire in his touch and all resistance flowed out of her. Instantly she was on fire for him. Ravenous and desperate.

She remembered that the house would be empty. Little Alessandra was staying the night with Rachel.

She shivered with anticipation at the thought of the menu of love-making he would be planning.

'Escape,' she whispered. 'Fast!'

In the car he stroked the soft insides of her thighs with teasing fingers, driving her to a frenzy of wanting.

Once in the house the growling explosiveness of his passion overwhelmed her, blotting out the agitated jumble of musical phrases that had been hammering on her brain, roaring and crashing through her consciousness. Now there was only Saul, his lips devouring her, his hands stripping away her clothes, his long fingers touching and probing so that her skin felt tinglingly alive with the sensation of a million tiny electrodes.

Tonight it was as though all their previous sex had been merely a long apprenticeship, some extended luxurious overture. And now, this was the real thing.

She found herself trembling violently as she lay sprawled on the bed and watched him loom over her. The intensity of the connection with him made her feel dizzy. For a crazy moment she sensed some previously unknown madness in him. Waves of fearful pleasure swept through her nerves.

'Let yourself go Tara,' he whispered. 'Trust me.'

There had been times before when he had been rough to the point of sadism, when he had left her with an aching body and a heady sensation of exquisite femaleness.

But tonight there was something new. Some demonic quality which thrilled and troubled her.

But she would trust him absolutely.

And as she laid aside her fear so he took her past pain through to high crests of pleasure she had never even dreamed of reaching.

But as he drove into her and the wild tempo increased she snapped back suddenly into the mundane realms of reality, realizing that she was unprotected inside, that she had not inserted her diaphragm.

She froze.

His thrusts paused and then intensified.

'Saul,' she gasped. 'Stop. Let me go.'

His hands grasped her arms. His body pinned her beneath him.

Tara felt herself melting, her resistance fading to a small, soft plea.

'I could get pregnant,' she gasped. But his mouth covered hers.

When it was over he gathered her to him.

'You frightened me,' she murmured.

He stroked her face with infinite tenderness. His lips pressed gently over hers. 'I love you completely,' he said.

# CHAPTER 18

Rachel and Alessandra were in the garden when Tara arrived.

Rachel had filled an old baby bath with fine damp sand and Alessandra squatted beside it stirring the contents with a large plastic spoon. Her smooth young face was grave as she concentrated on her task, totally absorbed.

Tara stood watching her, realizing how mysterious children were. What did she really know of Alessandra? She knew her firm, healthy body, but her mind was mainly hidden. And just at this moment she looked exactly like Saul.

Tara felt an urgent desire to be close to her small daughter, at one with her. She knelt down and wrapped her arm around her. Alessandra looked up at her in the way a kitten does when disturbed from its washing ritual. She turned back to the sand and her stirring.

'She cried for you last night,' Rachel said. 'So now she'll probably ignore you to punish you for going away and leaving her!'

'Did I used to do that?' Tara asked.

'Oh, sometimes.'

Mother and daughter stood together and watched the child in companionable silence.

Rachel felt uneasy. She sensed some disturbing new aura around Tara, a new solemnity, a new adult reticence. She reminded her of someone who has been in an accident, and though not physically injured, now sees the world as a more dangerous place than it appeared before.

Rachel wondered about the concert. How it had gone. She was not sorry that she had been unable to be there in person, that there had been the excuse of having Alessandra to look after. She did not think she could have borne the suspense of hearing Tara perform.

Privately she thought that Saul had placed a tremendous burden on Tara by setting her up to do such a bold and daring thing as appear as soloist at the Albert Hall. The musical world abounded with rivalries and jealousies just like the theatre or the world of films. A budding career could easily be snuffed out by a dud performance which had received maximum exposure.

Or people could simply despise and discount a young performer who was seen to be getting a leg up on the ladder of success through their connection with the kind of people who mattered.

On the other hand she supposed there was plenty of that about, so perhaps it didn't matter.

And Saul had been very good to Tara. He did seem genuinely to love her and care for her well being. And he was breathtakingly romantic; flying Tara around the world so that she could be there with him at his endless performing and recording sessions, wining and dining her

199

in exotic hotels and restaurants, taking her on exclusive cruises.

But to have in his gift an entrée into the world of music was perhaps the most precious and the most dangerous of his indulgences. The idea of such power made Rachel uneasy.

She recalled that it had always been Richard's dream for his child to play solo at one of the great concert halls; the dream being initially for Freddie and later for Tara. The occasion last night would have thrilled him, but how would he have felt about the way it had come about?

'I wonder what Alessandra will do with her life,' Tara said suddenly.

'What do you hope for her?' Rachel asked.

Tara paused, her face heavy with thought. 'To know what she wants. To feel the freedom to choose.'

'Does that mean you didn't?' Rachel said quietly.

'I got all mixed up,' Tara said, giving a swift impish smile. 'I screwed things up. I don't want her to be such a fool.'

Oh hell, thought Rachel. She went into the house, made coffee and brought it out into the garden. She and Tara sat in the chintz-covered garden swing and kept a loving and watchful eye on Alessandra who was still absorbed in her sand games.

Tara told Rachel about the concert. She struggled to convey simple delight and enthusiasm, not wanting Rachel to gain any inkling of the drone of anxiety humming ceaselessly within her.

'The audience reaction was simply marvellous. Unbelievable!' she said.

'And Saul's reaction. What about that?'

'He brought me back for an encore. So that must speak for itself,' Tara responded smartly, having anticipated this question and rehearsed the answer.

In actual fact she was stunned with dismay and confusion that Saul had not yet made any direct comment on her performance. She felt she had played well. Naturally there was always room in any performance to do better. But on the whole she had felt pleased and satisfied with her achievement. Until much later . . .

She could only conclude that privately Saul had considered her performance so embarrassingly pedestrian that he did not know how to break it to her. Always before he had been both fair and free with his comments, both positive and negative.

And then there had been that disturbingly demonic quality to his lovemaking afterwards, a brief moment when she had feared things might tip over into some dark area of human interaction that she did not begin to understand.

She snapped her mind away from the idea. She would not think about it. She would not believe it.

Today her body ached and smarted and tingled with a dizzy cocktail of pleasure and pain.

But she was disturbed. Subdued and dampened down. She knew that the gears of her relationship with Saul had shifted and changed, that nothing would be the same for them again.

And yet she had never felt so crazily desirous of his love and approval.

She looked at her mother and saw a new serenity in her

face: a calm, mellow satisfaction with life that had been growing over the last few months. She guessed that the new marriage had given Rachel some totally unexpected happiness, and she felt a rush of warmth towards Donald for making it come about.

With Saul, of course, one would never feel a sense of calm satisfaction. Saul was exciting, provoking, gloriously dangerous. Tara knew she could never be happy with someone as safe and good as Donald.

Saul was not safe. He was tricky and unpredictable. He battered her emotions. But he was as necessary to her as air to breathe. He made her feel alive.

She could not wait to be with him tonight.


Saul telephoned Tara in the early evening. She had not been home for long, was in the middle of bathing Alessandra and had to call him back.

She could hear the slight edge in his voice. He hated to be kept waiting. And he thought her persistence in managing on her own with the baby and refusing to engage a nanny was charming but hopelessly impractical.

'Darling, I want you to come up to town and have dinner with me and Roland,' he told her.

Tara's heart fluttered. A meeting with Saul's influential agent could only mean one thing. Surely!

'It's too short notice to get a baby-sitter for Alessandra,' she said steadily. 'Bring him here.'

A pause.

Tara imagined his face momentarily taut with annoyance at not having things go exactly as he had planned them. She really would have to start standing up for herself. 'I'll do a super little supper,' she teased. 'Terribly elegant. As good as the Ritz.' She really wanted to ask him if Roland had liked her playing but she could hardly bear to hear the answer.

'Of course you will,' Saul said seductively. 'You do *everything* superbly.'

Her heart racing Tara searched the refrigerator, praying that Mrs Lockton would have left something suitable to enable her to fulfil her reckless promise.

Mercifully there was a whole cooked salmon, assorted salads and a selection of excellent cheeses.

'Perfect!' Tara murmured, browsing through Saul's collection of wines in the stone-shelved larder and selecting two bottles she considered suitable.

It pleased her sometimes to be domesticated. The professional women around Saul were all rather helpless in that direction and she knew that Georgiana would be struggling to recall the ingredients and methods necessary to scramble an egg.

By eight Alessandra was fast asleep, the food all arranged, and a new recording of the Mozart G-Minor symphony number 40 with Saul and the Tudor Philharmonic on the turntable. Minutes later the Porsche roared up the drive closely followed by a sleek Mercedes convertible. Tara stepped out of the door to watch the drivers get out, curious to see the great Roland Grant in the flesh.

For a man who was the founder and president of the largest classical music management firm in the world he struck Tara as surprisingly unassuming. Unlike Saul, whose eagle features and black clothing marked him out in a crowd as someone special, Roland Grant was somewhat grandfatherly in appearance, anonymously dressed in a dark suit and a quiet silk tie. His manner was quiet also, gentle and charming like someone from a former era.

Tara guessed him to be around sixty. He was slim and silver-haired. He drank very little and ate sparingly.

But, in common with Saul, he lived and breathed music. From the moment he took her hand in his and squeezed it firmly he talked about it ceaselessly.

Through the pre-supper drinks and the meal itself a procession of famous names rolled off his tongue like butter from a hot knife. Household-name singers, renowned instrumentalists and a procession of great conductors. He seemed to know everybody, and to handle their affairs also.

'At Grant's we have a vast warehouse of talent,' Roland explained to Tara. 'We are interested in any artist, any fixture, no matter how small or how big. We supply great opera stars to the international stages of the world and we also supply has-beens and lesser talents to the provincial circuit.' He paused and smiled. 'Am I giving you a good enough idea of what we do?'

'Oh yes,' Tara said slowly. 'But where do I come in?' She glanced swiftly at Saul, but his eyes were at their most remote, staring into some unknown distance. He was not going to interfere in this particular dialogue.

'My telephone has not stopped ringing since you played last night,' Roland said evenly. 'Whatever it is you want you could take just at this moment.'

Tara laid down her knife and sat back in her chair. 'Such as?'

'Engagements to play with some of the great orchestras of the world. The New York Philharmonic, the Chicago Symphony, the Swedish Radio . . .'

Tara could not fully take in what he was saying. 'Am I really that good?' she asked, the familiar disbelief about her musicianship gripping her.

'Your playing has a good deal of individuality. You bring warmth and colour to the platform,' Roland Grant told her, his clear blue eyes holding hers.

He's talking about personality, Tara thought. She wanted to be told about quality of technique and musical interpretation.

Her eyes appealed to Saul. He stared back at her, his eyebrows faintly raised. He was like a harsh tutor watching a hesitant child making thrashing attempts in the water. *You must swim or drown.*

She turned back to Roland Grant. 'Do people want me because I'm a great player or because I'm Saul's mistress? A juicy celebrity?' she asked brutally.

Roland looked her hard in the eye, as though to say, *Does it matter?*

Oh yes it does, thought Tara.

She got up from the table and went to the kitchen on the pretext of fetching more wine. As she thrust the corkscrew into the bottle neck she heard Saul come up behind her.

'Tara,' he murmured, turning her innards to liquid. 'My sweet nymph.' He wrapped his arms around her, enclosing shoulders, ribs, breasts, heart. Everything.

Tara twisted in his arms and pressed herself against him, sliding her hands over his hard bones of his chest and encircling the firm flesh at the back of his neck.

'Roland Grant is interested in money,' she said flatly. 'Commodities that people will buy. I'm not interested in that. I want to be a musician!'

Saul smiled down at her. 'My darling, musicians are commodities. Whatever made you think otherwise?'

'Don't tease. And don't be so damn cynical!'

'You do Roland a disservice,' he said mildly. 'His love of music is entirely genuine – as are his proposals.'

'Cooked up between the two of you?' she suggested spikily. 'I would love to have been a fly on the wall when you chewed me over in the privacy of his office.'

'You would have been extremely pleased with what you heard,' Saul said evenly.

She squared up to him. 'So what *did* you think of my performance last night? You never said one word. Not one.'

'No. I was afraid I was going to lose you.' His grey eyes stared down at her with cool challenge.

Her forehead creased in a frown of perplexity. If only he would be direct. If only he would give her a straight opinion. There was no one on whom she would pin more faith.

'Your playing was impeccable Tara,' he said softly. 'You demonstrated all the required range, accuracy and precision. Your interpretation was full of spontaneous sensitivity and you created some superb chemistry with the audience. In short, my sweet one – you were delicious!'

She stared at him; she was beginning to be convinced.

'So? Shall I lose you?' he enquired, his eyes cool and probing.

'What do you mean?'

'Now is your chance to jump on the concert circuit bandwagon. Is that what you're going to choose?'

Tremors of apprehension seized her. She felt the quiet menace of Saul's will licking around her like a serpent's tongue.

'Is that what you want Tara?' he demanded coolly. 'Living out of suitcases, flying from one soulless capital city to another, playing the same dozen or so concertos time and time again?'

Tara was stunned. 'Are you trying to stop me?'

'You must make your choice. We all make our own lives, however close we are to each other.'

His eyes suddenly softened. 'Darling sweet angel,' he said gently. 'I would never try to stop you from doing what you wanted. I would be a fool if I did. That would be the certain way to lose you.'

'Is that why you were so . . . angry last night?' she asked. 'Because you were frightened of losing me?'

He pulled her close to him and sighed deeply. 'Oh my precious nymph,' he breathed into her hair, his fingers lightly caressing her neck. 'What would I do without you?'

Tara felt a lump of feeling lodge in her throat.

Slowly she disengaged herself from his arms. 'I'm a hostess,' she reminded him with a wry smile. 'I have my guest to consider!'

But whilst Roland and Saul talked together over brandy and coffee she sat a little apart, her mind roving over the myriad new possibilities for the future.

It struck her that for Saul musical talent was an every-day phenomenon. Commonplace. He had worked with countless brilliant singers and instrumentalists, a never-ending stream of them. And newcomers were surging up constantly.

Saul had already been through all the heady business of flying the world and absorbing acclaim. Success, prestige and wealth had been part of his everyday life for years. For Saul, the tight family unit he and Tara had formed here in this provincial English house with little Alessandra was something very special, utterly precious.

And yet, of course, Saul would have no intention of giving up his own career ambitions. Tara saw that it was the old story of the woman making compromises whilst the man had it all: career, worldly success and the satisfaction of family life.

And then she thought about the reality of an extended existence in soulless hotels, rarely seeing Alessandra once the child was old enough to go to school and could no longer be carted around like a pet dog . . .

She wondered if Roland Grant would press her to make some sort of commitment or, failing that, at the very least offer an indication of his hopes and intentions. But he seemed to pick up her troubled indecisiveness, and in the end made no attempt to put her under further pressure.

He took her hand in his before he left, thanking her for her hospitality, making it seem as though this evening had been nothing but a delightful social occasion.

Saul, as she had expected, declined to make any further comment. After switching off all the lights he sat down at the piano and began to play Debussy's *Clair de Lune*. The wistful evocative melody stole through the silent darkened room.

Tara stood beside the window and watched his long fingers caressing the gleaming keys.

Her eyes travelled upwards to move over his remote carved features, pearled now in the moonlight. She felt a tremble of pure ecstasy. The continued mystery of him bound her ever closer.

Later he took her to bed and made love to her with exquisite gentleness.

She could not think about anything but his nearness.

She would think about her career the next day.

# CHAPTER 19

The prospect of lunching with Saul at Claridges gave Georgiana a good deal of anticipatory pleasure.

It was some weeks since he had been in touch with her. She had begun to feel neglected.

In the beginning, just after he had cast her off, he had been very careful to maintain regular contact. He had made it his business to keep checking that she was not lonely, that she had enough social engagements and little trips to Europe to keep her happy. In fact it had seemed to Georgiana that he had cared for her well-being with a loving concern he had not shown her for some years.

She had liked the consideration and the attention. She had felt it as a warm blanket of love and appreciation settling delicately around her.

The pain and humiliation of his rejection had begun to ease. And since she had come to know Tara and darling little baby Alessandra, she had discovered an unexpected new interest in life. There was such a lot she could show them – about being a female. Such a lot she could give.

Tara had been in desperate need of a helping hand regarding her clothes and general presentation and

Georgiana had thoroughly enjoyed herself on their two or three trips around town hunting out amusing little items for her. Not that Tara had shown much improvement in choosing for herself so far. Her taste remained dubious and apart from buying chunky bottles of heady fragrances, lacy bras and skimpy panties, she showed no especial inclination to spend a lot of money – a pastime which Georgiana had always found most delightful.

But it was little Alessandra who provided the most pleasure and satisfaction. Georgiana spent hours searching out clothes and books and toys for the baby. Lavish parcels were regularly despatched to the Oxfordshire house. And Tara always responded with a charmingly grateful letter.

But as Georgiana's links with the baby and Tara developed so her contact with Saul decreased. Georgiana knew that Saul was busy. She had read in the newspapers that he was to conduct several concerts at the Proms and that he was also planning to make a series of films of the Tudor Philharmonic playing complete cycles of the Beethoven and Brahms symphonies.

Even so, she was offended and troubled that he had ignored her for so long. For whilst it was true that she was used to living her own life, and that she was more than relieved to have had the threat of sexual expectations finally lifted from her, she was still his wife. He still owed her some consideration.

Nevertheless being taken out to Claridges seemed some sort of olive branch, and she prepared herself for the event with great care.

Facing him across the table, enjoying the soft fall of

aquamarine blue silk around her flawless, toned body, she noted that he looked drained and tense. Older.

'You will wear yourself out,' she told him.

He made a low sound in his throat. It could have meant anything.

It would be all the sex, Georgiana decided. She thought about her husband's sex life a great deal, gaining a quaking thrill of pleasure from imagining him and Tara in the act of congress. Tara was an earthy type of girl, with her strong short-nailed fingers and her small bosomy body. There was something primitive and basic about her. She was the sort of female designed for all that grunting and thrashing about and sweating. Whereas she, Georgiana, was created from finer more delicate fibre. And pleased to be so.

'You should take care,' she said to Saul with a knowing smile. 'Middle-aged men can die of heart attacks in trying to keep pace with young girls.'

Dr Daneman had encouraged her in this new frankness. He had told her that she should give herself permission to listen to her inner thoughts, not to be afraid of them. Especially the thoughts about sex.

She could tell that Saul was startled, but he covered up well. 'It's kind of you to be worried about my health,' he said in a dry way, 'but there is no need.'

He fell into silence. They progressed from the fish to the duck. Saul was not eating much, she noticed.

'I want to give Alessandra a very special present for her first birthday,' Georgiana said. She began to tell Saul about her searches in little antique shops for Georgian jewellery. There was a chain and pendant she had seen. It

212

would make the perfect start to a collection that could continue through Alessandra's childhood and youth.

Saul's face went blank for a few seconds. Then he smiled at her patiently. 'There is no need for you to buy Alessandra extravagant presents.'

'I want to. There is nothing wrong in that,' Georgiana told him with sweet conviction.

'Spend the money on yourself my dear.' He dismissed the subject with that floppy wave of his hand she had seen him employ to dismiss orchestras on countless occasions. His smile indicated that the subject was really of little importance or interest to him.

Georgiana was not dismayed. She would do exactly as she wished.

The pudding arrived. Some exquisite dessert wine also.

'Georgiana, I want a divorce,' Saul said softly.

Georgiana blinked. Her blue eyes opened wide. She parted her lips and inserted a spoonful of lemon soufflé. She decided to say nothing.

'Did you hear me?' Saul's eyes were hard.

She nodded.

'Well?'

She shrugged. Inserted more soufflé. If she focused carefully on savouring the lemon tang, then the words that Saul wanted to drop into her ears would simply float away into the air. They would have no meaning. No consequence.

'Tara is expecting another baby,' he stated evenly. He said these words in such a way as to suggest that they explained everything.

Her eyes slid from his in panic. The breath jerked in her

213

chest. Tara was having another baby. Georgiana must have a divorce. As simple as that.

Georgiana saw splinters of iridescent red light dance in front of her eyes. She blinked, felt her innards swoop and glide dizzily. She stared back at her plate, examining the scrolls and swirls of silver chasing on the handle of her spoon.

She screwed up her eyes, following the lines of one of the swirls and detecting the shape of a feather. A perfectly symmetrical feather, the fronds precisely balancing on each side of the central spine. Beautiful, perfect, orderly.

She breathed steadily. Concentrated on the immaculate perfection of the feather.

The red lights began to fade. And after no more than a few brief moments they went away altogether. She continued with her pudding.

The muscles in Saul's jaw fidgeted with irritation. 'Georgiana. You can't just ignore this.'

She looked up at him. She smiled, opening her eyes wide. 'No,' she said, agreeable and vague.

He sighed, reined in his mounting anger. 'Do you want time to think about it?' he asked. 'I shall be more than generous with the settlement. You would be a very rich woman.'

She gave another shrug. Money was not an issue. She had always had plenty. 'Yes, I will think about it,' she said finally.

She was pleased about the dignified way she had said that. Dr Daneman would have been proud of her.

'Thank you for the lunch,' she told Saul as she offered him her cheek to kiss as they prepared to part.

'And you will consider what I said very seriously,' he urged.

'Oh yes.' She laid an immaculately manicured hand on his arm and then she was gone.

Tara prowled the house, opening doors, going into rooms, coming out again. Picking up a book. Putting it down again. Settling to nothing.

She felt herself cruelly trapped. Snared, netted and caged. She did not want to be pregnant again. Not just now.

She knew the exact moment of the conception: a new career and a new baby had been launched on the same fateful night. Her concert debut.

She wondered if Saul had engineered it deliberately.

And if that were true she was forced to admire his tactics. If he had wanted to keep her tied to him at home he could hardly have been more successful.

Being pregnant, feeling sick for half the day and finding it hard to keep up her practice schedule had made the prospect of a budding career as a soloist vanish into a distressingly distant future.

And what was more her doctor had advised against having sex, at least until the first few months were safely past.

Life was looking rather less rosy than it had for some time.

'He wants to cut me off,' Georgiana told Dr Daneman. 'He can't bear my being friendly with the girl and wanting to buy the baby presents.'

Dr Daneman pondered on Georgiana's persistence in placing herself at the centre of things, how it did not occur to her to consider her husband's many other motives in wanting a divorce. All those hours Dr Daneman had spent with her and still she was as purely and unequivocally self-centred as a very small child.

Whilst he waited for Georgiana to expand on her theme he took the opportunity to admire once again her elegant and streamlined body which transformed even the simplest clothes into haute couture. He imagined the way heads would turn when she entered a room. She had exceptional physical beauty. And he was sure that what she possessed beneath her clothes was equally inspiring.

This afternoon her fine buttery blonde hair hung down from her face in an incandescent stream of gold, lit from behind by the sharply metallic light of the midsummer sun. She wore a dress of soft wool challis in a delicate stippling of dove grey and ivory. Her eyes were shaded with soft russet shadow and her shoes, lying beneath the chaise, were an absurd confection of creamy coloured straps perched on three-inch heels. Around her neck was a single serpentine chain of gold. He had never seen her wear anything vulgar, sport even the smallest accessory that did not seem the essence of restrained good taste.

'How can it be bad to buy presents?' she continued. 'My parents used to say that giving beautiful presents was a wonderful way of demonstrating love. They were always buying things for me. I remember once when we went to the seaside house in Cornwall my mother bought me a wonderful doll that walked and talked. It was to keep me company so that I would not feel lonely in my strange bed when I went to sleep at night.'

'You were their child Georgiana,' Dr Daneman said softly. 'That is why they gave you beautiful presents.'

'Alessandra is Saul's child,' she replied. 'And I am his wife.'

Her thin fingers plucked nervously at the folds of her skirt, betraying some considerable inner agitation. The skin between her eyebrows puckered as they met in a frown of puzzlement. It was as though she were straining to hear whispered words that were just too faint to comprehend.

'Tara is having another child,' she announced suddenly. 'Alessandra will have a brother.'

There was a silence. It lasted for seven minutes. Dr Daneman timed the period and declined to say anything. The light on his tape machine winked as it recorded emptiness.

'Tara played at the Albert Hall a few weeks ago,' Georgiana volunteered. 'People said she was quite good.'

Dr Daneman saw an involuntary spasm cross her face. Despair? Envy? True pain?

'But they said she would be nowhere if it wasn't for Saul pulling strings for her behind the scenes.'

'And what did *Georgiana* say?' Dr Daneman asked.

Another long silence. 'I wasn't there,' she said eventually in a flat voice.

She closed her eyes and rubbed her hands across her forehead. 'Saul's agent wants her to build a career for herself. Play at concerts all over the world.'

'How does that make you feel?' Dr Daneman asked.

She appeared not to have heard his question. Her breathing was light and shallow now. She was almost panting. Her fingers folded into knobs and kneaded her closed eyelids. 'I can see these lights,' she said. 'They're red and blue and gold. Furry and shiny like the lights my mother hung on our Christmas tree at home.'

'Do you have a headache?' Dr Daneman asked.

She shook her head. In a sudden, entirely uncharacteristic surge of activity she swung her legs over the side of the chaise and stood upright.

Beads of sweat glistened on her face and the skin of her forearms. She passed a hand over her forehead. 'May I have a drink of cold water please?'

'Of course.' Dr Daneman put his notebook on the table and went into the small bathroom adjoining his consulting room. He filled a glass and brought it back to her.

She took it and drank it in one gulp.

He had not seen her so openly agitated before, flushed and in some disarray, with her skirt rucked up nearly to her buttocks where the fabric still connected with the edge of the couch. The sight of her like this had the effect of making him experience very unprofessional feelings towards her.

'I think you should come again tomorrow,' he told her.

She turned to look at him. She was like someone returning from a long airplane flight, disoriented and temporarily detached from reality. 'Yes. Yes, I will.'

Sometimes she was astonishingly obedient Dr Daneman thought. And very suggestible. It would be the simplest thing in the world to put her under hypnosis and seduce her right here on the chaise longue.

218

'You are very safe, Georgiana,' he would tell her. 'With someone who loves you dearly. Who would do you no harm.'

He imagined himself talking very softly to her, crooning and rhythmic, his voice a mistily penetrating anaesthetic. He saw himself slipping his hand along the length of her calf, over her knee, up the taut slender thigh. Reaching beyond, finding the moist rosy flesh. Dropping words into her ear that would make that flesh wet with longing.

The thought provided him with some mild amusement directed against himself and his shockingly salacious feelings towards his most beautiful, supposedly frigid client. Feelings which must, of course, remain secret and undemonstrated.

He looked at Georgiana with a mingle of professional and personal concern. 'Are you feeling better now?'

She had wriggled her dress down, stroked the folds into immaculate smoothness. She was slipping into her shoes, tugging at the straps. She had beautiful long feet, like those of a ballet dancer. She looked up at him and he was surprised to see her face suddenly transformed. A smile curved her lips and her eyes shone with an excitement and purpose he had never seen in them before.

'Yes,' she said simply.

'Would you like me to call you a taxi?'

'No. I think I'll walk.'

'Are you sure you are all right?' He was surprised at himself for the depth of concern he felt. Even though now she was smiling and outwardly quite recovered.

She gave a little chuckle and shook her head as though to

219

say that there was no need to be worried on her behalf. Her fingers closing around the brass doorknob, she turned to him and said, 'I've just thought of the most wonderful present to give Alessandra for her birthday.'

# CHAPTER 20

'God, I hate being a bloody brood mare again!' Tara raged, surveying the mouth-watering buffet that Mrs Lockton had prepared and feeling the immediate need to throw up.

'My darling, you're such a little lioness when you're pregnant!' Saul came up behind her and slipped his arms around her hips sliding them upwards and cradling her breasts with tender hands.

As his fingers squeezed her nipples she felt herself twitch with automatic ecstasy. She wrenched herself from his grasp.

'I'm going to be sick,' she gulped, desperately swallowing down the lap of nausea. She raced to the lavatory across the hall and hung over the bowl retching.

Only a thin white dribble emerged but she felt as bruised as if she had coughed up a four-course dinner.

Groaning, she turned the washbasin taps on full, scooping up handfuls of fresh water to her face, to wash away all the grim traces.

The face looking at her from the mirror was putty grey and decidedly unappealing. The symptoms of this pregnancy were far more pronounced than her previous one. She wondered why that should be. The books all said that you suffered less after the first time.

Already her waist had disappeared and her stomach had begun to swell. Her breasts seemed as big and hard as footballs.

Heaving a sigh she squirted herself liberally with *Femme* and went back to the drawing room which was now filling up with guests.

Saul had arranged a special party to celebrate the Tudor Philharmonic's triumphant appearances at the Proms which had been ecstatically received by both the audiences and the critics. His dreams for the orchestra were turning into reality. Engagements and recording contracts were flooding in. And the sales on existing recordings had soared, bringing significant financial reward to each player. The company was in decidedly buoyant mood. Tara reminded herself to look out into the drive when she had the chance in order to count the number of Mercedes.

In addition to the players in the orchestra Saul had invited a number of prominent soloists: a flamboyant bearded flautist, a brilliant bald cellist and a flutteringly gorgeous Danish soprano.

Tara went forward to greet them all. She was becoming very skilled at playing the charming hostess.

Around nine o'clock, when the consumption of supper was in full swing, one of the fleet of hired waiters glided softly to Tara's side, whispering to her that there was an important phone call. She looked at him, startled.

'Mr Roland Grant,' he explained politely.

She picked up the phone in the oak-lined study at the back of the house. 'Roland?'

'Tara! I'm sorry to ring so late.'

'Why aren't you here Roland? We're having a rave-up!'

'I know. I was fully intending to come. But you know how it is . . .'

'Not really. In fact I wish I did!'

He laughed. 'I've just had a call from David Bronfenbrenner. He's had a fall and sprained his wrist. Can't play a note. He was due to play the Elgar at the Golden Hall in Vienna three nights ahead. Can you fill in?'

The shock hit her like a swung plank. Bronfenbrenner was an established violin virtuoso. To step into his shoes was an awesome prospect. And the concert date was the day before Alessandra's birthday. But then it only took a few hours to fly back from Vienna. 'I don't see why not,' she said slowly, amazing herself.

'Those are the sweetest words I've heard all day,' Roland told her.

'I suppose it's a nightmare trying to get people to fill in with everyone being booked up for years ahead,' Tara commented, her voice a little unsteady now as the full enormity of her decision began to sink in.

'It isn't easy. But don't get the idea that you're a last resort. I haven't been ringing round the troops. I happen to think you are the ideal person for the job.'

Tara drew in a sharp breath. 'Had you ever considered a career in the diplomatic service Roland?' she enquired with an ironic smile.

'I *am* in such a service,' he responded.

223

Tara stood beside the desk after she had replaced the receiver.

Her heart was beating with great thick jumps and she felt sick again.

She heard a sound in the doorway and sensed Saul's presence.

She turned. He wore the blank, austerely remote expression that could still send a chill of desire and fear down her backbone.

'Bad news?' he enquired softly.

Her mouth went dry. She gave him the news in a nutshell; brief, unemotional and to the point. It felt like delivering a bombshell.

The muscles around his long curved mouth flickered under the skin. He gave one of his dry smiles. 'Congratulations!'

Tara could not believe he meant it. She felt defiant, touchy and on the defensive. Roland had offered her a hard earned prize and no one, not even Saul, was going to take it away from her. Although, to be fair, Saul was giving her no grounds for thinking that he would try. His tone had been perfectly reasonable, holding no hint of sarcasm or mockery.

'I'll be back in time for Alessandra's birthday,' she said, unable to stop herself justifying her actions.

'Good. Good.' His eyes held hers, relentless and unfathomable.

Tara felt herself quake internally. It must be this damned pregnancy.

'What about the sickness? Will you be able to cope?' Saul enquired in clinical tones.

'I just won't eat anything. Won't look at any food.' She tried to sound light hearted.

He nodded, his glance coolly assessing. 'So!' he commented. 'The gateway to the road to success – mmn?'

Tara felt deeply uneasy. She wanted to throw herself into his arms and be close to him, share with him this moment of triumphant anticipation. He seemed as distant and remote as that first time she had seen him on the podium the night of her father's death.

'You don't want me to go, do you?' she challenged him.

'I want you to feel free to make your own decisions,' he said enigmatically.

'You want me to stay here and breed children for you and act the perfect hostess!' she burst out.

'Tara!' His voice was low and gentle. But there was a note of chiding fatherliness which kindled a spark of deep resentment in her.

'You've got it made Saul, haven't you?' she continued bitterly. 'Success, critical acclaim, the licence to do exactly as you like. A wife, a mistress . . .'

She knew that she had gone too far.

'Darling, if you're in a state like this will you really be fit to play?' he asked evenly.

It was a perfectly valid question.

Tara refused to answer.

'My sweet, you must do what you want to do and not feel constrained by me,' Saul said softly.

'But I do. I feel as though you're holding me in bonds of steel,' she appealed.

'No.' He looked at her with such tenderness.

Her mind raced like a trapped animal. She suddenly

recalled that he had mentioned going to Copenhagen at the end of the week. 'We shall both be away the night before Alessandra's birthday,' she exclaimed.

His eyes stared into hers. 'Yes.'

She knew there was no question of his cancelling his arrangements. And she would not expect him to. What a conventional little woman I'm becoming, she thought scornfully. 'I'll ask Mummy to come and stay,' she decided.

'Good. And after the new baby I really think we must apply ourselves to engaging a suitable nanny, so that we can both pursue our work in peace.' He smiled and left the room quietly.

Tara took some deep breaths.

She returned to the party and forced herself to eat. She willed the food to stay down.

Circulating amongst the guests she whipped herself up into lively witty sociability. Her eyes sought Saul. He was watching her from across the room. He smiled at her, a deep intimate message. Her heart swelled. For a moment she considered calling Roland back and telling him she had changed her mind.

The moment passed.

Informal musical performances were now proceeding and everyone was having great fun.

The flautist entertained with dazzling extracts of Mozart and the cellist varied the mood with some touching Dvorak.

The blonde Danish singer hung back, wide-eyed and nervous as a woodland gazelle.

Saul sat down at the piano. He summoned her with that

deceptively casual flap of his hand which was irresistibly compelling.

Tara watched the singer approach the Maestro and incline her shining head towards his as he flicked through some song sheets. She knew that Saul was constantly on the look-out for singers. He needed a constant supply of new talent for his operatic work and for vocal recordings. She also knew that he had an inclination for sopranos with light, lyrical voices in preference to the more powerful typically 'operatic' ones. But tonight, with this gorgeous young woman, she sensed an extra unquantifiable dimension at work.

They started off with some Schubert.

The woman was desperately nervous. There were continuous little breaks in her exquisitely clear voice. A hush fell over the guests and heads turned in her direction.

Saul stopped her. 'You're working too hard. Don't try to give too much all at once. Mmm?'

She took a sip of water from the glass offered by one of the guests standing near her.

They started again. This time the voice flowed out unfettered; gorgeous and liquid. Sharp as carved crystal.

Tara marvelled afresh at Saul's skills as an accompanist. He was technically faultless but he also had an instinctive understanding of the needs and difficulties of the person he was playing with. Tara recalled playing the Ceésar Franck sonata with him that fateful day on which they had first made love, how she had been utterly seduced in the first instance by the act of making music with him. Her body glowed with remembered passion.

She heard him speaking to the woman over the music as he played. 'Hold back a little now, let yourself flow into the music. Good, good. Wonderful!'

The woman was flushed and her eyes shining as she reached a final top C.

Saul lifted his hands from the keys. 'Hold it, hold!'

She held.

Saul smiled. 'There you are! Perfection!'

Applause rippled through the captivated audience.

Saul looked the singer up and down, his eyes skating over the slender figure, the curved waist and the long thighs shown off tantalizingly in a long clinging jersey dress. 'So! Do you know Handel's oratorio, *Samson*? The aria, 'Let the Bright Seraphim?' Mmm? Will you sing it for me?' His fingers returned to the keys.

The singer gazed at him appealingly. 'It is a *bravura* piece,' she protested in her charming Danish accent. 'And all those difficult English words.'

Saul gave a dismissive chuckle. 'Don't be frightened. I'll make a fool of myself imitating the piccolo trumpet part on the piano.'

The voice rang out again. It was getting better by the minute.

Tara felt her blood heating up. She sensed a personal chemistry working between these two musicians as potently as though it were being injected into her own veins.

The expression on the singer's face was one of pure exhilaration and rapture. She was clearly bowled over by the response she was getting from the great Xavier. To Tara it seemed as though Saul were pulling the voice right

228

out of the girl's throat; any moment now she would be literally squealing with delight.

And if Saul should take her to bed! Well then she really would squeal. With ecstasy. Tara couldn't stop the awful thoughts from racing round her brain. Maybe this kind of thing was common in the early stages of pregnancy she told herself, struggling to fill her mind with anything but the word jealousy.

She went forward to give the singer her congratulations, which from a musical point of view were totally genuine. 'Come and have a proper drink now,' she told her. 'You've earned it.'

The woman's name was Margerita. She was really very likeable. In any other circumstances Tara would have been making arrangements to meet up with her and talk music and concerts and agents and conductors.

But tonight she was wary. And when Saul joined them she judged that her anxieties were more than the neuroses of a pregnant woman at the mercy of her hormones.

'Marvellous stuff,' he said. 'I'd like to give you a role at the London Met when I next direct there.'

Margerita gasped. 'Oh! My career will really set in flames then!'

'Ignite,' Saul corrected gently.

'Oh, sorry, is that how you say it?' She turned to Tara. 'I was so nervous to come here tonight. When your husband . . .' She paused here confused.

'Go on,' Tara smiled.

'When he asked me to sing I felt like I do at auditions. Very sick. Here.' She placed her hand on her enviably flat stomach.

229

'Auditions are the work of the devil,' Saul observed with a smile. 'People listening out for you to make a mistake. Predatory agents lurking in the wings, wicked conductors waiting to pounce.'

'Oh yes. That is so. Quite!' She stared at him with admiration.

Tara, looking on, felt as though she were growing older and wiser extremely fast.

Saul poured himself some wine. 'You see,' he told Margerita, sipping reflectively, 'in an audition the way to success is to tease your audience. Entice them. Have them on the edge of their seats to hear more of what you can do. It's rather like a striptease.'

He smiled into Margerita's eyes, raising his eyebrows.

'Violinists have the same problems,' Tara informed the starry-eyed singer. 'I learned to take my clothes off very slowly.'

In bed that night Saul reached for her.

Instantly her blood began to sing in her veins. The bovine sensations of pregnancy slid away from her and she felt like the most desirable woman in the world.

Still he could do that to her!

'My unborn child!' she breathed to him in mock protest.

'I am afraid my longings for you will have to take precedence even over that precious creature,' he confessed regretfully.

His fingers were already probing her with sensuous intimacy.

Tara rolled over on her back, forgot about Margerita,

forgot about everything, and allowed the rolling waves of pleasure to wash over her.

She refused to listen to the small inner voice that told her some kind of warning had been issued.

# CHAPTER 21

There were two works on the programme. The Elgar Concerto in the first section – with Tara standing in for David Bronfenbrenner as soloist – and a performance of Handel's oratorio *Israel in Egypt* in the second.

It was a concert for connoisseurs, demanding both stamina and musical sophistication from the audience who in turn would expect nothing short of excellence from the performers.

Tara's flight from Heathrow was delayed because of a bomb scare and when she eventually arrived at the Golden Hall the rehearsal had finished some time previously.

Fatigued, queasy and wracked with nerves she looked around the great ornate hall and felt completely overwhelmed. It was a place of opulent magnificence, a glowing golden palace of music. The fifty-foot ceiling was elaborately panelled around a series of ten central paintings depicting female figures draped in long floating robes. White, long-necked birds perched on the narrow balcony above the orchestra section whilst the rest of the balcony was supported on golden columns cast in the form of heavy-breasted Amazon figures naked from the waist up. Thirty-six of them formed an impressive ring around the hall.

Tara stared up at them. Their smooth faces, framed in shoulder-length ringlets, were cool and impartial as though they were constantly sitting in judgement. She had the feeling that they would give no quarter to inadequates.

Horrified panic at what she had let herself in for kept rising in her throat.

A small man with a mass of frizzy silver hair came forward to greet her. She recognized him immediately as Hermann Schalk, the octogenarian conductor who had been a mainstay of music in Vienna and Salzburg for over fifty years. Like Saul, his face decorated countless record sleeves and compact disc covers. Tara had also seen him many times on television conducting the great orchestras of Berlin and Vienna.

Schalk had worked with some of the great composer/ conductors of the early part of the century, including Richard Strauss and even the genius Gustav Mahler, who had noted the potential of the young Schalk when he was no more than a boy. It was like confronting a slice of living history.

'Tara, Tara, Tara!' He exclaimed. 'I hear so many wonderful things about you.'

'I think I'd rather you'd heard bad!' she said, shaking her head. 'Then at least I wouldn't be an awful disappointment.'

A grating guttural chuckle bubbled in his throat. He chuckled all the time, never stopped smiling. She began to feel better. He took her hand and shook it warmly, his eyes twinkling brightly from the heavy wrinkled folds of skin surrounding them.

'You are terrified!' he said, observing her trembling fingers. 'Quivering with fear.'

She nodded.

'This is how it should be! No one ever plays well without the demon of terror driving them from within.'

He placed his arm around her shoulders.

'The Elgar Concerto,' he mused. 'I always play it completely straight. You know? No conductor's frills. Just like your Xavier would choose to do. You will be quite safe with me.'

'I hope I do you justice,' Tara said simply.

Another chuckle from Schalk. 'My beautiful orchestra. You will love them. They will do everything to help. You take the music at your own pace – and I will bind you all together!'

Tara breathed deeply. He was talking about one of the great Vienna orchestras, one of the great *world* orchestras.

'What a wonderful challenge,' Schalk murmured, 'to play for an audience so spontaneously, so fresh.'

My God! Tara thought. He's going to let me simply go on and play. No impromptu run through just with him. Nothing! She wished she saw the situation in such a positive light as Schalk did.

In the white-walled dressing room she took out her photographs of Saul and Alessandra and placed them on the table beneath the mirror. Then she put on the simple toga-style dress of green silk that she had bought on Georgiana's advice on one of their recent shopping trips. It was a good choice, concealing all the ripening bulges. After that there was nothing to do but pluck at the tendrils of hair around her face and wait. She judged that she had gone beyond fear now.

Walking onto the stage she was aware of the stern formality of the occasion. Black ties and jackets were the uniform for the men, orchestra and audience alike, whilst the women formed a kaleidoscope of colour against which a firmament of jewels flashed. The auditorium throbbed with a low ripe murmuring. A heady cocktail of expensive perfumes hung in the air.

Schalk hugged her to him as he led her to the front of the orchestra. Then his hands invited the audience to welcome her with warm applause, acknowledge her courage in acting as stand-in at such short notice.

Tara stood in motionless concentration. And then her bow was carving over the strings and the joy of re-creating this majestically beautiful concerto blotted out all fear.

Schalk was as good as his word. He let her have her head and he took the orchestra with her. And as she played Tara knew that she was making contact with this exacting audience, that she was making Elgar's music sing to them. That she could do all this even without Saul.

Her breathing deepened. How she adored this exposure to an audience, how hungry she was to draw them into the magical circle of a composer's sublime artistry.

The music was burrowing inside her now, taking her on a deeply personal journey. The figure of her father seemed to materialize at her side. She was conscious of that loved, grave face watching her. Assessing, criticizing, urging her on.

'You will have Freddie's gift,' he used to say to Tara in

those sad months after her brother died. She had understood that it was her duty to rekindle her dead brother's snuffed-out torch and bear it out into the world for him.

She remembered the weight of responsibility which had fallen on her slight young shoulders at the sound of her father's words. Heavy words, pressing her down, crushing her own developing individuality. She had been a child of only nine.

She had tried so hard. She had so wanted to please her father, carry out his longed for wishes. Make it up to him for the loss of his son.

She had not understood that the task was impossible and thus must be quietly abandoned. After all, the message in her father's words was clear enough. Her childish spirit had struggled to make his hope come true. She had driven herself on. Always trying. Always failing. *Never good enough.*

Eventually despair had taken over. She had given up her mission and cast it away from her. All that uphill toiling. She would never be as good as Freddie. Not as a person. Not as an instrumentalist. After all he was dead. He was a saint who could never again do any wrong.

As she played the Elgar Concerto in the great Viennese hall she understood the anger and despair of her childhood with the rare clarity that can come with great emotional tension.

And with that understanding her spirit felt lightened. A burden was lifted.

No Daddy, she thought, not Freddie's gift, but my own. Me, Tara.

And then she was playing not for her father, not for any

of her teachers, not even for Saul. She was playing simply for the people who were here now with her in this hall. For the reticent English composer who had conceived the music. And for herself.

After the final chord, as Schalk lowered his baton, the orchestra exploded into spontaneous applause. The noise of their delighted enthusiasm clattered around her, rattling at her nerves, drawing her out of her reverie, propelling her on the journey back to the real world.

Schalk saw that his soloist was only slowly swimming up from that private place into which an artist can submerge themselves when playing. He turned her gently to face the audience. He took her hand, pressing it firmly. He took her in his arms, hugged and kissed, clapped his hands together as his arms linked behind her neck. The audience roared.

It seemed to Tara that history was recording a new beginning for her.


There were two telephone messages at the desk in her hotel. She read them when she finally got in at one in the morning.

The one from Roland said crisply, 'Tonight the foundations of a glittering career have been laid.'

And from Saul just one word. 'So?'

She slipped into bed, elation having turned to exhaustion. The music still crashed in her head. But tonight there was no Saul to enfold her with his body and his will and soothe it away.


On the flight back to London late the next morning Tara read the newspaper criticisms of her performance. Several

237

British journalists had attended the concert, it being a rather special event when a Viennese orchestra played an all English programme on their home territory. Reports had been phoned through to London to make the morning editions and copies had just arrived at the airport as Tara checked in.

The comments on her performance were unanimously positive and some went much further than that. 'Strong, muscular playing from the diminutive British soloist,' said the *Guardian*. And the stern critic in *The Times* went so far as to describe her interpretation as 'poetic – bringing a glow of fresh colour to an Edwardian masterpiece.'

Tara relaxed in her seat and closed her eyes, letting the praise trickle over her in warm streams. It told her that she was a player of worth and stature. And she had proved it out there in the big wide world all on her own. No Daddy looking over her shoulder and chivvying her on, no Saul acting as her beloved guardian and patron.

She was a player of individuality and quality. Finally she believed it. Because now she could see the reason behind her previous stubborn denial of her abilities – the long shadow cast over her by her talented dead brother from whose loss her father had never recovered.

She saw it so clearly now; how her father had unconsciously compared her with the dead Freddie. Maybe nothing had been said directly, she could not remember. But she had sensed it with a child's keen intuition – she could still call up the feelings of despair and inadequacy now.

And she could feel the anger of herself as a teenager when she had finally abandoned the task of attempting to give her father something that was not in her power to give. The only thing she had been able to do was rebel. Stamp on her musical talent and bury it in a dark hole. Open up a brittle, jagged gap between herself and her much loved daddy.

She could see now that it was no coincidence that the re-emergence of her longings to be a brilliant player had begun to flower after his death.

Then Saul had come into her life and become the guardian of all her hopes: emotional, sexual, musical. With cool clear-minded unsentimentality he had nurtured the green shoots of her reawakened ambitions. Without Saul it would not have been possible to reach the pinnacle she was perched on this morning.

But there was someone else besides her father and Saul who had played a crucial part in all this. Someone she had treated with dismissive disdain. Railed at. Abused. Her mother. Tara looked back once again into her childhood and saw her mother there as a shadowy presence, a warm anchor of stability and calm, acting as a foil to her father's obsessive ambition.

Whilst her father had been a ruthless driving force her mother had offered the very gentlest encouragement. She had always been there when the young Tara needed a shoulder to cry on. And she had never compared her to the dead Freddie.

Tara gave a little gasp as the jig-saw pieces of her childhood slotted into a coherent picture.

It was her mother who had been her greatest ally. Her mother who had borne the brunt and taken the flak. The rage and frustration Tara had felt for her father she had vented on her patient mother.

After her teenage rebellion the relationship with her father had become a curious mixture of the warmly loving and the reverentially distant. Tara had learned never to get into fights with him. The anger that swelled inside her; dark, uncomprehended and terrifying, must be held down at all costs. Far too dangerous to uncork.

There had been just one crucial, final engagement between them. A battle between a man with only months to live and a girl struggling to get a grasp of her own ambitions.

He had been cool and reasonable.

She had been a ball of rage, yelling until she tasted blood in her throat. She had let him know without a doubt that the last thing in the world she was ever going to do was practise her bloody violin. It could be broken up and used for bonfire fuel for all she cared.

Rachel had intervened. Staunching wounds. Getting lacerated herself. Carrying the future blame.

Tara thought of her mother in Saul's big country house at this moment, caring for little Alessandra, taking her through the initial hours of her first birthday. It would have been impossible to entrust Alessandra to anyone but Rachel.

Recalling some of her more brutal retorts to her mother over the years Tara gave a grimace. She determined to make a new start. She and Rachel would talk over the past together. Explore it at leisure and draw close to each other.

The triumph of the Vienna concert would be a gift Tara could offer her mother to mark the beginning of a new closeness between them.

She looked out of the window and saw the English

Channel gleaming grey and pearl-like below. Already Tara felt herself to be at home. She longed to see her mother. She ached for Alessandra. She burned with heat at the prospect of being reunited with Saul.

As for her career. Well, she would find a way. And Saul would help her.

'So?' he had said. She knew exactly what that cryptic communication conveyed. It was an enigmatic message combining the highest of praise with a dose of stern caution. She was beginning to understand at last how his mind worked.

OK, things would not be easy. But they would find a way. Tara sensed that she was not quite the same person who had flown out to Vienna the day previously. She was enriched, strengthened, emboldened.

The world was out there to be grasped. The future was suddenly not only shining, but controllable.

# CHAPTER 22

Georgiana's interest was caught by the stark beauty of the little country church, a black shape against a lowering, sulky June sky. She slowed her speed, her glance taking in the squat steeple and the grotesquely comical weathered gargoyles guarding the guttering.

Just outside the churchyard several busy figures were unloading their cars, emerging pink-faced and panting, their arms filled with flowers and ribbons and silver horse-shoes. The figures hurried down the mossy path, disappeared into the dark doorway of the church.

A wedding!

Georgiana's foot pressed firmly on the brake. She stepped with the grace of a dancer from the car, her eyes trying to pierce the gloom of the inside of the church. Fascinated. Irresistibly drawn.

She walked down the narrow path, paused in the stone-paved entrance and slipped a note into the wooden offertory box, whose notice hesitantly requested generosity.

The women were busy in the nave and at the chancel

242

steps. They glanced at her. Curious. Wondering if she was a guest misguidedly turning up hours too early.

Georgiana smiled in reassurance, shaking her head and pointing to an empty pew indicating a wish to do nothing more than partake of the consolation and tranquillity to be had in a church.

They smiled back. Nodded with relief. Continued their grapplings with vast swathes of tiger lilies, apricot roses and huge daisy-like chrysanthemums which were already shedding peppery yellow dust.

Georgiana knelt, her hands clasped in an attitude of prayer. She was not a religious woman. She did not attend church except for the three big life events: birth, marriage, death.

Nevertheless she appreciated the hallowed atmosphere of a church. It gave her comfort to contemplate the thread of possibility that there might be some hope for a life after death.

She found herself shaken with a tremor of revulsion. She hated to think about death. About ageing, the sagging of the face and the awful decay of the body.

It was this horror that had kept her from visiting her mother in California during the ordeal of Saul's rejection. Georgiana had not lied when she told Dr Daneman that her mother was still a beauty. She was indeed lovely. If one looked only at the right side of her face. A stroke two years previously had made the slightest but most malevolent alteration in the left side which Georgiana found horrifying. Crushingly depressing.

She and her mother had talked on the telephone, however. Many times. Her mother had been reassuringly and justly horrified about Saul's actions, whilst at the same time reassuring her daughter that he was bound to come to his senses sooner or later. She would get him back. She would have everything again.

Georgiana raised herself into a sitting position. She patted her hair, touched her face with tentative fingertips, grateful to find the contours still smooth and perfect.

She looked down the nave to the chancel steps. A white shaft of sun glinted on the brass stair rods. She blinked, checking that the glimmer was real, not one of those iridescent displays that were like hot grit beneath her eyelids, reverberating needles of fire at the base of her armpits.

Carefully she traced the spear of light to the arched window behind the pulpit. She smiled. Breathed deeply. There was nothing to fear.

The women were now busy looping swags of delphinium and cow parsley around the lectern. Country folk obviously. But the effect was rather charming, she had to admit.

She regretted that she would not be able to stay on and observe the ceremony, cast her eye over the bridal procession.

She and Saul had been married in a country church. It had been decorated with twenty dozen white roses. And, at a time when it was fashionable for brides to look like lace-festooned balloons with skirt hems frothing around their calves, she Georgiana, had worn a carved floor length sheath in heavy satin and carried a single orchid.

She smiled in the satisfied recollection of exquisite taste and setting a lasting trend.

Saul had been the perfect escort, a recipient entirely worthy of her loveliness. He had looked so austere, so imperial and untouchable in his grey morning dress. A trophy of handsomeness, lofty bearing and newly fledged talent.

Saul had only been twenty-three years old on their wedding day. He was already a virtuoso concert pianist, his engagement diary filling up in line with his wallet.

Georgiana looked ahead of her at the front pew just before the chancel steps. She had a dazzling image of the young Saul, standing bolt upright in the pew as she had started her walk up the aisle on her father's arm. He had turned to watch her. Smiling, astonished at her bridal splendour.

He had been a solitary and evocatively romantic figure. Saul had been an orphan. He had been brought up by his unmarried and aristocratic uncle, who had died when Saul was only sixteen. At the wedding Saul had wanted only one friend: his musical agent.

Georgiana's mother, concerned regarding the symmetry of the seating in the church, had worried about the bridegroom's lack of supporters. In the event there had been no embarrassment. Georgiana's family and friends had overflowed and filled the bridegroom's side of the church with no difficulty at all.

This solitariness of Saul, this mystery of his roots had never seemed strange to Georgiana. It had been part of his god-like fascination. She had always thought of Saul as having in some way invented himself.

And now Saul had created a real flesh and blood family, started a dynasty all of his own. The idea of it filled Georgiana with a rapturous, incandescent glow.

She bowed her head in a final prayer, asking whatever God might inhabit this church to give her a blessing.

# CHAPTER 23

Tara picked up her car at the airport and made her way through the complex jumble of London's outer circular roads. Once on the motorway she pressed her foot firmly on the accelerator and allowed the Jaguar's five-litre engine to show her what it could do.

Saul had taught her to drive fast and had recently provided her with a wonderful piece of engineering for the purpose. The surge of speed pressed her spine against the seat and brought a smile of pleasure to her lips. She hoped she was not slaughtering too many flies with her side windows.

She glowed with well-being. The persistent nausea of the early weeks of her pregnancy seemed at last to have vanished. She felt alert and fit, sharpened up with a new sense of her own worth and fresh purpose.

She promised herself that in the coming months she would practise for at least five hours a day come what may. Obviously she would need to put any ideas of playing in public on hold until after the baby was born, but there would be no need to hold back after that.

All of which meant she must start making plans in order

to be fully prepared. Tara decided that now was the time to go ahead and find a kind and affectionate nanny to care for Alessandra for some part of each day in order that she would have the mental and physical freedom to play for as long as she felt necessary.

Alessandra was steadily emerging from babyhood, reaching a developmental point where it was becoming possible to talk and reason with her on simple issues. Tara began to frame the words of explanation and reassurance in her head, confident that she could set things out to her little daughter in a way that would not make her upset.

She imagined Saul's eyebrows lifting ironically at the news, the mocking 'I told you so', expression in his eyes.

The car leapt forward seeming to sense the driver's urgency, her surge of longing to reach home and translate thoughts into action.

As she turned into the drive her heart lurched in consternation as she registered the presence of a police car parked outside the front door. She groaned, her mind leaping guiltily over the last twenty minutes when she had been averaging over a hundred miles an hour on the motorway.

But as she entered the house she knew immediately that something deeply serious and threatening was wrong. She could almost touch it in the atmosphere: a dense silence, an air of stillness, a heavy quality about the air, thick with dark expectancy.

Her mother came down the hallway to greet her. Her face was deathly white, her eyes hunted and fearful. She raised her arms, reaching out to Tara, and then instantly let them fall again so they hung slack by her sides.

'Oh Tara!'

Mother and daughter confronted each other in a silent moment of panic and horror.

'What?' Tara breathed.

'Alessandra,' Rachel said. Her eyes glittered with fever and panic. 'Little Alessandra,' she repeated in a low whisper. 'Oh my God, Tara. She's disappeared. Been taken.'

Tara felt the breath rush out of her body. 'Taken?' She stared at Rachel uncomprehendingly.

'She didn't sleep much last night. She was restless. She fell asleep this morning while I was playing with her in the garden. I settled her in her pram,' Rachel paused, needing to gather strength before she could continue.

Tara tried to concentrate on her mother's words. Their meaning slithered away from her before she could grasp it.

'I only went inside for a moment. The phone rang; I thought it might be you. It was a wrong number. When I got back, she'd gone.'

Tara stiffened. Her face felt frozen.

'Dear God in heaven, Tara, I'll never forgive myself,' Rachel said bitterly.

Tara shook her head. 'No. Don't say that. I've often left her in the garden for a minute or two.'

It was true but Tara knew that she blamed Rachel nevertheless, that if anything bad happened to Alessandra she would never be able to forgive her.

'Does Saul know?' Tara asked softly.

'Yes. He phoned from the airport around an hour ago, just after it happened. He'll be back as soon as he can.'

'How did he take it?' Tara's eyes widened with fresh anxiety.

'How can you ever know with Saul?' Rachel responded, turning her face away.

'This is all my fault,' Tara burst out. 'I should never have gone to Vienna. Never have left her.'

Rachel sighed. 'You need to talk to the police Tara.' She led the way into the drawing room.

A man and a woman were standing silent and musing in front of the Picasso. They turned when Tara entered.

She stared at them. Strangers in her and Saul's house. She found herself hating them because of what had happened to bring them here. Because they had not suffered the crushing grief and terror of having their child taken.

Taking deep breaths she controlled her savage feelings, reminding herself that there was only one human being on earth to blame for all this misery: the wicked, murder-deserving creature who had snatched her baby.

When she spoke to the police officers it was with impeccable politeness, admirable calm. She was a performer. She knew how to dissemble, how to cloak her nerves.

There were endless questions to respond to. Tara listened carefully and answered as best she could.

The officers took turns to fire questions at her.

Who were the people who had access to the house and garden? Who might know the routine of the household, times when the baby might be on her own? Was there anyone Tara knew who might have some reason to take the baby?

They came back to that last point on more than one

occasion. Tara tried to think. Her mind kept crying out, *Oh God, Oh God! Please!* Over and over. Racing like a hunted animal.

She forced her brain to perform. But she could think of no one who would do such a cruel and heartless thing as take a young child from its home.

She looked up at the cool, law-enforcing professionals. 'What do we do now?' she whispered, her eyes wounded and pleading.

They explained to her that press, radio and TV news conferences were already being set up. They judged it would be helpful if she and Saul would agree to appear on a TV news bulletin and make an appeal to the abductor to give the child back. It would be an ordeal, they agreed. Painful and distressing, but a ploy that had worked in previous cases.

'I'll do anything! Anything at all to get her back!' Tara told them.

She heard them communicating with their headquarters. Voices buzzed and rasped as the details of arrangements were discussed.

Rachel perched on the arm of a sofa, her face etched with misery. She looked at her daughter and felt the deep gulf between them expanding by the second.

Tara sat beside the window, her body hunched in despair. She had the sense that all the pain she had experienced in her previous existence had merely been a pale rehearsal for what she was feeling now. In her mind's eye she saw Alessandra's silken unblemished skin, the polished plumpness of her young thighs, the watery clearness of her innocent trusting eyes. She tried

251

not to allow her imagination to explore the little girl's feelings of bewilderment, shied away from any picturing of true fear or pain.

In a span of unmeasured time she registered the arrival of the Porsche, watched Saul leap out and run towards the house.

In the hallway she flung herself into his arms. He clasped her briefly. His body was stiff with urgency for action.

Rachel stood watchfully in the background.

Tara saw Saul's eyes move from her to her mother. It flashed into her mind that for a fragmentary moment he viewed them both as enemies; gatecrashers into his life, strangers who had allowed harm to come to his child.

He answered the questions the police put to him with barely concealed impatience and irritation. Tara saw that it was intolerable for him to be constrained to remain passive and still, placing himself in the hands of bland public servants. He needed to be on the move, to be doing something active and positive towards finding his daughter.

Tara was dismayed, but not surprised, when he declined to be transported in one of the police cars to the nearest station where a news conference was being set up, and instead strode out of the house towards his own car.

She ran after him, feeling the air around him crackling with pent up emotion.

'Wouldn't you rather do the orthodox thing and travel with the police?' he asked, looking up at her from the driver's seat with chilling coldness. He seemed a grim stranger, his spirit as far away from her as though it were locked in a box at the bottom of the ocean.

'I'll go with you,' she said, firmly resolved.

In the car he was grim and silent. She wanted to speak to him, to reach out and touch him and become close. But a deep instinct told her to keep still and quiet.

His breathing was heavy and agitated, his face full of steely purpose. Glancing at his profile it occurred to her that he knew something she did not.

His foot pressed down ever harder on the accelerator. The car swung around a big roundabout and down the slip-road of a motorway.

'This is going out to the west country!' Tara protested sharply.

'Yes.'

'Saul! We should be going into Oxford.'

'I've no intention of wasting my time at some provincial police station.'

Tara looked hard at him. 'You know where Alessandra is don't you?'

'I know *who* she's with.'

Tara's lips parted in astonishment. 'Who? For God's sake! WHO?'

'You haven't guessed?' Cold disdain.

'Oh sweet Jesus. Just tell me!'

'The woman you mistakenly tried to befriend. Your rival!' The scorn in his voice lashed her. Dimly she groped for the clues behind his words.

'Georgiana!'

'Of course.'

'I don't believe it!'

'No? Well, maybe it's hard for you to believe. You were always so keen to see her good points, to play the good samaritan, inviting her into the house and binding up her wounds.'

Tara flinched as though he had struck her. She had understood his reservations about her forming links with Georgiana. Had never guessed at all this caged animosity seething within him.

His foot pressed down relentlessly on the accelerator. The speedometer registered ninety, a hundred. Still accelerating.

'Saul!' She put a hand on his arm. He shook it off.

'*Saul!*' Now there was a chill of alarm. Primitive, self-preservatory fear.

Ahead of them was a clear road. No obstacles, no danger. There was a sudden blast beneath them. A black crackle and then the scent of rubber and fire. Grey smoke spiralling. The car veered towards the central barrier, crab-like and crazy.

There was no way of stopping.

After the grating blasting impact there was silence.


The double tragedy of Saul Xavier's car crash and the abduction of his baby daughter on her first birthday made the front pages of all the next day's newspapers. It emerged from the stories beneath the dramatic headlines that Xavier's young live-in lover Tara Silk, a talented violinist, had been in the car with him and that her side of the vehicle had absorbed most of the impact.

Xavier had been discharged from hospital after only a

few hours but Miss Silk had been detained. Medical personnel were able to reveal that she had sustained a number of injuries but that it was as yet too early to disclose further details.

# CHAPTER 24

Dr Daneman was startled from sleep by the warble of the telephone. It was four in the morning. A luminous grey light pierced his eyelids. In his ears was the enthusiastic oratorio provided by an army of birds proclaiming the wonder of a drizzly midsummer dawn.

His mind uncurled from a state of unconsciousness induced by a single measure of malt whisky on retiring and maintained by a modest ten milligram capsule of Temazepam.

He took a deep breath. Inhaled slowly and deeply, then let the breath go. His was not a profession in which one was required to be 'on call', aroused from slumber at any moment of the day or night at the whim of some unknown sufferer.

He experienced a perfectly proper and normal alarm.

He manoeuvred the receiver to his ear. 'Yes.'

'Your patient, my wife Georgiana Xavier, has abducted my daughter,' the voice on the other end announced with brutal disregard for preliminaries.

Dr Daneman shook his head like a slapped dog. It then took him no more than two seconds to snap from drugged somnolence into a state of red alert. 'Mr Xavier!'

'Did you know this would happen?' Cold. Accusatory.

'Of course not.'

'You should have warned me.'

'I would have done. If she had given me any specific indications.' Dr Daneman found himself backed up against a wall. He tried to rally into some semblance of assertiveness. 'Are you sure your wife is the abductor?'

'For God's sake, the evidence is staring us all in the face.' The lacerating contempt transmitted in the icily reasonable voice made Dr Daneman understand how Xavier was able to put the fear of God into orchestras.

'I'm afraid it's a definite possibility,' Daneman said lamely.

'I suppose it was only a matter of time.' Suddenly Xavier sounded overwhelmed with weariness. 'In fact I'm surprised neither of us thought of it before.'

Dr Daneman maintained a cautious silence. The ultimate defensive weapon.

'I want you to come with me to get Alessandra back,' Xavier commanded. 'I don't think I trust myself to handle matters calmly.'

'You know where Georgiana has taken her?'

'To her parents' old holiday cottage in Cornwall. It's the obvious place.'

'Yes.' The doctor was forced to agree.

'Well?'

Daneman passed a hand over his forehead. 'I'll leave a message for my secretary to cancel today's appointments.'

Sitting beside Xavier in a silver Jaguar an hour later Dr Daneman observed the great conductor with a mixture of professional detachment and personal interest.

Xavier bore no outward signs of a man who was undergoing a cruel ordeal. His hands on the wheel were steady, his reactions keen, his speed nerve-chilling.

He spoke little for the first few miles. Then he said abruptly, 'Alessandra is my only flesh and blood. My parents are dead. I have no close family.'

So his child is more important than anyone, anything, Dr Daneman thought. His clinical eye saw in Xavier a man who had spent years in ferocious slavery to his growing talent, single-mindedly devoted himself to his massive drive for fame, power and glory. He would have regarded the people in his work and social orbit to be little more than shadows; hazy satellites revolving around the sun of his ambition. But now there was another human being he could truly care for; flesh of his flesh, bone of his bone. What an intensity of feeling would be focused on that child.

Dr Daneman did a quick mental run through of Georgiana's accounts of her husband's background and genealogy. Both of which had been extremely hazy. Daneman had put the vagueness down to Georgiana's extraordinary self-absorption. Now, observing Xavier's demonically disciplined features, recalling the almost menacing emphasis of his statement – *My parents are dead* – he experienced a surge of fresh interest. The analytical part of his mind began to conceive new theories.

'You never knew your parents?' he said quietly to Xavier, gaining confidence as he slipped back into the familiar role of therapist and priestly confessor.

'No.'

The silence prickled.

'That must have been hard.'

'Not at all. From what I see of the children of my colleagues, a parent can be one of the greatest crosses some children have to bear. I'm often surprised at how resilient they are, turning out so well when their parents are so pathetically inadequate.'

'We are all a strange and unique mixture of our genetic inheritance and our experience,' Daneman remarked in a professional manner. Neutral. Unchallenging.

For most people such a comment would have been an irresistible invitation to tell their life story. Xavier made no response. Then he said abruptly, 'I never talk of the past.'

'Of your childhood?'

The hooded lids drooped slightly, indicating conceal-ment, a shutting out of the external world.

'Silence is sometimes the best way of dealing with painful memories,' Dr Daneman said, a knee-jerk clin-ician's response. The moment the words were out he wished he could draw them back.

'Don't patronize me,' Xavier said softly.

'I'm sorry.'

'I take it your interest in me is professional?'

'I am a human being, besides a psychologist.'

'It is personal then?'

'I don't think that is what I said.'

'You should practise the art of making up your mind Dr Daneman.'

Daneman winced. As a psychologist he had learned to view the human condition with an impartial eye and an openness to a variety of differing interpretations. *On the one hand this, on the other hand that.* No single, absolute truth. A most elegant dispassion.

As far as Xavier was concerned such flexible attitudes were probably to be written off as contemptible vascillation.

Xavier was speaking again. 'I suspect that your interest in me and my past is very personal indeed. Based on your interest in my wife, which I am sure strays far beyond the professional.'

Daneman found himself shocked and impressed by this cool analysis, this capacity for an almost psychopathic clarity of thought in the face of impending tragedy.

No, not tragedy, Daneman told himself desperately. It will be all right. Things will turn out all right.

'Alessandra will be safe,' Dr Daneman told Xavier. 'Georgiana only wants to possess, not to destroy.'

'Please God you're not mistaken.'

'Amen to that!' Dr Daneman voiced silently, sending up a fervent prayer.

'The baby Tara was expecting was aborted last night,' Xavier announced with brutal unexpectedness. 'And there won't be any more children.' There was an unnerving cold detachment in his tone. He seemed to be issuing some kind of threat.

*If anything should happen to my only child . . .*

Daneman felt great pity for Tara. And no mean pity for himself at this moment.

His mind ran forward to the possible scenario at the cottage and a grey mist of apprehension descended on him, its droplets crawling down his spine with the tread of a poisonous spider.

# CHAPTER 25

Georgiana could not understand why the child would not stop crying. '*I* am to be your new mother. You are Georgiana's own lovely darling,' she told her. 'There's no need to cry.' And later on, more sharply, 'You mustn't cry any more, my precious.'

Things had gone very well to begin with. Alessandra had been happy to go with Georgiana in the car. But at lunchtime when they stopped at a country hotel she would not eat her food. She kicked out her limbs and stiffened them to rods of steel as she wriggled to get down from the high-chair.

The waiter brought puréed beef and vegetables and semolina pudding, which Georgiana knew were the child's favourites. But Alessandra simply spat the food out, her face red with disgust and outrage.

Georgiana had been dismayed. And deeply embarrassed. The eyes of all the diners had been on her and the child. Assessing, disapproving eyes. She had never experienced anything quite like it.

In the car later Alessandra had yelled solidly for over an hour and then suddenly fallen into an exhausted sleep.

Georgiana began to breathe more normally. Her panic and escalating anger gradually dissolved. She was sure things would go smoothly once they got to the cottage.

She had made her preparations with meticulous care. She had spent hours in Harrods selecting the most luxurious and stylish pram, the smartest pushchair, the most splendid cot. All of these were safely installed in the cottage. The Mercedes now sported a baby seat, and its boot was packed with little dresses, dungarees, anoraks, toys and books. The refrigerator at the cottage was stocked with baby dinners, milk and eggs.

Georgiana felt that she had made a full and exhaustive consideration of a child's needs.

In doing this she had let her thoughts run back to her own childhood and followed the blueprint of her parents' care. Her mind fastened entirely on their example.

In their life at the cottage *she* would be them and Alessandra would be *her*.

How could they fail to be happy?

Alessandra slept until they got to the cottage. As the car drew to a halt she woke up, registered her situation and started to howl once more.

Georgiana's heart beat like a drum. Blood raced through the veins in her temples.

There followed seemingly endless, nightmarish hours of screaming.

The child's face was red and contorted with rage. Georgiana's eyes raced over her features and saw first Saul and then Tara. She blinked in confusion. But then she touched the child's buttery blonde hair and felt reassured.

By midnight she was frantic for the opportunity to sleep. Alessandra seemed to have an iron grip on consciousness. She was exhausted from fear and sobbing but each time she drifted into a preliminary doze she wakened herself up with a start and recommenced her howling.

Georgiana's eyes hurt. Her skin prickled. The veins in her arms and legs twitched.

The baby supper on the table was rejected and congealing, the little jars of puréed beef, mushy carrots and apple slush giving off a uniformly malty smell which turned Georgiana's stomach. There was a smell of warm wet nappy too, a result of her half-hour struggle to change the squirming, thrashing Alessandra and make her clean and sweet again.

When she had tried to feed the child, the food had ended up spattered all over her dress. Her stockings felt sticky and her shoes were streaked with glinting threads of drying food.

It was late now and the child's continuing cries were like scalding needles piercing her. Even the brief silences were torment. One never knew when the peace would be shattered.

Georgiana decided to put the child in her cot and leave her. Even if she yelled the place down. Even if all the village came battering at the door.

She must sleep. It was unthinkable not to be able to sleep. How did parents manage when children behaved like this? Could it go on for days? Weeks? She decided to undress in the downstairs bathroom, running both the taps at full so as to activate the noisy plumbing and drown out the human cries coming from above stairs.

She recalled reading reports of parents who had battered their young children, killed them even. Suddenly it was possible to comprehend.

A rosy glow was creeping up over the knobbly Cornish coast as Saul Xavier and Dr Daneman came within striking distance of the town. The steep road leading to the centre was glistening with early morning moisture.

'How long since you were last here?' Dr Daneman enquired, maintaining a conversational tone. His palms were damp with anxious anticipation as if he were on the runway in an accelerating jet.

'Ten years. More possibly. I don't care for the English idea of country life.'

'And Georgiana?'

'She hated it. The reality of it. Of course there were all the golden memories of childhood wrapped up in the place. Neither she nor her parents ever let go of those. The cottage should have been sold long ago but her mother wouldn't hear of it.'

He parked the car at the side of the road. A beech hedge screened the lower part of the house. There was a sizeable English country garden to the front with roses and gladioli flowering in colourful abundance. Sitting on the narrow paved driveway was a sleek dark blue Mercedes.

'Ah yes, she's here,' Xavier said darkly. He paused, looking up at the first floor windows. The curtains were still drawn. 'So? What now?'

Dr Daneman felt the chill of those penetrating grey eyes. 'We shouldn't do anything to alarm her. We should simply act as friendly callers.'

Xavier made a guttural sound of derision. 'Impossible. I think I might kill her.'

'I'll go in,' Dr Daneman said, closing the car door soundlessly behind him. Dread clutched at his guts. His experience had taught him that human behaviour was made up of a high degree of predictability coupled with a hefty dash of spontaneous impulse. And when the personality became disturbed the tendency to obey the edicts of blind impulse was more pronounced. He had spoken the truth to Xavier when he had said that Georgiana's wish was to possess not destroy. But general trends in motivation were no more than a small part in any life story.

His ears strained for the sound of a child's cries as he stood outside the front door. His stomach curdled with fear.

He tapped gently on the door. Waited. Tapped again. Knocked. Eventually activated the heavy iron knocker.

The noise seemed to shatter the early morning calm. It reverberated in his ears like gunfire.

The door opened and Georgiana stood before him, immaculate and lovely in an aquamarine satin négligé.

Her face through the perfect make-up showed little sign of strain, although there were faint creases between her brows and tiny lines fanning out from the corners of her lashes that he had not noticed before.

She looked at him uncertainly. Behind her the house

appeared darkened and dead looking. There was a terrible doom-laden silence hanging in the air.

'Georgiana!' he said, taking her hands in his. 'I've come to see your holiday home.'

Slowly she stepped to one side.

'You're looking very lovely,' he told her, moving smoothly into the narrow hallway. 'At your most beautiful.' He laid a protective hand on her shoulder, allowed the pressure to increase before he removed it.

She took him into a recently restored kitchen full of stripped pine and oatmeal-coloured tiles. There was a hideous, slum-like mess on the table. A soiled nappy screwed up on one of the chairs. A sour stench.

At the sink Georgiana fiddled with the kettle.

As Dr Daneman surveyed the outer scene and contemplated the internal squalor in Georgiana's head he was surprised to find himself both shocked and sickened. He had thought he was beyond all that. But this was not the consulting room. This was life.

'Your holiday home,' he commented soothingly, staring around him appreciatively.

She nodded.

The silence was becoming unbearable.

Georgiana paused as she turned off the taps, tilting her head sharply like a watchful lone animal on strange territory.

'You feel happy here?' Dr Daneman suggested calmly.

'I couldn't sleep,' she said pitifully. 'I got no sleep. There were no beautiful dreams.'

Automatically Dr Daneman paused to consider the appropriate response.

Georgiana stiffened. Her eyes slanted towards the door, towards the stairway. Dr Daneman followed her gaze. He felt himself immobilized, stripped of all power of action.

With a swift and vicious movement Georgiana slammed the kitchen door shut. She looked around her, her eyes blinking and puzzled. In time she crossed to the cutlery drawer. Slowly, deliberately, she lifted out a long bread knife, then took bread from a pretty hand-painted stone jar. It was sliced bread Dr Daneman noted. She grasped the blade of the knife and stared at it, examining it carefully, turning it over so that the blade flashed with pale white light from a thin struggling sun beyond the window.

Her fingers moved experimentally over the glinting serrations. A thread of blood darted across the pad of her thumb. She looked up, her eyes connecting with those of her doctor. She looked back at the knife.

Dr Daneman breathed deeply, held himself still.

Georgiana turned and looked out of the window. Following her glance Dr Daneman saw Xavier coming up the path towards the door. He flinched inwardly, fearing some dramatic response from Georgiana when her husband challenged her.

'Saul is here!' Georgiana exclaimed.

'Yes.' He watched her uneasily.

She went swiftly out into the hallway. 'Saul!' she exclaimed once more, her voice bright with anticipation.

Saul held his arms out to her and she moved into them with a long sigh. 'You've no need to worry any more now,' he told her. 'I'll take care of everything. Mmm?'

'Thank God. Oh, *thank God*!' She wound her arms up around his neck.

Dr Daneman watched Xavier gently disengage the knife from her fingers and allow it to slide to the floor.

Suddenly there was a shrill scream of terrified infant rage from the upper floor of the cottage.

Xavier flung his head up, a great sigh easing itself from deep in his chest.

The noise of the baby's crying intensified and accelerated, hammering through the fabric of the cottage.

'I couldn't sleep!' Georgiana complained to Saul pathetically.

'Ah – my poor darling. What torment. You always needed your rest so badly. Well you must have it now. I shall take you to bed and then I shall take care of the baby whilst you have a lovely long sleep.'

Georgiana gave a sigh of blissful relief. Saul was back and suddenly everything was simple again. Saul would know what to do to stop the baby crying. Saul would take care of everything.

He led her upstairs and and propelled her to the frilled four-poster bed in the main bedroom. He wound the bedclothes tenderly around her and kissed her cheek. Then closing the door behind him he raced into the next room.

Alessandra stood in her cot, a pathetic, deserted figure bellowing in despair and misery. Her soiled, soaked nappy was entwined around her feet and the stench of urine coming from the bedding was rancid and powerful. Her face was laced with the tracks of countless unstoppable tears and her lips were purple with distress.

Anger to see his beloved child subjected to such a painful and humiliating ordeal swirled viciously through Saul's head. Alessandra stared at him in distrustful bewilderment for a few seconds and then she threw out her round baby arms towards him. 'Dad-dee!'

Saul held her very close. He felt her heart ticking frantically against his collar bone. His eyes closed as a surge of feeling engulfed him.

Dr Daneman moved up and down the kitchen attempting to put together some kind of breakfast. Saul sat down at the table with the damp Alessandra on his knee.

She appeared ravenous, snatching up fingers of toast and cramming them into her mouth. Saul cradled her head in his hands from time to time and kissed her brow. 'Thank Christ she's safe and well.'

Dr Daneman looked at the child's face, smooth and serene once more as though the negative feelings had simply drained away and dissolved into the air.

Suddenly he felt very tired.

'I need to get back to London,' Xavier said abruptly. 'Will you deal with things here?'

Dr Daneman nodded. 'She'll need to be seen by the local doctors for a start. They'll probably recommend a period of in-patient treatment.'

'I want the best clinic there is. She couldn't bear anywhere coarse or brutal.'

'There's no shortage of good places.'

'Will you see to it?'

'Yes.' Dr Daneman gave the answer automatically and then thought about it. 'I'd be happy to.'

Xavier stood up, clasping the child closely against him. 'Poor Georgiana – I had no idea how desperately ill she had become.'

That is one way of looking at it, Dr Daneman agreed without voicing the words.

Watching Xavier prepare the child for their journey he was impressed with the almost maternal ease with which he handled her. He had thought that the charismatic, worldly-successful Xavier would be a man encapsulated in a protected adult world, a man with little tolerance of the ceaseless, irrational demands of a child. He saw instead the strong bond between father and daughter, the trust in the child's eyes, the tender protectiveness in the parent's. All the complex mesh of shared blood and genetics.

Xavier, a man alone in the world. No parents, no family. A man of his own creation. But he had his child. Warm flesh. Pulsing blood.

'Thank God,' Daneman kept repeating silently.

Xavier eventually left, Alessandra safely harnessed into the seat he had wrenched from Georgiana's Mercedes.

Dr Daneman listened to the note of the Jaguar's engine as it faded into the distance. As Xavier's presence withdrew from the house so Dr Daneman felt his own personal freedom and professional competence slowly seeping back.

He waited for an hour or so and then made fresh tea. He mounted the stairs to Georgiana's room.

She lay on her side, tranquil and lovely, one golden-skinned arm resting outside the covers.

Dr Daneman sat on the bed and stared down at her for a long moment, stroking her cheek with lingering fingers. Then, very gently, he pulled the covers back and slipped his hand on the curve of her waist.

# CHAPTER 26

Tara struggled back into consciousness. The first thing she registered was the reassuring figure of her mother sitting close by the bed.

Rachel smiled. 'Hullo!'

Tara reached out her hand and Rachel grasped it.

'Alessandra's safe,' Rachel said. 'She's with Saul.'

'Aah!' Tara felt the wall of her chest contract. 'That's all that matters.'

She registered the grinding ache of emptiness in her belly and knew that the baby had gone. But the feeling was nothing stronger than mild regret. Alessandra was safe. Life could continue. Nothing would ever be so bad again.

She pressed her fingers against her forehead. 'There are lots of things I need to say to you.'

Rachel smiled.

'About the past.'

Rachel shook her head. 'There will be all the time in the world.'

Tara started to frame some thoughts but the words would not come.

'They'll wait,' Rachel repeated.

They looked at each other. Suddenly Rachel dared to take her daughter in her arms. They were clasping each other, laughing. Weeping with joy.

It is like a resurrection, thought Rachel.

'Is my brain damaged?' Tara demanded, struggling against the muzzy feeling in her head.

'Your brain is fine. You're in shock from the accident, and they gave you sedatives for the pain. It takes time to get going again.'

'You didn't say who took Alessandra,' Tara said, fighting hard against the urge to drift back into a doze.

'She's safe,' Rachel repeated, knowing that only Saul could speak to Tara about what had happened and what it meant.

After Rachel had left Tara lay staring at the ceiling. The events of the last forty-eight hours swam in and out of her memory; the recollections of having been in Vienna to play at a concert jostling with the chilling image of Alessandra in some terrifying unidentifiable danger.

I shall never leave her again, she kept telling herself. Never! She had a powerful sense of her life having swerved away from the direction she had recently steered it into.


Saul looked through the glass partition and saw Tara lying propped on a mound of pillows. Her face was calm, her expression strong and accepting and brave.

She should not have had to suffer and endure like this.

He recalled all the times he had hurt her, holding her away from him through his need to withdraw into himself. How he had too often silenced her need for simple affection with commanding sex. How he had dared to smite her with his disdain on that last fateful drive.

And still she loved him. And sadly he knew he must hurt her further.

He placed the armfuls of flowers in a mound at the foot of her bed. She held out her arms to him, tears wetting her eyelashes.

'Where's Alessandra?' she asked him.

'At home asleep. Rachel and Donald are standing guard.'

'I should never have gone to Vienna,' Tara said, angry to find herself openly tearful.

'It would have happened some time, whether you had gone or not,' Saul said, not quite believing it.

He told her what had happened. How Georgiana had been up to her old tricks of watching the house and garden from her car, how she had seized on the brief opportunity to snatch Alessandra.

He went on to describe the scene at the cottage. He told her about Dr Daneman's offer to ensure that Georgiana received all the care she needed.

Tara listened to the flow of words with a sense of revulsion and horrible guilt. She looked into Saul's face and read the thoughts behind his carefully constructed phrases. She understood that there would no longer be any question of a divorce. He would never say so openly. But his heart would no longer be in it. They had destroyed Georgiana and now they must pay for it.

So be it! Tara thought. I shan't make any demands. Alessandra will always be ours, and that is enough.

The next day when he came, he pulled her hard against him, a gesture of deep love, an insistent desire that must make itself known, even if it could not be immediately satisfied.

Tara put her lips against the hard warmth of his cheek. As his fingers pressed into the bones at the base of her neck she held herself still, schooled herself not to cry out.

The tingling down her arm intensified, small needles of sensation stabbing like tiny electric shocks in the tips of her middle three fingers.

Saul stiffened. Gently he pushed her away from him, looked deep into her face. 'What is it?'

She shook her head. Shrugged.

'What is it? Tara!'

'I have this terrible stiff neck.'

He flinched. 'So?'

'There could be some damage to the nerves in the vertebrae.' She reached up and touched the place. 'It's only minimal, not serious. It'll probably get better over time.'

She recalled the discussion with the consultant an hour before. An analysis of the scan she had undergone the day before and kept fiercely secret.

He had talked to her for some time, his voice low and calm.

'A slight loss of sensitivity in the middle three fingers of your left hand,' he had said. 'Maybe a little numbness in the tips. Maybe in time very little that will bother you at all.'

'I'm a violinist,' she told him. 'A concert soloist.'

She had seen that the doctor found it difficult to meet her gaze.

'It's all right,' she had told him. 'I shall deal with it. My little girl is safe.'

Saul rattled her shoulder. 'Tara, speak to me. Surely it's treatable?'

'No! There's nothing can be done. It will make very little difference to my everyday life. It will probably simply go away on its own.' She stared at him, steely in her courage, in her challenge and defiance.

He took her hand. Her left hand. Her precious hand that sought the strings on her violin and made them sing. The three crucial middle fingers looked entirely normal. But outward appearances could be cruelly deceptive.

He looked up at Tara. She shook her head. Stretched out her fingers and examined them. 'Something has happened,' she said. 'Something permanent. I simply know.'

He was silent.

She smiled at him. 'It's very unlikely that anyone will notice – as long as I don't walk onto a platform and try to play my violin.'

'Oh my darling!' he groaned, closing his eyes in grief.

'No more concert performances,' she said drily, wondering if deep down he would be glad. She wasn't sure yet what she herself felt; the shock was keeping her numb.

She had this strong sense of the two of them having committed a sin for which they were now being punished in various ways. Thinking about things in that light and admitting the faults of the past brought a curious relief. And with it the freedom to begin building another life.

She knew without a doubt that it would be necessary to build afresh. The idyll that she and Saul had shared was over.

*Part Three*

# CHAPTER 27

Saul was leading a seminar of student conductors at the Music Centre in Tanglewood, Massachusetts – the summer location of the Boston Symphony Orchestra.

The cream of music students throughout the world were drawn to Tanglewood each year, a significant proportion of them being students of conducting.

Saul had been guest conducting the Boston players for five summers now, and between rehearsals and concerts he would spend time with emergent young conductors as they tried out their skills on the student orchestra.

On a vivid August morning, heralding the start of yet another swelteringly hot day, the students were assembling in the theatre-concert hall, a shed-like building with corrugated steel doors, incongruously set in the sedate greenery of the Tanglewood grounds. Having unpacked their instruments they were now seated on the stage, excited and keyed-up. The student conductors sat in the front row close to the stage, their eyes riveted to the scores on their laps.

Tara, sitting on her own in the middle of the auditorium noticed how young they all looked, most of them in their late teens and early twenties. Every year the students looked younger as she and Saul got older.

On the programme was the Schubert Symphony Number Five and Stravinsky's *Petrushka*. Two of the student conductors would each conduct one work, whilst the others would watch and hopefully learn.

Exactly a minute before the starting time of the rehearsal Saul arrived at the main entrance to the hall and made his way down the auditorium.

Eyes fastened on him. A reverential silence fell.

Vaulting athletically onto the stage he went to sit beside Gustav Siegal, the coordinator of the conducting course, and instantly nodded to the first student conductor to start proceedings.

The young man was tall and beanstalky with a mop of tight auburn curls. Tara was interested to hear how he would tackle the challenge of Schubert's deceptively delicate music. She had talked with the young conductor at length over a number of beers and coffees during the past couple of days. She liked his openness and sensitivity, loved his wide-eyed enthusiasm. She had a strong wish for him to do well, not only because she judged that he was good, but also because she knew that she would feel unnerved and angry were Saul to unleash his venomous sarcasm upon the young man's trusting head.

She breathed a sigh of relief as the student took the orchestra effortlessly through a sensitively warm and honest rendering of the piece. Not even Saul could fault that. She noted with pleasure how the would-be conductor was openly grateful for playing that pleased him, how he requested things of the players rather than making demands, how he coaxed rather than ordering.

She judged he would go far.

At the end the players applauded their conductor with warm spontaneity and Saul inclined his head in gracious acknowledgement of a task well done.

The next student set the orchestra off with arms whirling like windmills and a bending and stretching at the knees more suited to a rigorous exercise regime in a gymnasium than directing from the podium. His clumsy verbal commands to the players: 'Loud', 'Soft', 'Short', 'Long', were clearly audible over the music.

Tara bent her head towards the score balanced on her knee so as to hide her amused astonishment.

At the close of the piece Saul and Gustav summoned both students and talked them through their performances. Tara heard Saul's dry, sardonic tones biting deep into the unfortunate last performer.

'So, I see you're an all action man. Maybe if you don't make it as a conductor you could pursue a successful career directing the rush hour traffic in Trafalgar Square.'

Tara did not stay to hear any more. She went softly out of the auditorium and made her way into the gardens beyond. Saul would not notice her exit. He would be entirely happy for the next hour or so. He had one student good enough to spend time with, yet not so brilliant as to be any real threat to his own prowess, and another who was sufficiently dismal and wooden to merit the marshalling of all the skills in his baiting repertoire.

She wondered if there would be time to make a quick phone-call to England and speak to Alessandra. It was now half-past twelve, almost lunch-time. Back home it would be half-past seven in the morning. Alessandra would just be coming in from her early morning ride, ravenous for a hearty breakfast.

Alessandra had always demonstrated a great fondness for her maternal grandmother. She got on well with Donald also and stayed with the two of them whenever Saul and Tara went away.

Soon after their marriage Rachel and Donald had bought a cosy thatched cottage in a Bedfordshire village. It had two acres of land including a huge paddock and ample grazing for two or three horses. Close to the back of the house was an old barn and some airy loose boxes. Alessandra preferred to keep her bay mare Tosca there rather than at the Oxfordshire house belonging to her father, where the garden was more formal and the grazing space limited.

Tosca was always given as the reason for Alessandra's increasingly frequent and ever longer stays with Rachel and Donald. But Tara suspected that the horse was only one factor in the equation and that Alessandra simply felt more comfortable and relaxed in the easy-going atmosphere of the Bedfordshire cottage than in her parents' house.

Suddenly Tara longed to hear her daughter's voice. She ran up the dirt path towards the cafeteria beside the main gates and put coins in the pay phone.

Rachel's voice answered, miraculously clear and sounding no further away than the next town.

She handed her straight over to Alessandra who was full of news of Tosca's latest achievements. Listening to the

284

joyous enthusiasm in the girl's voice Tara felt a warm glow of happiness. Whatever might be wrong between her and Saul, at least their daughter was experiencing a stretch of untroubled happiness in this summer of her thirteenth year.

'Grandma and Grandad have taken me to heaps of gymkhanas. Tosca's won absolutely loads of rosettes. We did a two-foot-six course yesterday. It was fabulous!'

'Wonderful news darling. Well done.'

'I'm going to put her out in the field today. She needs a rest. We've got more shows lined up for the weekend. Grandad's ace at driving the horse box. And he wants me to teach him how to pick Tosca's feet out and tack her up just in case he's needed. I've bought some new exercise bandages because the old ones are getting grubby and one of the judges at the shows said I should try her in a martingale so I'm thinking about that.'

Tara smiled, fighting to get a word in. It was almost impossible to stem the flow of Alessandra's conversation once the subject of Tosca came up. She would chatter happily about the horse for hours. In fact for Alessandra at present, any topic that did not include Tosca was of little interest.

Saul found this obsession with horses puzzling and more than a little irritating. It annoyed him to see Alessandra distracted from giving her whole-hearted attention to the more serious business of schoolwork and singing practice.

Alessandra was showing promise as a vocalist, but since her passion for horses and riding had developed so her interest and motivation regarding singing had declined.

'Putting her under pressure won't make her want to sing any more,' Tara would explain to him gently, watching Alessandra storm off in tears after one of her father's sardonic lectures on the merits of music as against the inanity of jumping about on horses. 'If anything it will make her worse, more inclined to kick against you.'

Tara knew all too well the retort that framed itself in Saul's head in response to that kind of remark: 'Like mother like daughter – you also wasted the years of *your* adolescence.'

The words were never spoken but were heard by both of them; one more set of spikes in the uneasy collar of their complex relationship.

'She does practise for an hour every single day,' Tara would point out to him, in Alessandra's defence. 'That's perfectly satisfactory.' And truly heroic for someone who didn't seem to enjoy it very much and would far rather be doing something else, she added to herself silently.

'We won't be back until the end of next week, darling,' Tara told Alessandra, bringing their conversation to a close. 'Daddy's been invited to make a special guest appearance at the New York Met. And I thought I'd go with him.'

'You always go everywhere with him,' Alessandra said in a matter-of-fact voice. There was a short pause. 'Will you be back by Sunday?'

'Early Monday morning I would guess. Why?'

'There's a really super open jumping class on Sundays at the riding school. Grandma and Grandad said they'd take me if I was still here.'

'Don't worry, you will be! Quite safe from the parental presence!'

'Oh Mummy, I miss you terribly.'

Like hell you do, Tara thought with a wry smile. A bit, but not very much if Tosca's around. And how very healthy that is.

'Is Daddy there to talk to me?' Alessandra asked.

Tara thought she traced anxiety behind the question. But maybe she was getting over-sensitive. 'He's busy in a conducting seminar. He sends his love.'

'Oh! Right. Give him mine too then.' There was no mistaking the tone of relief.

Ah well, thought Tara, it was understandable. Saul had never been the most relaxed person to chat to on the phone.

She wandered slowly back to the music theatre, reflective and subdued. She understood what a disappointment it was to Saul that Alessandra had shown so little spontaneous enthusiasm for music.

He had been so keen to share the passion of his life with his only child, bathing her in classical music from babyhood. At weekends the house would be filled with the sound of live music played by some of the world's greatest instrumentalists, and whenever Saul was at home there would be great symphonic works blasting from the multitude of high fidelity speakers positioned round the house.

Watching Alessandra grow up Tara saw the child's early devotion to Saul gradually transform itself into an awed and distant respect. It was the intensity of his wish for her to share his obsession with music that lay at the heart of the problem. Alessandra had never shown any great interest in either listening to music or playing an instrument, despite Saul's encouragement. As a small child she had loved to sing, but once Saul arranged for coaching lessons with one of his opera star contacts, her enthusiasm and confidence had rapidly deteriorated.

Tara had watched with growing dismay as the little Alessandra grew more and more tense, overwhelmed with the enormity of her father's musical knowledge and skill, shying away from his obsessive need for her to display genius.

On a number of occasions she had tried to explain to Saul how the child might be feeling, but he had brushed aside her tactful suggestions with polite dismissiveness. 'One never achieves anything without pain.'

Tara saw herself and her own father all over again; the pattern of parental pressure relentlessly repeating itself.

Arriving at the door of the theatre she saw that the rehearsal had drawn to a close. Saul and Gustav were making their way out of the auditorium, the two student conductors following behind.

'We're going to get some lunch,' Saul told her. 'We were coming to find you.' He raised his eyebrows in a gesture that let her know he had been wondering where she had been.

Tara fell into step with him and slipped her hand through his arm. 'I've just been checking that they're all alive and kicking at home.'

'Ah. And?'

'They're all fine.'

'Ah.' There was a brief pause. His face clouded. 'I would have liked to have spoken to Alessandra.'

'Yes. She was terribly disappointed that you were busy. I said we'd ring later.' Tara was acutely aware of the soothing and cajoling quality in her voice, as though she were a kindly parent humouring a clever but emotionally delicate child.

And this is what we have come to, me and Saul, she grieved inwardly, reaching up and pressing a kiss on the side of his neck.

She saw the auburn-haired young man's eyes on her, registered the gleam of speculation in his eye. He was a romantic; he would look at her and Saul and see a couple who had once intrigued the musical world with their scandalous love affair and had now settled into mellow devotedness.

She smiled.

After lunch Saul led a seminar of around twenty conducting students. He and Gustav sat on a Victorian sofa facing the class who sat in neat rows on metal chairs. Behind them were two grand pianos, their lids propped open. On the wall opposite was a life-size portrait of Arturo Toscanini, Saul's former mentor.

Gustav had attempted to prevail on Tara to join the sofa group but she had laughingly declined and retreated to her preferred place in an unobtrusive corner of the room.

Saul went to the piano and played the opening bars of Stravinsky's *Petrushka*. 'So! We heard our young friend bring the orchestra in with a flourish that would have halted the traffic in London's rush hour. Maybe not the most subtle, mmm? Who would like to offer some alternative suggestions?'

The next half hour was spent in a discussion of the ways to start big orchestral works. Saul had brought the score of the Mozart Symphony Number 29 in A-Major to use as an illustration. He employed his usual tutorial methods of tempting his audience with snippets of information without ever revealing his own personal convictions. He teased and taunted them also, leading them gently down certain pathways and then suddenly demolishing all the ideas he had planted with derisive scorn.

'You didn't believe all that did you? No, not for a moment!' His mildly sarcastic jests were accompanied by flourishing runs on the piano.

Tara, watching the eager, puzzled, anxious faces of the students, felt increasingly sorry for them.

The discussion moved on to aspects of interpretation and the gulf between the work of current composers and the old masters. Now suddenly he was serious. He explained to them that conductors must always be prepared to conduct new works however inaccessible they seemed at the time. 'Remember, if we ignore all the new composers there will be no "old" music in the future for anyone to conduct.'

There was a round of applause. This was Saul at his best; stunningly clear with no axe to grind.

He invited questions from the audience and an hour flew by with everyone enjoying themselves.

Then suddenly Saul was bored with it all. He looked at his watch. 'So. I think we've all had enough, mmm?' he announced abruptly, giving his floppy dismissal wave. 'Go away and lead your lives. There is life beyond music you know!'

But possibly not for Saul Xavier, thought Tara with a wry little grin.

Later on, after Saul had disappeared with Gustav to discuss the next day's programme of events, and the students had all drifted away, she stayed on in the gracious seminar room, staring out of the windows at the glassy-surfaced lake and beyond to the wall of blue mountains.

The auburn-haired student peeped round the door and stole back into the room.

Tara looked up and smiled in welcome. 'Hello!'

He sat beside her, his eyes fixed on the open score of the Mozart symphony which rested on her lap.

'How would *you* start it?' he asked softly.

She laughed. 'Why are you asking me after all you heard earlier?'

'Because Xavier never answered the question. But I felt sure you'd tell me. I've watched you conducting on those training videos you made for A-Level students. I bought every one of them. You're wonderful!'

Tara breathed in deeply, startled to find herself truly moved to be offered such genuine, heartfelt praise.

'Thank you. But I'm no authority on setting off orchestras on Mozart symphonies.'

'You'll do for me,' he said bluntly. 'So tell me!'

She stared at him.

'Tell me!'

'All right.' She looked down at the score, then looked up and fixed him with a steady stare. Raising her hand she gave a minute downbeat and a virtually invisible nod. He saw that her eyes gave a message too but it would have been impossible to describe it in words.

'Exquisite!' he said.

'It only takes about three years to learn, two more to perfect!' she told him mischievously. The admiration beaming from his face warmed her. Not only was he talented, he was charming and gentle – and very young.

And I'm turned thirty, Tara thought. Really quite old.

'Why aren't you a tutor in these conducting seminars?' he demanded. 'You'd be marvellous.'

She gave him a tolerant smile. 'I've done very little besides making the training videos.'

'What about conducting the student orchestras at the music schools? Doesn't that count? And if you say "no" then it means you don't think students are important – and I don't believe that of you.'

Tara smiled. 'I see that I'm trapped. I had no idea I was going to be so fiercely attacked whilst I was sitting here thinking about Mozart and watching the mountains.'

'You're wasting yourself,' he told her with exasperation.

'And you're trespassing on delicate areas you know nothing about,' she warned.

'I'm sorry.'

A silence. They both stared at Mozart's score.

'Do you aim to be a great Maestro then?' she asked playfully.

'I just want to make great music.'

'Ah.'

'That whole Maestro thing, the worship of the charismatic musical dictator who plays no instrument and makes no noise himself is an anachronism,' he declared solemnly, clearly quoting from some text which had impressed him.

Tara smiled. 'You strike me as being a little confused,' she told him patiently. 'You want to be a conductor but you don't want to be tarred with the brush of the great men who have made a success of it.'

'Those old style conductors, they are tyrants,' he burst out, his cheeks flushing with dark colour. 'They demand a level of obedience from their orchestras more than any army commander and collect a fee for a concert that adds up to as much as the whole orchestra is paid.'

He pulled himself up and glanced hesitantly into her eyes. 'I'm sorry,' he repeated and the image of Maestro Xavier rose up between them.

She smiled and shrugged. 'Don't apologize. I remember having the same ideas myself once upon a time.' She had the feeling this young man understood quite a lot more than he expressed.

'I'm just starting out,' he said with feeling. 'I'm not interested in whopping bank balances and racing round the world in my private jet. I just want to communicate music. I love it so much! Some of the pieces – I could just die for them!'

Tara looked him straight in the eyes. 'Don't lose that. That wonderful joy in the mystery and sublimity of music.'

He pressed his hands together. 'I came here to get some tips from you, but now I'm ashamed to ask.'

'Don't be. Ask!'

He twisted his hands together uneasily. 'You were a violinist weren't you?'

'Yes.'

'My tutor at music school knew you. She told me about what happened – the accident.'

'Yes?'

'You never recorded anything did you? What a waste!'

Tara understood that this young man had stumbled on her story and seized it as though it were a fairy tale. He had made her into a heroine; a mythical creature to worship.

He was *very* young.

'No. I didn't ever record my playing. And I regret that. But it is not a tragedy. There are other violinists to bring the great works to life. Music goes on you see – a shared thing. Not some individual instrumentalist's ego trip.' She smiled at him. 'And Saul was right when he said that there was life beyond music.'

There was a long, thoughtful silence. The young man was not at ease. His glance surreptitiously moved over Tara's long dark waves of hair and her smooth creamy skin. He could not bracket together this warm, sensitive creature with the disparaging, lip-curling Xavier. And worse, he sensed that she knew exactly what he was thinking!

'What instrument do you play?' she asked.

'Clarinet. And the piano of course.'

'Good. Well, I'll give you a tip for free!'

'Yes?'

'Hold onto that. Your playing. Hold onto it every minute you're conducting. Don't ever stand in front of an orchestra telling them how to play without remembering how bloody hard it is! '

He shook his head. 'No.'

294

She smiled. 'I don't think I needed to tell you that. I think you knew already.'

He reached out and took her hand. 'And *you* mustn't let it go,' he said meaningfully. 'All your marvellous talent.'

The tall figure of Saul appeared at the door. 'Darling, I've been looking all over for you.'

'I'm just coming. Got a little tied up.' She withdrew her hand gently from the student's eager clasp.

As regards her own aspirations she felt there was no need to spell it out to him that within certain confined spaces there was room for only one Maestro.


In New York, forty-eight hours later, Tara watched Saul as he lay stretched out on the bed in their hotel room, mentally preparing for his appearance at the Metropolitan Opera that evening to conduct *The Flying Dutchman*.

The dress rehearsal had not been happy. There had been tears from the lead soprano, who fled temporarily from the stage protesting that Xavier was a heartless sadist, sulks from the lighting crew into whom the Maestro had lashed with a serpent's tongue, and glum resignation from the orchestra who seemed unable to do a single thing to please him.

Tara knew that he was deeply ill at ease with himself. He had, of course, always been tyrannical: brilliant, egocentric and utterly powerful. But now the brilliance was becoming tarnished with bitterness and cynicism. He had conquered the world, but he had maimed his wife, robbed his mistress of her musical talents and alienated his only child. The guilt was there with him constantly, generating a self-hate which was now beginning to turn outwards onto others.

He drove himself mercilessly. He never stopped working; setting himself new goals, seeking out new interpretations. Demanding the same level of obsessive excellence from all those who worked with him.

Tara sat on the bed beside him and stroked the long bones of his face. They seemed to become more hollow, more deeply sculpted as each year passed. His face and his spirit seemed to be slowly sinking into them, the whole effect making him more arrestingly attractive than ever before.

She leaned down and kissed his forehead in a tenderly reverential manner as though saluting an historic hero. His monumental drive and his breathtaking knowledge of music and conducting still inspired her with awe and respect. There had been so much to learn from him over the years, so many benefits.

Her fingers traced over the grooves running from the flare of his nostrils to the corners of his firm mobile mouth. He made a slight noise, a faint groan.

Tara pressed her lips on his.

He opened his eyes. For a moment he seemed not to register her presence.

'It's all right,' she told him with a smile of irony. 'There's still an hour and a half before curtain up.'

'Ah.' He lifted his hand and slid it inside her robe.

As he caressed her she wondered which of the problematic aspects of the evening's performance was exercising him most. He had always had the capacity to do more than one thing at a time with consummate skill.

His lovemaking remained technically perfect, ever more refined and imaginative. But there was a growing restraint to it, a curious throb of sadness.

Sometimes she wondered if he would prefer to abandon the flesh and live the life of a monk.

# CHAPTER 28

It was winter. Alessandra had several songs to prepare for the prestigious Christmas recital being organized by her singing tutor. Tosca required frequent exercising in preparation for the county-wide cross country event taking place at the riding centre in the same week. The latter was taking up far more of her time and effort than the former and Saul was not at all pleased.

Driving Alessandra across to the Bedfordshire cottage to exercise Tosca, Tara wondered how to tell her daughter about Saul's recent suggestion of a family skiing holiday to be taken in the mountains above Salzburg the following spring. She knew how important it was for him that Alessandra should be there.

Hesitantly, diplomatically she broached the subject.

'When?' Alessandra snapped angrily.

'February probably – half-term.'

'The riding school have got all their best open competition events arranged for then. I can't possibly miss those.'

'It would only be for ten days,' Tara urged encouragingly. Alessandra rounded on her. 'That's a bloody lifetime!'

After a prickly silence, Alessandra said, 'I'm sorry.'

Tara sighed.

'You go Mummy. You know I hate trekking round the world.'

'It's only Europe!'

'You and Daddy'll enjoy it just as well without me.' She was trying desperately to be reasonable. Tara could see her whole face shrieking out 'don't make me do this'.

'I think Daddy really wants you to go,' Tara said quietly. 'He sees so little of you.'

'And whose bloody fault is that? He's never at home!'

'Neither are you,' Tara shot back.

Alessandra jerked her head away from her mother and stared out of the window. 'He doesn't really want me there. He just likes the idea that I'll be around. He won't spend any time with me. You know what'll happen. He'll get bored of sticking to the novice runs and go off on his own. Anyway I loathe skiing; it's a waste of time when I could be riding.'

Tara heard the truth in her words.

'Oh God!' she groaned to Rachel, having deposited a stormy, pink-faced Alessandra at the entrance to the paddock. 'How long does it take for them to get through adolescence?'

"With you it went on from around eight to twenty-one. So I should prepare for a long siege!' Rachel said drily.

Tara stirred cream into the coffee Rachel put down in front of her. She wondered if Alessandra and she would eventually find the harmony she herself had discovered with Rachel.

'I feel so helpless!' she burst out suddenly, thumping a

299

clenched fist on the table. 'I know what he's doing to her. And yet I don't seem to find a way to do anything about it. And anyway, for all I know I'm just as bad for her as he is.'

'You're both good parents,' Rachel commented, which she considered to be broadly the truth, taking into account the impossibility of the general task of parenthood. 'And he feels a huge bond with her, he really adores her.'

'Is that the problem?' Tara wondered.

'Too much love, too much neediness?'

'Yes.'

'Probably.'

'History repeating itself,' Tara mused.

Rachel had often considered this very issue. 'Maybe some similarities.' But Richard had been nothing like Saul, she thought privately. Richard had been a fine instrumentalist and a committed musician, but he had never been driven. And he had at least made the attempt to look at things from the other person's point of view – even if he had not always succeeded.

Rachel had been truly shocked when Tara presented her with her own version of the relationship between her and her father. She had never had any inkling of the child Tara's feelings of inadequacy in comparison with her dead brother. The realization that she and Richard might unwittingly have been the cause of Tara's lost opportunities – both musical and personal – had been a bitter pill to swallow.

But there had been a huge compensation. She had been emotionally reunited with the daughter who had seemed determined to cast her off for ever.

'It'll sort itself out,' Rachel said practically.

300

'I suppose something will turn up to push her decision one way or the other. It usually does,' Tara said with faint resignation.

'I'm surprised *you* agreed to go. Since when did you like skiing?'

Tara shrugged and laughed. 'Oh, well. I'll try anything once!'

Rachel shuddered inwardly. How pliant and pragmatic Tara had become, using up all her skills and energies in negotiating the dangerous swirls and eddies of her relationship with Saul and her daughter.

'What's your programme for the coming six months?' she asked Tara. 'Your personal music programme, not your packed social life with Saul?'

'The usual. Charming huge amounts out of the Arts Council for the Tudor Phil and I'm pretty hopeful of getting some hefty funds out of the local council as well.'

'You've been the best ambassador for that orchestra that Saul could have hoped to get anywhere!' Rachel observed.

'Yes, I have, haven't I? I've done a good job on his behalf. But then of course if it hadn't been for Saul I'd never have had the opportunity. We are good for each other you know,' Tara told her mother archly, knowing exactly what she was thinking – that Saul called all the tunes and thought of no career but his own.

'Then what? Are you teaching at the Chetwind School again?'

'Yes. I've got regular weekly slots through January and February, coaching the orchestra. And we'll be giving a special concert for the children's charity event in March.'

'Mmm,' said Rachel.

'It's enough,' Tara told her calmly. 'Enough in terms of my time and my level of abilities. I was a good player and I lost that – and now I'm a good teacher.'

Yes, but if you weren't chained to Saul Xavier you'd be thinking about other things than teaching, thought Rachel. It grieved her to see Tara like this, so outwardly brave and cheerful but in truth fettered and isolated, her creativity stifled. Humouring an irascible tyrant couldn't really be much fun. Her friends were all his, her time was all his. Her fierce talent too. She had given him everything.

'Don't be worried about me,' Tara said gently. 'Truly there's no need.'

She placed her hand over Rachel's: her left hand where the fingertips were still numb, the middle three digits slightly wooden-looking.

They sat for a time in silence.

'I'll have to persuade Alessandra to go on this holiday,' Tara decided. 'He'll be so . . . hurt. Anyway it's not good for any kid to have all their own way.'

'Hah!' said Rachel, bursting into sudden laughter.

# CHAPTER 29

Saul was in the basement, which had been turned into a vast work space where he could carry out editing work on his film project.

Projection machines, cutting racks and all the paraphernalia of film editing were ranged around the walls. Saul perched on a high stool at the centre of the cutting table in front of the controls of the cutting machine which could be activated in three ways – forward, fast forward and reverse. Tara, acting as his assistant on his secretary's night off, carefully loaded up the raw 'takes' through a maze of rollers, ensuring that each was in perfect synchronization with the other.

When all was prepared Saul set the projection machine rolling.

Three images came up on three small screens positioned side by side just behind the table. They each showed Saul conducting, filmed from three different angles. Two cameras had picked up a hazy chequerboard of black-and-white-clothed orchestra members, whilst the third carried an arresting image of Saul starkly outlined against a backcloth of slender waving bows.

303

It struck Tara how completely he dominated the frame on all the screens, how he was the continual and vital focal point of the shot.

Saul watched the film intently, his eyes narrowed in assessing slits. Around every forty seconds he switched the machine into pause mode and then decided on the cuts he would make. Using a thick grease pencil he sketched marks on the film accordingly.

After they had been working for half an hour a considerable length of film had been loaded and assessed. Looking up at the screen Tara saw that the images on the screen had not changed much; Saul was still there in triplicate from three different angles.

Sitting behind the table Saul monitored the triple images of himself conducting. One hand glided with the music – Beethoven's Fourth Symphony – whilst the other made random stabs at the air in front of the screens.

'We don't want any gimmicks,' he muttered. 'The viewers mustn't be distracted from the music by pretty pictures. It's got to be the music that counts.'

Tara looked at the dominant, arresting images of Saul's granite features and wondered. Nevertheless there was no denying that the sound was fantastic. The new video disc, with its vivid visual image, carried advanced fidelity laser tracking which produced an uncannily brilliant and sparkling sound light years away from the old tapes.

Saul had always been fascinated with musical technology, and his life-long love-affair with recording – begun years before Tara had met him – had persisted unflaggingly and was now something of an obsession.

The products of his years of work and effort were

stacked around the walls of his ground floor study: hundreds of thick old 78rpm records, then a further army of LPs, firstly in mono and then in stereo sound. After that the compact laser disc had come along and he had started all over again.

Tara would sometimes take down one of the old vinyl records and place it on the turntable of Saul's cherished 1950s hi-fi equipment. Whilst listening she would survey the huge collection, marvelling at the sheer volume of work Saul had undertaken so as to constantly update his repertoire, re-recording as many of the great works as possible each time a new technological advance was made. The cycles of great symphonies, Tchaikovsky, Brahms, Bruckner, Beethoven, Mozart, Schubert, Mahler were all there, and countless other things besides.

His interest in video recordings was the newest development. He planned to begin yet again and put all his 'core' repertoire on film. 'The medium of the future,' he had told Tara decisively.

Wanting to have entire control of the operation, artistically and financially, he had formed his own film company and set about the task without delay. He had started with the cycle of nine Beethoven symphonies. 'Beethoven has been my bread and butter,' he liked to joke. 'But on video disc he will be the jam.'

Now, after three hours editing work, Tara stretched her stiff limbs and gave a small groan of fatigue.

'When is Alessandra coming home?' Saul asked suddenly, surprising her. She had been convinced that he was totally immersed in the music.

'In the next day or two.'

305

'You said that the last time I asked.'

'You've been away yourself since then.'

'That is because of my work. She should be here. This is her home.'

Tara felt her heart lurch.

'She must bring the horse back here,' he said. 'I'll be interested to see how she is progressing with it.'

'Saul, in the past it suited us for Alessandra to stay at Rachel and Donald's whenever we went away together. If she chooses to stay there off her own bat from time to time I think we have to respect her wishes.'

'She virtually lives there. She must come home. And the animal also.'

Tara agreed that he had a point. She wanted her daughter back too. But she knew this was basically an issue between Saul and Alessandra. She decided to point this out to him. Rather sharply. He listened attentively.

'So! It is all my fault. Very well, I shall take the responsibility to change things.'

Years ago she would have given him a playful squeeze and said something zippy like, 'Use a little tact Saul. She's not an orchestra!'

Tonight she considered a number of responses and said nothing.

Watching the film reel relentlessly on she said, 'Are you sure people will want to buy films of nothing but symphonies being played?'

'Absolutely convinced. They will be a resounding success. But if not, well – they are *there*. If in a hundred years people want to know about Saul Xavier, the films will tell them.'

306

Tara stared at him, a cold hand gripping her innards. He was talking about a memorial. For the first time she felt that the music had somehow slipped down the priority list of his mind.

This was a Saul driven by a new motive – the terrible fear of dissolving into obscurity.

She stepped up to him and put her arms around his chest. It was time to go to bed. At least she could give him a particle of comfort there.

He dropped a kiss on her hair. 'Will you stay with me and look at a new set of reels?'

She breathed in deeply, began loading again.

Her weariness was swept away by the unfamiliar and arresting images which swam onto the screen. This was the first of Saul's new project on the filming of opera. The one on screen was Mozart's *Magic Flute*. Tara had not seen this particular production which had been filmed in Munich only days before.

She watched in fascinated anticipation. At first. Then with a creeping sense of cold dismay she saw that the film was seriously flawed – over-literal and lack-lustre. The pace was slow. The image of the singers was ugly and disturbing, there were too many close-ups of contorted mouths singing and veins on necks swelling grotesquely. Operatic singing had always struck Tara as a very physical activity. Singers needed to be seen from the distance of the auditorium, not at point blank range.

The outdoor scenes were no better, containing too many lingering views of inky skies populated only by a grossly artificial moon.

And as for the dramatic scenes with dragons and

monsters they were ludicrous to the point of ridicule.

She glanced at Saul but he seemed perfectly satisfied. Maybe he even enjoyed seeing the singers portrayed as ridiculous.

Her blood felt icy. Was Saul losing his touch? That couldn't be. He was still comparatively young. In his full mature prime in fact.

She had seen him irate, arrogant, tetchy, despotic. But never weak or inept. It was unthinkable.

'Darling I'm absolutely whacked. I've just got to get some sleep,' she told him.

He turned abstractedly, gave a distracted wave. 'You go up. I won't be long.'

She almost ran from the room. At the top of the basement steps she paused, leaning against the door and breathing heavily whilst her heart thumped in her chest.

She recalled his telling her that he wanted to do a whole series: *Carmen*, *Rosenkavalier*, all four operas in Wagner's cycle *The Ring of Nibelung*.

Dear God!


Two weeks later Saul was directing a special rehearsal of *The Flying Dutchman* prior to the filming of a live performance that evening.

The idea of putting all the great operas on film had taken a grip on Saul with a ferocity of purpose not even Tara had seen him display before.

Anxious about his general well-being she had attempted to accompany him on all his work assignments where possible, acting as his personal assistant, confidante and unequivocal ally. They were constantly together, the inseparable couple. They made a handsome pair and the newspapers frequently carried photographs of them: the saturnine Xavier and his faithful consort Tara Silk, her dark eyes gazing up at him, her long hair swinging back from her face in a thick luxurious sweep.

Sitting in the front row of the stalls half listening to Saul unleashing his most bitter sarcasm on the hapless wind section of the orchestra, Tara was distracted by thoughts of their daughter, wondering what she was doing at this moment. Alessandra had evaded the issue about bringing Tosca home with the usual protests about events at the prestigious riding centre just down the road from her grandmother's cottage.

'Darling, have you given up on us?' Tara had asked playfully when she last telephoned.

'Of course I haven't. The shows will be over soon. After the weekend. And anyway Tosca needs a rest. Daddy can come and fetch us.'

'Yes. Right. Or I'll come if he's busy.'

'He *never* comes!'

Tara laughed. 'Well . . .'

'Why can't he have days off like other people? Or maybe turn his brain down a few notches so he's on the wavelength of lowly earth creatures like me!'

'Alessandra!'

'He's like someone possessed. Sometimes I think the music will kill him.'

'Alessandra! Stop it!'

'Oh – bloody hell!'

'Bloody hell back!'

The phone had crashed down.

Tara knew that she was digging herself into a dangerous hole, lavishing time and care on the father at the expense of her daughter. And deep in her heart she also knew the reason; that it was necessary to be more and more with Saul in order that the gap of outlook and philosophy yawning between them did not widen into an unbridgeable gulf.

She pulled her attention back to the rehearsal. The atmosphere was becoming ever more tense. Saul seemed unable to stand back and allow the players and singers the free rein they fully deserved. After all they had been performing the opera regularly twice weekly for some time now. All that was going to happen tonight was that the cameras would run. It was a technical exercise surely, not an interpretative one.

She pressed her fingers on the bridge of her nose as Saul took issue with the young soprano singing the role of Senta, the girl who falls for the Dutchman. It was some minor artistic point. The singer, unnerved and edgy, flashed retorts back at him. Anger crackled from the stage.

Saul laid down his baton and vaulted up onto the boards. The cast watched him with wary and hostile eyes: the great Xavier, ambassador of music, a priest of his profession – a dictator with an ego the size of Canary Wharf and a heart of stone.

Sweat prickled in Tara's palms. She watched Saul cradle the girl's neck with his fingers, cringed as he gave her a playful yet vicious pinch. Catching her breath she waited for the inevitable exit of the victim in tears.

And then astonishingly Saul had leapt down from the stage, picked up his jacket and with an unmistakable gesture of farewell was striding away down the auditorium and through the rear exit doors.

A hush fell on the auditorium. Everyone was temporarily frozen.

The leader of the orchestra looked at Tara with mingled exasperation and mute appeal.

She breathed in deeply. 'I'm sorry,' she said automatically.

The cast began to shift about, a murmuring started.

The leader spoke softly to her from the orchestra pit. 'You take over Tara. We can't afford to waste time.'

The cast partially heard, instantly realized the sense in the suggestion.

José Moll, playing the Dutchman, stepped forward and called to her. 'We need to get this thing turned round,' he said. 'Good feelings manufactured. Time's going on. And that's money in this day and age. Help us in our hour of need Tara!'

Tara stood up. 'Fair enough.'

She knew the opera's score inside out. She knew the stage play inside out. She adored the music. She had conducted countless music school and youth orchestras.

So be it! she thought grimly, taking her place in the pit and retrieving Saul's baton.


Half an hour before the performance the cameras were loaded up, the orchestra present, the audience arriving. But Saul was nowhere to be found.

Tara, deadly calm with shock and concern as to his safety and whereabouts, was still making telephone calls.

She had been sure he would have gone to make his peace with Alessandra but Rachel had seen no sign of him.

'Alessandra's upstairs doing her homework for once! So if he does turn up she'll be here safe and sound.'

'Don't let her know there's a problem. There's no need to worry her unnecessarily.'

'Right. And don't *you* worry my sweet. Conductors are an indestructible breed.'

Feeling sick with anxiety Tara put in a further call to Roland Grant. It was the fourth or fifth time she had done so in the last few hours.

'Any news?' she asked desperately.

'Nothing.'

'I can't believe it, he never misses an engagement.'

'He's been driving in the fast lane for an awful long time. Maybe he just needs a break. He'll be fine Tara. You know Saul.'

A long shuddering sigh. 'Yes.'

'And you can handle the performance tonight with no problem at all.'

'You haven't found anyone else?'

'No. And I have to confess that I didn't try too hard. This is quite definitely your baby. Not only can you do it – you've earned it.'

'I just hope that is what *he* will think when he finds out.'

The audience had assembled, the members of the orchestra were taking their places. The camera crew were in place, their director outwardly calm and relaxed in jeans and T-shirt.

Tara sat in her dressing room taking a last-minute look at the score.

It was five minutes to curtain up. She could hear a distant medley of trills and scales, the magical sound of the orchestra warming up: mournful notes from the oboes, flitting cadenzas from the violins, deep-throated rasps from the double basses. A classic jumble of musical anticipation. Her spine tingled.

She had especially requested that there would be no announcement at the last moment of her standing in for Saul, but rather that written notification should be placed in prominent positions in the foyer so that those who wished could leave and no one would feel cheated.

Two minutes to go. Anticipation mounted in the front of the house. Behind the curtain tension sizzled.

Tara recalled the night in Vienna at the Golden Hall. It seemed like another life. Tonight there was no nervousness about demonstrating brilliance. Simply a job to be done – and done well. And then, please God, a reunion with Saul.

Wearing the simple black dress that had been hurriedly found for her in the costume section, she threaded her way through the crowded pit and to the podium.

The audience were hushed. They had not instantly registered her presence. She was slight, modest, smiling. Not yet a heroic figure.

The orchestra welcomed her warmly with a ripple of applause and a gentle stamping of feet. The audience pricked up its ears, craned forward and then broke out into a delighted storm of applause.

Tara turned briefly to acknowledge them. She was more

interested in checking that the camera crew were ready, that the orchestra was unified and steady.

Turning back to face the stage she raised her hands and gave a barely perceptible nod.

# CHAPTER 30

Detached and self-possessed Saul made his way to Georgiana's apartment in Mayfair.

Focusing on nothing more complex than placing one foot in front of the other he arrived at the glass and brass entrance to her block. As he raised his hand to the row of entry buzzers the beginning of his journey and the deserted podium in the orchestra pit flashed momentarily across his mind. I shall get my come-uppance later, he thought with a grim smile. But much later.

A disembodied voice came metallically through the entry phone in answer to his terse announcement.

'Saul! At this time?'

'Yes. Saul.'

There was a low buzz. 'Come up.'

The smoke-tinted outer glass door swung silently open at a touch from his finger and he stepped through into an oak and marble foyer. Banks of fresh flowers captured in wire and polished greenery lined the walls.

In Georgiana's lavishly decorated drawing room preparations were in hand for some imminent entertaining. Tables bearing small savoury delicacies were dotted around, and in the adjoining dining room her Italian manservant, Tullio, could be seen gliding about with trays of tall champagne flutes.

Georgiana kissed Saul on the cheek. 'I was expecting you tomorrow. It's Tuesday today. Are you all right Saul?'

He sat down on one of her vast, plump sofas and stretched out his long legs. 'I'm sorry to interfere with your schedule. I know Wednesday is my designated calling day. What time are your guests arriving?'

'Not until six. It doesn't matter anyway. Why not stay on?'

'I think not.' He gave a dry smile.

'It wouldn't do to be seen visiting your wife in secret?' she suggested archly.

'Quite.' Tara had no idea about his regular visits to Georgiana which had been going on for the past five years. He never spoke her name to Tara and in turn Tara and Alessandra were barred subjects when he was with his wife. He had no idea what Tara's feelings about Georgiana were these days. The kidnapping incident had receded into the past, but for all he knew she might still retain some of the shock and revulsion she had demonstrated at the time. Whatever was the case he did not think it helpful for her to know.

Georgiana's black toy poodle emerged from the kitchen and paddled its twiggy paws against Saul's leg. He bent and gave it a single pat. Sensing that it was to be ignored the dog went into a corner of the room.

Watching Georgiana's face Saul judged that she was a happier woman now than she had ever been. Now in her late forties Georgiana had acquired a sleek look of undented self-assurance. She was a woman of means. She was still beautiful: hair still long and blonde, caught at the back with a velvet bow, figure still slender, encased in a designer creation of peacock blue silk. In addition to all of that she had the potential of the older woman to be unnervingly intimidating if she chose.

And she was still Mrs Saul Xavier. He knew she would not have survived if he had robbed her of that.

Georgiana passed her days amusing herself with an endless round of socializing: giving and attending parties, frequenting art galleries, and in recent years becoming very accomplished at playing bridge.

Although she lived alone there was the little dog to keep her company. And more important a succession of hired hands. Tullio, her latest, with his showy dark good looks and his sensitivity to her every wish and command, was obviously the perfect servant and household companion.

In Saul's eyes, the combination of Dr Daneman's care together with occasional visits to an exclusive clinic in the north of England, had restored Georgiana to the woman she had been prior to the breakdown of their marriage. Saul presumed that she lived a life of dainty celibacy and he recognized that there were many who would describe her as an empty shell. But at least she was functioning well on a daily basis. He need not reproach himself with having destroyed her.

'I've got some splendid 1976 Bollinger,' Georgiana said. 'Tullio will open it.'

Commandments were issued.

'Alfreda and I have booked a cruise,' Georgiana told him, conscious of a growing silence. 'The Caribbean.'

'I hope you checked on the climate at this time of year. It can be terribly wet.'

'Of course we checked. And *you* could do with a holiday. It's long overdue.'

'I'm a workaholic – one of a dying breed,' Saul announced abruptly, staring into his glass of leaping bubbles.

'You are my darling. The ones coming along now are just pale imitations.'

'Monkeys dancing to the organ grinder's tune,' Saul commented. 'Hedging their bets between the incompetents on the orchestras' managing boards, kow-towing to all the puffed-up performing prima donnas.'

'Absolutely,' Georgiana agreed, never considering for a moment that his view might be distorted or that he might simply be wrong.

'Idiots, the lot of them,' he growled. 'I've just about had enough.' Anger smouldered within him when he considered the instrumentalists who demanded ever more power in decisions about programming and player selection, singers who thought they knew best how to interpret the great operatic roles. And that was before one started doing battle with the administrators!

Even his daughter chose not to listen to him. Preferred to direct her attention up a horse's nose.

'I walked out of the "Dutchman" rehearsal this afternoon,' he said casually. 'And I don't think I'll go back. They can manage without me.'

Georgiana stared at him in horror. 'Impossible!'

He pressed his lips together. 'They'll struggle through.'

'But how . . . who?'

'Tara will probably take over.' He gave a tight, complex smile. 'She will probably do quite well.' After all, I've set everything up, he thought. All she need do is activate the starter button. He gave a wistful smile, his mind running back through the years, recalling the young Tara, his plump pixie, his rebellious elf. And now she was a slim, poised and elegant woman in her thirties, making her way very nicely in the world of music. It was hard for a woman in the conducting field, but she would make a strong mark, he was sure of it.

Georgiana was horrified. It was not so much the sound of Tara's name on Saul's lips – although that was bad enough. It was the idea of a mere slip of a young woman usurping Saul's role. For Georgiana Saul was a true emperor of music. A god.

Having never earned a penny in her life, and relied always on the proceeds of wealth generated by men, Georgiana belonged to a sisterhood of women who would defend the basic superiority of the male to the death.

'Oh what does it matter?' Saul exclaimed, suddenly deeply weary. What did *anything* matter?

'She may muddle through,' Georgiana protested. 'But she will never be even mentioned in the same breath as you by true connoisseurs of music. You are the Maestro. The king of all maestros,' she concluded grandly.

Saul laughed. 'Thank you for that. But I am afraid yours may be a lone voice in making such proclamations!'

He stood up in preparation for leaving. In the mirror-walled lobby an infinity of Georgiana's faces stared into an infinity of his. Looking down at the flesh and blood woman he wondered how long it would be before her

319

beauty melted away. She was quite remarkably youthful, her skin seemingly untouched by the unseen finger of time which could sketch out its lines with such cruelty.

He bent down and kissed her lightly on her mouth, interested to note that the rosy, firmly plump lips aroused no emotion whatever.

He walked through the London streets, meandering and desultory, detached from the pressures of the present. He found that his earlier anger had abated. Some tight cord within had stretched and broken. He had a sense that his perspectives on the outer world, his ability to make a clear analysis of reality, were all slightly awry. He felt himself to be a spectator looking down from a height; the view was tilted and misty. A frightening sensation of empty resignation gripped him.

He had said to Georgiana that he was one of a dying breed. So! Maybe that was something to be glad about. He often felt that he had no wish to be part of the new order, that the days of his golden glory were gone.

Well, let them go, he told himself. Simply savour what has been. It was hard, however, not to indulge in wistful recall of the early days of his youthful brilliance. He was doing it more and more, remembering the young Saul who had been not only talented but gloriously impetuous. At twenty-five, invited to conduct the Czech Philharmonic in Prague, he had walked out onto the platform having just discovered that the solo pianist was seized with a migraine and was unable to move from the dressing room. Without turning a hair he had sat down at the piano and played Prokofiev's phenomenally difficult third concerto whilst directing the orchestra from the keyboard.

It had been a sensational experience. Orgasmic. It had driven him on to even greater feats. A flame leapt in him at the recollection.

He thought of Tara in her thirties, ready for the world to roll itself out at her feet. Whereas he was a man over halfway through his life, existing in a world all too well explored. Had the hill been crested, he wondered?

He recognized that much had been achieved. But for what? All that struggle and energy and effort. Expending. Giving. What had it all been for?

He knew that such grossly self-pitying thoughts were to be stamped on hard.

Tullio aimed a mainly harmless kick at the little poodle before bending to wipe up the shiny pool of urine under the dining room table.

The dog made a menacing gargle in its throat and nipped at the aggressor's Gucci loafers, succeeding in penetrating the soft leather.

'Tullio, don't tease him,' Georgiana said.

'You should house-train him,' Tullio told her, pulling his thick black brows together and looking stern. An expression he knew she liked. 'And see, he's made a little prick in my shoe.'

'I shall buy you another pair,' Georgiana told him, making her lips pout and twitch. Something which she knew *he* liked.

Tullio sulked for a moment or two.

The entry phone buzzed.

Georgiana glanced with meaning at her servant.

He picked up the receiver, placed his hand over the

mouthpiece. Employer and employee stared hard at each other.

'Will you be wanting me later?' Tullio asked Georgiana, his brown eyes kindling.

Georgiana turned her head slightly, giving the young man a view of her creamy white neck, smooth and baby-soft from years of massage and pampering. She tilted a glance of girlish coquetry at Tullio. And then she arranged her features into cool severity. 'My guests are waiting to be let in,' she said to the manservant, pointing an accusing finger at the receiver, reminding him of the task to be done. Of his position as a hired hand.

Through the evening Georgiana and Tullio engaged in a tantalizing game of concealed flirtation. Nothing more than the occasional connecting glance, the split-second touch of fingers as a glass was offered and taken. But with each tiny, secret connection was an accompanying sizzle of sensation, the brief fizz of short-circuited electricity.

When the guests had left, Tullio stacked all the glasses, plates, dishes and ash-trays on a tray and took them into the kitchen. He folded down the legs of the green baize card table and put it in the store cupboard in the hallway. Methodically he loaded the dishwasher, placed left over food in sealed containers in the refrigerator and opened up windows to let out the smell of stale cigarette smoke.

When all his tasks were finally completed, he combed his hair, splashed on a little cologne and knocked softly at Georgiana's bedroom door.

'Come.'

She was sitting at the dressing table. Tranquil, serene. Tullio saw that the woman gazing back at her from the mirror had the expression of a woman very pleased with what she saw.

He went to stand behind her. Placed his slim, tanned fingers on the slippery crêpe-de-chine draped and tied around her. He felt her bones beneath, jagged and brittle.

Tullio moved his fingers across the fabric, sliding it away from the stem of her neck, revealing shoulders, then long arms. In the mirror he saw her girlish, bud-like breasts revealed, white like a pearl with delicate rosy nipples – already pleasingly erect.

Tullio, at twenty, found no difficulty in becoming erect himself at the sight of beautiful female nakedness. Even if that nakedness was well in excess of forty years old.

He knelt, laying his cheek against Georgiana's marble-like back, passing his arms around her. As his hands began to creep upwards from her waist, he took the precaution of asking very politely, 'Is this permitted tonight?'

In the mirror he saw his fingers approach the faint curve under her breast.

She breathed in deeply.

Instantly Tullio paused. He knew her to be as easily alarmed as a deer. Even now. When he had penetrated her on countless occasions.

He must proceed each time with caution. Woo her afresh. Never give the impression of presuming, of taking her for granted. Always assume a reverential gratefulness for whatever gift was to be bestowed.

It did not irk Tullio to do this. It was an amusing entertainment for him, an intriguing diversion. Learning how to control one's fellow human beings was endlessly fascinating.

And when he had eventually brought her to the slippery point of breathless begging, then he gained his own satisfaction in the easiest and swiftest way imaginable.

Mrs Xavier preferred a simple straightforward performance, nothing fancy. Man on top. Conventional penetration. The minimum of thrusts. He got his satisfaction with very little effort.

And as if that were not enough there were all the other benefits which accrued.

Rich older women tended to show their appreciation in the most gratifying ways. Gifts of hand-tailored suits, leather jackets, silk shirts. He had already had those in abundance. Bonuses on his monthly salary.

He judged that if he played his cards right there could be richer pickings still. Which was why he had got into the habit of scanning the Sunday newspaper columns for the perfect classic car to suit his taste.

He glanced into the mirror and saw that Georgiana's eyes were closed. He permitted his fingers to stray onto a nipple. Georgiana gave a little groan – her consent to allow proceedings to develop.

Tullio lifted her from her stool and laid her on the bed.

As he covered her, and the bones of her greyhound-slender body stabbed into his muscle-toned bulk, he thought of his little Rhona, a young Scottish nurse who comforted him on his nights off. Rhona's bones were hidden in a gorgeous cushion of spongy flesh and, being a medical worker, she had no squeamishness about the performing of certain services a lusty young man found utterly enchanting.

Georgiana tilted her head back. She began to breathe

faster. Dainty, shallow gasps. Nearly, nearly there, she whispered to herself. Sometimes it happened. Sometimes not. Tullio should really have learned by now how to arrange things so it happened for her every time.

Nevertheless it pleased her to hear the groans announcing his own satisfaction. To know that she was still supremely lovely and desirable.

She lay still and passive beneath him, reflecting on the curious way in which she had discovered a renewed curiosity in sex at this stage of her life. She had tried many times to pin-point the beginning of this renaissance of interest and motivation. But with no success.

She had tried to relive some of the experiences at exclusive and luxurious clinics in the heart of the English countryside. Attempted to call up the details of the treatments she had been offered, thinking that surely these must be in some way connected. But no matter how hard she prodded her mind to function, she could remember nothing of significance. There had been constant and interminable group discussions on the issue of sex. Oh yes, she could remember all those. She was sure they hadn't helped a jot, and quite frankly they had bored her stiff.

No, the talk sessions were not the spring that had activated her renewal. There was no key to be found there.

Georgiana had a strange notion of there having been some moment of sudden healing. A puff of smoke, a flash of light, some magical process that had conjured up the realization that even she, the terrified Georgiana, could let a man into the temple of her body. And take pleasure from doing so.

When she tried to uncover the mystery, her mind would dig deep into itself, curling its tail around buried sensations. Almost, almost, almost. But the heart of the mystery had never yielded up its secrets.

Tonight, as Tullio rolled from her to creep respectfully back to his own room, she found herself thinking of Saul. She recalled that sense of invasion that had used to terrify her during the latter years of her marriage.

But how would it be now? Sex – with Saul?

There was a stab of intense excitement.

To make love with Saul? To have him enslaved to her beauty. In her power as he had been, just a little, just for a while, at the beginning of their marriage.

Then as swiftly as it had surged up, the excitement muted. Anxiety prickled.

Georgiana frowned. Bewildered. Suddenly uneasy. As the night progressed to that cold empty point when a woman on her own can feel most cruelly alone she saw herself being swept remorselessly on into the future like a little particle of dust. Insignificant. No one to care for her. Her father dead. Her mother ageing. Saul no more than a visitor. Saul virtually gone.

Saul gone, she whispered to herself. Forever?

Georgiana was suddenly convinced of the impossibility of moving forward into the future alone.

She needed guidance. The ear of someone who would listen, and share and sympathize. Someone with the capacity to unravel the twisted threads of her doubts and hopes and lay out the way ahead.

Her mind clicked down old pathways, made a series of connections. A fresh thought presented itself. And then a decision. Again there was a tremor of excitement.

She smiled to herself in the darkness.

Beyond in the hallway she heard Tullio walking with the stealth of a cat through to the kitchen. He would be after the remains of the uncorked champagne.

Well, he was welcome to it. He'd earned it. And who else would drink flat Bollinger?

TullIo was quite an agreeable boy all in all. He was not Georgiana's first young lover. She rather fancied, however, that he might.be the last.


Saul waited at the stage door, standing back in the shadows so that he would be hidden. He had no wish to suffer the annoyance of being recognized, of having to withstand the inevitable surprise and concern that would be forthcoming.

Eventually Tara appeared. To his utter relief she was alone. She walked forward, oblivious of his presence, her firm steady steps ringing in sharp rhythm.

He moved towards her.

When she saw him an expression of huge relief came over her face, like that of a mother whose wayward child has run off and got lost, and now is found.

'Saul!' she said. 'Oh God! Thank heaven!'

He placed his arm around her shoulder and allowed his fingers to press and caress the flesh encasing her delicate bones.

'So! How was your evening little maestro?'

# CHAPTER 31

Saul had booked a ski lodge perched high in the hills overlooking the Grundlsee lake east of Salzburg. An amphitheatre of mountains protected the lake, deep and breathtakingly blue under a cloudless daytime sky. At night the sun dropped behind the stony walls of the hills, turning the lake to the shade of blood as it sank into its own vast dying glow.

In the mornings the alpine slopes dazzled, white and crusty, zigzagged all over with the network of grey tracks marking the ski runs.

The lodge was a long low wooden chalet, built on a flat shelf of ground and girdled all round with a wide railed terrace which caught every minute of the sunshine.

Tara would stand out on the terrace in the mornings, breathing in deeply and looking down through the empty air to the still deep lake. The air was sharp and bright. It smelled of pine and cold.

Inside the chalet all was warmth and comfort. Central heating, log fires, TV, radio, answerphone, fax machine.

It was a situation that could well be described as idyllic. Something Tara wished she could get across to Alessandra who, when not distracted with the immediate excitement of being perched on skis, shambled around the chalet, wearing the look of one who is suffering greatly. And in silence.

Saul had not fulfilled her prophecy of abandoning her in order to indulge his own skiing prowess. He was behaving impeccably.

He had taken her off each morning to rendezvous with her instructor and had stayed around to observe and encourage.

Tara felt that he was pulling out all the stops to play the role of the good and interested father. But perhaps the appearance of trying too hard defeated its own ends. Perhaps Alessandra was uneasy to be the focus of such paternal attention. Or perhaps Alessandra was merely aching with longing for Tosca.

Whatever undercurrents were at work Tara had the sense of living with a barrel of unexploded gunpowder.

She had made no attempt to ski herself, having long ago decided that the sport was much too cold, wet and hazardous for her liking. The days passed pleasantly enough sipping coffee at the wickedly expensive café at the summit of the ski lift and catching up on her reading.

Five days into the holiday, just as she was dressing in preparation for her morning patrol of the terrace to view the sunrise, she was interrupted by the trill of the telephone bell. It was seven-thirty in the morning. And the caller was Roland Grant.

'Are you sitting down?' he asked. 'Because if not I think you should. Are you on your own?'

'Yes. And yes. Roland you're making me very jittery.'

'The Golden Gramophone Award was announced late last night. They've chosen your video disc of *The Flying Dutchman*.'

'Oh,' said Tara.

'That is not the expected response,' Roland observed with dry humour.

'It's the old dilemma of wondering whether to laugh or cry.'

'Why should you cry? It's news to make any normal mortal shout for joy.'

She made a brief low noise in her throat.

'Is Saul about?' Roland asked with sudden urgency. 'Just say yes or no.'

Tara held the receiver from her ear. She could hear the hum of the shower heater, the hiss of hot water. 'Yes. But I can still talk!'

'Is that the problem for you? Saul, what he'll think? How he'll react?'

'Of course it is!'

'You're worried he'll feel his nose put out of joint. Oh, come on Tara.'

'Come on Roland! That video was his baby. Until I snatched it from his arms.'

'Until he walked out on it and handed it to your safe-keeping.'

'Things can sound beautifully simple when you phrase them like that.'

'Tara, Saul will do nothing but applaud your achievement. And in any case, you had a lot to do with the preparation and directing of this performance. Don't put yourself down.'

'No, no. Perish the thought.' She laughed out loud now.

'The important thing is that in the end you were the one who directed the final rehearsal and conducted the performance. You brought everything together and made it hum. Made it into a huge success.'

'Thank you.' Tara smiled into the mouthpiece. An acerbic and ironic grin. Tara knew all about Roland when he got the bit between his teeth.

'Saul will get full credit for the part he played,' Grant insisted. 'But it's your award. Yours only.'

Oh God! Tara thought.

'Saul's too big a man to cast a shadow over this,' Roland concluded.

'Yes, of course you're right.' Tara thought it wise not to say anything directly to Roland about her growing anxiety on Saul's account. Of how brittle he seemed, how his mood was occasionally so dark she felt she could no longer reach him at all.

Those things were deeply private. And if they turned out to be more than a passing phase, Roland would soon sniff them out for himself.

'I'm simply not used to being in the spotlight,' Tara said eventually, hoping that would satisfy Roland.

There was a pause. 'Ah well! That's something I'm hoping we shall be able to put right at long last.'

Tara replaced the receiver, heartily glad that Saul had not been around when this particular call came through. The news of the award had shaken her. Delighted, shocked, alarmed.

Her mind kept swerving back to Saul's reaction. She had no doubt that outwardly he would display all the

331

enthusiasm and also warm congratulations appropriate to her achievement.

But how would he feel in his heart? Would he judge himself to have been beaten at his own game by his young, inexperienced mistress? Is that how he would view it? And if so how would he bear it? Might he even end up hating her?

She let out a sigh of dismay. She needed to get out of the chalet for a while, have some time on her own to explore her feelings further. There was no question of facing Saul before she had had time to think.

In the breakfast kitchen she scribbled a hasty note and propped it up against the coffee pot on the breakfast table.

'*To my two dear ones –*

*I've gone for a pre-breakfast walk. Carry on without me. See you soon. Love, love, love . . .*'

She walked out of the north-facing door of the chalet, through the car parking space and out onto the cleared and heavily salted lane which wound down the mountainside into the village below.

The morning was ripe with the sound of cheery, hopeful birdsong. A luminous white haze hung over the lake like a giant cover. In an hour it would have cleared away completely and the sun would burnish the water to a clanging copper brilliance.

Tara breathed in deeply, mindful that the majority of the rest of the world's creatures were not so privileged as she to be a spectator of all this wonder.

But even this reflection did not quell the drone of anxiety within her.

She stamped on, her boots making a ripe creaking sound

in the powdery snow. She clasped her hands behind her, thrust her head down as she pondered. Pictures paraded in the portrait gallery of her mind: Tara Silk in the glare of the spotlight and glory. Running lightly onto a platform amidst a blaze of lights in order to receive a glittering trophy. Saul Xavier in the shadowy background, applauding her quietly, just one anonymous figure in the midst of an admiring audience. Saul's name written in small letters at the back of the video display sleeve, just one more name swelling the credits list.

Was that how it would be?

After an hour's tramping in the snow, she was still not sure what her feelings were about Roland's news. She made her way slowly back to the chalet, feeling no sense of hurry. Saul and Alessandra would already have left for the morning's skiing. There would be no need for any direct confrontations until she met up with Saul at lunchtime.

She stamped the snow from her boots at the rear entrance to the chalet then wandered onto the wooden veranda to look down at the lake. The mountains rose in the background like rows of clenched white knuckles. Their snowy tips flashed platinum bright in the sunlight and in the basin of the valley the lake glistened blue-green shot through with gold.

Tara was surprised to see Alessandra sprawled on a chair at the far end of the terrace. Completely ignoring the exquisite panorama rolled out before her, Alessandra was engrossed in the latest issue of *Horse and Pony* magazine. Her long blonde hair slid forward over her face and from time to time she tossed it back with an impatient thrust of her head, curiously reminiscent of Tosca.

'I thought you'd be up on the slopes with Daddy by this time,' Tara commented surprised.

'So did I.' Alessandra did not look up; the equine head tossing continued.

'So why aren't you?'

'He's got better things to do.'

'Yes?' Tara struggled to keep calm.

'He's gone into Salzburg.' Alessandra's lips were tight. She flicked over a page of the magazine and assumed an expression of supreme detachment and disdain.

There was a lengthy silence.

'Well, do you know why?' Tara asked.

'Yes.'

Another silence. Dear God in heaven, was I like this too in my adolescent days Tara wondered, knowing that the answer was sadly yes.

'Alessandra! Just tell me. Please. In plain and simple language.'

'Something terribly, overwhelmingly important has come up.' Raw bitterness threatened to break through the studied indifference.

'Such as?'

'The opportunity to conduct one of the *world's greatest orchestras*.' The mimicry of Saul's detached, measured tones were breathtakingly accurate.

'The Vienna Phil?'

'Something like that. Or was it the Berlin lot?' Alessandra shrugged. 'I can't see why he's so bothered. He's had his evil way with both of them millions of times before.'

Tara could feel her daughter's anger, frustration and deep hurt throbbing in the air around her.

'Why do they need Daddy?' Tara enquired calmly, playing for time and sticking to practicalities whilst she considered how to tackle this delicate situation.

'The reigning baton-waving tyrant had a stroke in the night. Or was it a nervous breakdown? Something of that sort. The kind of thing that stops people conducting orchestras. Daddy heard about it on the early morning news. He was on the telephone like a shot, offering to gallop to the rescue.'

'Blast!' fumed Tara. 'I wanted him to have a proper rest on this holiday.'

Alessandra looked up. Eyes flashing with fire, glinting with the prickle of tears. 'Hope springs eternal,' she mocked.

The two of them contemplated their thoughts for a while.

'He wanted me to go with him. Breathe in the hallowed atmosphere. Watch him in action. Listen, mark and learn,' Alessandra commented.

Tara could imagine.

'Well, I suppose you have to look at it from his point of view,' Alessandra continued. 'You stood in when he stormed out of the Dutchman rehearsal. Anything you can do he can do better!' This experimentation with sarcasm was still quite new, but Alessandra was going to be terribly good at it once she got into her stride.

'Did you overhear my conversation with Roland this morning?' Tara demanded sharply.

'Yes. I picked up the extension in case it was Grandma with news from home.'

'Did Daddy hear?'

'No. And I didn't breathe a word.'

'Did you and Daddy have a row?'

'No. He went off to his orchestra and I stayed here. Perfectly OK arrangement.' Alessandra rattled the pages of her magazine.

Tara sank down on a chair beside her daughter, stretched out her legs, closed her eyes and released a long despairing sigh.

'And by the way, congratulations Mummy,' Alessandra said warmly. 'I'm really proud of you.'

Tara felt her daughter's long strong fingers clasp her own limp hand and press it warmly. She roused herself.

As she sat up, her eyes connected with the open notebook at Alessandra's feet. Next to the beautiful sketch of a horse's head was a carefully drawn chart. A brief diary, representing the duration of the Xaviers' stay here in Grundlsee. Chunks of it were coloured in red; the days that had already passed. Alessandra was crossing off the hours and days, counting the minutes until she could return home.

'Oh darling!' Tara picked up the little book and stared at it in dismay.

'I only came because he seemed to want it so much. I could have been in the riding centre's spring show. And now he's buggered off to do his own thing.'

Alessandra sniffed, suddenly childlike and deeply vulnerable. 'He's not bothered about spending time with me at all,' she exploded.

'That's not true!'

'Nothing can compete with the bloody music and all that buzz he gets from being King Kong in the concert hall.'

Tara gazed at her shocked, then suddenly she could not help bursting into laughter.

Alessandra sprang up and flung herself into Tara's opened arms. 'Mummy I do love him. I do. But he's so difficult. So . . . *far away*.'

Tara arranged for Alessandra to go up onto the slopes with the American family who were staying in a nearby ski lodge. She then swiftly changed her clothes, brushed her hair, jumped into the Range Rover Saul had hired for her use and roared off into Salzburg. It was a drive which normally took an hour and a half. But even with the snow chains, on this particular morning, she made it in just under eighty minutes.

Driving through the streets to the Grosse Festspielhaus it struck her with particular force what a curiously unattractive town Salzburg was. Small, parochial, a shameless prostitute for tourists, it nestled like a squat grey pebble in the bowl of the mountains. Songs from *The Sound of Music*, jostling with fragments from Mozart's piano concertos, oozed from a line of loudspeakers on the bridge over the river. And in the cafés near Mozart's birthplace one had the dubious privilege of consuming coffee and a cake at a price which would buy a full meal in Vienna.

Tara recalled that the young Mozart had hated the town in the 1770s. She guessed he would smile to see his judgement vindicated if he returned to see it now.

Or maybe she was simply seeing things through jaundiced eyes.

She went straight through to the auditorium of the

337

Festspielhaus and found Saul in the orchestra pit with a handful of players and some anxious looking administrators. Behind them a vast and exotic stage set depicting mountains of gold stretched up into the darkness of the roof arch.

Placing her hand on the long curved railing which separated the pit from the audience Tara called out Saul's name. Just once.

Heads turned towards her. She beamed Saul a steely look that not even he could resist. He turned from his colleagues and came to stand beside her. She took his arm and guided him away from the curious band of watchful spectators who immediately turned back tactfully to their previous deliberations.

'Your daughter needs you,' Tara told him crisply.

His grey eyes were as hard and shiny as weapons. 'And *I* need this.'

Even after all her years with Saul, Tara still found herself staggered by the diamond-hard purity of his self-will. Or was it self-preservation?

'Letting her down like this will drive her away from you,' she told him.

He raised his eyebrows. 'Then our relationship is of little worth if it can be damaged so easily.'

'For Christ's sake Saul. She's thirteen. She adores you. But you have to bend a little.'

'She has her own life. And I'm not "letting her down". She and I discussed this. She was very firm that I should step in here if they needed me. She said she was not a baby who needed her father to be a nursemaid.'

'God Almighty! She was *heartbroken!*'

'No.'

'She was just putting a brave face on things because she knew you would do what you wanted anyway.' Tara could feel herself flailing about in desperation.

Saul shook his head. 'You are always so dramatic about things Tara. It does no good.' He paused, staring down at her. Utterly sure. 'Alessandra and I understand one another.'

Tara felt her mouth drop open. The progress of this conversation was entirely unexpected. Baffling.

'I shall be here rehearsing all day and then for the performance this evening. After that we shall all be together again.'

'But that is not the point Saul,' she protested, knowing that she had already lost the battle.

His face was stripped of all emotion. Chilling.

'I have two tickets for tonight's performance. Premier seats. *Das Rheingold*. One of the most thrilling operas in the repertoire. Alessandra will love it.' He held out the long thin slips. 'I hope you will both come,' he said in formal, courteous tones.

Tara took his offering. She burned to find some words, make some kind of gesture that would bring her back into living contact with him. She felt that it would give her satisfaction to strike him. To slam the back of her hand across his aristocratic features and leave wounding imprints on the flawless olive skin.

Without warning he leaned down and kissed her mouth very tenderly. An incredible shiver of feeling shot through every vein of her body.

'One more thing,' she said sharply, reclaiming his

attention as he turned back to the small group anxiously waiting for him. '*The Flying Dutchman* disc has picked up the Golden Gramophone award. Roland telephoned me this morning.'

He swung back. His features registered a restrained mixture of speculation and amusement. 'Well, well. Your slender shoulders are going to have to brace themselves for the heavy burden of honours that will be heaped upon them. Congratulations, Tara.' He stared at her for a long moment, then smiled. 'So!' he murmured softly.

Tara was pleased to find Alessandra in a surprisingly happy frame of mind after her day on the slopes. The American family had been very welcoming. The children had been joky and good fun and the parents not intimidatingly proficient at skiing like her own father. They also had several hundred acres of Texan land and a racing stud back home. Alessandra had been told she was welcome to visit whenever she liked. In fact they were insisting she should go in the summer.

Alessandra settled her mother on the sofa and poured her a large glass of white wine.

'Don't look so tragic,' she told Tara.

'Is it that bad?'

'No, not really. You do look a bit zapped though. Have you told Daddy about the Grammy Award yet?'

'Yes.'

'And?'

'He was very pleased.'

Alessandra flopped down on the floor and tickled Tara's feet. 'Of course he was. Honestly Mummy, it's absolutely fantastic news. I told everyone about it. They were simply knocked out.'

Tara stroked Alessandra's hair. How her mood had changed. Lightened and softened. One day without the watchful challenge of her father. Was that what had done the trick? Her heart dropped like a stone in her chest.

'You know Mummy it's the best thing that could have happened for you. It's about time you did something for yourself!' Having been taciturn and moody for days Alessandra now seemed unstoppable.

'I feel Daddy ought to share the prize,' said Tara. 'The project was his original idea. He did all the planning and the spade work.'

'Don't forget that you were there digging away with him. As usual. Grandma was forever worrying about how hard you were working. Slaving in the shadows whilst he stood under the spotlight.'

'Really? The cheek of it. You two, chewing me over.'

'Donald joined in. We all agreed.'

Tara sighed. Took a huge gulp of wine. Sighed again.

'Oh for goodness sake. Don't be so saintly,' Alessandra exclaimed. 'Daddy would hate to see you brooding like this. And in any case he'd have nothing to do with sharing the award. He's an all or nothing man.'

Tara was inclined to agree. She dropped a kiss on the top of Alessandra's head, feeling proud of her daughter's emerging shrewdness.

'More wine?' Alessandra enquired.

'No. I shall be driving later.'

'Oh?'

Tara drew in a deep breath. She decided now was the

time to broach the subject of the performance at the Grosse Festspielhaus that evening.

'It's a very exciting opera. Very dramatic,' she told Alessandra persuasively. 'Mermaids and dragons. No horses though as far as I can remember.' She found herself holding her breath tight in her chest.

'OK,' said Alessandra with casual cheeriness, as though the morning's bitterness had been nothing more than a sharp frost which had melted away in the sunshine.

Maybe Saul was right. Maybe I *am* over-dramatizing the situation between him and Alessandra, Tara thought.

'Why the tortured face and more of the big sighs?' Alessandra demanded.

'You and Daddy,' Tara said frankly. 'I sometimes feel as though I'm trapped between the hammer and the anvil.'

Alessandra leaned her head on Tara's lap. Her eyes slanted up into her mother's face. 'Never mind the Golden Gramophone award,' she exclaimed, rueful and whimsical. 'You deserve the Nobel Peace Prize. For divine tolerance. And for not committing violence on my father.'

# CHAPTER 32

Dr Daneman stirred cream into his early morning cup of coffee at the same time glancing down the list of names of possible new clients which his administrative assistant had printed out and left on his desk.

One name sprang out at him. Caused a slight acceleration of pulse, a feeling of dryness in the mouth.

He pushed the button on his compact switchboard, thought better of it, and walked through into Celia's office, the list in his hand.

Celia looked up at him smiling. She liked her employer. He was even-tempered, genial and unflappable. She had never seen him irritable or moody. She had been with him for six years. Celia judged she knew when she was onto a good thing and had no intention of leaving.

'This referral – Mrs Georgiana Xavier?' Dr Daneman queried. Definitely on the sharp side – for him at least.

'Yes.' Celia had been rather excited to speak to Mrs Xavier when she had telephoned out of the blue, the day before. Being an avid devourer of glossy magazines Celia was well aware of Mrs Xavier's progress around the fashionable parts of London, forever changing her apartment, her furniture and drapes.

Celia considered Mrs Xavier an excellent subject for the magazines. She was wonderfully photogenic; she was glamorous, elegantly dressed, discreetly jewelled. She was also eternally wistful on the subject of her defected husband Saul Xavier. Always hinting at a possible reconciliation. The ever-loving, forgiving and tolerant wife. So romantic.

'This isn't a new referral,' said Dr Daneman. 'It's an old case on which I spent a good deal of time.'

'Oh!' Celia felt a blush creep up her cheek. She had a sense of having been precipitate, not having checked thoroughly enough. 'I'm very sorry, Dr Daneman. I'm afraid I just assumed it was a new assessment. I checked on the computer. We've no records on the data base. And it is a very unusual name.'

She gazed at him anxiously.

He nodded, realizing that it must have been well over ten years since he had seen or heard of Georgiana Xavier. Her name would be very unlikely to be found on the comparatively recent database.

'It's all right,' he said to Celia, smiling with reassurance. 'Go ahead and send out the standard invitation for an initial appointment.'

Celia felt a little warm after Dr Daneman had returned to his consulting room. She undid a button on her neat blouse and opened the window a fraction wider. Maybe she was getting to that difficult stage in a woman's life.

Georgiana stood before the full length cheval mirror in her dressing room and took stock of her naked body. She turned sideways, observing the firm curve of her breasts. She looked at her stomach, breathing in to tighten the

344

muscles further, flattening her belly almost to concavity. She twisted slightly, a movement which accentuated her high hip-bones and allowed her to admire the indent of her waist and the swollen tautness of her small buttocks.

Spectacularly good for a woman of her age she judged. It had been hard work of course, this constant attention to the details of self-preservation. Even with perfect bones and an excellent skin one could never let up on the relentless effort.

Her eyes still on the mirror, she pulled on champagne-coloured silk underwear: bra, french knickers and suspender belt, then rolled sheer flesh-coloured stockings over the smooth skin of her long legs.

Her dress was a simple cream sheath, skimming over her figure, drawing attention to slenderness, hinting at female curves. The matching jacket had a drifting quality to it, dreamy and a touch mysterious.

She spent an hour in making up her face so that it appeared not to be made up. The long blonde hair, still in its severe and classical style, swung and gleamed as she tilted her head.

Opening her jewellery box she took out a gold pendant and held it against her neck. Staring in the mirror she fingered the delicate chain thoughtfully before replacing it in the box and then unfastening the pearl studs from her ears.

She stepped out of her apartment with a feeling of satisfaction in the beauty of perfect simplicity.

Dr Daneman looked at his watch. He had an odd sensation in his stomach, an echo of the hollowness he used to feel as a boy when he stood on the high board above the swimming pool and stared into the wobbling turquoise depth of the water below.

He smiled to himself. The sensation was by no means unpleasant, in fact quite the reverse. It was some time since he had experienced any significant emotional turbulence. In fact in recent years it had sometimes crossed his mind that the tranquil, unvarying nature of his moods and feelings bordered on the pathological.

Celia, in the reception ante-room, was in a flutter of anticipation, looking up at the clock and smoothing her eyebrows with a moistened finger.

Mrs Xavier did not disappoint her. She glided, rather than walked through the door, as graceful as a prima ballerina, with all the presence of the high born and privileged.

Intensely blue eyes fastened on Celia, unnerving her a little, as though the queen herself had unexpectedly walked in.

The blue eyes skimmed Celia's efficient, unremarkable face and pillow-like body. 'Mrs Saul Xavier,' she announced with a faint smile.

Celia took Mrs Xavier through to Dr Daneman and closed the door softly behind her.

Breeding, thought Celia, settling once more behind her desk. Class. Quality. She felt no envy, no malice. The world needed magical figures like Mrs Xavier to brighten up the general greyness of things.

Dr Daneman rose from the impressive leather chair behind his vast desk and offered his hand. Georgiana's fingers rested in his for a moment.

For a split second their eyes locked together.

He waved her into a chair positioned at the front of his desk.

'Not the couch!' she exclaimed. Chiding, coquettish.

'Not until I know what you've come about.' He raised his eyebrows. Very much the impartial clinician.

'You're not angry that I've come are you? I didn't expect you to be angry with me,' she said, opening up her blue eyes.

'I'm not angry.' But, my God, am I curious, he told himself.

'You certainly look rather stern,' she said. She gave a little laugh.

'I'm simply reflecting on our need to understand each other and be very clear what is at issue here.'

'I need help,' she said.

'Clearly. I understand that. But we can't simply start where we left off, if that's what you're hoping for.'

'Why can't we?'

'A considerable time has passed. And you had extensive treatment from a number of other consultants, of which I know nothing.' This was all flannelling. Dr Daneman had only to pick up the phone to gain access to all the information he needed about Georgiana's various therapies following the kidnap incident.

He wondered how much Georgiana recalled of the nightmarish scene in the Cornish cottage. How much she had managed to block out. His own memories of the incident were certainly a cause of discomfort. There was a sense of professional failure. A fear of having been not fully in control of his patient. He recalled Xavier's withering scorn.

And there was another memory also. One which was both fascinating and utterly taboo.

All of which made him very doubtful of the wisdom of becoming involved again. It was surely safer to let sleeping dogs lie. His mind started to run through a catalogue of alternative clinicians whom he could recommend her to approach.

'I need you,' Georgiana announced. She said this with such calm simplicity that he was taken aback. Instantly disarmed.

'I need you to . . .' she paused, frowned, 'I need you to help me explore my feelings,' she concluded.

She had learned the relevant jargon, Dr Daneman thought, amused and curiously touched. Poor innocent Georgiana, she would have been exposed to an endless procession of analysts and therapists during the long months of residential treatment he had arranged for her. All of them mouthing jargon at her, which she would have obediently swallowed.

'Georgiana,' he said softly, causing her to flicker her eyelids at the sound of her name on his lips. 'If you're feeling a need to explore possible routes of getting back to Saul, then I'm afraid I'm not able to help you.'

He timed the minutes of the silence.

'That's not what I'm wanting.' She swivelled her eyes to his, locking into his feelings, refusing him permission to look away.

He was startled to find that the sheer visual appeal of the wide, china-blue gaze still had the power to move him.

Dr Daneman laced his fingers together and forced his mind to move at speed. 'I'm prepared to offer you five appointments,' he told her, calm and firm. 'I suggest we go right back to the beginning, looking again at the reason you first came to me. We can examine that a little – and then take things from there. At the end of the fifth session I'll be happy to give you my opinion on the best way forward. Mmm?'

'I came to you because I was frigid,' Georgiana said. 'But that's no longer a problem.'

'I see.' He was becoming more and more fascinated. He reminded himself to maintain his features in an expression of supreme impartiality.

'You cured me,' she said.

Dr Daneman's heart gave one violent buck, and then was steady. He would choose to ignore that statement. 'You're telling me that you don't want to follow my suggestion of going back to the original problem?'

'What would be the point? I've had several lovers in the past few years. I'm no longer frigid you see.'

'You enjoyed these sexual encounters?'

'Yes.'

'Is that the truth?'

'Yes.'

'You reached orgasm?'

'Not always. Most times.'

Dr Daneman was beginning to feel slightly breathless.

'I got bored with them,' Georgiana said. 'They were all the same really.'

'So what is it you're wanting now?'

She stared at him, frowning at his obtuseness. 'I'm not quite sure what I'm wanting. That's the whole point of coming to talk to you.'

'Yes. Of course.'

'You'll take me back won't you?' Her eyes were hunted and fearful. 'You will take me back!'

Aah – what one could read into that, Dr Daneman thought, his emotions now thoroughly aroused.

'Yes – I'll take you back.'

'I want it to be just like before,' she insisted. 'I shall lie on the couch and you will sit beside me at my head. I'll look out of the window and see the line of cherry trees. And the little light on your recorder will throw a red glow on the wall when it's a cloudy day.'

My God! Such recall. Such needs. Impossible to resist. Dr Daneman knew that he had no choice but to capitulate totally. 'Yes. You shall have all of that, Georgiana.'

He asked her to make a further appointment on her way out.

As she reached the door, she turned. She did something she had never done before. She asked him a question about himself. She asked him if he were married.

He told her that he was not. That he had never been married. She nodded and seemed satisfied. She parted from him looking far more composed than her therapist now felt.

He sat down at his desk and wound the audio tape back to its starting point. He pressed the play button and leaned back in his chair.

In the room beyond, Celia, brimming with anticipation and curiosity, waited for Dr Daneman to bring her the tape of the interview which she would then transcribe onto the word processor. Usually he brought tapes through straight away. But to her disappointment this did not happen.

When she slipped in with the cup of coffee she always offered her employer between appointments she noticed that he was in the act of dropping a cassette into his personal briefcase, with its secret locking code.

Georgiana looked forward to her visits to Dr Daneman with all the excitement and eagerness of a child anticipating a visit to the Christmas pantomime.

She sensed that she was on the brink of some great discovery.

Towards the end of the fourth appointment she told Dr Daneman about this strong premonition and asked him what he thought it meant.

He shook his head. 'Only you have the key to unlock the answer to that question,' he said.

He looked along the outline of her body, tracing every known and admired hollow and curve. Today she wore an oatmeal Chanel suit with a cream blouse. It struck him that one really could love a woman who was so perfectly beautiful.

She smiled. 'You love to tantalize,' she said.

'By not answering your questions?'

'Yes.'

'Does that make you angry with me?'

'Maybe. No, I don't think so. I don't think I've ever felt angry with you,' she added.

'You have one more session remaining of the five we planned, Georgiana. Are you any nearer finding out what it was you were searching for?'

'No.' She paused. A shadow passed over her face. 'I need you to give me more time.'

'Do you want to talk more about your young lovers?' Dr Daneman would certainly like her to talk about them some more. Her descriptions of the various encounters had, quite frankly, pitched him to dizzy heights of vicarious satisfaction.

'No.' She frowned. Concentrating hard.

He waited. The red light glowed.

Her eyes stared up at the ceiling. Glazed. 'I thought I wanted Saul back. I dreamed about him at nights. After I'd been with those young men, I often dreamed about Saul.'

'You dreamed of making love with him?'

'No! Never that. I couldn't! Couldn't! I still couldn't.' Tears brimmed suddenly from her eyes. They slipped across her cheeks, making a glistening trail.

Dr Daneman placed his hand over hers. 'There's no need to be afraid, Georgiana. You will never need to make love with Saul again if you don't want to.'

'I was afraid of Saul,' she said. 'I was terrified.' Little pants and gulps accompanied the words.

'Yes.' Go on, go on, Georgiana. You're getting there. Nearly, nearly.

'He never hurt me. He never shouted.' Her head turned slowly. 'I was so afraid.'

'Saul could make you do anything. He could make you feel anything.'

'Yes.'

'He did that to you through the power of his will.'

'Yes.'

'Saul is a very powerful man. An exceptional man.'

'He swallowed me up into his mind. He covered me with his body and went deep inside me. Pushing, pushing. I felt as if I was suffocating. And I must give him a child.'

'Ah yes, there was that too. Giving Saul a child. But you were terrified of having a child weren't you? Of swelling up and being ugly? Of getting lumpy veins and stretch marks? Of suffering pain?'

'Yes. Oh yes!'

'Yes, Georgiana. All of those things made you afraid. You were afraid of having a child, but you were even more terrified of your feeling that Saul was swallowing you up and crushing you. That's why you couldn't enjoy sex with him. Why you could never enjoy sex with him Georgiana, not even now. Even after your good times with all those young men.'

'No, I couldn't.' She sighed. As though his words had brought great relief.

'The young men were good for you because they were in your power. *You* had control over *them*.'

He permitted a long pause. He wondered if he had gone too fast for her. Heaped on too much pain all at once.

'Georgiana,' he said, calling her gently back from her reverie. 'In the past you used to be terrified of losing Saul because you thought that without him you would lose everything.'

'Yes, yes!'

'That you would be nothing. If you couldn't have a child, and you couldn't keep Saul then you would be nothing.'

'Yes.'

'But you know that isn't true any more. You don't need Saul any more.'

'No.'

'Georgiana! Listen to me. Listen!' He touched her shoulder. The glaze over the blue eyes softened and split like a torn transparent skin.

'Tell me the truth,' he commanded softly. 'Was the real reason for your coming back to talk to me a wish to get Saul back? Did you lie to me before?' He knew he was slipping from the professional to the personal.

'I did believe I wanted to get Saul back. I'd always believed that.' She breathed very deeply. A sigh of huge weariness. 'I couldn't let him go.'

'No. You couldn't let him go Georgiana. But that's a very different thing from wanting him back.' Firm now. The true professional speaking.

'I'm growing old,' she said after a time, taking him by surprise.

'You're still a very beautiful woman.'

'Yes. I think I always will be. But I'm alone. All alone.' She turned to him in appeal. 'I'm so frightened.'

Dr Daneman found himself stabbed with feeling; a prized and pleasant sensation. He felt himself drawn once again to Georgiana Xavier. They were suited. Emotionally, they were a match.

Dr Daneman knew himself to be shallow. He had never felt the huge surges that he read about in books, in plays, in poetry. He had never been stirred to tears by a great symphony, a sublime painting or an immortal sculpture.

It was perhaps the act of sex that had been the prime

emotional experience in his life. Sex with a procession of discreet, married mistresses who would never make psychological claims on him. Who would leave him free to devote himself to the furthering of his career and the accumulation of money and style.

He was by no means a cruel or heartless man. The misery of his clients had often jarred his feelings and wearied his spirit. But he had never found himself approaching the brink of some personal crisis or breakdown, as he had seen happen to a disturbingly high proportion of his colleagues in the helping professions.

Georgiana, of course, was shallow, narcissistic, and basically a child. Yet she was not vicious. She had little calculation and virtually no malice. Even when pushed to the limits of her limited endurance she had not been prepared to commit a violent act.

Georgiana, in fact, was most pleasingly bland. Like him she preferred the even keel to the pitching and tossing between soaring heights and plunging depths. And like him she was alone, being propelled relentlessly into a cold future.

He took out a freshly laundered handkerchief and gently mopped her cheeks.

Reassuring her that he would not leave her for long, he walked quickly into the reception area and left Celia in no doubt that she had most certainly earned the bonus of finishing work half an hour early for once, in return for all the times she had stayed late.

As Celia closed the front door behind her Dr Daneman returned to the couch, sat behind Georgiana's head and then leaned down to press his lips on hers.

Georgiana sighed. She arched her back and her hips burrowed against the leather of the couch in a languidly inviting manner.

Dr Daneman placed a hand on her waist, stroking her for a while, before transferring his attentions to the smooth globes of her knees and the long sweep of her inner thigh.

All the time he was talking to her. Rhythmic, soft phrases. Words of praise, comfort and reassurance. Over and over. Soft, sighing, singing words.

Sending her mind down a sweet-smelling grassy staircase. Long flights of steps. Leading down and down. Inviting her to imagine herself in a sun-drenched walled garden filled with cream lilies and purple iris.

'So still, so peaceful,' he whispered to her, his hand moving slowly upwards.

Georgiana felt herself lapped in a wonderful sense of security. There was a sense of all this having happened to her before.

And it was then that the flash of realization came to her. This was the key. The means to unlock the mystery of her premonition.

Dr Daneman himself was the key. He, the person, the man.

She stared up at him as he mounted the couch and straddled her hips. She held out her arms to him and then clasped them around his waist. She murmured in pleasure.

As Dr Daneman entered her with gentle authority, he thought about the cottage in the little village in Cornwall. The scene of Georgiana's childhood idyll. The scene of her ultimate humiliation and rejection.

He could smell once again the curious blend of Georgiana's lily-of-the-valley fragrance and the sour mushy scent of vomited baby food and unwashed baby.

In his mind's eye he saw Saul Xavier erupting grimly from the cottage, clutching his child. How Xavier had hated his wife on that day.

He saw the limp body of Georgiana stretched on the bed. A woman who had blotted out the horror of her fall from grace through a momentary flight into unconsciousness, a state the lay person would call madness.

And he, Dr Daneman, had taken it on himself to initiate the start of the healing process through the hypnotic suggestiveness of his caressing voice. He had spoken to her of the beauty of the sexual act, of the way it could offer pleasure and consolation. He had reassured her that there was nothing to be afraid of, that there would be no invasion, no pain, no baby, no guilt.

Slowly and tenderly he had continued his treatment with the application of techniques more physical than talking.

In time he had slipped inside the covers with her. Slid softly inside her body.

He had set her on the road to recovery.

As he thrust inside Georgiana, now, all these years later, he reminded himself that there were certain secrets which must never be shared, not even between a doctor and his patient.

# CHAPTER 33

Roland Grant had faxed Tara with the full details of the Golden Gramophone Award whilst she, Saul and Alessandra were still in Austria. She had looked through the names of the other prizewinners and been astonished to see one which instantly conjured up old memories. That of a person she had not seen for years.

Bruno Cornwell.

Bruno had won a special award for best newcomer of the year with a disc of his newly formed choir, the Renaissance, performing fifteenth and sixteenth-century church music for unaccompanied voices.

On returning to England, Tara had immediately bought a copy of the disc and had listened to it in the privacy of her car.

She had been enchanted by what she heard. There were just ten voices, five male, five female. They blended together in a unity of sound which had a breathtaking purity and stark ethereal beauty.

According to the accompanying notes Bruno Cornwell had spent a number of years digging out yellowed and fusty-smelling manuscripts in the music libraries of London, Florence and Venice. Motets and anthems that had been written centuries ago to be sung in Europe's great cathedrals and monasteries for the glory of God.

Bruno had not only chosen the pieces for the disc, he had also formed and selected a very special choir to sing them. He had taken the unusual step of electing to include mature female voices rather than the original practice of using boy trebles or counter tenor male singers to provide the higher register singing.

Tara judged that Bruno had been very shrewd. The female voices he had chosen had many qualities in common with those of a mature boy treble. All the clarity and purity, but with no trace of distortion in the high register fortissimo passages. And, of course, with mature female sopranos singing in his choir he was not going to have to lose sleep at nights wondering which young lad's voice was going to break next.

As Tara listened she became convinced that the sound produced by this mixed sex adult choir was not only pleasing, but unique. Most other directors of early music had chosen to stick with authenticity and exclude female performers as a matter of course.

Well done Bruno! she kept saying to herself, smiling with pleasure as the music permeated the car. How clever he had been, and how cunning to choose William Cornish's *Salve Regina* as the initial track. It was a perfect hook into the rest of the album; a work of sonorous and dramatic splendour with a hefty dash of Tudor flamboyance.

Listening later on to the the ringing and jubilant *Sing Joyfully* by William Byrd, Tara guessed that Bruno could have a runaway best seller on his hands. She saw the disc leaping up the Classic Countdown charts and sitting perched there for quite a while.

Well, well. Good old Bruno, she thought affectionately. He had certainly kept his light hidden under a bushel. She had heard nothing of his choir until now, but then that was not surprising. It had only been formed a year before and, according to the biographical notes on Bruno himself, he was still an amateur in music, juggling his interest in early vocal church music with a full time career as a barrister.

Oh yes, she could well imagine. Good old Bruno, still fulfilling his parents' fond ambitions.

She wondered if Bruno would have to make a change now that he and his disc had shot with astonishing speed from shadowy obscurity straight into the spotlight.

She played the recording to Saul who listened with intent interest.

'What do you think?' she asked him.

'Remarkable!' Emotionless, giving nothing away.

'You don't really like it do you?'

'A little thin-blooded for my taste.'

'The music?'

'No, no. The music is wonderful.'

'The ensemble then?'

'Five men and five women?' He arched his eyebrows. 'Not even a cricket team, is it?'

Tara laughed. 'Whereas you like a small army under your baton. Eighty plus in the orchestra, a choir of hundreds . . .'

'Quite.'

For a moment she had thought he was going to relax. Let his guard slip, laugh at himself.

The smile that had flickered on the edge of his features faded and stilled. He moved to the piano, began to play some stark and sombre Ravel.

Tara listened, spellbound. She closed her eyes for a moment and let the sound enfold her.

Opening them again, she stared at Saul's face. Her heart contracted at the sight of those classically carved, impartial features.

*So far away*, Alessandra had said.

As Tara watched him now, his gaze directed straight ahead of him, his hands moving with quiet command over the keys, it struck her that every day he was moving further. Further and further away.

The hall was steadily filling up as Saul and Tara – with a proud and faintly embarrassed Alessandra lurking in their shadow – arrived for the award ceremony. They progressed through the throng of guests, smiling greetings, acknowledging congratulations.

Saul, having previously decreed that this was to be Tara's night, placed himself discreetly half a step behind his consort and declined to allow the flow of adulation which washed over Tara to be deflected in his own direction.

Tara, her adrenalin surging in response to all this enthusiastic recognition of her achievement, looked up at Saul from time to time and found herself aching with fresh love and a strange yearning.

She gazed around her, curious to identify Bruno. For

the first few moments she saw no one remotely resembling the portrait in her memory. And then the figure of a bear-like man, balding, bespectacled and constantly smiling caught her attention. She stared harder. The man turned. His own recognition was instant. Detaching himself from the throng he came towards her.

The two former lovers looked into each other's faces. There was a brief shared stab of regret: recollections of a youth and innocence long ago lost. There had been something precious and shared for a time, but they had moved away from each other. Moved on.

Tara looked at Bruno and saw that he was established in the world. Successful, prosperous and confident. And happy too, she judged. Yes, there was a strong emanation of well-being and contentment from those good-natured features.

She stretched up and put her arms around him, hugging him close, pressing a light, dry kiss on his cheek.

As she pulled back her glance was drawn to the woman at his side, a woman observing this affectionate reunion with the indulgent smile of a wife entirely confident of her husband's love and loyalty.

'Tara, meet Clare,' said Bruno, his face warm and animated as he drew his wife forward.

Clare wore a full-skirted dress of calf-length mulberry taffeta: sweetheart neckline, leg-of-mutton sleeves, strained creases at the waist. Like Bruno's her waistline was spreading in anticipation of the creeping onset of middle age.

Beside the lithe Tara in her clinging ankle-length scarlet gown, daringly slit up one side to mid thigh, Clare looked comfortably unadventurous and dependably conventional.

Conversation began to flow. Laughing mutual congratulations, general music talk.

Bruno looked beyond Tara and registered Saul Xavier. Tall and gaunt, the skin pulled tight over those sword-like bones, Xavier struck Bruno as a man little altered by time. Except that possibly the great conductor was even more terrifyingly compelling than before.

Saul shook Bruno's hand warmly. 'Many many congratulations. And to think that I'd once imagined I was setting a young man on the road to the timpani section in some provincial orchestra!' he commented drily. 'Just look at you now! Fame and fortune!'

'Oh, well. Hardly. Not yet.' Bruno waved a diffident hand.

Tara thought she saw a faint blush on his cheek.

'You wait!' Saul commented.

Bruno watched with interest as Saul Xavier drew a girl forward: a lovely leggy colt with a great mane of blonde hair and glinting green eyes exactly like those of her mother. The girl's gaze was frank and penetrating, disturbingly adult.

'This is Alessandra,' Saul said. 'Our daughter.'

Bruno took the girl's hand. He was sickeningly nervous. Sweat tingled in his palm. He hoped the girl did not register revolting clamminess.

'Hi!' she said with a grin. 'Congratulations.' She looked towards the stage, simply adorned with a black rostrum and a backdrop of draped gold curtaining. 'I hope they get on with it,' she announced, looking impatient. 'And then we can all go home and get stuck into supper. I'm already famished.'

'These young sprouting shoots. Always thinking of their stomachs,' Tara commented, smiling at her daughter. 'Do you have children?' she asked Clare with interest.

Clare's face glowed as though an inward switch had been thrown. 'Twin boys. Marcus and Rupert. They're seven now. Too young to bring along tonight. Children need their sleep at that age, don't they?'

Tara smiled to herself. She had Clare marked down as a nice woman; sensible and practical. A good woman. A woman who would never have got herself up the spout and run off with a sexy married maestro before she had even grown up properly.

She glanced at Saul and was pierced with a sudden and vicious dagger of desire as she recalled her own youthful impulsiveness and folly.

The ceremony progressed on oiled wheels. Speeches were given, praises sung, gracious acknowledgements made.

When it came to his turn, a quaking Bruno was surprised to hear his carefully prepared words of thanks proceed from his mouth with smooth fluency.

As he sat down, so Tara rose to accept her award. Her speech was short and to the point: a crisp and witty performance that had the audience chuckling appreciatively.

Bruno watched her with interest, this gracious, wand-like version of the curvy voluptuous girl he used to toss over his shoulder. Her dress shimmered softly as she moved and her long dark hair cascaded freely over her shoulders. Easy to understand how he had been captivated all those years ago.

He looked across to Clare and let his eyes travel with love over the dear, familiar, wholesome face. How right she was for him. How good things had been for them as a couple. His mind conjured up an image of the two sleeping boys at home. He breathed in deeply, reached out and pressed Clare's hand warmly. She turned to him and smiled.

Still retaining her hand Bruno looked from Saul to Alessandra and then back again. His brows contracted slightly. The seed of an idea planted itself. A notion, a wild fancy. Surely not, he said to himself. And yet? What if, what if? He instructed his mind to call up certain details of the past.

Tara was coming to the end of her speech. On more than one occasion she had mentioned Xavier's name as she spoke. Now, as she spoke it again, she paused meaning-fully, and the spotlight operators had no option but to train the light on the dark, saturnine figure in the audi-ence. Xavier got to his feet and took a brief bow.

Bruno watched Tara descend from the stage. Applause clattered around her like gunfire. He watched her as though in a daze, his mind still struggling to bring misted past memories into sharp and precise focus. Eventually he was forced to abandon his search as his attention was fully claimed by the here and now.

A procession of faces moved across his line of vision. Through a haze of unreality he heard talk of new recording contracts, of a proposed TV film about the formation of the Renaissance Choristers, of the possibility of tours in the United States and Japan. Someone called Grant wanted to represent him.

Bruno found himself bemused. He mouthed suitable words of response, indicating a need to consider at length, consult with his advisors. He was, after all, a man who had always, up to now, trodden a path of caution and security.

It was something of a relief when Xavier cut through the insistent throng and came to his rescue with an invitation for him and Clare to come without delay to his London apartment for a celebratory supper.

Alessandra stood in the kitchen of her father's London pied-à-terre, looking at the posters she had pinned to the wall a couple of years ago. All of an equine nature. Some of them made her smile now. The interests and knowledge of thirteen are somewhat different to those of eleven.

Nevertheless the large coloured diagram entitled 'Points of the Horse' was still of interest. Alessandra unpinned it from the wall and laid it on the table.

She frowned in concentration, running her finger along the finely drawn lines. Slowly, with wonder, she traced the connections of the cannon bone down to the fetlock joint in the right foreleg. What a complex, cunningly constructed animal a horse was.

Bruno came through the doorway, crossed to the sink and filled his glass from the tap. He looked at the absorbed girl.

'You're a keen rider I take it?' he said to Alessandra. She gave a slight start, automatically framing a defensive retort. She paused long enough to appreciate the complete absence of any patronizing adult superiority or hidden criticism in Bruno's open face.

She relaxed. 'Yes. Very keen.'

'I know hardly a thing about horses,' he told her. 'Not even enough to have a stab at asking you a sensible question without risking putting my foot in it.'

'I'll bet!'

He smiled. 'Let's see. Are we talking about show-jumping here? Or maybe eventing?' His eyes twinkled behind the Franz Schubert glasses.

Alessandra snorted. 'We're talking about dressage. Have you heard of that?'

Bruno nodded.

Alessandra turned back to the diagram. 'Dressage riding's a tremendous discipline,' she told Bruno. 'For the horse and the rider. Hours and hours of work. Day after day. Just to get to the point of knowing if you'll ever be just a little bit better than a load of rubbish.'

'Sounds like the music treadmill,' Bruno said.

Alessandra glanced sharply at him, her smile snapping off. She considered. She looked again at him. Her smile slowly returned.

Bruno sat down beside her, swivelled the diagram so that he could see it properly. 'Whoever designed the horse had a good deal of optimism,' he commented. 'All that bulk balanced on such frail stick-like legs.'

'Yes.' Alessandra stared intently over the diagram. 'That's true but you see if you think of the weight distribution over the four limbs . . .' She began to explain to him.

The two heads bent towards each other in contemplation.

In the big drawing room the swirling clumps of guests were having a splendid time with the aid of copious supplies of champagne and the intoxicating presence of their host, Saul Xavier, who was generously entertaining them on the piano with some thunderous Liszt.

Rachel, circulating dutifully, heard the general chorus of praise for the great maestro.

*What a truly marvellous man. So delighted with Tara's success, so far above petty jealousies,* she heard more than one guest opine.

Don't you bloody believe it, she retorted to herself privately. He's controlled everything very nicely from the word go. And now he'll control the scale of Tara's success.

Rachel's feelings about Saul were still uneasy and ambivalent. She wished he were more accessible, more relaxed. Easier.

But then he wouldn't be the Saul who held Tara in thrall. And Rachel knew that Tara was still helplessly, deliriously in love.

Bruno and Alessandra came through the door side by side, rejoining the main company. They sought out Clare and Tara who were talking together, standing against the curved end of the piano.

'Are you a pianist Alessandra?' Clare asked, following the girl's gaze as she registered her father's interpretation of Mozart's Rondo in A Minor.

Bruno too was watching Alessandra, fascinated by the

confusion of feelings battling on her mobile young face as she was confronted with her father's brilliance.

This was late Mozart Xavier was tackling, a piece some musicologists described as the most perfect Rondo ever written. It required the exquisite lightness and clarity of execution common to all of that particular composer's keyboard music.

Bruno noted that Xavier was not using the sustaining pedal at all. And yet the lyricism of the piece was entirely intact. There was no trace of starkness. Nothing jarring. Everything flowing.

Xavier's left hand, which had moments ago been mountain climbing with Liszt, now danced over the keys with almost birdlike delicacy.

Follow that! thought Bruno ruefully.

Clare was watching Alessandra, waiting with interest to hear her reply to the question she had posed.

'No,' Alessandra said shortly.

Tara longed to intervene. She stopped herself.

'Not at all?' Clare pressed, gently tenacious.

'I have lessons,' Alessandra admitted. Her eyes took on a wicked glint. She arranged her face into an expression of weary resignation. 'Each week my teacher says: "Now then Alessandra, I'm looking forward to hearing the results of your practising. Yet another triumph of hope over experience." '

Bruno hooted. 'Well if you abandon the piano you could always get yourself a reputation doing impressions.'

'I do sing a bit,' Alessandra told him, astonishing Tara who had never heard her daughter confess this to anyone before. 'That's your thing, isn't it Bruno?'

'I simply direct. I don't make any sound myself,' Bruno told her, his face mockingly grave.

'Oh, like Daddy when he's bullying orchestras,' said Alessandra with a show of gritty scorn. But when she looked across to her father at the piano there was pleading and aching and need in her face.

Tara resisted the impulse to reach out and hug her daughter. Things had not been easy in the last few weeks. After they had returned from Austria Alessandra had tried so hard to build a bridge to Saul. She had spent hours with him in the projection room acting as his willing slave and dogsbody. But he had seemed hardly to notice her, been completely absorbed in the editing of the films.

Increasingly, it seemed he had interest in little else when he was not actively engaged in conducting work.

Tara sensed that he was in the grip of some conflict, some fathomless personal despair.

Being Saul he put on a good front, whatever was troubling him. He never made any show of anger or displeasure. As ever there were no displays of violent emotion. He was unfailingly courteous, correctly loving. And yet Tara knew that Alessandra, like herself, had a chilling sense of his moving away from them, slipping into a private world of music over which he wielded total power.

Tara felt that it would be only a matter of time before Alessandra blew up and stormed out on him. Maybe packed her bags and went off to live with Rachel and Donald.

And why not? How could she be expected at her age to

put up with what amounted to constant rejection? Let alone try to understand it.

Tara felt a hand on her arm. It was Roland. 'I need to have a word. Not tonight. But very soon,' he said softly. 'There must be no more missed opportunities.'

'OK. Fine. I'll call you first thing tomorrow.' She reached up and kissed him, chuckling at his sternly raised eyebrows.

Roland turned to Bruno. 'And I hope that you will call me too.' He laid his hand briefly on Bruno's shoulder, as if in blessing.

Bruno is made now, Tara thought with pleasure and affection. Once Roland touched you everything you did turned to gold.

Her head buzzed with dizzy sensation and the evening's plentiful glasses of champagne. She thought of the new career that would inevitably unfold for her, of Alessandra's desperate needs, of Saul's frightening alienation. How was she going to cope with all of this when it was the morning and she was sober?

The Mozart was drawing to a close. Roland stole up to the piano and leaned over Saul. The two men left the room quietly together.

Thank God, thought Tara. If anyone can pull Saul round, Roland can.

Bruno wandered up to the piano and started tinkering. He noticed Alessandra watching him. He smiled. She moved to stand beside him, drawn by his gentle and reassuring manner.

Some of her music lay open on the stand.

Bruno flicked through the sheets and then played a few

371

cheeky bars of *The Harmonious Blacksmith*.

Alessandra bridled. 'I do sometimes think of other things besides horses!'

'Sorry.' Bruno grimaced apologetically. He picked up the song sheet of Schubert's *Rose among the Heather*.

'Will you turn the pages?' he asked Alessandra. 'I expect you do that for your father.'

'Daddy never needs sheet music. His memory is phenomenal.' Alessandra said.

'Mine is abysmal,' Bruno lied cheerily. He played the opening bars and grunted out the words in his deep baritone voice.

'Dreadful!' Alessandra exclaimed. She looked swiftly around her, automatically checking on the whereabouts of her father. Realizing he was safely off the scene she felt herself able to relax. Amidst the hubbub of laughter and conversation she began to sing.

Tara strained for the sound of her daughter's voice above the buzz of conversation. Her eyes filled with tears.

'Bruno will be inviting her into his choir,' Clare said, tilting her head, kitten-like, as she listened. 'He's always on the lookout for young female singers. I tell him I shall get terribly jealous.'

Tara felt certain that jealousy was the last thing Clare was feeling with regard to Bruno. Her conviction in the security of her wifely status glowed around her like a halo.

Saul came back into the room. As always his presence brought about a subtle change in the emotional atmosphere.

Alessandra sensed his presence even before she saw

372

him. Her singing faltered. She was suddenly attacked with a fit of coughing and had to disappear to get some water.

Bruno finished his accompaniment, placed the sheets of music neatly together and returned to stand by his wife, throwing an affectionate arm around her shoulder.

Tara, strung up with nervous tension and growing fatigue, found herself considering how pleasant and comforting it would be to lay her head on Bruno's fatherly, well-cushioned shoulder and blurt out all her problems. Just as she used to when they were first year students together.

She drained her glass and laughed at herself. Too much champagne could make one very soggy and sentimental.

She stretched out her hand and placed it in Saul's, needing to make physical contact with him.

The strong dry pressure from his fingers instantly reassured. Pushed away every other need.

'What a lovely daughter you have,' Clare said to him. 'You are so lucky. We didn't manage a girl.'

'We are indeed lucky,' Saul said quietly.

'She's already taller than me,' Tara said ruefully. 'My authority diminishes with each passing day.'

'She has very striking colouring,' Clare went on. 'Such wonderful hair. So unusual with those dark green eyes. Bruno used to have blond hair, didn't you darling? Right up to being a teenager. And see him now. Just a few little mousy brown tufts!'

Tara felt a slight alteration in the pressure of Saul's hand. She looked up at him and saw a blood vessel flickering in his jaw. Her mouth went dry.

Excusing herself she went into the small office next to the kitchen. Her cheeks and forehead burned with heat. Throwing open the window she sought the coolness of the night air. It was the past that seemed to rush in.

Alessandra crept up behind her. 'I think I'll go to bed now Mummy.'

'Are you all right?' Tara asked, concerned.

'I just got a frog in my throat. It's nearly gone now.' She coughed convincingly once or twice.

'Good.' Tara put her arm around Alessandra and kissed her tenderly.

'Isn't Bruno *sweet*?' Alessandra exclaimed suddenly.

'Yes. He is.'

'Like a great big cuddly teddy bear! Have they any kids?'

'Twin boys. Seven years old.'

'They could do with a daughter to control Clare's dire fashion sense. That dress! If she went out in a wind she'd take off like Mary Poppins. Grim! Well. I'll be off.' She was all brittle cheeriness. She walked to the door. Turned. 'Is Daddy all right?'

'Fine.'

'He was great tonight, wasn't he? He looked so proud when you went up for the award. Really pleased. Honestly, he did.'

'Of course he did.'

Tara stood at the window, unable to make herself go back to the party. She tried to clear herself of all feeling, to empty and purify herself.

She wondered how long it would be before Bruno decided to confront her. Tomorrow, next week? Never?

He was already in the room. He closed the door behind him.

'Tara,' he said, as though it were an endearment.

She was silent.

'Alessandra is a wonderful girl.' His voice was thick with some pent up feeling.

'Yes.'

A long pause. Tara closed her eyes. Saliva poured into her mouth.

'Is Alessandra mine?' he asked softly. 'Is she my child?'

'No.'

'Can you be sure?'

'No. I just know.' The words were simple and brutal. She heard his breathing, jerky and harsh.

'Don't imagine things Bruno! Don't hope!'

'She could be mine. It's possible.' He was suddenly strong. Fiercely determined. 'It is possible. Isn't it?'

Tara let her head sink into her hands. 'Alessandra belongs to Saul,' she whispered.

'It's possible,' Bruno repeated.

'Yes,' Tara admitted flatly. 'It's possible.' She had always known it was possible. She had also never had a shred of doubt that she had been impregnated by no other man than Saul.

'Alessandra is Saul's. She is his legacy. *Whatever!*' Tara cried in protest. 'Oh for God's sake Bruno. Look at her. Listen to her. It's obvious!'

Suddenly she couldn't wait to get away from Bruno and his earnest, considerate ponderings. Pushing past him she stumbled to the door.

Saul stood behind it. Silent. Knowing.

What had he heard? Anything? Everything? She knew that he would never demean himself by referring to it.

She collapsed against him, shuddering, her eyes burning with grainy dry tears that refused to be shed.

Later, when the guests had gone and she and Saul were undressing for bed, he began to talk calmly to her about plans for the future. Spelling things out clearly and logically. There would be offers for her to take on the musical directorship of an orchestra with national prestige. Build it up, forge new and exciting paths. How would she feel about that? It would be a marvellous challenge, although riddled with pitfalls. But he would be there to give her all the help she needed.

She did not want the precious time with him eaten up on professional discussion. She wanted him close, their hearts beating in unison. She wrapped her arms about him, moved her hands over the stern line of his vertebrae. The hardness of him, the smell of his skin brought back sensations of their past love-making, all its spinning intensity, its hypnotic enchantment.

'We'll think about it tomorrow,' she murmured. *And all the other things.*

She slid into bed, worn out, but eagerly waiting for him. Saul was pacing restlessly. He was often sleepless nowadays. She held out her arms to him. He bent to kiss her. 'I think I'll take a short walk,' he said suddenly. 'Clear the head of champagne.'

She heard him get into the lift which opened up just outside the entry door to the apartment. She heard the whirr of the mechanism as it went into descent.

When did Saul ever go for a walk, she asked herself anxiously. A run maybe, a hard drive, a whirling scurry down a mountain slope. Never a walk. And she doubted that he had drunk more than half a glass of champagne.

Sure enough after a short pause she heard the engine of his new Porsche Turbo roar and whine into life in the street below.

His new toy. No wraparound stripes. Stark and black. More powerful than any car he had had before. He said it made him feel young again.

Well, at least he would be happy behind the wheel.

Exhaustion claimed her. Her muscles relaxed and she fell into a deep sleep.

She was pulled back into consciousness by a relentless banging on the entry door to the apartment. She screwed her eyes up. Shook her head, blinking away the blankness.

A thin grey light penetrated the curtains. Birds were shrilling out a dawn chorus.

She went to the door, her heart dipping and swooping with premonition. Behind her, a white-faced Alessandra padded up on bare feet.

Two police officers stood behind the door. They looked grave.

'Mrs Saul Xavier?' one of them said.

Tara flinched. Sighed. 'Well . . . yes.'

'I'm afraid we have some bad news, madam. May we come in?'

# CHAPTER 34

Tara and Alessandra sat together after the police had gone. Stunned. Numbed. Temporarily suspended even from pain. That would come soon enough.

Alessandra stared ahead of her. She began to comb her fingers through the long strands of hair. Over and over, strong downward sweeps as though she were grooming Tosca's mane.

Tara sprang up. 'We mustn't be like this!'

Alessandra's obsessively moving hand stilled. 'What? What do you mean?'

'It's not a death. We mustn't behave as though it's a death.'

'His car's been found all mangled and burned. There's no sign of him!'

'Yes, yes. But . . .'

'For goodness' sake, Mummy!'

'You heard what the police said. Officially he's simply missing.'

'Who are they trying to kid?' Alessandra stared at her mother, furious and bitter. 'They just won't say the word *dead* until they've got a body to gawp at.'

'No.' Tara moaned softly, covering her eyes with her hands.

'Look, it was obvious what they were thinking. Why would they have kept banging on about all those other "cases" where drivers have gone missing and then been found in a river somewhere. Dumped by some drunken truck driver who didn't want to find himself on a charge of manslaughter.'

'No.'

'That's what they think has happened. The driver of the truck that crashed into Daddy's car dragged him out of the mess and then . . .' Alessandra faltered. 'Mummy. Don't live in cloud cuckoo land!' she finished, burning with fury and grief and impotence.

Tara gasped as though Alessandra had punched her and crushed all the air from her chest. She sat down again. She began to tremble, shaking uncontrollably.

'Mummy! Oh, Mummy.' Alessandra panicked, a little child again at the prospect of her parent's breaking down completely. 'Don't, don't.'

She cradled Tara's head in her arms.

In time Tara was calm. Herself again. She looked at her watch. 'Eight-thirty. You should be thinking of school.'

Alessandra sighed. 'It's Saturday. And we're in London, not at home.'

Home! The mock Tudor monstrosity. How Tara had come to love that place. She wanted to be back there. In the big sparse drawing room: Saul's room, filled with his music collection, his piano, his presence. She wanted to fly there and draw the atmosphere of the place around her like a blanket of comfort. She longed for the ministrations and refreshments of the kind and loyal Mrs Lockton.

Alessandra was watching her mother anxiously.

Tara smiled. 'It's all right. I'm not about to disintegrate. Look, if it's Saturday, that means you'll be entered for the equitation classes at the riding centre.'

'It doesn't matter. Not today.' Alessandra's eyes swung from side to side, not knowing where to look. Hating to be wanting trivial pleasures when a black cloud of tragedy hung in the air. And yet longing for that pleasure as the only shred of comfort available.

'Of course it matters,' Tara said briskly. 'Get ready. I'll drive you there right away.'

Tara helped Alessandra unload Tosca from the trailer. Alessandra got out her grooming kit and set about the horse with a will.

Tara watched. She found herself strangely comforted.

It struck her that Alessandra was rapidly outgrowing her beloved Tosca. They would have to consider another horse. Saul would have a few words to say on the subject, she could imagine. She halted her thoughts in horror. Saul! Saul!

Tara grasped one hand tightly with the other, praying that Alessandra had not heard her high-pitched mew of distress.

'It'll be ages until we're in the arena,' Alessandra said. 'Don't wait Mummy. Go and see Grandma. Come back later.'

Friends drifted up to make horsey talk with Alessandra. Tara looked on with an uncertain smile, then slipped quietly away and drove straight to Rachel's.

'He's a survivor,' Rachel said with dry practicality, having served up coffee and then listened to Tara's long story without making any interruption.

'But he'd have been in touch by this time. He wouldn't leave me in this hell of uncertainty if he were alive,' said Tara. She looked at her mother. 'Would he?'

Rachel picked up a biscuit from the plate in front of her, staring fixedly at it as she crumbled it into little pieces. 'You don't believe he's dead do you Tara?'

'No.' Tara looked up with hunted eyes. 'Oh, I don't know. Alessandra doesn't want to hope. She keeps saying the awful word: dead, dead, dead.'

'Of course she does. If you tell yourself to think the very worst there's nothing else to fear.'

'Yes. I know that's right.'

'He loved you,' Rachel told Tara gently. 'He was absolutely besotted.' She recalled the journey with Saul to the hospital when Tara was fighting for Alessandra's life. 'And if he's alive, he'll still love you. But he's one on his own. He has the capacity to think and act and feel in ways other men don't.'

'Do you think he did it on purpose?' Tara asked suddenly. 'Tried to kill himself?'

'No. Certainly not.' Rachel judged this was a time to be firm, whatever uncertainties hovered. 'Do you?'

'The police said the HGV driver was well over the limit. The road surface was wet and slippery.'

Tara kept reminding herself of this. It was an accident, not Saul's fault. Not his doing. Yet she couldn't help thinking that if only Bruno's wretchedly chatty wife hadn't opened her mouth about Bruno's bloody blond boyhood hair . . .

She recalled her words to Saul when he had taken her for a spin on the motorway after Monica Heilfrich's master class. *You believe your life is important. You would never put yourself at real risk*. Words she had spoken fifteen years previously. Had they been crookedly, grimly prophetic? And was a particle of doubt about Alessandra's parentage the final twitch on the trigger of a pistol which had long been cocked?

She groaned out loud, thinking of her beloved, beleaguered Saul. The pain was cutting through the numbness now. She had to brace herself against the conjectures revolving in her mind, grinding relentlessly into her spirit.

Rachel comforted herself with the thought that Tara was still young. Even if Saul were dead her sadness would not be forever.

Rachel's inner thoughts of Saul were bitter. From his lofty pedestal he had dangled his adoring satellites, Tara and Alessandra, on strings of steel and they had danced around him in worshipful adoration, keeping in strict rhythm with every tune he called. If he had gone, then now there was a chance for them both to be free. Fulfilled in their own way, on their own terms.

Rachel got up and filled the kettle in preparation for yet more coffee. No, she thought. That's not right. That's just my way of looking at it. Tara's will be quite different; Alessandra's too.

'You need your work,' Rachel told Tara bluntly. 'You need Roland Grant. You need an orchestra and a trunk load of music.'

'I can't. Not now. Not yet.'

'That's something *he* would never have said,' Rachel stated brutally.

The police had agreed with Tara that they would maintain an embargo on issuing any public statements. At least for twenty-four hours. After that it would not be possible to maintain silence any longer. They had pointed out their obligation to publicize details regarding missing persons. They had indicated their hope of someone coming forward with information leading to Mr Xavier's being found.

Tara did not disagree. She knew, however, what would happen once the press got onto the story. She had wanted Alessandra to have at least one day of peace.

A breathless quiet hung over the house at the start of Sunday morning, thirty hours after Saul's disappearance. Tara grimly braced herself for the storm that would break over her and Alessandra once the news broke.

Alessandra, worn out with grief and the nervous elation of coming second in her equitation class with Tosca, slept on well past breakfast time.

Tara walked out into the garden, her mind full of Saul. The thin white cloud that had dominated the early summer weather for days seemed about to be banished by a luminous disc of sunshine. Tara looked up at it, her eyes dazzled and aching.

She wandered underneath the dipping branches of the monkey-puzzle tree, past the lawns and down the driveway, idly touching the glossy leaves of the bordering bushes. At the gates she stopped, looking out into the road. The gates were standing open. She and Saul had long ago decided that security was a matter of caring and trust, not locks, alarms and searchlights.

A silver Mercedes coupé rounded the curve of the road, slowing, signalling it's intention to turn, passing between the gates. The driver, not noticing Tara, drove on, making for the house. But Tara had taken notice. As she ran up the drive she was conscious of a strong need to get to the front door before Georgiana announced her presence and was confronted by a half-asleep Alessandra.

Surely, she said to herself in a rush of panic as she ran, it couldn't be possible that Georgiana knows something of Saul's whereabouts.

A bolt of joy surged up. Maybe, just maybe, there was hope.

Georgiana was still arranging herself before she got out of the car. Tara saw the blonde hair swing to and fro as its owner stroked fingers over cheeks and hairline whilst staring in the rear view mirror. A pale hand brushed at the shoulders of her dress.

The car door opened and two elegant legs swung out. The rest of the figure unfolded itself, standing erect, cat-walk svelte in dark navy silk.

Tara called out, 'Georgiana!'

Georgiana turned. Hesitated, and then walked forward. Tara stood stone-like and astonished as Georgiana leaned forward and pressed each of her cheeks in turn against Tara's.

As Georgiana pulled back Tara looked into the big china-blue doll's eyes of Saul's wife and knew with a terrible sinking of her heart that Georgiana knew nothing. She came bearing no significant news which could bring her, Tara, back into full life again.

'Come in Georgiana,' she said automatic and polite.

Georgiana sat on the big white sofa. Her wraparound skirt slid away to the sides, revealing an expanse of tanned leg.

'I had hoped to see Saul,' she said, calm and amiable.

Tara had an urge to burst into raucous laughter. 'I'm sorry, he's not here at the moment.' She stopped. How to go on, she wondered. A wave of nausea seized her.

'I've tried the London apartment, left a number of messages on the answerphone,' Georgiana said.

Tara straightened her spine, marshalled her resources. 'Georgiana, I think you can help me. Will you help me?'

Georgiana blinked. 'I'll try.'

'Saul had a car crash in the early hours of yesterday morning. He's missing. I've heard nothing from him.'

Georgiana stared. 'Oh,' she said. 'Oh dear.'

'You haven't heard from him, have you?'

'No. Not for a week or two.'

So, he had still been visiting her. Tara had always suspected as much. The bastard, she thought vicious in her rage for a brief moment. The nausea welled up again. Oh if he were only still alive. Even the thought of a blazing row was like some dream of bliss.

'He'll be all right Tara,' Georgiana said. 'He's had more scrapes in his cars than I can remember. He always comes out without a scratch.'

Tara flinched. 'He hasn't been in touch. Not a word. Not a call. Nothing!'

Georgiana caught the torment and hint of menace in

Tara's voice. Her hands fidgeted with the navy silk of her skirt.

'Where might he have gone? Do you know?' Tara asked urgently.

Georgiana shook her head helplessly. 'I'm sorry.' she said.

Silence.

'Dr Daneman, my doctor, he would say . . .' Georgiana paused, as though regretting having embarked on this line of thought.

'Yes?'

'That anyone who goes missing is searching for their past.'

'What?' Good God, that old cliché. But then clichés were often born out of life's truths. 'And where is his past?' Tara wondered. 'I know he was brought up by his uncle. He never said much beyond that.'

'No,' Georgiana agreed. She lowered her head, fussed with her big ruby ring.

'We don't know very much do we?' Tara said dismayed.

'Poor Saul,' Georgiana said. 'No parents, no family.'

Tara looked at her curiously. She had the impression that Georgiana's words carried genuine feeling. But then she had always understood that Georgiana had truly loved Saul in her limited way, had always felt herself something of a thief in Georgiana's presence. 'Why did you come this morning?' she asked her.

There was a hesitation. 'I wanted to tell Saul that the divorce can go through. I want to remarry – my doctor.'

Tara groaned aloud. The terrible cruel irony of it. And maybe, at this moment, Georgiana was in no need of a divorce from Saul. Maybe she was already his widow.

'Oh Tara, I'm so very sorry,' Georgiana said.

They could no longer think of anything to say.

Some futile murmurings were made. Eventually Georgiana stood up to go. In the hallway a pyjama-clad Alessandra was leafing through the Sunday press.

She looked up. There was a shivery pause.

'Oh my dear!' exclaimed Georgiana. 'But you're beautiful!'

Alessandra's eyes smouldered like explosive.

Tara swiftly shepherded Georgiana out. 'Good-bye. I'll let you know if . . .' She turned away, ran back into the house.

'Oh, Mummy. Poor, poor Mummy!' Alessandra cried, grasping at her. 'That awful woman. Coming here. Oh, grotesque!'

'Truly, I don't think she meant any harm.' Amazing, thought Tara. 'Listen Alessandra, the press will be arriving soon. In droves.'

'Yes. It's OK. We'll cope.' Alessandra smiled. Suddenly she was terribly strong. She padded off into the drawing room.

To her amazement Tara heard the piano begin to resound with a Schubert impromptu. Very pleasingly executed, most interesting in its interpretation.

## CHAPTER 35

Alessandra came down to the basement to find her mother. She tried to avoid looking at the screen monitors where the image of her father's face dominated in triplicate. It was more than three weeks since he had disappeared.

'Mummy, you've got to stop doing this. You're driving yourself into the ground. Look at you, your clothes would be tighter on a twig.'

Tara reached out and enclosed her daughter's waist. 'This is his monument.'

Alessandra rattled Tara's shoulder roughly. 'Just leave it for a while. You can come back to it later. It's grim being down in this dungeon for days on end.' She took up a ribbon of film and slid it through her fingers. Her expression was puzzled and bitter. 'I wish Roland Grant would just come and take the whole lot away,' she said, tossing the celluloid to one side.

Tara flicked switches. The film stopped rolling. The images on the screen faded to a blank.

She was well aware of the obsessive nature of her compulsion to do this editing work for Saul. Carrying on where he had left off. She was more and more convinced that he had been on his way from London to his projection room on the night he had faded from her life. She had to finish the work. She was learning so much from it. And his face was there all the time. His spirit. She had to carry on, even though it felt as though it were killing her.

'Come on,' she said to Alessandra. 'Let's go out for a walk. Or were you going to exercise Tosca?'

'Done it already. Let's go for a drive, blast the village with loud pop music!'

Tara tried to relax behind the wheel. She kept her pace steady. The notion of speed no longer thrilled her. 'What do you want to do for your birthday?' she asked Alessandra cautiously.

'Nothing.'

'Well, what about your present? Another horse?'

'No. Not now. I can't take any more changes.'

'How about taking friends to a disco? A film?'

'Can I have something at home? Some friends in? A few spritzers, lagers for the boys?'

'Oh heavens!' Oh if only you had a father to ask. Tara gave a small laugh. 'Yes. Of course you can.'

The birthday loomed large for both of them. Only days away. Alessandra would be fourteen, a fully fledged teenager.

Tara recalled the days of June fourteen years before. Her heart leaked a drop of blood.

The insistent thump of African-style drums throbbed through the house. When it wasn't the drums it was

Irish wailing that made Tara think of green bogs and slaughtered innocents.

'It must be torture for you, having to put up with all this modern music,' Mrs Lockton said to her sympathetically.

Tara laughed. 'There's some so-called "serious" contemporary music that has the edge for awfulness.'

'Is that a fact?' said Mrs Lockton, unconvinced. She had finished her work now, prepared and set out a magnificent supper for a dozen or so ravenous young people intent on growing a few inches in the next few months. She was reaching for her anorak, shrugging into it.

She cocked her head, listening again. 'They seem a nice bunch of kids really,' she said. 'I just hope they take care with Mr Xavier's sound equipment. It must be worth a fortune.'

'I've told Alessandra that if there's any damage to the sound system or his piano, heads will roll. Actually she's pretty protective about his stuff. I don't anticipate any real trouble.'

Mrs Lockton nodded in approval. 'Well, good-night Tara.' She picked up her bag. She turned. 'I hope . . . I hope . . . Oh!' Mrs Lockton couldn't say the words. She made a sudden lurch forward, hugged Tara fiercely then disappeared swiftly through the back door.

Tara went through into the dining room, surveying the magnificent feast of Italian, Chinese and Indian cuisine and the huge, horse-shoe shaped birthday cake with its fourteen candles captured in mock stirrup holders.

Returning to the kitchen she sat down at the table. Empty and weary. Frighteningly alone. She felt that she had lost a part of herself, that there was a gaping hole inside her.

She looked at the calendar. Four weeks now. Hope was slipping away, the occasional glimmers of optimism appearing less and less frequently. Panic constricted her chest.

She threw her head back. Turned to look outwards. To the garden at the back of the house. Pale green light leaked from the rain-soaked leaves. It had poured earlier on. Now the garden was rinsed and clear.

It was seven in the evening. The sun was still high, but frail, not yet sure of its power against the clouds. A shadow moved into position on the wall of the entrance porch. A long shadow. Dark. Perfectly still.

The skin under Tara's hair crawled with sensation.

She sat. A stone without feeling.

The shadow shifted. He came through the door. He was thinner than before, his face pale, his skin luminous, almost translucent.

Tara's hands soared up to her face, covering her eyes, blotting out the power of the beloved image.

He made no sound. No move. He was watching her. Just watching.

Tara got up. The unimaginable was happening.

She went up to him. She reached out her hand and touched his breast bone. He was real. Flesh, blood, bone.

Her chest heaved. Blood thundered in her head. Red waves beating. Joy, fury, rage.

'You bastard,' she whispered. She struck him across the cheek with the back of her hand. Raised the other hand.

He stood quite motionless whilst she rid herself of all her rage and anger and hurt.

She was not a big woman, but she was strong and her emotions fuelled her. In time he moved to the table, sat down, sank his head against the wood and covered himself in protection with his arms.

'Aah!' Tara leaned over him, slid her hands over the loved form and pressed kisses into the skin of his neck, into his hair, his ears.

With the sudden slippery lash of a python she gripped him in a final burst of rage. 'God, I'd like to kill you.'

His hands moved behind his head, reached up and pulled her head down to his. 'I had hoped you might forgive me,' he said.

She leaned against him. Leaned into him. Saul. Her Saul. Found. Returned. Oh joy, joy!

He sat up. She looked at him; soaked a cloth in cold water and dabbed at the livid marks of violence on his face. Their eyes came to rest on each other, granite-grey into green. The fear of meeting was immediately banished into a living, dissolving, union.

He allowed her to bathe his cheeks, to sweep the hair back from his forehead and search for damage.

He started to speak. To begin his explanations.

Tara stopped him. She threw out her hands, framing a globe shape as though cradling his head. 'No. Don't. Just BE.'

She wrung out the cloth in the sink and carefully hung it over the tap to dry like Rachel always did. Her legs felt soupy and disobedient. She sat down and pulled her chair close to him. She took his hands in hers. She breathed deeply.

Time passed, unheeded, uncharted. Wordless.

The African drums continued relentlessly. Saul's eyes glimmered, his gaze swivelling to hers. They smiled with the conspiracy of those who had intuitive access to each other's thoughts.

A door in the hallway opened and closed, the music surging through in a huge burst and then receding. Alessandra erupted into the kitchen, her face flushed. 'I just wanted to tell Mrs Lockton she's performed miracles with . . .' Her gesticulating arms dropped down by her side. She stood rigid. Light flared from her eyes. There was disbelief in her face and then the most intense concentration as the truth inserted itself into her mind, which had told itself not to hope.

Saul got slowly to his feet.

'Daddy,' Alessandra said. 'My daddy.' Her voice shook. 'My *daddy*!'

Tara watched as the two of them merged together, heads touching, arms tightly wound about. Her vision blurred, a swimming image, a glimpse of perfect harmony. 'Happy birthday,' she heard Saul murmur.

The music swelled, deafening now as a straggle of young people filtered into the hallway, sniffing out the whereabouts of food like hungry dogs. Eyes glanced curiously into the kitchen. Looked away in confusion.

Tara smiled, walked through into the hallway, closing the kitchen door behind her. She led the way into the dining room. 'This way to the fatted calf,' she told the famished guests.

He had been briefly stunned. Dazed. Instinct had propelled him out of the car onto the road. Porsches under

393

attack were like tanks, he said, bruised but not shattered. He had crawled across two moving lanes of the motorway to the hard shoulder. A miraculous survivor. A cat with ten lives.

He had watched the car flare into a great sheet of fire; spitting and growling in its death throes. He had stumbled into the dry scrub at the hem of the motorway, found his way into a meadow and slept against a gate.

When consciousness had returned he had found himself in a world where everything was slightly askew and tilted. He had forced his stiff limbs to move. Had walked for hours, eventually reaching a motorway service point. He had bought food. A razor. A fresh shirt.

Tara placed her hand over his lips. 'No more. Later. You're here now, that's enough.' *That's everything.*

They were in bed. They had sneaked off, hand in hand, tip-toeing up the stairs. Furtive fugitives from the serious business of teenagers braying at the trough.

They had needed the simple glueing together of sex.

Tara lay in his arms, her body liquid and satisfied, recklessly uncaring about anything except his presence.


Reasons, motives, explanations. They filtered through slowly. Dribbling unevenly like wholesome soup through a sieve.

At breakfast the next day Alessandra had watched him with steady eyes. Assessing, joyous. No longer afraid.

Tara sat down between them.

'Where did you go to, Daddy?' Alessandra asked suddenly.

His glance moved from one of them to the other. 'I

walked through fields for days and days. Slept up against walls or in barns. A tramp.'

'You must have been concussed. Ill!' Tara exclaimed.

'Likely. But I was already in some disarray before the accident, as you both know. I eventually ended up in a smart anonymous hotel near Henley. Business conferences, a fax in every room. Piped Sinatra through the speaker system. No one recognized me.'

'Were you wearing a bag over your head?' asked Alessandra.

He smiled. 'I lay low. The place wasn't always a hotel,' he added evenly. 'It used to be a private house. My uncle's house. Where I spent my childhood.'

Tara reached out her hand to him. 'Oh, Saul.'

His eyes hardened. 'There's no need for pity. I was not desperately unhappy there.'

Alessandra shifted in her chair.

Saul turned to her, his smile gritty and ironic. 'I can tell when I'm boring people. The pouring out of human frailty isn't the most exciting topic.'

Alessandra began to protest. He cut in: 'Look it's enough that we all still love each other. You don't have to stay and listen to all this stuff. Go and feed that great horse. I'll come and join you in a minute.'

Alessandra got up. She kissed Saul on his forehead. She looked at the yellowy-brown bruise on his cheekbone and shook her head.

Passing Tara she murmured: 'Nobel Peace Prize withdrawn.'

Tara smiled briefly. She was watching Saul intently.

'This is something I want to say just to you, Tara. I

went to that place because there was something I needed to remind myself of. It was there that I learned to be totally reliant on myself, to be fiercely self-sufficient, utterly contained.'

'How old were you when you learned that?'

'About six. I'd already started on music lessons. My uncle was not a loving man you see, but he was an excellent musician. He didn't offer warmth, but he did offer the gift of music. I grabbed on to music as my emotional lifeline.'

'Dear God!' She studied her fingers, flexing them, recalling her own childish isolation after Freddie died. And she had had loving parents. 'You were so alone Saul. I suppose that's why you married so young?'

'Georgiana was the perfect wife for a man who needed a beautiful mate. A mate who wouldn't penetrate that fragile inner part of him that needed to be closed and secret.'

Tara nodded, understanding. At least some of it.

His eyes glinted. 'You were dangerous Tara. You pierced the container I'd sealed inside me. You made me vulnerable, exposed me to neediness again.'

'And oh God you were sometimes so angry with me,' she cried.

'Yes. Because I love you so fiercely. So hopelessly.'

She drew his head down between her breasts. She rocked him like a child. 'And when you heard Bruno trying to claim Alessandra was his. What then?'

'My God!'

'You didn't believe it?' Her eyes blazed.

'Of course not. I know Alessandra is mine. But seeing

396

you with that nice, open young man, thinking of what you'd shared together. The sickening jealousy. And thinking of what a pleasant easy time you could have had with him . . .'

Tara cut in. Savage, insistent. 'I didn't want an easy time. I wanted to be engulfed and bewitched. To be with you in the rapids, steering my precarious little craft, negotiating the rocky shoals, never knowing from one minute to the next how deep it was underneath – infinite or just a few dangerous inches. Oh God! How I loved you.' She stared at him. 'How I do still, God help me!' She released a long sigh. 'Saul, it was right that you came back. If only because Alessandra is your very own flesh and blood. And no one can take that from you, whatever else happens.'

He raised his head. His face was chilling and austere. 'Alessandra must have her own life. She doesn't belong to me. To either of us. You are my flesh and blood Tara. You and me. Sex, flesh, birth, blood. Man and wife. One flesh.'

'Aah.' She groaned as he gripped her upper arms in fingers of steel and pressed his lips over hers. 'I am not your wife, Saul,' she murmured.

'Oh yes. In spirit you are my wife. And you will be soon in reality. If Georgiana won't finalize the divorce I think I shall kill her.'

Through the intensity of her emotions an impish smile broke out on Tara's face. Saul looked at her outraged.

She told him the news. That Georgiana had a betrothed. Some doctor or other. That she sported a very handsome ruby ring.

He made no comment. Tara did not press him. She knew there was a part of him that must always be left secret and untouched. But there was more than enough that he would give to her in return.

They walked out into the garden, making for the stable block Saul had had built for Tosca the year before.

Soon the world would crowd in: Roland Grant, the press, the rebuilding of an established dazzling career, the construction of an embryonic one. But just now she had him to herself.

She pulled his arm around her. Held him very close.


Alessandra was invited to supper at a friend's house. Saul said he would drive her there in Tara's Jaguar.

Tara went out with them into the driveway and wagged a warning finger at him. 'No rally driving in my car!' She looked pointedly at Alessandra as she said so. 'Precious cargo,' she mouthed at him, her eyes then travelling meaningfully over his own person.

On his return to the house Tara heard him go down to the basement. She followed on, hesitant, apprehensive. She knew there would always be that anxiety with Saul, that because of it she would always be drawn to him, held irresistibly.

He had the recording system up and running. Three differing images glowed on the screens. 'You've done all this,' he said, fingering the container of completed and edited film, whilst staring at the three faces of the tortured Saul conducting.

'I did it because I thought you were dead,' she told him with an upsurge of new anger.

'You did all this for me. Even though you knew it was the sick work of a man intent on destroying everything he had loved. You, Alessandra. My art. Your generosity makes me feel humble, Tara.'

He swung round on his stool. They looked at each other. Tara closed her eyes briefly. The power of his feeling overwhelmed her.

'Do you remember at your father's funeral that you said you wanted to roar and howl?' he asked her.

'You told me to weep a flood. That it would prevent years of painful leaking later. I've always remembered that.'

'It was something I heard from a very famous psychiatrist who I met when I was on tour in Europe years ago. It stuck in my mind.' He looked down, his long arms hanging slack.

'Saul!' Tara called him softly back to her.

'When I was walking in those fields the days just after the accident, that's what I was doing. Sobbing, howling. It just happened. I would force myself to stop. And then it would start again.'

She gathered up his hands, held them protectively in her own. 'What were you sobbing for? The little Saul? The lonely little boy in the big house doing his piano practice?'

'My uncle didn't want me there. I was there on sufferance.'

'What do you mean?'

He gave a harsh, gritty laugh. 'My very aristocratic parents, with their international pedigree, were not quite as they seemed. My mother was indeed Grecian and beautiful, my father clever and well connected. It was just that she was the household's parlour maid who my very young father happened to make pregnant. She died of a haemorrhage just hours after producing me. My father went and joined the Air Force and got himself shot down. My very much older and wiser uncle was left holding the baby, so to speak. I don't think it was ever possible that he could love me. But he did do his best.'

Tara pulled him to her and held him close. She had long ago come to appreciate that every living person is a product of their past. 'So Saul Xavier decided that he could take the world on all on his own,' she said to him. 'That he needed no one, only his music.'

'Oh yes. And he did very well for quite some time. Perhaps until he met someone he couldn't stop himself from loving.'

Saul turned from her, confronting the stilled images of himself on the three screens. He made a sound of disgust. 'I was beginning to loathe myself,' he told her. 'I fancied that everything I did led to a plunge into disaster. I was a downhill racer, hurtling on to the destruction of everything I cared for.'

He picked up a snake of film from the floor and pulled it through his fingers, his face savage.

'I felt myself growing older, terrified I'd lose all I'd struggled for in those years when I just relied on myself. So finally there was one person left to destroy. Myself.' He glanced with loathing at the distorted, harsh faces on the screens. 'I began to tear at the essence of my being. I would seize my precious art by the throat and squeeze. You see, Tara, if you destroy all that is precious then

400

nobody else can step in and do it on your behalf. And when everything is torn down there is nothing more to fear.'

'Oh yes,' said Tara. 'I see that very well.'

He turned away from her. His shoulders were rigid with feeling. He wrenched the ribbons of film from the three parallel rollers and flung them onto the floor in a shiny heap, grinding at them viciously with his foot.

He swung back to Tara. 'Now I start building again.'

She sighed. 'Please God, yes.'

He saw her weariness, her need for comfort after all she had endured for him. He took her in his arms. 'Only you can help me do it Tara.'

'Yes. Oh Saul, it must have taken such courage to come back.'

He held her tight against him. 'You know it's not in my power to change, don't you? The essence of me, the Saul Xavier you first got to know, I can never change that.'

Tara considered. Warmth stole through her. 'Which of us can change ourselves? Rebuilding is far more real and precious.'

It was the winter of that same year. Morning frosts were laying a crusty white covering over the ground and each evening the sun sank in a blaze of rose and gold.

On the day before Tara and Saul were to be married, the bride-to-be went in search of her daughter. She carried two pairs of gloves in her hand, wanting Alessandra to help her decide which would be most suitable to complement her simple cream bridal suit.

Approaching Tosca's stable, she saw Alessandra

brushing mud from Tosca's tail – always a tricky task – and Saul standing at the horse's head, two fingers around Tosca's cheeks, two hooked into each side of the head collar.

'Try to make her keep still Daddy.'

'I am.'

'You're pretty good with her. She kicks terribly sometimes.'

'I might take up riding. I can't remember ever being up on a horse.'

'No,' said Alessandra.

'No?'

'You'd be desperately good at it after about ten lessons and start coming home with rosettes and silver tankards. Do keep her still!'

'Mmm.'

There were some moments of silence.

'Daddy?'

'Yes.'

'You know that Schubert impromptu? The one in A flat?'

'Yes. '

'Well, I was listening to a couple of old recordings of it. Your vinyl discs. Brendel and Barenboim.'

'Well?'

'They each use an entirely different tempo in the first movement.'

'Really? I must listen again. And what are Schubert's instructions?'

'He says *allegro moderato*.'

'So? How do you like to tackle it?'

'Like Schubert says of course. But then how do we know exactly what he meant by *allegro moderato*? Was it the same as Beethoven meant – or Brahms?'

'Ah, now that is a fascinating question.'

Alessandra began to speak again. Offer a further opinion. Confident, prepared to be innovative.

Tara crept away. She laid the gloves on her dressing table to show to Alessandra later.


Tara had told Saul that she was too old for net and frills, but she promised to look radiant for him.

Alessandra was stunning as the only attendant, wearing a jacket in hunting pink and a cream bowler complete with veil.

It had been meant to be a family occasion; a few friends, well wishers from the village. The news had leaked out. The church was crammed.

Dr and Mrs Georgiana Daneman slipped in discreetly at the back and slipped away equally unobtrusively as the bride and groom moved into the vestry.

The Tudor Philharmonic turned up in force and during the signing of the register the first violinist played the Chaconne from Bach's Partita Number 2 and then the wistful Air on a G string.

Saul held Tara so fiercely against him as they walked down the aisle, man and wife, that she found it hard to breathe.

At the reception Alessandra watched proceedings with a coolly mocking fourteen-year-old gaze, trying to conceal the swelling surges somewhere around the region of her heart.

'Honestly,' she complained to Rachel and Donald, eyeing the happy couple, 'Most of my friends' parents are at each other's throats all the time. And mine are always down each other's.'

'Alessandra! Where do you pick up such coarseness?' said Rachel, amused.

'Ever heard of school? The media? Books? I bet Mummy was much worse when she was my age.'

There was no easy reply to that. Rachel just smiled.

Roland Grant rose to his feet to toast the couple. He sketched out the bright musical future ahead for both bride and groom. Saul would be taking the Tudor Philharmonic on tour through Japan in the spring, playing an exciting programme of music from the baroque period and the twentieth century which the orchestra were to make their speciality. Meanwhile Tara had accepted the invitation of the Eastlands Symphonia to take over as their music director and chief conductor. A truly remarkable duo, was Roland's conclusion as he raised his glass.

They spent the first night of their marriage at the house in Oxfordshire.

In the morning Alessandra woke them with her clattering in the kitchen below.

Clad in jodphurs and boots ready for a morning canter, she brought up tea on a silver tray.

'First day of married life,' she said briskly. 'The sun is shining. The world is out there to be taken by the throat. So!'

They heard her running down the stairs.

'Like father, like daughter,' Tara chuckled, about to say more but being silenced by her husband's kiss.

An outer door slammed. And then there was the sound of Alessandra's clear treble voice striking out clean and free into the coming day.

# THE EXCITING NEW NAME
# IN WOMEN'S FICTION!

## PLEASE HELP ME TO HELP YOU!

Dear *Scarlet* Reader,

As Editor of *Scarlet* Books I want to make sure that the books I offer you every month are up to the high standards *Scarlet* readers expect. And to do that I need to know a little more about you and your reading likes and dislikes. So please spare a few minutes to fill in the short questionnaire on the following pages and send it to me. I'll send *you* a surprise gift as a thank you!

Looking forward to hearing from you,

*Sally Cooper*

Editor-in-Chief, *Scarlet*

# QUESTIONNAIRE

Please tick the appropriate boxes to indicate your answers

1 Where did you get this Scarlet title?
Bought in Supermarket ☐
Bought at W H Smith or other High St bookshop ☐
Bought at book exchange or second-hand shop ☐
Borrowed from a friend ☐
Other _____

2 Did you enjoy reading it?
A lot ☐   A little ☐   Not at all ☐

3 What did you particularly like about this book?
Believable characters ☐   Easy to read ☐
Good value for money ☐   Enjoyable locations ☐
Interesting story ☐   Modern setting ☐
Other _____

4 What did you particularly dislike about this book?
_____

5 Would you buy another Scarlet book?
Yes ☐   No ☐

6 What other kinds of book do you enjoy reading?
Horror ☐   Puzzle books ☐   Historical fiction ☐
General fiction ☐   Crime/Detective ☐   Cookery ☐
Other _____

7 Which magazines do you enjoy most?
Bella ☐   Best ☐   Woman's Weekly ☐
Woman and Home ☐   Hello ☐   Cosmopolitan ☐
Good Housekeeping ☐
Other _____

*cont.*

And now a little about you –

8 How old are you?

Under 25 ☐     25–34 ☐     35–44 ☐
45–54 ☐     55–64 ☐     over 65 ☐

9 What is your marital status?

Single ☐     Married/living with partner ☐
Widowed ☐     Separated/divorced ☐

10 What is your current occupation?

Employed full-time ☐     Employed part-time ☐
Student ☐     Housewife full-time ☐
Unemployed ☐     Retired ☐

11 Do you have children? If so, how many and how old are they?
_____
_____

12 What is your annual household income?

under £10,000 ☐     £10–20,000 ☐     £20–30,000 ☐
£30–40,000 ☐     over £40,000 ☐

Miss/Mrs/Ms _____
Address _____
_____
_____
_____

Thank you for completing this questionnaire. Now tear it out – put it in an envelope and send it before 31 December 1996, to:

*Sally Cooper*, Editor-in-Chief

SCARLET
FREEPOST LON 3335
LONDON W8 4BR
Please use block capitals for address.
No stamp is required!        THMIS/6/96

**_Scarlet_ titles coming next month:**

## MARRY ME STRANGER Kay Gregory

Being newly married is difficult enough, but when the couple concerned are strangers . . . difficult becomes impossible! At first, though, it seems that Brand and Isabelle will make their marriage work, until, that is, real life intervenes . . .

## A QUESTION OF TRUST Margaret Callaghan

Billie is everything Travis Kent claims to despise in a women: she's an impetuous tomboy, who lives in a ramshackle cottage with a mischievous cat. Throw in Travis' suspicious fiancée and the outcome is anyone's guess. But one thing is certain . . . passion is the most important ingredient!

## DECEPTION Sophie Weston

Ash believes that _all_ men should be treated as enemies, Jake has other ideas: he wants something from Ash . . . something she isn't prepared to give! Jake sets out to melt her resistance and, against her will, Ash begins to turn into the sensual woman she was always meant to be . . . until she remembers the saying 'Once bitten, twice shy!'

## IT TAKES TWO Tina Leonard

No woman has ever dared to refuse Zach Rayez . . . particularly when he decides he wants something! So when Annie says 'no', Zach is determined to win his battle of the sexes with this feisty lady. Annie can't believe that a successful man like Zach is interested in a country mouse like her, but if he isn't, why does he keep finding reasons not to leave her?